TRACON

Paul McElroy

JAPPHIRE

For information address:

Japphire Inc.
6947 Coal Creek Parkway SE – No. 1000
Newcastle, Washington 98059
www.japphire.com

Japphire is a trademark of Japphire Inc.

PRINTING HISTORY
Japphire paperback edition / August 2000
Japphire hardcover edition / August 2001

BOOK DESIGN BY AMY M^cELROY

Publisher's Cataloging-in-Publication Data
(Provided by Quality Books, Inc.)

McElroy, Paul.
    Tracon / Paul McElroy. -- 1st ed.
    p. cm.
    LCCN 00102328
    ISBN 0-9679963-1-7

    1. Air Traffic Controllers' Strike, U.S., 1981--
Fiction. 2. Professional Air Traffic Controllers
Organization (Washington, D.C.)--Fiction. 3.
Information technology--Social Aspects--Fiction.
I. Title.

PS3563.A2935T73 2001   813´.6
                    QBI01-700406

PRINTED IN THE UNITED STATES OF AMERICA
10 9 8 7 6 5 4 3 2 1

To John S. Carr, and his brethren,
unseen shepherds of the skies.

ACKNOWLEDGEMENTS

Nearly 100 professionals in the aviation community and elsewhere graciously provided background for this book. I'm grateful to all of them for demystifying their world, and I bear full responsibility for any errors in adapting the material to this story. With apologies to those not mentioned, the following individuals deserve recognition for their exceptional generosity:

Chicago O'Hare International Airport
TRACON

John Carr	Ken Mallot
Ray Gibbons	Robert Nicholas
John Gratys	Bob Pywowarczuk
	Bob Stone

Tower

Bob Richards	Jim Veronico

Boeing Field — Seattle
Tower

Paula Crooks
Mike Maikowski
Dan Olsen

Seattle-Tacoma International Airport

Tracon

Randy Bachmann	Ed Gass
Tom Bergin	Ann Gilchrest
Mike Callahan	Hugh "Bo" Watson

Tower

Lisa Eidson
Paul Hadler
Jerry Whitsett

Others

First Officer David L. Hinman / American Airlines
Capt. Charles E. Boswell / American Trans Air
Judy and Capt. Gary Ostrowski / American Trans Air
Bill Fischer / The Boeing Co.
Lt. Earl W. Zuelke Jr. / Chicago Police Marine Unit
Capt. Dwight Lubich / United Airlines
William Arnold
Bob Bachmeyer
Connie and Rich Halstad
Kathryn O'Neal
Richard Rush
Rebecca Teagarden
Chris West

Finally, my profound thanks to Amy,
a true friend who patiently showed me the way.

AUTHOR'S NOTE

The pilot was in a panic. Untrained to fly in the clouds, he'd been blinded by an unexpected weather front. Beside him in the cabin of the small plane, his terrified toddlers—a 3-year-old and 2-year-old twin daughters—fidgeted wide-eyed in their seats. As the pilot succumbed to vertigo watching the ground evaporate in a white haze, the Piper PA-28 careened through the sky like a roller coaster.

In the O'Hare radar room in Elgin, Illinois, 40 miles from Chicago, air traffic controller Chuck Knox watched the green blip on his scope disappear. Now that the plane had descended below radar coverage, it was a mere 500 feet above the Chicago suburbs.

"Do you see the ground?" Knox asked the pilot.

"Yes—a freeway," he responded.

Based on his location, Knox deduced the pilot was flying above Interstate 88 and told him to continue west toward Aurora Municipal Airport. He kept talking quietly and steadily, hoping to help him regain his wits. But the seconds ticked by and the voice on the other end of the radio remained silent. With a sinking feeling, Knox feared the plane and its precious cargo had crashed. Then came the pilot's stricken scream.

"I almost hit some high-tension wires!"

And a desperate plea. "Help me save my children."

The disoriented pilot bounded into the clouds several times more. During one perilous descent, Knox said urgently, "Just let go of everything." An experienced pilot, Knox knew the plane could level off and virtually fly itself. He also knew the aircraft would spiral into oblivion if it had been in a steep bank.

Knox was legally prohibited from issuing such an order, but his gambit paid off. The Piper pulled out of its dive about 300 feet above the ground and the pilot regained control. He spied another road and Knox guided him safely to Du Page Airport, ending the 45-minute ordeal. Three days before Christmas 1996, Chuck Knox, a supervisor named Terry Hall, and several controllers who'd been helping on the sidelines had just given one family the present of a lifetime.

I am neither a pilot nor a controller, but aviation fascinates me. Like many travelers, I can't resist peeking in the cockpit when boarding an airliner. That's only part of the picture. A host of professionals in the air and on the ground help ensure our safe passage.

Controllers are among them. News accounts periodically focus on air traffic delays and equipment breakdowns, but we rarely hear about the people hunched before radarscopes in darkened rooms, guiding the thousands of flights a day that crisscross the country. This is their story.

P.M. / April 2000

Perspectives From The Front Line

A foreword by John S. Carr,
president of the National Air Traffic Controllers Association

Twenty years ago, almost 12,000 men and women walked off their jobs and into history. The Professional Air Traffic Controllers Organization called for a strike—an illegal strike, at that—and the membership responded in overwhelming numbers.

Fed up with poor equipment, oppressive, autocratic management, and incredibly stressful working conditions, our nation's air traffic controllers left high-tech government jobs in protest and frustration. They gambled their careers trying to make a difference in their profession.

The Federal Aviation Administration had been making strike contingency plans for well over a year when the walkout hit, and an emboldened agency urged President Reagan to take a hard line. In response to the illegal job action, Reagan fired the strikers and began hiring replacements. Several months passed, and it became clear to everyone that the strikers were finished, the union destroyed.

The PATCO strike of 1981 was a watershed event in American history. Organized labor was decimated by the president's aggressive maneuver. Private industry took its cue from the administration and the term "replacement workers" grew into the lexicon. Pilots lost their jobs when airlines were forced to scale back to operate in the FAA's downsized and severely constrained system. As the nation slid into recession, the men and women who struck were banned for life from federal employment.

In that blizzard of hiring, training, and deployment following the strike, the feds offered a position to a scrawny college student with four years of Navy controlling experience under his belt and a job at a discount store. I gratefully accepted.

Six short years after the PATCO strike, I joined many of my fellow air traffic controllers in forming a new union, the National Air Traffic Controllers Association, or NATCA for short. We organized for many of the same reasons as the banished strikers: to improve our abysmal working conditions, and bring new technologies and equipment into our profession. The fact that the FAA's management culture remained brutally Jurassic helped NATCA blossom, and on June 19, 1987, we were certified as the exclusive representative of our nation's air traffic controllers.

The lessons of the PATCO strike were not lost upon the new union, and we grew in strength and influence very rapidly. Today, just fourteen years after our founding, we are the strongest union in the federal sector. We have the fastest-growing Political Action Committee (PAC), our membership continues to expand as we add new bargaining units, and, unquestionably, we have the best contract in federal-sector labor history.

I was active in NATCA from the start and fortunate to rise within the union's ranks, first in Kansas City, then in Chicago and Cleveland. In 2000, I was elected to a three-year term as my union's national president.

I'm proud to lead a group of professionals whose mission is to ensure the safe, orderly, and expeditious passage of the nearly two million people who fly everyday in the United States. Air traffic control is a delicate science. It blends the physics of applied technology with the artistry of ballet. It requires split-second coordination, steely nerves, keen eyes, the ability to think in three dimensions and carry on at least half a dozen conversations at once, a cast-iron gut, the swashbuckling bravado of a pirate, and an aura of invincibility. It is, in every sense of the word, a young person's game.

The men and women who perform these feats are a rare breed. They come from every walk of life, and science will never replicate the knowledge, skills, and abilities that flow from their minds in the few seconds that stand between normal and fatal during every hour of every shift.

Air traffic controllers are prone to living and dying at Mach 3 with their hair on fire. It's been said that controllers at busier facilities produce more adrenaline asleep than most people do in their waking hours. Controllers do everything hard, whether it's work or play. If they smoke, they smoke a lot and love it. If they're occasionally prone to a cocktail or two, why, they know how to socialize. If they cuss, no Navy sailor could have said it any better. And if they're on your side, then you might as well head on down into that fictional valley because they're not fearing any evil, so why should you?

Controllers are fiercely independent, demanding people. Their job description requires perfection as the minimum acceptable level of competence, and they're notorious for expecting perfection from others. They are routinely disappointed in that regard. Divorce rates are high, and spouses and children of controllers can tell you a thing or two about being ordered around like an airplane. It should come as no surprise that some of us can only find true happiness with those who really understand us—other controllers. My wife, Jill, is a controller, and a damn good one. You'd be hard-pressed to find a better soul mate. I love her dearly, and it is for her that I get up in the morning to greet the day.

The work of an air traffic controller is transitory, and in that sense, not very rewarding. The planes come in, the planes go out, and the only time there is evidence that you "did something" is if you did something wrong. When that happens, the evidence is customarily found on page one of the morning papers.

Air traffic control is, of course, an inherently governmental function, and should always remain so. ATC is replete with safety and national defense implications. Shortsighted attempts to commercialize or privatize the FAA should be routinely dismissed.

The air traffic control system in this country is a national treasure, and it belongs to the citizenry. Your tax dollars have paid for the infrastructure, ranging from hardware to software to the limitless boundaries of the human capital which is its workforce. It would be reckless and naïve to commercialize something so intrinsically linked with the public's best and safest interests.

A privatized system would balance the financial bottom line against an air traffic controller's bottom line: the safety of the flying public. The privatized air traffic control system in Australia recently circulated an internal memo discussing the possibility of "curtailing services to aircraft in distress due to liability concerns." In other words, they're thinking of turning their backs on pilots and passengers at the very time they need help the most. I'm sorry for waxing sanctimonious, but decisions involving life and death should never come down to dollars and cents.

Pilots, corporations, and other users pay hefty landing fees, fuel surcharges, and other taxes to operate in our system, which even our staunchest opponents will admit is the safest in the world. "User fees" are simply well-disguised new taxes, and most pilots will agree that what our system does not need is a new tax. User fees will destroy aviation in this country, wrecking twenty years of economic growth and prosperity.

Our system is not perfect, and we are straining under the weight of unfettered discretion. Anyone can add demand to a finite system of runways and taxiways without consequence, and the greatest economic growth in American history has turned the "transportation mode of the elite" into mass transit. You can look above your head and see the limitless sky, but unfortunately the same cannot be said for our nation's airports. They are limited not only by geography but by the economic, political, and ecological ties that bind. "Not In My Back Yard," or NIMBY, has become the battle cry over power plants, prisons, and airports, as well.

Travelers are not fed up with air traffic services. They are fed up with waiting for air traffic services. Unfortunately, until the public policy debate turns away from laying blame and toward laying down some new runways, delays will continue to mount and passengers will continue to suffer.

In the 1950s, President Eisenhower set this nation on a path to greatness when he founded the interstate highway system. It is long past time for our elected leadership to set a course for this country's safety, security, and economic future by embracing a blueprint for aviation growth that will take us not only past next summer but into the next century. I have long advocated concrete solutions to our nation's aviation infrastructure dilemma, and by that I mean concrete. At some point, we've got to stop talking about this problem and start pouring some new pavement.

Aviation is a good news, bad news story. The good news is the delay problem has gotten so acute that Life magazine ran a cover story titled, "Stack Up: Danger and Confusion of the Air Traffic Jam." The bad news is the story ran on August 9, 1968—thirty-three years ago. I sincerely hope real and lasting change to our nation's delay problems can be made in my lifetime, and I hope to contribute to making those changes. You can help, too, by making sure your elected leaders know how important aviation is to the lifeblood of this country.

The air traffic control world is off-limits to most of you and, consequently, often misunderstood. In that regard, Paul McElroy's novel, *TRACON*, is a triumph. It captures the essence of the profession, resplendent in all its glory and its scars. Paul managed to create a fictionalized account so accurate and chilling in its realism that it strikes people in the aviation business as a narrative summary of actual events.

This book accomplishes what many other media accounts, newspaper articles, magazine treatments, and movies have tried and failed to do: get into the minds of the men and women who are responsible for more lives in an hour than most surgeons are in a lifetime.

Paul has written the book I always wanted to write, and written it perfectly. There has never been a better, more accurate novel about the air traffic control profession. So, before you turn the page, I recommend you fasten your seat belt, and keep your tray table in its upright and locked position. You've just signed up for one hell of a ride.

J.S.C. / Washington, D.C.
August 3, 2001
www.natca.org

CONTENTS

"One of the first things an air traffic controller learns is that we can't make mistakes. . . . The computer should be held to the same standard."

— *Ryan Kelly*

O'Hare International Airport

The locale of *TRACON*

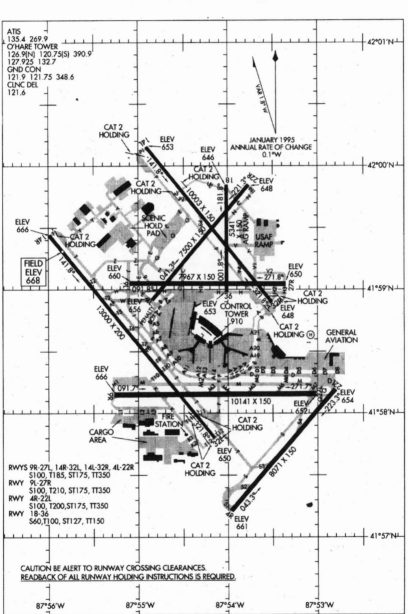

ONE

THE FLICK

R YAN KELLY WAS STRETCHING A LONG ARM DOWN to loosen his shoelaces for the third time that Monday night when the radarscope in
front of him flickered and darkened.

Shit—the beacon's out.

With a fleeting electronic gasp, a coded array of airline flight numbers,
aircraft types, speeds, and altitudes vanished. Nothing remained but a muddle
of anonymous green blips marching relentlessly across the large round glass.
Kelly's brown eyes swept around the dim windowless radar room at O'Hare
International Airport, his wide mouth curling into a frown. Every other
scope was equally barren. Eighteen black holes. The customary background
hum of controllers talking into their mikes and bantering with each other
off the air fell silent momentarily, then resumed in a flurry of laconic
commands.

Sighing heavily, Kelly leaned his elbows on a narrow wooden console
and stared at the jumble of targets to memorize identities before the pattern
changed and confused him. When faceless passengers clouded the image,
he blinked to chase them away. It's just a video game, he reminded himself,
one the Federal Aviation Administration had let him play for fourteen years.
He never dreamed as a boy growing up in a Minnesota farm town that one
day he'd juggle airliners with the same easy calm as the performers he marveled over at the county fair, casually tossing their flaming sticks in the air.
Cool reserve born of an intolerant father who wielded a stinging backhand.
But now, he felt that familiar tightening inside, an acid rush, a burning gut.

Don't drop one.

A sudden oppressiveness thickened the air of the warm subterranean room, barely illuminated by small downlights in the ceiling and low-level lamps on a couple of desks. Kelly unconsciously undid the top button of his red cotton shirt while scanning several colored displays glowing around his scope. Everything else appeared normal. In his periphery, he saw the taut, lime-tinted faces of the men on each side of him making the same checks.

Frank Pepperidge, a burly, bearded controller everyone called "Bear," bellowed irritably from across the room. "Christ, Sammy, the beacon's out again!" At the area manager's desk behind them all, Samantha Sanchez was already reaching for a telephone.

Sitting next to Kelly, Greg Webber clenched a fist but kept his voice low. "Goddamn it, that's twice this month."

Kelly smiled sardonically. "Twice for the radar. The radios went dead last Friday."

"And it took forever for the backup system to kick in," Webber said. "The only thing holding this place together is baling wire and spit."

"And some heroic efforts from the techs," Kelly added. He adjusted a frayed piece of maroon carpet beneath his elbows that someone had placed on the console for padding, his mind straying skyward.

High above him nearly 100 airliners were screaming through the cool cloudy night, zigzagging over the vast metropolis at three to five miles a minute like balls spinning across a three-dimensional billiards table. A flock of aluminum birds carrying thousands of lives he rarely allowed himself to think about. Unsuspecting passengers who were downing the last of their drinks, handing in headset cords, and gathering belongings for that rush to clog the aisle the moment their plane reached the gate. *Ladies and gentlemen, we've begun our descent into Chicago. Please put your seat backs and tray tables in the upright position . . .* Travelers who breathed easier at the sight of a silver-haired captain in the cockpit, but had no idea the traffic cops orchestrating their arrival with choreographed precision coped with rickety equipment that belonged in a museum.

Kelly's slender frame shifted slightly on a dingy, worn swivel chair, making it squeak in protest. Behind him, an ancient Teletype machine churned out printed strips of paper about incoming flights with an irritating chatter. Carelessly, he ran a hand through his long but well-groomed black hair to brush away frustration. Now was not the time to ponder grim realities and wallow in self-pity.

Using his left foot, he pried off the other shoe and wriggled his toes in relief. The dark brown deck shoes were new, with stiff leather laces that constantly unraveled. Kelly kept tying them too tightly, forcing him to fiddle when his feet began to throb. The annoying process made him wish he'd bought those slip-ons the salesman suggested. He clenched his jaw in renewed concentration and forced his attention back to the scope.

Let's run through them again. Number one on final is Delta 1172, then American 1650 behind him. From the northeast is . . . Coastal 540. Or is it Continental 267? His stomach twisted a notch. *Christ, that better be Coastal.* Over there is Prairie . . .

He glanced down at a rack of flight strips on the console. Each plastic strip contained a pale green slip of paper with cryptic abbreviations about one of the airliners. Normally, the six-inch-long strips served as a backup to information displayed on the scope. At times like this, they were invaluable.

. . . Oh, yeah, Prairie 838. His eyes flicked back and forth between strips and scope, darting among the cluster of targets that blinked and danced with each sweep of the radar. Look away an instant too long and the whole house of cards could collapse. After confirming the positions of all ten planes in what he prayed was the correct order, he pressed a hand switch to key the boom mike on his headset, his words quick and his tone confident.

"Delta 1172, descend and maintain seven thousand. Report reaching seven."

His earphone crackled alive. *"Out of eleven for seven, Delta 1172."* He scribbled "7 R/R" on the flight strip and sighed once more. This time, Webber noticed and arched his head toward Kelly.

"As usual, Bear was the first to cry. He's getting to be a weak stick."

Everyone knew Pepperidge was burning out. He'd been playing the game for more than two decades, an eternity in the world of air traffic control. But to Kelly, he was a friend who didn't deserve public condemnation— yet. Despite Webber's disdain, he was still a good controller. You couldn't get away with mediocrity in this profession. Even so, it'd be difficult to hang on until retirement in three years. Hard time at a place like O'Hare. Webber was right about one thing. Above all else, the first priority was your traffic. He tossed off the accusation with a shrug.

"Someone had to sound the alarm."

At the desk behind them, Samantha Sanchez barked into a telephone connecting her with the FAA's Airways Facilities Department. "We've lost the beacon! What's going on?"

"Automatic shutdown. We had a power surge."

The technician's frazzled voice told Sanchez he wasn't in the mood for a discussion but she needed to know more. One of their lifelines was gone. A hand flew to her generous hip and several fingers tapped impatiently. "We're running naked on commercial power? What about the UPS?"

Electricity for O'Hare's radar room and control tower was fed through an uninterruptible power supply that provided steady continuous current. Without it, sensitive radar and computer equipment was dangerously vulnerable to voltage spikes and electrical failures.

The technician's reply tumbled out in exasperation. "We had no choice. We took the main unit off line for routine maintenance this afternoon and found a bad bearing. We've ordered a replacement but it won't be here till tomorrow. Then the spare we plugged in started overheating, so we had to shut it off. It's not my fault we have only one spare—blame the bean counters. And the longer I talk to you, the longer it'll be before I can bring the system back up."

Sanchez groaned, silently cursing the ninety-four planes expected to land this hour despite the FAA's brain-dead budgeting. "Okay, okay. We're in the middle of a west arrival rush, so get it back as quick as you can."

She dropped the receiver back onto its cradle and carefully surveyed the room. Glancing at the clock, she sighed. Her two kids would trundle off to bed in another half hour and she envisioned the disappointment on their faces if her regular good night call to them didn't come in time. She loved her job, but the schedule made it difficult to balance a life at home. She looked at the phone, then at the darkened scopes around the room. Watching, waiting, barely breathing.

Briefly taking his eyes off the West Arrival scope, Kelly glanced at Webber, who was exuding his usual poise again, and the controller seated behind them, nervously smoothing a thick black mustache. "You guys got the flick?" That was the secret to this game. Maintain a mental picture of who everyone is and where they're going. Never—ever—lose the flick or you're liable to make it on the six o'clock news.

Webber shuffled his flight strips with the polished flair of a casino dealer. "In Technicolor."

As feeder man, he accepted two flows of inbound airplanes from Chicago Center in the far western suburb of Aurora and reduced their altitude from 10,000 feet to 7,000 before handing them off to Kelly for sequencing onto final approach. He also monitored the traffic on final in the unlikely event that Kelly missed something. They worked side by side at their own scopes, Webber passing a steady stream of flight strips to Kelly.

"Yes."

The hesitant rasp was all Gene Lombardi could muster as he worried his mustache. Lombardi had tried to gird himself for O'Hare's legendary traffic before transferring from Hopkins Airport in Cleveland a year ago, but it still occasionally shocked him. And the constant equipment breakdowns were unreal. They always happened at the busiest times—or perhaps it was just that they were always busy.

The uncertainty didn't surprise Kelly. Lombardi was struggling through the one- to two-year training process of becoming an FPL, a Full Performance Level controller certified to work every position in the radar room. This was his first day checking out on Arrivals. Welcome to the major leagues, my friend. Watch and learn.

"I'm taking points off if your spacing goes to hell." Webber emphasized his threat by licking the tip of an imaginary pencil.

Kelly snorted. "I'm watching your traffic, too, pal. It's the poor craftsman who blames his tools."

Beneath their bravado and barbs was mutual pride in maintaining the safe, orderly, expeditious flow of traffic. That was the controller's credo, and equipment breakdowns bought them no latitude. Just because the computer had crashed, Kelly wouldn't dream of letting his spacing get sloppy and make more planes burn a hole in the sky waiting for their turn to come down. When the beacon system was working, he could press a few keys to display distances between aircraft, right down to hundredths of a mile. Now he had to eyeball them, plus estimate speed and verify altitudes with pilots to keep everyone apart.

His eyes narrowed on a trio of blips heading toward a dotted line on the scope that designated the electronic localizer for runway 14 right. The Delta 727 he'd spoken to moments ago would be down to 7,000 soon and ready to turn onto final approach. From there, the localizer would funnel the pilot through a standard descent path to landing. An American MD-80 and Coastal Airlines 737 were converging from behind.

"Chicago Approach, Delta 1172 is level at seven."

Kelly scrawled a check mark on the flight strip. "Delta 1172, turn right heading one-two-zero and intercept the runway one-four right localizer. Maintain one-eight-zero knots or greater, please. You're number one."

He engaged in a mental debate while listening to the pilot's response, not ready to commit his memory to the blip he planned to move behind American. Is that really Coastal? Or is it Continental? Pick the wrong one and you're checkmated, pal. And don't take all day to decide. In twelve seconds that jet barrels another mile through the friendly skies.

His thumb wiggled on the mike switch. After a moment's hesitation, he pressed it and told Coastal 540 to turn onto final.

A high-pitched hum accompanied the reply and then Kelly held his breath, following the bright green line of the radar beam as it swept around the scope. When the correct target pirouetted behind American and Delta, he quietly let out his breath and nodded imperceptibly.

All three planes were now in a string homing in on the runway. As he talked with each pilot, Kelly arranged the flight strips on his rack according to their position on final. He placed the one for Delta at the bottom, slipped American's in on top of it, then Coastal's.

"Delta 1172, contact O'Hare Tower on one-two-six-point-niner."

"Good day."

Webber passed another strip to Kelly, who glanced at it and looked back at the scope. Note American and Coastal closing in on Delta. In quick succession, he told the two pilots to reduce speed. Now it was time to slow Prairie so Continental could slip in behind Coastal, a constant weaving of targets into a string of pearls. He called the pilot, but his earphone remained silent. Come on guys, listen up. He waited a few seconds and repeated the call.

No response.

What the hell—has the radio gone out again? He tried another flight. "American 1650, contact O'Hare Tower on twenty-six niner."

"So long."

Not the radio, but Prairie's gonna blow into Coastal's airspace real soon.

The radar beam swept around and the target jumped another quarter inch on the scope, another 1,800 feet in the air. Kelly turned to Webber. "You talkin' to Prairie 838?"

The feeder man shook his head and called the pilot, but still no one answered. Kelly pursed his lips at the prospect of a renegade jet and radioed Coastal with an alternate clearance to keep him out of the way. The pilot was responding when Webber waved a hand.

"It's okay. Prairie just called me back. Went to the wrong frequency when I sent him to you." Webber repeated the correct one into his mike, crisply biting off each number.

Kelly shook his head. One digit off on the radio and this guy's in nowhere land. We can get through this, but everyone's gonna have to stay sharp.

"*Chicago Approach, Prairie 838 is with you at eleven thousand.*"

A trace of sheepishness seeped through the pilot's metallic voice. Kelly felt a twinge of sympathy now that they'd re-established communication. An easy mistake given all the frequency changes we put them through. He issued descent clearance and as he'd done with the other pilots asked to be advised when the flight reached 7,000 feet.

"*Roger to seven, Prairie 838. Approach, uh, do you copy our Mode C read-out?*"

Kelly had been expecting the question. The beacon system—which they also called the ARTS, for Automated Radar Terminal System—received the altitude information it displayed on the scope from an aircraft's Mode C transponder. Except for verifying altitude when first accepting a flight, he usually didn't have to ask for confirmations unless the transponder failed.

"Negative, 838. Our beacon system is out."

The words had barely left his mouth when the radarscope flickered again and green computerized data tags for each plane reappeared next to the blips. Kelly laughed and looked at Webber, who grinned in bemusement. A few more seconds and the pilots would not have known anything had been wrong.

"Prairie 838, looks like your question just fixed it. I show your altitude at ten-point-six, descending."

"*Glad to help.*"

Gene Lombardi sank back in the chair behind them and blew out his cheeks. "Sure nice to have the alphanumerics back. We were out six minutes."

Kelly sneered inwardly. He didn't know much about Lombardi other than having watched him survive training on other positions in the radar room. It was a fact of life at O'Hare that most journeymen controllers waited to become friends with developmentals until they were fully certified. Too many washed out after a few months and were gone, so why waste the effort? Lombardi was said to be one of the stars in Cleveland, but you had to prove yourself all over again at a new facility. Probably an "ARTS baby," one of those techno-types who was lost without the luxury of the computer. The display deceived some of the newbies, making them forget there was still a lot of instinct and improvisation involved. Just like some store cashiers who don't bother to count change and blindly hand over whatever amount the register tells them. Not a big deal at the supermarket. Here, it was a recipe for disaster.

Kelly leaned back in his squeaky chair and put one foot up on the console in a rare display of cockiness. "Yeah, it's a pain in the ass without the ARTS, but don't rely too much on all this computer shit. Show me skin paint from the primary radar, give me a radio that works, and I'll bring them in all day long without the alphanumerics. That, my friend, is what air traffic control is all about."

Webber chuckled while handing Kelly another flight strip. "Piece of cake tonight. Remember last month?"

Kelly's head reared back at the heart-stopping memory. "I'll never forget it. I heard later a construction crew was digging a public swimming pool, for God's sake, when they chopped through our fiber optic cable."

He'd been working East Arrivals on a perfectly normal day when suddenly they had no radar, no radios, no telephones, no lights. *Nothing.* There was a moment of eerie silence while everyone in the pitch black room grasped the situation, then twenty people began shouting helplessly at each other. Webber felt his way to the door and dashed down the hall to use a pay phone to scream at Chicago Center to shut off arrivals. Kelly sprinted close behind on his way to the tower cab 200 feet above to get them to handle the remaining planes on final. He'd never been so grateful to see a functioning radarscope, panting over it in jubilation after racing up the final flight of stairs.

Webber gently massaged his aching eyes. "Some days I think I'm getting too old for this crap. I'm thirty-four, you know."

A young man's game, yes. At thirty-six, Kelly found it took more effort to handle everything, too, and he wondered how it would be at forty-six—if he could gut it out that long. He winked at Webber. "I'd say you're good for another month or two."

Across the room at the East Departure scope, Bear Pepperidge adjusted his bulk in the chair with a disgruntled sigh and shouted at their supervisor again. "Hey, Sammy, you trying to make us work harder for the same money?"

Samantha Sanchez didn't flicker, despite the misuse of her nickname. Bear loved reminding her that the radar room was a predominantly male bastion, regardless of the FAA's official policy of sexual equality. Long ago she'd learned to hide her irritation over such taunts and so tonight her voice remained light once more. "Just keeping all of you on your toes. It's evaluation time, you know."

Kelly spun around while listening to a pilot repeat his clearance. "She gets kickbacks from the Hilton."

Bear nodded and stroked his beard thoughtfully, anticipating the traditional stop for beers at the Sports Edition bar in the airport hotel after their shift. "Now that you mention it, I am pretty thirsty. I might even buy the first pitcher."

As he called an airplane a familiar stench wafted around him. He crinkled his nose and let out a long breath. Then he fanned his face with a hand, but it was futile. Pungent flatulence tainted the air and there was no escape. Overcome, he pushed his chair back from the console and roared with imperious disgust.

"Goddamn it! Who farted?"

The moment Bear heard the echo in his headset, his craggy face suffused in embarrassment. His foot must have inadvertently stepped on the floor pedal and keyed the mike. It was only the third time in his long career that he'd said something accidentally over the air.

The controller sitting next to him recoiled in mock horror and windmilled his arms. "Whew, yeah. Major cheese action here. Crank up the ventilation, Sam. I think it's Bear and he's just trying to divert attention."

Before Bear could answer, his headset came alive. *"Chicago, this is USAir*

1221. Negative on the fart."

He shook his head in disbelief.

"Chicago, negative on the fart for American 1730. How about you, Northwest?"

"Ah, Northwest 172 is negative on the fart."

Bear's lips spread into a grin. He flicked a switch to put the frequency on the speaker, prompting guffaws from everyone in the room as the roll call of denials continued. A half dozen more pilots proclaimed their innocence before he could vector a departure during the lull. He was laughing so hard his ample belly jiggled and his eyes welled up with tears. He wiped them again and was trying to bring the scope back into focus when a Detroit-bound DC-9 called just after takeoff.

"Chicago, this is Prairie 492. We've got a hydraulic failure and have to come back."

Immediately, Bear's face turned serious and he sat up straight. "Hey Sam, I need a supe at East Departure."

Two
TCAS

THE SILENCE IN THE *Chicago Chronicle* LIBRARY was broken only by the soft whirring of a microfilm machine while Sharon Masters impatiently scanned old news clips. One month away from graduation at Northwestern University, the intern reporter was tracking down a detail for a story, the year a city alderman had been convicted of graft. Her slender fingers cranked the wheel that fed a roll of film through the viewer, pages whizzing by in a blur until she paused intermittently to check her progress back in time. The jerky rhythm was dizzying, prompting her to curse the *Chronicle*'s limited electronic archives. Nothing written more than ten years ago was on computer, making this search laborious.

Her hand eased up on the wheel again and the parade of pages gradually slowed until she found the date at last. Though eager to leave, she conscientiously rewound the film and turned off the machine, stuffed the reel back into its box, and replaced the box in its correct slot in a file cabinet.

Masters strode back into the city room and maneuvered through a yawning maze of gray and mauve cubicles. Each sprouted a computer terminal, many of which were nearly buried beneath mountains of books, files, and papers. A toy rocket awaited liftoff atop one of the terminals—the science writer's desk—and a jury-rigged wanted poster of the crime reporter was plastered on the side of another. Much of the newspaper was prepared during the day, so only a few reporters were still here. In one corner of the room, several editors huddled over the metro, national, and foreign pages for the next morning's edition. Nearby the night city editor concentrated on Masters' story. She approached him and waited for the right moment to interrupt.

Several radio scanners on the desk tuned to public service, marine, and aviation frequencies chattered incessantly. When Masters was hired at the *Chronicle* last fall, she could barely comprehend the dispatchers who spit out their jargon in a torrent, often garbled by static. Since then, she'd developed her ear and begun to understand the routine. Endless police traffic stops. So many fire calls that she'd learned to listen for the second and third alarms before getting excited. Domestic disputes, where anything could happen. And so on.

"*—got a hydraulic failure and have to come back.*"

The words caught her attention and she bent closer, pressing a button to hold the scanner on the frequency. Static scratched harshly from the speaker.

"*Roger, Prairie 492. Are you ready to return right now?*"

"*Affirmative.*"

"*Prairie 492, do you need any assistance? Do you want the equipment standing by?*"

"*Negative. We just need to come back and get on the ground. Is your beacon system still out?*"

"*Negative, 492. We're in business again. Stand by and I'll give you vectors in a moment.*"

Masters straightened and looked at the night city editor, still engrossed in his work. "Did you hear that? A plane's in trouble and has to land right away. Must be O'Hare or Midway. Sounds like air traffic control had a problem, too."

Mark Shepherd's bored eyes remained glued to the computer screen. "What year for the alderman's conviction?"

"Nineteen eighty-six." She hesitated, then pressed the point with quiet determination. "We should call the airports. It could be a good story."

Shepherd finally looked up, admiring Sharon's soft face and short silky blonde hair styled in a bob. He yearned to be single again. "I heard it, too. What makes you think air control had a problem?"

"Their beacon system apparently failed. That's part of the radar."

The editor's stare glimmered with journalistic interest. He'd only been half-listening to the scanners. "And how do you know *that*?"

Masters shrugged nonchalantly, hiding the pleasure of a small victory. Shepherd usually rejected her ideas out of hand, an attitude that once drove her to indignantly proclaim she wasn't a bimbo. He responded with a dismissive laugh, which made her livid until she realized he treated everyone with the same indifference. "My dad's a pilot. You want me to make some calls?"

His eyes dropped back to the computer screen. "No. I may have more questions about this story. I'll shout for you if I do. Thanks for the info."

Shepherd followed her lissome figure as she shuffled away. He respected her for not mentioning that her dad also happened to be a U.S. senator from California and a heavyweight in the aviation community. Sharon had raised some eyebrows in the newsroom for refusing to trade on his well-known connections. To the contrary, she seemed to avoid them in order to establish credentials on her own. It was a good tip if she'd heard the radio correctly. He'd missed whatever was said about the beacon and wouldn't have understood it anyway. But he prided himself on combating the overeagerness that too often sent reporters chasing worthless leads. It was bad enough when his bosses panicked and created an unnecessary frenzy. He particularly refused to let a college kid see him react with too much interest.

Across the city room Robert Duncan hung up the phone for the fiftieth time that night. He hated cop checks. Call a police station, ask if anything's going on, get the usual "no," move on to the next. Sure, the calls panned out sometimes, but usually it was sheer drudgery. As a diversion, he mentally undressed Sharon when she walked by, his pulse quickening over her long legs and the shapely sweep of her sweater. Perhaps tonight he'd ask her out for a drink. Impress her at a couple of clubs and then—

"Duncan!"

Shepherd's summons shattered the fantasy, but Duncan didn't mind when he heard his assignment. Anything was better than cop checks and this one sounded good. His excitement was tempered only by the editor's final missive. "Hustle, young man. Deadline's in forty-five minutes." Duncan scrambled back to his desk.

On the news desk Christy Cochran removed a stylish pair of eyeglasses after reading a story she'd just gotten from Shepherd. The glasses were a recent concession to the rigors of age and staring at computer monitors for ten years. She was still self-conscious enough that she wore them only when reading, but her constant fussing was becoming a bother. Twirling the glasses in one hand, she knew her charade would end soon and she'd simply wear them all the time.

"Is the alderman still your lead?" asked the layout editor for the metro section, interrupting Cochran's musing.

"Hmm? Oh yes, Sandy. That picture of him at his indictment this morning will play well in three columns."

As news editor, Cochran was the ranking executive at night and responsible for what 650,000 readers would see on tomorrow morning's front page. The decision about what to run had been made earlier by several editors, including herself, at the daily four o'clock budget meeting. Now, she had to determine exactly where everything would appear.

Sandy laughed scornfully. "These clowns never learn. This is the same real estate swindle he got nailed for the first time."

"Be kind. It's not polite to disparage someone who helps us sell so many papers. By the way, I'm running Sharon's sidebar about his first conviction out front, too."

"Okay. Leaves me more room for the rapid transit hearing."

Cochran slipped her glasses back on, brushed a lock of auburn hair behind an ear, and typed a few commands on the keyboard. Different-colored rectangles appeared on a computerized page dummy in front of her to indicate placement of the headline, photo, and text. Then she pressed the SEND key to move the story to another directory in the Atex system so the copy desk could edit it and write the headline.

Just after the file disappeared off the screen, the wire editor leaned across her desk, looking somber. "We've got a plane crash, Christy, and they're saying fatalities."

✈   ✈   ✈

IN THE DIMLY LIT RADAR ROOM AT O'HARE, Bear Pepperidge raised a thick hairy arm and handed Samantha Sanchez a flight strip. "Prairie 492 needs to come back. Hydraulic failure."

The supervisor absently scratched her head with the plastic strip while deciding how to weave the plane through the labyrinth of other traffic. Behind them the hubbub had returned to its normal mixture of swiftly spoken commands over the radio and wisecracks among the controllers. She tapped a fingernail on the glass of the scope, first at a nearby target departing from Midway Airport on Chicago's South Side, then at a couple of others over Lake Michigan.

"He'll level off at five thousand and he's goin' to seven and he's at eight, so climb Prairie to six. Turn him northbound and switch him to Arrival. He's gonna get two-seven left."

As Sanchez stepped away, Bear shoved a ballpoint pen at her, his petulant voice rising a few decibels. "Say, Sammy, can we get some pens that work? It's bad enough the radar goes out all the time. The least you can do is give us decent writing utensils."

She froze in stony silence. Although Sanchez's husband accused her of being overly sensitive, she doubted Bear would make such a demand of his male colleagues. Bitterly, she recalled her promotion into management, an accomplishment she'd proudly relished until derisive remarks from several controllers turned it bittersweet. Skill, they reminded her, had little to do with the decision. The FAA cared only that she was a Hispanic woman, double bonus for an agency under pressure to satisfy equal opportunity quotas. Four years later, no matter how fair and level-headed she tried to be as a supervisor, some of the controllers would never accord her much respect.

"Hey, Neanderthal, get your own pens. You can use the exercise."

It was Ryan Kelly, hollering from across the room with a smirk for Bear and a wink at Sanchez. The Neanderthal raised a finger in response.

Sanchez smiled appreciatively at Kelly, then scowled at Pepperidge. "I'm not the supply sergeant. I don't order 'em and I certainly don't deliver them. There's a box in that cabinet." She gestured to the right and marched away before he had a chance to reply.

Bear grunted and mimicked her rebuke, his head swaying. When he spoke into the mike, he made no attempt to hide his irritation. "Prairie 492, Chicago Departure. Expect runway two-seven left. Climb and maintain six thousand and turn left heading three-six-zero."

While listening to the readback, he rotated his chair and glared at Kelly. *The guy's a star here, so how come he's sucking up to management? Could it be that our fair-haired boy wants to become one of them? Too bad, because then we'd have to stop being friends.*

✈   ✈   ✈

AT THE EAST ARRIVAL SCOPE, Pete Rykowski was finishing a transmission when Sanchez handed over the flight strip. "You're getting him back on a three-sixty heading at six."

He barely glanced up. "Okay."

Rykowski had eight other planes coming in from the north and south over the Lake Michigan shoreline before they turned west onto final approach. His stubby index finger beat steadily on the console while he determined how to squeeze in the unexpected arrival. His immediate concern was a Coastal Boeing 727 descending from the southeast. Its path would intersect 1,000 feet above Prairie's, the legal minimum for vertical separation. After Prairie checked in on the frequency, he advised both pilots of their proximity so they could look for each other in the sky.

Rykowski was relieved to have the ARTS back in operation. He felt more comfortable now that the scope was displaying aircraft identifications again and updating altitudes once every second. The two-digit numbers displayed in hundreds of feet. He saw Prairie's flash 58 before turning another flight onto final approach. Okay, time to slow USAir 758 to create a gap for Prairie, now level at six and looking good. A hole in the arrival flow opened and Rykowski's finger slackened its pace. This is gonna work.

Hey—wait a minute.

The altitude readout on Prairie's data tag flashed 62, riveting Rykowski's attention on the scope. Why didn't he stop at 6,000? *Sam said he was cleared to six, didn't she?* His mind raced to recall her instructions. He didn't think he'd made a mistake. Maybe the plane's Mode C was sending bad information. It happened occasionally. He cleared another plane onto final, then watched with rising concern as the readout flashed 63. At the same time, Coastal's data block dipped from 70 to 69.

Fuck. They're *both* busting altitude!

Beep-beep-beep-beep. The Conflict Alert system began blaring insistently over the loss of separation and the two targets blinked in unison.

"Coastal 1638 is descending. We've got an RA."

Rykowski immediately keyed the mike, his voice level but urgent. "You'd better climb. You're descending into traffic. A DC-9."

He gritted his teeth because the warning was futile. The pilot was following the dictates of an onboard computer called the Traffic Alert/Collision Avoidance System. TCAS monitored the surrounding sky for traffic and issued a Resolution Advisory if the digital sentry deemed that two paths would converge, commanding the pilots in a recorded voice to climb or descend. The policies of most airlines mandated that pilots follow the computer, regardless of anything controllers said.

The two targets continued blinking in persistent accompaniment to the shrill beeping of the Conflict Alert bell. As if drawn by a magnet, they moved toward each other unerringly. Rykowski used a round trackball to slew his cursor on them and pressed a few keys to turn off the alarm. Then there was nothing else he could do but stare helplessly at the scope.

The readouts flashed again. Coastal now at 67, Prairie at 65.

Rykowski shivered in a sudden cold sweat. Everything had been running smoothly until these two runaways threw his carefully constructed traffic plan into chaos. They were seconds away from colliding now, yet part of him still refused to accept the horror, the ultimate disaster he'd trained and strived every working moment for eight years to prevent. It was a nightmare that he always knew could happen but didn't want to believe would happen to him. In the one other incident like this that he'd suffered through, the two planes never got closer than about 700 feet. There hadn't been any real likelihood they'd hit.

He sprang out of his chair and paced before the scope in an unconscious effort to dissipate nervous energy, hugging himself to stave off the shakes as the full import of the moment dawned on him.

He'd never seen two targets co-locate on the scope.

The radar swept around again and the pair of green blips and overlapping data blocks merged. In the black sky above Lake Michigan, Coastal and Prairie were flying so close together that the rotating ASR-9 radar dish at O'Hare could no longer distinguish the two planes. Confused by its inability to sift information from the converging transponders, ARTS lapsed into "coast status" and simply displayed CST on the data blocks.

Rykowski's left hand held his forehead. If only two targets come out the other side, I win. If it's more than two . . . *Jesus, I can't think about that.*

The sweep seemed to crawl. His eyes followed the pencil beam of light on its four-second lap around the compass, willing it to move faster. He clutched the mike switch with a clammy palm.

"Coastal 1638, say your altitude."

There was no reply.

"Prairie 492, say your altitude."

No reply.

His gut roiled. Come on, guys, I'm sure you're busy but one of you please say your altitude because I don't think I can bring myself to ask again and I need to know. I want to hear those sweet voices of yours and know that you're not in a thousand flaming pieces right now. He scanned his other traffic to make sure no other crises were developing and noted the potential conflict with USAir 758.

✈   ✈   ✈

THE CAPTAIN AND FIRST OFFICER in the cockpit of Coastal flight 1638 leaned forward, their faces nearly touching the windshield while they urgently searched the night sky for the "intruder" traffic that set off the computer. Behind them the flight engineer monitored the TCAS display they called the fish-finder. He looked out the window, too, but couldn't see as much from his position. The fish-finder was dotted with white diamonds signifying other planes in their vicinity, each accompanied by a readout of the difference in their altitudes. The intruder, highlighted by a red square, appeared on the lower left.

"Should be in our eight o'clock position," the flight engineer announced. "Four hundred feet below."

"Increase descent—increase descent!" The synthetic voice of TCAS rang out stridently.

The captain pushed harder on the control yoke and a muffled clatter sounded on the other side of the cockpit door from flight attendants securing the galley. The nose of the Boeing 727 pointed toward a gently curving line where the inky void of Lake Michigan melded with a grid of twinkling lights that stretched to the horizon. Directly ahead, glittering office towers that formed the Loop thrust skyward. The panoply of lights, partially obscured by scattered ghostly white clouds, made it difficult to pick out the other plane.

"Three hundred feet," the flight engineer said.

The first officer squirmed in his seat. "I don't like this."

The captain's seasoned eyes squinted, alternating between the sky and the TCAS display that told him how fast to descend. Watching the distance diminish between their plane and the conflicting traffic made him uncomfortable, too, but he had a lot of faith in TCAS. He loved the radar display that let them see other planes nearby instead of having to rely solely on controllers. He'd caught them making mistakes too many times.

"It'll be okay. The computers are talking constantly with each other to coordinate the maneuver. They're not going to let us hit. Just keep looking."

"*Two* hundred feet."

"There! I got him." The first officer's arm flew across the cockpit. "Wait a sec—" His view was momentarily obstructed while they punched through a cloud. "Okay, there he is."

The looming profile of the T-tailed DC-9, in a steep climb, mushroomed on their left. Just as quickly, the plane streaked above them, out of harm's way. The first officer ducked instinctively and swiveled his head to follow the other aircraft, soaring to their right.

"Christ, that was close."

The captain said nothing, his body rigid. Several moments later, when his sweaty hands began slipping on the control yoke, he slowly wiped one and then the other on his navy blue trousers.

✈   ✈   ✈

PETE RYKOWSKI RESTED HIS CHIN on clasped hands and prayed. After another radar sweep, the beacon re-acquired the transponders and two targets jumped apart.

Sweet Jesus.

Gingerly, he sat in front of the scope. The data blocks resumed their normal display, showing Coastal at 6,000 feet and to the west of Prairie, now at 6,800. He squeezed his eyes closed and reopened them, breathing deeply after reassuring himself there'd been no disaster. Then he remembered the conflicting traffic.

"USAir 758, I need you to level at eight thousand. Traffic two o'clock, five miles northbound."

"We'll hold at eight and . . . the traffic is in sight, USAir 758."

Thank you, sir, now don't pull a fast one on me.

"Approach, Coastal 1638 is level at six and we show the traffic eight hundred feet above and to the right of us now. We got the RA and had to follow it . . . but then he went right in front of us."

Rykowski's already high blood pressure skyrocketed. He hadn't misheard

Sam. The goddamned computer had fucked up again, this time nearly splattering several hundred bodies all over Lake Shore Drive. He gripped the
mike switch, his voice constricted with anger.

"Understand, Coastal 1638. Maintain six thousand and turn right heading three-six-zero. Prairie 492, uh . . . climb and maintain seven thousand.
Turn left heading two-four-zero. You're cleared for the ILS runway two-
seven left."

"Seven thousand, left to two-four-zero and cleared for approach on the left,
Prairie 492. We got an RA, too, that told us to climb."

"Roger, Prairie. We'll get a hold of you. It's going to be a TCAS near miss
instructing you to climb and Coastal to descend into each other."

Rykowski called another airplane farther out on approach, barely hearing the pilot's response over the rapid pounding of his heart. His mouth
was cottony and his gut felt like a cauldron ready to boil over. He needed
off the scope—*now*. He turned around to holler for Sanchez and saw her
standing right behind him. Jodi Jenkins sauntered up and plugged her headset jack into the console.

"Fucking TCAS, Sam! It damn near spot-welded a couple."

"J.J. will take over for you," she said quietly.

Sanchez watched them run through the transition checklist and noted
that Rykowski's hands were trembling as the short stocky controller eased
out of his chair. Small wonder. She couldn't wait to find out how close the
two planes passed when they analyzed a radar track of the incident.

Kelly looked up at Rykowski and Sanchez, shaking his head grimly. "Close,
but they didn't scrape paint."

"Yeah, well, it's bound to happen someday," J.J. said as she settled in
front of the scope. Then she fixed Kelly with a melancholy stare. "And
when TCAS does run a couple together, guess who they're gonna blame?"

"It was someone else's turn tonight."

Kelly, J.J., and Rykowski all turned toward Sanchez, whose nutmeg face
hung toward the floor.

"Coastal bought it in Dallas. Dropped one on final to DFW. It just
happened, so I don't know any more details." She paused, her words sinking heavily while each of them contemplated what might have gone wrong
and succumbed to a moment of relief that they weren't involved. At length,
she touched Rykowski's shoulder. "Let's go listen to the tape."

THREE
DEADLINE

CHRISTY COCHRAN, THE *CHRONICLE*'S NEWS EDITOR, shuddered inwardly at the mention of a plane crash. So many souls snuffed out in seconds. It's what made her nervous about flying, never mind that those metal contraptions were supposedly safer than driving a car. Comforted by the knowledge that her son and sister were safely on the ground this evening, she gazed serenely at the editor leaning across the desk.

"National wire?"

"First news alert came in a few minutes ago."

Cochran tapped on her keyboard and scanned a dispatch from The Associated Press:

U,A,4—AM-COASTAL CRASH,   04-10 0083
URGENT
Coastal Airlines jet crashes in thunderstorm
DALLAS (AP)—A Coastal Airlines jetliner crashed this evening near Dallas-Fort Worth International Airport while trying to land in what appeared to be a flash thunderstorm. At least a dozen people were believed killed, but apparently there were some survivors.
Airport officials said the McDonnell Douglas DC-9, Flight 1521 from New York, went down in a residential area about two miles from the runway.
Fire and rescue crews were on the scene trying to douse the blaze and get survivors out of the wreckage.
MORE
AP-WS-04-10-00 2128EDT

She stored the file and searched the directory for additional takes, but none had been sent yet.

The wire editor watched expectantly. "Are you taking it out front?"

Cochran toyed with her glasses, glancing at the clock. It was 8:37 P.M. and they had to send their last page to the composing room by 10 to close the first edition on time. Details were scant but this would definitely develop into a bigger story. The question was whether they'd get more information before deadline. Three paragraphs weren't enough to vault it onto page one. Such meager coverage would look embarrassingly incomplete by morning when the tragedy would dominate TV news. Gambling that the wires would send more in the next hour, though, seemed a good bet. The crash occurred in a major U.S. city, not some remote jungle. Reporters were probably swarming over the scene already.

"Yeah, I'll take it."

She was deciding how to shuffle the stories on the page when the night city editor appeared at her side. "We plan to give you something on a radar outage at O'Hare. Sounds like the control tower had a rough time of it for a while. Duncan says he'll turn about fifteen inches."

She shot him a quizzical glance. "Is there a full moon out? We just got word of a plane crash in Dallas."

Mark Shepherd raised his palms as if to indicate the obvious. "Always in threes, Christy. One more to go."

"Thanks for the sage warning. What else can you tell me about O'Hare?"

"All the aircraft identifications disappeared from their radar screens for several minutes. The FAA is downplaying but it sounds serious. Our lovely intern, by the way, is the one who caught this on the scanner."

Sandy, the metro section layout editor, overheard their conversation and leaned across her desk to join in. Cochran assessed her page dummy yet again. The two aviation stories were a natural pairing and fresh news. The *Chronicle* had covered the alderman's impending indictment all last week and the only new angle was his appearance in court. It made sense to push the story inside. She felt her adrenaline kick in because they had a lot to do in the next eighty minutes. Looking up at Shepherd, Sandy, and the wire editor, she ticked off their orders.

"Okay, Mark, I need Duncan's story no later than 9:25. Lee, I can handle up to twenty inches on the crash, but get it to me by 9:20, please. That'll be the main headline and I'll stick the O'Hare piece underneath. Sandy, you'll have to take the alderman package in metro. Give it good play. I'll keep the photo out front and refer to your stuff from the caption."

Shepherd heeled around and the other two editors hustled back to work. Christy snatched her phone and dialed an extension for the Art Department.

"Hi, Rich, it's Christy on the news desk. Can you make me a one-column locator map of the airport in Dallas? No, not Love Field, the big one. Yeah, DFW. There's been a plane crash so the wires may move something. This edition. Thanks, Mr. Magician."

She hung up and leaned back in her chair. The plan was in motion. Now, if all the pieces came together in the next hour, they'd have a solid front page that would boost tomorrow's street sales. She reached for the phone again to update her boss at home and absently watched Robert Duncan across the room.

Seated at his desk, the young reporter's hands darted across the keyboard in a blur. He used only his two index fingers yet he typed very quickly. In staccato bursts of creativity and thought, the words blossomed into sentences on his green computer monitor. He'd promised the desk fifteen inches and had a third of that, but he needed to know what caused the outage at O'Hare and was unclear about some other details. He tried to ignore Shepherd looking restlessly in his direction, anxious for the story. This is why they call newspapers a first draft of history. If that FAA flack doesn't call me back in another ten minutes . . . He reviewed the notes he'd typed earlier and continued writing. When the phone rang, he nearly dropped the receiver by grabbing it too fast.

"Duncan here."

"Hi, Bob. Grant Miller at the FAA again. I've done some more checking for you. The radar malfunction lasted just six minutes. There was no loss of separation. Safety was never compromised."

"What constitutes loss of separation?"

"Controllers in the TRACON are required to keep aircraft apart by a thousand feet vertically and three miles horizontally. If two planes break that bubble, it's what we call an operational error or loss of separation. There's no real danger, but the safety margin has been compromised so we mount an inquiry to find out what happened. If they get closer than a thousand feet and one mile, that's called a near miss and there's a more detailed investigation."

"What's the TRACON?" Duncan repeated the unfamiliar term slowly, pronouncing it *tray*-kon.

Miller's voice oozed with patience. "Our abbreviation for Terminal Radar Approach Control. It's the radar room where the malfunction occurred. The controllers there are responsible for handling arrivals and departures in airspace around O'Hare. They work in concert with our boys in the tower, where the planes are cleared for takeoff and landing."

Duncan stopped typing abruptly. "I thought all this happened in the tower. Weren't those computers affected, too?"

"Some of the systems are linked, but the tower wasn't really impacted."

Duncan shook his head to clear up the fundamental misconception. "So this TRACON is at the airport?"

"It's at the base of the tower, one level below ground. We have 185 TRACONs across the country and most of them are located at airports. However, when the new tower opens up here at O'Hare, the radar room will move twenty miles away to Elgin. The latest schedule indicates—"

"Thanks, but that's another story. What caused the outage?"

Miller's lengthy explanation of the uninterruptible power supply was far more technical than Duncan needed. He typed a few notes and thought about how to describe the breakdown in layman's terms, stealing a peek at the clock.

9:15. Deadline.

"You say that Prairie landing was routine?"

"Touchdown was normal."

The phrasing of Miller's answer made Duncan skeptical. His sixth sense, honed by extracting the truth from too many sources bent on hiding it, told him he wasn't getting the whole story. He fought the urge to just say "thanks" and hang up so he could finish writing.

"Anything else you can tell me?"

"I'll put it in perspective for you, Bob. Incidents like hydraulic failure, engine failure, gear that won't retract—they happen fairly often. When they do, pilots want to get right back to the airport in case something else goes wrong. But the actual danger usually isn't that great because of the redundancy built into these aircraft. Even though Prairie lost its System A hydraulics, it still had System B and an auxiliary system."

"So it was the equivalent of a flat tire?"

Miller chuckled. "That's an oversimplification, but not too far off the mark."

Duncan still sensed the FAA man was holding out on him, but there wasn't time to pursue it. "Okay, then. I appreciate your help, Grant. Bye."

He threw the receiver back onto its cradle and pounded the keyboard, hastily revising his lead paragraph. Instead of peering out windows in the tower, the controllers were now hunched over radarscopes in darkness, desperately trying to overcome a computer breakdown and avoid a midair collision.

"Duncan! Where's that story?" Shepherd, yelling from across the room.

"In a minute."

It was another five before he hit the SEND key. Out of material, he was dismayed to discover he'd written just ten inches, even with information about the Prairie flight. *The desk will have to live with it.*

Shepherd quickly scanned the copy to make sure no major questions were unanswered. He grimaced at Duncan's overly dramatic writing style and changed a few words to tone it down.

On the news desk, Cochran drummed her fingers. Her page layout now included a file photo of a DC-9 and the map she'd requested pinpointing Dallas-Fort Worth Airport. The wire editor had sent along the national story about the crash, including several more takes containing quotes from witnesses on the ground describing how the plane nose-dived to earth. All that remained was Duncan's piece. When it finally arrived—ten minutes late—she was chagrined by its length.

"Shepherd, this story is five inches shorter than you promised."

"I know, but it's everything he gave me."

Cochran sighed. The last thing she wanted to do was revise her layout yet again. There were editions when everything fell naturally into place. Tonight, she'd had to wrestle with each story and picture to make them all fit. Her voice rose pleadingly. "Can you make it grow at all?"

Shepherd stood and placed both hands on his hips for emphasis. "Christy, that story is not Pinocchio's nose."

She swore under her breath and rapidly assessed the page. Instead of two columns, Duncan's story would fit nicely in one. The DC-9 photo that went with the Dallas crash next to it could be blown up to fill the gap. A one-column headline would be harder to write, but more radical layout changes would cause a ripple effect on several other pages and there wasn't time. She added a deck head to give the copy editor some room to elaborate and punched the SEND key.

As Christy expected, the editor grumbled about his difficult task and she listened sympathetically. Writing headlines that accurately summarized a story while also conveying a dash of color and wit was an art akin to poetry. An art frequently crafted under severe time contraints. After a minute of fretting, he smiled mischievously.

"Since I can fit only one or two words per line, how about 'O'Hare blows a fuse?' C'mon, Christy. You wouldn't let me use 'Texas toast' on the crash story."

She knew he wasn't serious but she glared anyway. Outrageous headlines were constantly volleyed around the desk. None made the paper. It was merely a way for copy editors to have fun and cope with deadline stress.

"We're not the *New York Post*, Ken." She began thinking aloud. "Something about no radar . . . outage turns scopes to black . . . scrambling to keep track of targets."

Ken picked up on the theme. "Have to get the 'no radar' angle in. They couldn't see who was who. They were handicapped . . . crippled . . . blinded. That's it. How about 'O'Hare blinded by outage'?"

Christy snapped two fingers. "What about the deck?"

The minutes ticked by while Ken played with the words, repeatedly shuffling their order like one of those puzzle games with movable tiles until he finally composed something that made sense in the allotted space. "Okay, here we go. 'Air controllers scramble after radar failure' is the best I can do for now. We're outta time."

"I like it."

Christy sighed with satisfaction as the copy desk chief sent the story and headlines to the composing room to be set into type. They'd made deadline with seconds to spare. While cleaning up the clutter of papers and unused pictures on her desk, she noticed Sharon Masters walking across the city room and waved her over.

"Shepherd mentioned you gave him the tip about the O'Hare story. Thanks for the nice work."

Sharon smiled bashfully, reminding Christy how the younger woman seemed much like herself when she was in college, studying and struggling to get started in journalism. She hoped Sharon would avoid the same mistake that nearly derailed her career before it left the station. Motioning her closer, she spoke in a guarded tone.

"Here's a tip for you. Mind Duncan's tentacles. He'll put the moves on and then toss you aside like a used tissue."

Sharon nodded knowingly. "I thought that might be the case. Thanks for the warning. Too bad. He's kinda cute."

✈   ✈   ✈

AT THE SPORTS EDITION BAR in the O'Hare Hilton, Bear Pepperidge followed through on his earlier offer and bought the first pitcher of beer. Ryan Kelly, Pete Rykowski, and Jodi Jenkins clustered around the small table while he filled their glasses. Over the din of blaring music and boisterous crowd of travelers, he shouted a typically crude toast.

"I'm sure glad this fucking night's over."

They each gulped a long swig, slowly uncoiling from the breakneck pace of the TRACON. Several pairs of eyes swung to Rykowski, who avoided looking back. He usually enjoyed stopping here after work. It gave him a chance to come down from his adrenaline high before heading home. But he knew they'd dissect the near miss and he needed more time, more beer, before he'd feel ready to delve into it. He pointed accusingly at Bear.

"I loved your little fart comment. I've never heard so many pilots respond to one radio call." He only half-succeeded at sounding cheerful.

Bear scowled, still embarrassed by his miscue.

Kelly took pity on him. "Remember the time I was training J.J.? Didn't pay attention for a second and she turns an airplane to some strange heading. When I look back at the scope and see it, I lean over and say, 'Where does that shithead think he's going?' Of course, I'd keyed my mike so now a dozen pilots are wondering who I'm talking about."

They all laughed, J.J. rocking hysterically on her cowboy boots. "I couldn't make a radio call for the next five minutes without cracking up."

Bear's bloodshot eyes regarded her contemptuously. "Excuse me, Miss Manners, but you'd say just about anything on the radio when you were at

Albuquerque Center."

J.J. stared back defiantly. "Bear, I refuse to engage in a battle of wits with an unarmed man. Besides, if you're referring to what I think, it was one brief comment."

Kelly sipped his beer and snickered. J.J. had transferred to O'Hare four years ago and quickly established herself as the queen of sarcastic comebacks. Controllers who tried goading her with insults or sexual taunts were invariably skewered by her acid tongue. Nevertheless, he wasn't going to pass up an opportunity to hear one of his favorite stories again.

"Some comment. Are you going to tell them or do I have to?"

Bear was watching her with anticipation and she shrugged at the inevitable.

"Part of the Center's airspace includes the White Sands Missile Range. When there's a launch, the range is hot and closed to civilian traffic. A pilot I was handling had been really difficult, questioning every one of my clearances. When I made him deviate around the range, he said, 'That's going to hurt us.' So I lost my patience and told him, 'Not as much as a missile up your ass.' "

"She forgot to mention she was a developmental at the time," Kelly interjected.

"That's why I got away with it. My instructor said it showed I wasn't going to let myself be browbeaten by an unreasonable pilot."

Rykowski smiled faintly. He swallowed more beer, half emptying his glass, then refilled it. He moved deliberately, a distinct change from his usual frantic pace, and wrapped both hands around the glass as if to steady them.

"Yeah, the things we say on the air—or would like to. I had a few choice words in mind tonight. Fucking TCAS. I'd like to personally rip it out of every god-damned cockpit I can get into. It was a classic Dallas Bump. I told Coastal to descend to seven and Prairie was climbing to six. Everyone was happy till TCAS shit the bed because it doesn't know the pilots' intentions."

After the anti-collision system went into widespread use several years ago, numerous incidents like tonight's plagued Dallas-Fort Worth Airport. Two planes rapidly climbing and descending toward each other spooked the computer into thinking they were going to hit because it had no way of knowing the pilots would safely level off 1,000 feet apart. With disturbing frequency, the resulting evasive maneuver sent both planes dangerously close to each other. DFW's longstanding traffic patterns helped cause the phenomenon, which was dubbed the Dallas Bump-Up Effect. It was also prevalent at Atlanta Hartsfield, LAX, and elsewhere.

J.J.'s lean face contorted. "I'll never understand why TCAS sometimes tells the pilots to increase their climb or descent so they shoot past each other. If they just leveled off, they'd stay a lot farther apart."

"Maybe there was something weird about the geometry of this encounter," Kelly mused. "TCAS must have seen other traffic in the area and figured that was the best solution."

"Some solution," Rykowski snapped, staring into his glass and rotating it in precise quarter turns. "According to the data run, they came within two hundred feet and a quarter mile."

Bear whistled. "Whoa. At least no one made the national news."

"Not here," J.J. said. "I wonder what happened in Dallas?"

Dwelling on the dark side was making Kelly uncomfortable and he could tell Rykowski wished they'd change the subject, too. "Some idiot reporter will have it all figured out in the morning. I heard you're going to Vegas again, J.J."

She was a notoriously good card player—a much sought-after and feared bridge partner in the TRACON break room—and consistently came home several thousand dollars richer from blackjack. "Yeah, a two-day hop next week. Get me some spending money for summer clothes."

Bear poured her more beer. "Take me along. I could use some of your good luck. My alimony payments are killing me."

"Sorry, guy, but I always gamble alone."

"Gambling and most everything else, it seems."

He frankly appraised her. No tits, but her skintight blue jeans hugged a trim waist and firm ass. Bear lit a Marlboro and pictured her naked. A pipe dream, he knew, because J.J. wasn't the least bit interested in him. For that matter, he'd never seen her cozy up to any man. Probably a dyke. It would fit with her hard-edged attitude. He decided to test the theory.

"How come you don't have a husband?"

J.J. laughed shrilly. "And end up like you? Anyway, I did for a while before I came here and decided once was enough." She jerked a thumb.

"Pick on Rain Man. He's never been married."

Bear revised his assessment—so she's bi—and squinted at Kelly through the smoke wafting from his cigarette. "No, but he played house for a while. Still puts the babe up on a pedestal, even though she dumped him for some other schmuck."

Kelly shook his head, both at the unhappy memory and Bear's characteristic bluntness. "Carol wanted kids and I don't. I couldn't blame her when she left me."

"Your sensitivity is touching. Really."

"Why don't you want kids?" Rykowski's astonished tone betrayed his upbringing. He was a devout Catholic who'd married his high school sweetheart, promptly produced four offspring and never stopped doting on them. It was beyond his comprehension that people could be happy any other way.

"They're a complication I can do without. I'm just not interested in them."

And afraid I'd be a tyrant like my old man. His frequent backhand rang in Kelly's ears like he'd been slapped only yesterday. He ignored Rykowski's condescending smile, the same kind others gave him who deemed his decision a profound mistake rather than carefully considered freedom of choice.

Bear swallowed the last of his drink and reached for the pitcher. "I think you're just not interested in women anymore. Haven't seen you date one in months. What I don't get is why you always stick up for 'em. Did it with Sammy tonight." He arched a bushy black eyebrow suspiciously. "You banging her? Might be good for your career. It was for hers."

J.J. elbowed Bear none too gently in the ribs, making him spill beer on the table. "Why am I not surprised your third wife just left you?"

Bear Pepperidge was a throwback to the days when the FAA was a "brown shoe" agency filled with macho types from the military. A chauvinist who reinforced J.J.'s decision to shun serious relationships with men. Still, the controller in her worried about him. He was easily fifty pounds overweight, his beard had more hair than the top of his head, and deep lines of stress creased his face. She also knew that his bombastic attitude had blossomed in direct proportion to the perennial equipment breakdowns. And so, like everyone else in the TRACON, she kept a close watch on his scope.

"Sam deserves respect," Kelly said evenly. "She's a good manager and was a good controller. Anyway, even if I wanted to, she's married." He pointed to his ring finger and took a long draft of beer.

Bear mashed his cigarette in an ashtray and massaged his bruised side. "As if that makes a difference. I bet you can't get it up anymore."

Kelly noticed J.J. smile discreetly and looked directly at Bear. "Bend over and find out, asshole."

For the first time after his shift, Rykowski laughed. J.J. feigned disgust. Controllers ridiculed one another mercilessly, often with the intellectual prowess of teenage boys trading taunts in the locker room. But their bandying in no way lessened the religious ferocity with which the TRACON's brotherhood looked after its own. When someone got in trouble on position, they all rallied to help. Given their close working conditions and long hours, it was inevitable that they knew intimate details about each other's lives, sometimes more than the spouses at home. These people weren't just drinking buddies. They were family.

J.J. was particularly fond of Kelly, one of the most talented controllers she'd ever known. When the traffic was overwhelming and the winds were wreaking havoc and the rest of them were sweating, he'd slouch in his chair and move airplanes like someone playing a friendly game of chess. It seemed his only concession to the stress was a sprinkle of gray spreading through his straight black hair. He was confident but not cocky. Assertive without being abrasive. Authoritative yet lacking arrogance. Most of all, she admired him for never lording his talent over the others. Physically, his broad shoulders and ruggedly handsome face appealed to her and she loved his endless supply of stories.

"This DC-8 had been holding near the coast for about forty-five minutes because Seattle was still fogged in," Kelly was saying. "So I called the pilot and offered to vector him to Mount Saint Helens or Rainier so his passengers would have a better view while they waited. But I hadn't noticed this was a forty-three series—a freighter. The pilot comes back on the radio and says in this long Southern drawl, 'Well, I don't think six thousand chickens *care* what they're lookin' at.' "

J.J. roared with the rest of them and caught Kelly's attention with a knowing gleam in her eyes. He nodded slightly while flagging the cocktail waitress for a second pitcher. It was another hour and too many stories later before they all left the bar. In the section of the O'Hare parking garage reserved for FAA employees, Kelly sidled up to Rykowski.

"You gonna be all right, Rykrisp?"

"Sure."

"Will you be in tomorrow?"

He didn't answer right away, instead looking down at his shoes, at the cars, anywhere but at his friend. "I dunno. I'll see how I feel in the morning."

Under different circumstances, Kelly would have lobbed back a wise-crack. But it was perfectly understandable if Rykowski took a day or two of sick leave to steady his nerves. The TRACON was no place for uncertainty, where the relentless pace demanded split-second decisions founded on un-wavering confidence. A stellar example of Darwin's theory. The insecure quickly and inevitably went down the tubes. He slapped Rykowski on the back.

"I'll call out the cavalry if we don't see you in a few."

The shrill screams of jet engines reverberated off the cement floor and ceiling and the acrid aroma of burning fuel saturated the air as Kelly strolled on to his car. Perversely, he'd liked the smell ever since flying caught his fancy as a boy. He savored it now like a wine connoisseur inhaling the bouquet of his favorite vintage. While settling in behind the wheel of his Acura, he noticed J.J. flash her parking lights. So he'd been right about her glance in the bar. She wasn't ready to end the evening. He flashed his park-ing lights back, one of several signals they used to conduct their relation-ship without the other controllers' knowledge.

With a squeal of tires, J.J. weaved out of the parking garage. She was an aggressive driver who looked for holes in traffic like she did on the radar-scope. He hustled to stay close behind as she sped beneath taxiways Alpha and Bravo that crossed over the expressway leading in and out of O'Hare, and wound through a cloverleaf funneling them onto the Tri-State Tollway. Then they peeled off along the Northwest Tollway, past the hotels huddling the airport boundary, Rosemont's imposing Horizon stadium, and the golden arches of McDonald's U., where hopeful franchise owners learned how to flip Big Macs into big bucks. After they pulled off the tollway at the exit for Schaumburg, he watched her taillights dance into the distance when he stopped at a gas station.

✈   ✈   ✈

KELLY WALKED THROUGH THE FRONT DOOR of J.J.'s one-bedroom condo without knocking and wasn't surprised to find her naked except for the blue and white checkered blouse she'd worn to work. The only illumination in the living room came from a pair of eyeball fixtures recessed in the ceiling that accented a colorful Southwestern tapestry hanging above the fireplace. The blouse was already unbuttoned. Reflected light cast her boyish figure in a warm glow as she casually slipped it off and dropped it on a chrome and glass coffee table while approaching him. She grasped his shirt and pulled it out of his black jeans.

"What took you so long?"

He nuzzled her neck, whispering in one ear. "I had to stop and buy gas."

J.J. kissed him hungrily and ripped at his shirt buttons while his hands caressed her with practiced familiarity. Her breasts were little more than nipples but delightfully sensitive to his touch and the left one quickly hardened when he squeezed it between two fingers. She moaned and reached down, smiling wickedly.

"Feels like you can still get it up. Think you can keep it that way?"

Tugging on his belt, she yanked down his jeans and they tumbled to the carpeted floor in the archway between the living and dining rooms. His lips grazed the smooth soft skin of her shoulders and he planted kisses on her neck. Open and impatient for more, she rolled over and sat astride him.

"God, yes. Give it to me."

J.J.'s brown and white beagle circled them with concern, his tail wagging while their moans swiftly crescendoed and subsided. Then the beagle settled down next to them as they lay side by side on their backs and waited for their breathing to return to normal. Kelly reached out to put an arm around J.J., but she was already grabbing her jeans.

"I'm hungry. You want an omelet?"

"Why are you running away so fast? Stay here awhile."

"What can I say? Drinking and sex make me hungry."

"Can't you cool it just for a minute?"

She stopped wriggling into her Levi's, looking down at him with steady green eyes and a firm voice. "You wanna snuggle, get a Beanie Baby. We fuck and that's it. You know that's all you get with me." She zipped up, fetched her blouse from the coffee table, and padded through the dining room into the kitchen.

Sighing longingly, Kelly got up and dressed, too. He eased onto a wooden stool at the short breakfast bar in the kitchen, a pensive smile playing on his lips as he watched her crack several eggs into a bowl. The fork clanged jarringly while she whipped them into foam, showing no hint of what they'd just done. That was the nature of their relationship. J.J. had been explicit about it before they first went to bed. "I want you sexually but that's it," she'd said at the time. "I don't get more involved with men because I can't stand the inevitable complacency and boredom. So let's not mess this up with lies about love or bragging in the locker room."

Kelly agreed readily, a bachelor's dream come true. No obligations. But the lack of intimacy gradually began to gnaw at him. J.J. never allowed him to spend the night, fearing it would imbue their liaisons with unintended substance. And so now it bothered him that he'd drive home soon. It bothered him, too, that sex between them had deteriorated into rapid rote couplings.

She glanced at him over her shoulder. "Thinking about Pete?"

"Yes."

He'd begun to question whether their affair was worth continuing and it surprised him that he'd consider giving up such a convenient outlet for his libido. But without the added dimension of real affection, he went home feeling physically sated yet emotionally empty.

J.J. shuttled efficiently between the stove and refrigerator. "Pretty scary, but he'll be okay. He knows the near miss wasn't his fault."

Kelly forced himself to change mental gears although he didn't want to discuss it, preferred not even to think about it. Far easier to view the job as just a game. Check that. Necessary to view it as a game. Otherwise, he'd go crazy worrying about the consequences. But there were moments when he couldn't escape the stark reality. Half to himself, he murmured, "Yeah, not his fault."

He knew that wouldn't matter if two planes ran together.

FOUR
DUMP ZONE

KELLY COULD BARELY BREATHE. His chest felt constricted. He was leaden, unable to move as he watched the two targets creep toward each other. Overtaken by a surrealistic sense of detachment, he knew he had to call one of the airplanes but couldn't key his mike. There was a heaviness in the air and something else, something that wasn't right but he couldn't put his finger on it except that he felt fear and danger, knew he must key the mike and call those airplanes because they were going to smack unless he did something—*could it be a gas leak?*—so he tried to move and didn't, tried again, urging, willing his fingers to cooperate and key the blessed mike.

The meow snapped him out of it.

He jolted awake and felt the oppressive weight of the rotund cat settled on his chest. Blearily, he focused on a small alarm clock on the bed stand, its hands edging past ten-thirty. He looked around the room to draw reassurance from familiar sights. His favorite lithograph on the wall—Hiroshige's *Rain Shower on the Ohashi Bridge*, a crystal sea nymph sculpted by Lalique forever pouring water from her jug atop the armoire, oak trees whispering in the morning breeze outside the window. Slowly, the effects of last night's near miss receded. The cat blinked deliberately and stared at him.

"I suppose you're hungry."

Rudy stood and stretched, grinding both front paws and all of his eighteen pounds into Kelly's chest. "Ouch." Kelly unceremoniously shoved the cat aside and sleepily pulled on his trademark black jeans and a heather gray turtleneck.

"Okay, Tubbo, let's go force some food into that emaciated body of yours."

Rudy charged down the spiral staircase leading to the main floor of the house with remarkable agility, eagerly anticipating his twice-daily feeding. The strict dietary regimen so far had failed to make the slightest dent in the black and brown tabby's substantial girth. Now, as always, he barely waited until the mix had been poured into his bowl before inhaling it.

Kelly put a pot of water on the stove to boil for coffee and strolled outside to retrieve the newspaper from the end of his long driveway. Oaks and maples hugging each side of the gently curving asphalt were finally blooming after a long harsh winter. Still laden with dew, the leaves glistened under a dazzling azure sky. The stillness of the morning was broken only by the chatter of birds nesting above and the dull thud of Kelly's footsteps on the pavement. He drank in the fresh air and felt the cool morning on his face. When scouting for a site to build a house several years ago, he'd been taken by this pastoral hilly area on the outskirts of Woodstock, sixty miles northwest of Chicago. His five-acre property was split by a meandering stream and heavily wooded, shrouding it in privacy. The hour-long commute to the airport could be tiresome, but he liked living far away from the noise and congestion of the city. The tranquillity helped him cope with the frenzied pace of his job.

He waved at his neighbor in the white-fenced pasture across the road, out for her daily horseback ride and a few stolen minutes of peace and quiet while the kids were at school. The woman's husband was an attorney in town and had reviewed the numerous contracts Kelly signed when he bought the land and built his house. Longtime residents in the community, the family's driveway was often filled with cars of guests attending the many gatherings they hosted.

Kelly pulled the *Chronicle* out of its box and his arm froze in mid-swing when he saw the headlines: "O'Hare blinded by outage" and "Air controllers scramble after radar failure." Skimming through the first part of the story, he shook open the paper to scan the jump and then crumpled the pages closed. He strode back into the house and flung the *Chronicle* on the kitchen counter, burying a stack of mail that typically went unopened for a week at a time because of his irregular schedule.

Kelly had little patience for ineptitude. He couldn't understand why reporters bungled so many fundamental facts whenever they wrote about aviation. Television was worse, prone to oversimplification and sensationalism. Certain technical concepts were difficult for journalists to grasp, to be sure, but this kind of sloppiness would never be tolerated in the TRACON. The *Chronicle* overstated the danger of the outage, incorrectly described the ARTS, and didn't even mention the near miss. Most galling of all was its implication that he and his colleagues had lost control of the situation.

Kelly was still simmering when he arrived at the airport several hours later. Bear spotted him striding through the break room on his way to the TRACON and held up a dog-eared copy of the paper.

"Did you see this piece of shit?"

"The usual crap, Bear. I think those morons make up half of it."

"They must because this ain't reality. It practically says we had no idea where the airplanes were and that they managed to land only through the grace of God. If my mother read this, she'd be terrified."

"Your mother is already terrified knowing you work here."

"Only because she's keenly aware that I have to put up with assholes like you."

Before Kelly could fire off a retort, Gene Lombardi walked over, nodded hello, and pointed at the paper. "I wonder why they didn't say anything about the near miss?"

Bear deigned the trainee an irritable glance, grimacing at his loud yellow plaid shirt and brown corduroys. Where did this hayseed learn to dress? "They always do that. Make something out of nothing and ignore the real story."

"Maybe we should call and find out why. It'd be a chance to warn people about TCAS."

"We've been warning them since TCAS came out," Pepperidge snarled. "Rykowski even testified before that senator and those idiots on his committee. It's done absolutely no good. They just think we're worried about losing our jobs to automation."

"I bet our people held out on them," Kelly said. "The agency wouldn't want to admit to a reporter that TCAS screwed up." He checked his watch and motioned at Lombardi. "Look, I hate to end this debate, but it's two o'clock and we're due in the TRACON. Ready to move some airplanes, Gene?"

"You bet."

They left Bear to grumble alone and took over on East Arrivals. Lombardi was both excited and nervous when Kelly told him to work the position. Checking out on Departures and North Satellite had been tough enough during the past year. Now he stared humbly at the scope, acutely aware that this was the final and most difficult phase of training. The hardest position in the TRACON—in all of air traffic control—was Approach, where controllers who could really move the metal left the amateurs behind. He was given up to 200 hours to certify, every one of them under the watchful eyes of a journeyman controller who was jacked in with a headset and could override what he said at any moment. Lombardi lived for those hours. He averaged only a few a day because developmentals weren't put on position when it was busy or they were short-staffed, which seemed like most of the time.

The first hour was easy. Targets popped up on the scope at a comfortable pace and blinked, indicating the planes were entering his sector and Chicago Center was ready to give them to Approach. Working on his right, Jodi Jenkins slewed her cursor onto each new blip and tapped ENTER on a small illuminated keyboard on the console to stop the blinking and acknowledge that they'd accepted the handoff. Kelly sat behind both of them, monitoring closely. Their final expanded to eight airplanes and nudged the twenty-five-mile ring around the airport. This was the boundary of the "Dump Zone," where arrivals began making their final descent toward O'Hare.

"Keep your spacing tight," Kelly admonished. "Two-and-a-half miles. Otherwise, your final gets too far out. Then J.J. will have to work harder and she'll be less likely to buy us a beer later on."

Lombardi hunkered down and tuned out the myriad voices around him. He kept one channel of his brain open to hear anything critical, but the bulk of his attention homed in on the targets and the echo of Kelly's offhand reminder. East and West Arrivals would handle about ninety planes in the next hour on the two runways in use. The only way to get everyone down on time was to pack them as closely together as safety permitted. Otherwise, he knew, airplanes would start holding and force a lot of people to work harder, including himself. This job was easiest when everything flowed smoothly. He noted the speed and distance of the first plane on final, then keyed his mike to call the next one.

"United 685, maintain one-seven-zero knots."

"Hundred seventy, United 685."

Another target sprouted on the scope and J.J. slewed to accept the handoff.

"Prairie 004, descend and maintain three thousand."

"Down to three, Prairie flight 004."

Another target sprouted and J.J. slewed to accept.

Lombardi's attention darted constantly to each of his planes, assessing their current and projected positions. Now United was ready to dump onto final and he issued a textbook clearance, struggling to work quickly and efficiently but still feeling himself falling behind.

Another target sprouted and J.J. slewed.

Lombardi's right leg began pumping like a jackhammer. Delta 370 was ready to dump and there was room to squeeze in American 389 if he slowed Air Canada 725 a little to create a gap. Better be quick about it, though, or he'd miss his chance. But Prairie 004 needed a traffic advisory for an arrival flying overhead on its way to the parallel runway. Telltale pressure ballooned under his ribs.

J.J. shot a flight strip across the console. "Better talk faster, Pizza Man. You're going down the tubes."

Kelly, too, saw Lombardi nearing his limit. That was part of the process. There's only so much you can teach in a classroom. Put a guy on position and throw a bunch of airplanes at him until he reaches capacity, then relieve him. Wait a little longer next time, allowing him to build up his ability and self-assurance. The trick was knowing when to step in. Do it too soon and he'd never really learn, deprived of opportunities and demoralized by his instructor's lack of confidence. Wait too long and the consequences could be catastrophic. The tightrope imposed more strain on instructors working an already stressful job. Few controllers walked it, despite the ten percent extra pay. *If he doesn't slow Air Canada now, we'll miss that gap for American.*

Kelly leaned forward and kept his voice gentle. "Use official phraseology, but don't dot every i and cross every t. Just tell 'em enough so they understand."

Lombardi nodded and keyed the mike, ripping through his advisory like a recording on fast forward. "Prairie 004, traffic twelve o'clock, two miles southbound. Crossed over you at four-point-three, descending, a TWA goin' to his final."

"We got him in sight."

"Zero-zero-four, maintain visual separation."

J.J. cackled. "Nice going. You just kissed that hole for American goodbye. Shoulda called Air Canada first."

Kelly winced. Even though she was right, her needling was flustering Lombardi. He poked her chair with his foot. "Would you like to take over as his primary instructor?"

J.J. got the hint but couldn't resist a comeback. "I figured he forgot that jet fuel's not cheap. If he keeps blowing holes, it won't take long for the airline mucky mucks to start screaming at us about delays. I suppose he'd be doing the local economy a favor, though, because the passengers he strands here would have nothing else to do but sit and drink—"

"Enough, J.J."

Unchastened, she flashed her dimples at him and turned innocently back to her scope.

Kelly rolled his eyes. "Think ahead forty miles, Gene. It'll give you space to plan your moves and enough time to talk to everyone."

Lombardi's brow flushed with anger—at J.J. and himself. This job was like tending to a group of wind-up toys, all buzzing in different directions. Stay on top of the situation and he could easily control them before they hit something. Fall behind and he felt this tense breathless feeling of running up to each one just as a crisis was about to break. All it took was one domino to start a chain reaction. A pilot who missed his call sign and forced him to repeat a transmission. The unpredictable winds. A traffic plan that didn't work. The list was endless. Falling behind was easy. Catching up was a bitch. He gulped for air, keyed his mike, and spewed.

"Prairie 004, turn left heading two-five-zero. Three miles from Ridge. Maintain three thousand till established. Cleared for the ILS two-two right. One-seven-zero till Ridge. Tower at Ridge twenty-six niner."

"We got it all, Prairie 004."

Lombardi knew the short response wasn't legal—the FAA required pilots to repeat instructions verbatim—but it saved precious time on an overloaded frequency. Prairie was a commuter airline that flew in and out of O'Hare hundreds of times a day. Its crews were intimately familiar with the procedures. If there were a crash, though, he knew the lawyers would nail him for not insisting on a full readback.

Targets continued flashing on the scope like crackling popcorn. He unconsciously stroked his mustache, fretting over how to fit the arrivals into an orderly plan. *Should I dump Air Canada next? American's in position, too. What about United and those other jumbos coming in from the northeast?* His mind reeled and he tucked his chin against his throat in a renewed effort to think. *Make a move. Any move.* It was a trick he sometimes used to help to uncover a pattern for everyone else. He drew a blank and his attention wandered—*don't forget to take the car in for an oil change tomorrow.* The momentary distraction shattered his concentration and the color drained from his cheeks.

I'm losing the flick!

The blinking targets inched along relentlessly, mocking his indecision. Lombardi shifted nervously in his chair and the sweet tang of sweat stained the air. *I've got to do something now.* Hesitantly, he took the flight strip for a United 747 and positioned it as the next arrival on the rack.

"I'm getting bored." Kelly, sounding pleasantly casual.

Relieved, Lombardi scooted his chair over and let the veteran slide in front of the scope. Looking at the radar from a different perspective, away from the furnace of the hot seat, he was shocked to realize they were working fourteen airplanes. Still, his head hung in shame and he hoped J.J. wouldn't ridicule him again. *Even though I deserve it,* he thought. *There aren't any equipment failures to blame like last night. This is just the normal traffic load.* A familiar fear seeped through him. *I can't hack it.* With growing admiration, he watched the targets transform from chaos into order.

As if conducting an orchestra, Kelly's fingers danced briefly in the air to help him visualize his plan. One by one, he then directed the pilots into a logical pattern. Instead of turning the 747 onto final, followed by Air Canada, Kelly slowed the "heavy," a term controllers used for planes weighing more than 300,000 pounds. Then he stuffed the smaller Canadian DC-9 in the gap and told a pair of jumbos arriving from Europe to follow United. His reprimand to Lombardi was low-key but succinct.

"Don't waste a mile."

Lombardi had heard the mantra many times and scolded himself for missing another gap. Every single mile was a precious resource they considered sinful to throw away. Five miles of spacing was required when smaller lighter jets followed jumbos, due to wake turbulence from the larger planes.

That could be cut to four miles when a heavy followed a heavy. Kelly's shuffle meant another arrival would land this hour.

Targets continued to cascade from the north and east, rhythmically flashing and falling neatly into place after Kelly dumped them. As they lined up on final approach, he pressed the ASTERISK key, then spun his cursor onto each one and tapped ENTER. The "splat" function displayed the distance and bearing between each aircraft on the preview area of the scope.

Lombardi's eyes widened. In every single case, the planes were precisely two miles apart. Like abbreviated phraseology, he knew two-mile separation was illegal. Nonetheless, it was common practice at O'Hare. Running airplanes that close was still considered safe, but it demanded the utmost vigilance and skill because there was scant time to react if something went wrong. He waited for a break between transmissions.

"Anyone ever have a deal going to two miles?"

A deal meant loss of separation. The FAA followed up with a detailed investigation and reams of paperwork—plus retraining if the controller did something wrong.

Kelly smiled thinly. "The agency's tried a few times. Never sticks. They know we do it and the airlines know we do it. But the bottom line is the public wants to fly at convenient times so the carriers bunch up their schedules. Which means we do what we gotta do to get them all down without sending them into the hold. If we ran it legal, everyone would accuse us of a work slowdown." He glanced sharply at Lombardi. "But we never cheat on wake turbulence. If the rules say five miles, give 'em five."

J.J. prodded his arm with another flight strip. "Keep up the pace, Rain Man, or you'll be buying me the beer."

Her caustic comments—first to Lombardi and now to him—had exhausted his tolerance. He recalled her crude reminder the night before about their personal relationship and bristled. "I can keep it up just fine. How come you're always in such a goddamned hurry?"

Fury flashed in J.J.'s green eyes. She immediately grasped the double-entendre and was loath to discuss it, not in private and especially not here in the TRACON. Lombardi glanced uncertainly at them both.

Kelly studied the scope and called an airplane, annoyed for allowing his frustration to bubble to the surface. Dismayed by how their affair had degenerated. He could remember a time when they couldn't get enough. When hurrying was the last thing on her mind. He stirred at the memory of one particularly sensual evening, the only time he'd ever seen J.J. wear a dress. They were seated outdoors at an Italian restaurant. Tiny white lights framed the latticework enclosing the terrace and candles on the tables flickered in the mild evening breeze. While he gave the waiter their order, her hand covertly guided his up one leg and along the inside of a warm thigh until he discovered she'd worn nothing underneath the dress. Dinner turned into a two-hour tease that had them both panting over their cordials. Back at her condo, they lunged at each other the moment the electric garage door banged shut and never got farther than the hood of her car. A time long ago, it seemed, when they enjoyed prolonging pleasure.

He forced himself back to the present and out of the corner of his eye saw J.J. shuffling her flight strips with unnecessary force. With a deep calming breath, he turned to Lombardi.

"You missed a gap awhile ago, but the real reason I took you off position is because we needed two-mile spacing. I didn't want to risk you slowing someone without allowing enough reaction time and suddenly he's cold-nosing the guy in front of him. Then we've got ourselves a deal and it'd ruin my whole day."

Lombardi nodded. In such cases, supervising controllers took all the blame because developmentals were protected by immunity. He watched Kelly work and marveled over his relaxed demeanor, how he carelessly racked the flight strips, the way he made the job look deceptively easy. The guy knew I was losing the flick but he didn't say a word. Few instructors are that charitable.

"I was a transmission behind you back there."

Instantly, he regretted the admission and waited for J.J.'s rebuke. When checking out on North Satellite, he never would have let a comment like that slip in front of Pepperidge, who pounced on him with ferocious glee at the slightest sign of weakness. But there was something about Kelly that made him feel comfortable and unthreatened.

"Then you've got no business being here, stonehead."

Lombardi cringed. His former instructor was towering behind them, a blue T-shirt stretched across his formidable torso that was imprinted with the slogan, "Old age and treachery will triumph over youth and inexperience."

Kelly glanced up with a look of annoyance. "Bear, did you come over here to work or just harangue us?"

"Sammy told me to relieve you guys because you couldn't handle it."

"She sent you over here because all the traffic's died down."

Bear scoffed and plugged his headset into the console. "Move over, Rain Man, and watch an old pro in action."

They went through the transition checklist and Kelly jacked out. He nodded curtly at J.J., who stared resolutely at her scope. Then he walked to the break room with Lombardi for the customary debriefing. They sat in a quiet corner, away from the table where several controllers were playing cards. A few others were sprawled on a sofa watching a Cubs game on television. Kelly pushed away lingering irritation with J.J. and reviewed their session on Approach.

Lombardi looked down apologetically. "The traffic swelled in a hurry, but I know I've gotta do better."

Kelly inspected his fingernails. Indeed, my friend, or we'll send you back to Cleveland with your head between your legs. There's no such thing as an average controller here. We're the best because we have to be. Few people in the world can do what we do. But he wouldn't say it—not yet anyway. His father had relied on bullying and insults as a teaching technique. So did Bear, J.J., and some others, motivated by their ego to wash out as many new people as possible. An attitude that helped maintain the club's exclusive membership. Kelly strove to turn it around. If they were truly the best, they should be able to train almost anybody. He put one foot up on the edge of the table to tighten a shoelace and tried to sound sympathetic.

"The usual three o'clock rush. I've seen you work Departures. You'll get used to the traffic and how fast you need to talk. You'll come to appreciate the ones who know the routine and don't repeat everything."

He chuckled, remembering an incident some years back, and recounted it now to help break the ice. "Bear was working a lot of traffic one day and had to keep repeating instructions to this pilot, who just so happened to be a woman. She was putting him in the hole because of all the time he had to spend with her. Finally, he asked, 'Ma'am, is there a galley on that aircraft?' She made the mistake of saying yes, so he growled, 'Then why don't you get back there where you belong.' "

Lombardi shook his head. "I suppose they decertified him. Or at least gave him a suspension."

"The Regional Office called ten minutes later, but we were so short-staffed they couldn't even afford to put him on the beach for three days. All he got was a letter in his file. This was before Anita Hill; it'd be different now. I like to think I would have been more diplomatic, but I couldn't really blame him. Pilots who don't listen can put you in the hole and you'll have to work like hell to dig out."

"We had rushes in Cleveland, but the pace here is definitely faster most of the time."

"You came from the TRACON at Hopkins, right?"

"Yeah."

Lombardi remembered how the traffic at O'Hare blew him away at first. The FAA rated facilities on a scale of one to five, based on their number of operations. Hopkins was a Level Four and O'Hare a Level Five, but he hadn't expected such a dramatic increase. "After seeing what it's like here, I think O'Hare should be a Level Ten. It's no wonder you guys have a reputation for being cowboys. You're all crazy."

Kelly chuckled and permitted a trace of pride to seep into his voice. "We have to follow the same rules everyone does, but we don't separate airplanes from airspace. We separate airplanes from airplanes, which partly accounts for our bad-ass attitude. The difference between here and most other places is that the traffic rarely stops. It can be five A.M. and we'll have thirty-five red-eyes coming in across the prairie from the West Coast. I'm sure you worked just as hard in Cleveland at times."

"Well, I have to admit the traffic's why I wanted to come here, to see if I could cut it. Took me awhile to suggest it to my wife, though. I was afraid she wouldn't want to uproot the kids and risk the move. You know, because of the washout rate. It's something like half, isn't it?"

"More like sixty percent."

Lombardi winced. "Worse than I thought. Anyway, I forgot her folks live here in Evanston. She loved the idea of having our kids closer to their grandparents."

His mind drifted back to that fateful week before Easter last year when he struggled through O'Hare's screening process, praying he'd be accepted for training. Orientation was on Monday, followed by three days of instruction on arrival concepts. On Good Friday, when Rachel and the girls flew in to hunt for houses on the assumption that he'd pass, he grappled with simulated traffic problems.

"How many kids?"

Kelly's interest surprised Lombardi, who'd grown used to being ignored by most of the FPLs. Now, gratefully, he felt a wall crumbling. He pulled a snapshot of the children out of his wallet. "Jennifer is seven and Megan's four."

They'd spent Easter weekend exploring neighborhoods they liked. "Just remember, they haven't said they'll take me yet," Lombardi warned each time they drove past a house that looked appealing. "Of course they'll take you," Rachel replied, almost defiantly. Sitting in the back seat, Jennifer mimicked her mother. "Of course they'll take you, daddy." Megan nodded enthusiastically, but Lombardi remained cautious. "Well, *if* they do, we'll rent for the first year or two until we're really sure we'll be staying here."

He'd sweat through more simulated traffic problems the following Monday and Tuesday. On Wednesday, when Lombardi left to fly home, his instructors told him he could grasp concepts quickly and that he showed a lot of potential. "We'll be in touch," one said with a hint of optimism.

Kelly politely studied the picture, then handed it back. A typically happy family portrait. "Very cute." He hoped the kid survived the last few months of training. Changing homes and schools was upheaval enough for families, never mind the backlash from controllers wrestling with failure. The stress of his job was a major reason why Kelly avoided serious relationships. He'd seen too many marriages break up and didn't care to experience it firsthand. He appreciated his uncomplicated arrangement with J.J. No emotional baggage.

"It wasn't raining when Noah built the Ark."

With this solemn pronouncement, Pete Rykowski dropped into the chair next to them. He seemed relaxed, but his eyes revealed a hint of strain.

Lombardi raised his eyebrows questioningly until Kelly explained. "Mr. Rykrisp likes to start each day with a so-called profound thought. Makes him feel like Plato, I guess." He leaned over and spoke softly in Lombardi's ear. "Frankly, I think he reads this stuff off the sides of cereal boxes."

Rykowski pretended not to hear. "Did you read this morning's *Chronicle*?"

"Yeah," Lombardi said. "That story made it sound like we were helpless. Typical. All they want to do is sensationalize and sell papers. I'd call to complain, except it'd sound better coming from a controller who's been here longer."

"Rykrisp's our facility rep," Kelly said. "An official union spokesman. He'll call."

Rykowski grunted. "I know I should. I'm just not feeling up to it today. Besides, I doubt it would do any good. Why don't you call, Rain Man?"

Kelly played with an ashtray on the table. The cynic in him agreed it would be a waste of time. Some clerk at the paper would listen politely, offer a bland apology, then hang up and promptly forget about it. But he'd been personally involved, giving him a strong urge to set the record straight. As he mentally debated, the voice of a TV news announcer drifted over to them between innings of the baseball game.

" . . . say the DC-9 may have crashed because air controllers in the tower at Dallas-Fort Worth Airport failed to alert the pilots about the turbulent storm. Details at six."

Kelly slammed a fist on the table, sending the ashtray bouncing across the surface. "Where do they get off making us the fall guys so soon? The wreckage isn't even cold, for Christ's sake!"

Rykowski lifted his middle finger at the TV. "See what I mean. It's hopeless."

Kelly stood and swiped a *Chronicle* off a nearby table. "Well, I'm not gonna take it anymore."

Smiling expectantly, Rykowski watched him charge off toward the union office. "They're in for an ass-chewing. Rain Man's a slow burn but once he gets mad—stand clear." He swiveled back to Lombardi and noted how the trainee self-consciously fussed with his mustache. Although it was his duty as the local union chief to keep tabs on developmentals, he also did it out of genuine concern. "How's the training going?"

Lombardi stopped fidgeting. "Good. He and I get along."

"You're lucky he's your primary instructor. He's got more patience and understanding than the rest of us put together."

"I've found that out already. Why do people call him Rain Man?"

"Someone gave him that nickname because he came here from Seattle. That's not the reason anymore." Rykowski paused, his face turning reverent. "Kelly's a natural controller. He moves airplanes as fast as Dustin Hoffman counted toothpicks in that movie. The patterns on the scope just fall into place for him like he has perfect pitch. Most of us have to work a lot harder." Suddenly, he held up a hand in warning. "And if you ever tell him I said that last bit, I'll deny it."

Lombardi smiled. Another wall was crumbling. "Roger. He's a nice guy, too."

"Yeah, well, nobody's perfect."

FIVE

CONNECTIONS

C HRISTY COCHRAN WAS IDLY SCANNING STORIES on the national wire at the *Chronicle* when her telephone rang. The display indicated it was an outside call and she wondered if her son was on the line. By now, class would be dismissed for the day, meaning Jason was practicing with his baseball team. Or attending a ham radio club meeting. Or sitting at a PC in the computer lab. Christy couldn't keep track of his schedule but she was relieved he stayed busy. That had been one of her ulterior motives when she encouraged him to get involved in school activities. A single mother's ploy to keep him out of trouble. Because she worked a swing shift, Jason spent his evenings at her sister's house, where Christy picked him up on her drive home from the paper. She reached for the phone, hoping that nothing was wrong.

"News desk, Cochran."

"Cochran, you say?" It was a male voice, strong and impatient, definitely not Jason's. "I asked for Duncan and they told me he's not there. Since I insisted on talking to a human instead of voice mail, they connected me with you. Am I wasting my time with some flunky or can you really help me?"

She adjusted her glasses, leaving them on as if they protected her against what sounded like an irate reader. "That depends on what you want. I'm the news editor so I have a little more authority than the janitor."

"Are you familiar with this morning's article about O'Hare?"

"Yes. What—"

"I'm calling to let you know it's a piece of crap. First of all, your headlines are misleading. We weren't blinded. Even without the beacon, we could still see targets on our scopes." The voice grew more belligerent with each sentence. "And the article is total bullshit. I can guarantee you we weren't scrambling to avoid a midair. These outages happen from time to time and we manage to handle them just fine without panicking."

Christy's face flushed as she remembered ruefully how they'd hurried the story in on deadline. "I take it you're a controller at O'Hare?"

"For fourteen years now, and I speak for the lot of us here when I say we're tired of seeing the news media misrepresent what we do. Stuff about us is always screwed up. You people don't have a clue."

Christy rarely talked with readers. The paper's ombudsman normally handled these calls, but she knew he was on vacation this week. While she didn't enjoy listening to someone complain, it helped to remind her that what they published affected real people. A basic concept sometimes forgotten in their daily rush to fill the paper. She took a deep breath and tried to avoid a defensive tone.

"Sir, I didn't write the story, but I'm sorry if it wasn't totally accurate. I did play a part in the headline and must tell you that it was a difficult count—I mean the copy editor didn't have much space to say anything. We based our head on the story, of course, which we presumed was correct. Apparently, it made your situation sound worse than it was."

"Seems like a pretty lame excuse to me."

"I'm just trying to explain how it happened. Obviously, our headlines should be accurate, but we also try to make them interesting enough to draw you into the story. It's a fine line. Sometimes, we step over it."

"More like all the time." There was a pause. "Well, that's probably an exaggeration. I'm sure I don't understand what you do, either."

She was relieved to hear him soften. Glancing at the clock, she contemplated how to end the call gracefully and get back to work. Yet part of her was curious about the real story. "What's your name, controller?"

"Ryan Kelly."

"Mr. Kelly, you said the problem last night happens from time to time. That sounds almost routine."

"It's never routine," he replied with a chuckle. "The equipment is old. Sometimes the computers just flip out. Whatever the reason, there are a lot of breakdowns and we've gotten used to dealing with them."

"I wish that angle had been in the story. If it had, our headline might have been different. Again, I'm sorry."

An editor across the desk who'd been eavesdropping made a fist and jerked it obscenely back and forth. Christy stuck her tongue out at him and faced the other way. She wasn't above apologizing to get rid of a caller, but this time it was sincere. If they'd had more time, maybe they would have considered a different headline. If Dunderhead hadn't botched the story . . .

"Thanks for having the decency to say that, Ms. Cochran. The irony is we almost had a midair last night but not because of the beacon going out—and that part didn't even make it into the paper."

She gripped the receiver. "You say two airplanes almost collided?"

"They came awfully damn close. One of them was that Prairie flight in your story. Maybe our press people didn't know about it at the time." There was another chuckle. "Or maybe they just didn't bother to tell your reporter."

"Do you know how it happened?"

"TCAS."

Christy rolled her eyes. Government workers had abbreviations for everything. "What's that?"

"It's a computer that's supposed to keep airplanes from whacking each other. The FAA won't admit it, but TCAS doesn't always work right."

"What went wrong?"

"TCAS saw Prairie and another plane heading toward each other and thought they were gonna hit. They weren't—the pilots had been told to stay a thousand feet apart. But the computer doesn't have the ability to know this, so it ordered an evasive maneuver. By law, the pilots had to follow it, even though a controller who could see the big picture warned them they were flying right into each other." He took a deep breath and resumed indignantly. "Ms. Cochran, those planes came within two hundred feet and a quarter mile. We're supposed to keep them apart by a thousand feet and three miles. If I messed up like that and as often as TCAS does, I'd be thrown out on my ass."

"This has happened before?"

"More than I care to think about. To be fair, TCAS saves us from mistakes once in a while. But a lot of times it's just trigger happy because it doesn't know the intentions of the pilots flying the planes it sees. It doesn't recognize terrain, either. After a plane took off from Southern California last month, TCAS got nervous about traffic and ordered a descent—right into the San Bernardino Mountains. The pilots couldn't see 'em because it was cloudy. Fortunately, they finally responded to the controller pleading with them to climb."

"You're kidding."

"I wish I was."

Christy's professional skepticism made her wonder what this controller wasn't saying. The *Chronicle* periodically ran other stories about malfunctions with the nation's air traffic control system, but she doubted the FAA would rely on a renegade computer that created the havoc he described. And yet, he sounded credible. He hadn't made a lot of vague insinuations or tried to tease her with double talk. Despite his frustration, what he said seemed plausible. Either way, she figured he was right about the FAA flack holding out on Duncan.

"I wish we'd been aware of all this last night, Mr. Kelly. May I put you on hold for a moment while I try to hook up with our transportation reporter?"

"Sure."

She tapped a few buttons and watched Ellen Sanders answer the phone on her desk across the city room. "Sanders here."

"Ellen, it's Christy. I've got an air controller on the other line who's telling me some hair-raising stuff about a computer that nearly causes midair collisions. Do you have time to talk with him?"

"Is this about TCAS?"

"You've heard of it?"

"I did a story on it a few months ago and we buried it in metro. Supposed to be a great system that pilots swear by. I guess there were some near misses at first because they didn't follow the computer's instructions soon enough."

"He says it happened at O'Hare last night—the near miss anyway. I don't know about the pilots. Might be worth another story." She saw Sanders paw through some papers and her voice sounded distracted.

"Maybe. To be honest, Christy, the controllers like to bad-mouth TCAS because it takes away some of their authority. Besides, I'm hip deep in the transit hearings. Why don't you ask Duncan to do the follow-up?"

Christy doubted he'd be welcome at the airport and considered whether to make another pitch. Although Sanders might be right about controller resentment, she sensed they were missing a good story. It was worth checking into at least. But the reporter answered to the city desk, not to her, so she decided to pursue it through other channels.

"Thanks anyway, Ellen." She punched the button for Kelly's line. "Sorry to keep you waiting. Ah, can someone call you back for more information?"

He reeled off a number. "That's the NATCA office—our union. Ask for Pete Rykowski. He's our facility rep and the controller who was involved last night."

She typed the name and number in a file on the paper's computer system, and hoped she wasn't making an empty promise. "Someone will definitely call. This sounds serious."

"We think so. You should come out to the airport sometime and see for yourself. I'd be only too happy to show you around."

"Thanks, but that's not my job."

"You don't do windows, is that it?"

Now it was her turn to laugh. "Something like that. I'm an editor, not a reporter." Then she remembered Jason's recent fondness for airplanes. Every other week, it seemed, her son was consumed by a new interest. Several times lately, he'd cajoled her into driving to O'Hare, where they'd wander through the crowded terminals for a few hours so he could drool over all the jets. "On second thought, if you'd be willing to include a twelve-year-old boy in the tour, I'd like to take you up on your offer."

"If it'll help enlighten someone from the news media at the same time, I'll be glad to show the kid around."

She made an appointment for Friday afternoon at four, her day off and late enough that Jason would be out of school. The prospect of an insider's peek at the airport intrigued her and she knew Jason would be ecstatic. "Thank you very much, Mr. Kelly. I'll look forward to it."

✈   ✈   ✈

ON THE OTHER SIDE OF THE CITY ROOM, the phone on Sharon Masters' desk rang and the young reporter prayed her source was calling back.

"Hello, Pumpkin. How are you?"

Sharon brushed a lock of blonde hair off her forehead and sighed peevishly. "Dad, I'm twenty-one. Isn't it time you stopped calling me that?"

"You'll always be my Pumpkin. You never seemed to mind when your mother said it."

"She stopped years before she died. Don't you remember?"

"That was a long time ago. A lot has happened, a lot to forget."

His words invariably fell into the rhythm of a trite campaign speech and Sharon's neck tensed. It always did when they talked. "Like your daughter. You hardly ever call me. What's the occasion?"

"I know I don't call as much as I should. It's busy here in D.C. and you're never home when I want to let you know I'll be flying through Chicago."

Just the right touch of conciliation, she thought. The same way he must sound when trying to persuade a political foe. "I have an answering machine. Ever used one?"

There were a few seconds of pointed silence on the other end of the line. When her father's voice came back on, it was deep and annoyed. "I'm trying to have a civil conversation, Sharon. Your birthday is coming up in a few weeks and we should get together."

Politics came first and family second in Senator Richard Masters' world, which was why it irked her when he tried to force intimacy into their relationship by using her childhood nickname. "Dinner with me in between fund-raisers?"

"It won't be like that. I'll be flying back to California. No meetings, no schedules."

Sharon gazed blankly out the window and across the murky green Chicago River at the traffic streaming along upper and lower Wacker Drive. "The last time we got together consisted of me joining you for that rubber chicken dinner when you gave a speech to the AMA." Cameras whirred every time he drew her to his side, a poignant prop for the widowed senator.

"No fund-raisers, I promise. I'll be there on the fifth of May. I know you're busy, too, but set that evening aside."

"Dinner with me and then the red-eye to L.A.?"

"Sharon!"

She sulkily flipped through the pages of her Day-Timer and penned a notation. "Okay, dad. *Cinco de Mayo*. I'll make sure I don't have a hot date. In fact, I haven't had one in months and thanks for asking."

"We'll have plenty of time to talk when I'm in Chicago. I'm sorry, but my assistant is waving at me and I've got to go."

"Sure. Talk to you whenever."

Sharon listened to the click and tried to believe he meant well. He'd always made sure she went to the best schools and sent her enough money to live on. He'd wanted to use his connections to get her an internship at the *Washington Post*. Recollecting that moral struggle prompted an ironic smile. Writing for the *Post* likely would have launched her career on a fast track. After much agonizing thought, she resolved to succeed on her own and spurned his offer, which infuriated him and further strained their already tenuous relationship. Even so, Sharon was objective enough to recognize that her determination and drive came from him—and fair enough to be thankful.

No, her present dissatisfaction wasn't about any of that. What bothered her was that his actions were always politically motivated. He'd made that devastatingly clear when he used her mother's death thirteen years ago to catapult his career into national prominence. She'd never forgiven him.

The phone rang again and Sharon picked it up. This time it was her source.

✈   ✈   ✈

"SORRY TO INTERRUPT, SENATOR, but Tony Martinelli is on line three and insisted on talking to you. Oh, and Bob Chalmers of the FAA called you back."

Masters reached out to snatch a one-page computer printout from his administrative assistant, a woman in her thirties who reminded him of his daughter. If only Sharon showed more interest in his work, perhaps she'd realize how much pressure he faced. She was just like her mother, who'd never missed a chance to harp on him for spending too little time at home, never understanding, never appreciating the sacrifice that public service required.

"Thanks, Laura."

The assistant left, quietly closing the ornately paneled door to his office behind her. Masters brushed a piece of lint off his crisply pressed trousers and reviewed the profile on Martinelli. Wealthy developer in the Los Angeles area. Last known project an office park in Riverside. First contributed to Masters' campaign twenty years ago when he was running for state representative on a pro-growth platform. Married to Rose. Four kids. The senator laid the printout on his desk and pressed the button next to the flashing red light for line three.

"Tony, how's the weather in Southern California?"

"Hot as usual." Martinelli's voice was gruff and impatient. As usual.

"I know what you mean, Tony. Those Santa Ana winds can be brutal. How's the project in Riverside coming along?"

"We finished last fall. Occupancy's ninety-five percent. The market here is supposed to be saturated. I'm expecting eighty and I get ninety-five. Go figure."

"That's terrific. I'm happy for you."

Martinelli grunted. "I'd be happier if I could get this hotel off the ground. It's a nice little complex I'm trying to build. I've got the land, I've got my architects working. I can see where maybe we can do this for reasonable money. Things are moving along like they should and then the FAA tells me I can't build what I want. They tell me fifteen floors is too high for that location because it's near John Wayne Field. If I don't chop it down to ten, I can't get the permit I need from them. Jesus, if I do that, the return on the place won't be worth squat."

"Sounds like a dilemma, Tony."

"I'm used to dealing with Building and Zoning. These FAA pricks are a new breed for me. They've got another whole book full of rules I've never seen."

Masters pulled his PalmPilot off the desk and started jotting on the small screen using an elegant black pen with a plastic stylus. The hand-held computer transcribed his handwriting into electronic notes. It also contained an appointment scheduler, contact and to-do lists, expense log, and a wireless modem for e-mail and Web surfing. The senator's penchant for gadgets was renowned on Capitol Hill and the Palm was his latest favorite.

"What exactly did the FAA tell you?"

"Some shit about a safety waiver."

Masters grimaced. Martinelli had the subtlety of a sledgehammer. "Tony, I can't help you if—"

"Yeah, yeah, I know. The hotel is under the approach path for one of the runways so they said they'd have to review my plans. Six months later, they say they're still reviewing but I can't wait any longer so I go ahead and break ground. Now they say they can't issue the waiver unless I knock off five floors. The bank is all over me because I've stopped construction and those bastards at the FAA always take forever to call me back."

"I'm writing all this down. What's the address of the place?"

"It's called the Roseland Inn. I'm sure they'll have a fat fucking file on it."

"Naming it after your wife? That's a beautiful gesture, Tony. Who are you dealing with out there?"

"Regional Office in Hawthorne. Most of the time it's a guy named Eckhardt, but he's getting yanked by someone back there." There was a pregnant pause before Martinelli's voice dropped a notch. "Senator, I need your help getting some relief from these guys. They've got no conception of my timeline and financial constraints."

"I'll look into it and see what I can find out. How's Rose?"

"The same. I've got to finish this hotel, Senator."

"We'll get this resolved, Tony. I'll call you back soon. Bye for now."

Masters replaced the receiver and pressed the intercom button for his administrative assistant. "Laura, ring Bob Chalmers."

"Yes, Senator."

He ran his fingers back and forth along the polished edge of the French provincial desk. Martinelli and his problem could not be ignored. He was an influential constituent who'd donated thousands of dollars over the years and ran with a crowd who'd determine whether Masters stayed in office after the election this fall. Now was not the time to make him unhappy.

The intercom buzzed. "Bob Chalmers on line one, Senator."

"Thanks, Laura." He pressed the button. "Hi, Bob, glad we could finally connect. I'm just checking on that Coastal accident in Dallas. Terrible tragedy."

As chairman of the Senate Subcommittee on Aviation, Masters maintained an official relationship with the FAA administrator and was in close contact when a plane went down. Unofficially, he and Chalmers had been friends ever since they met twelve years ago at the nonprofit MITRE Corp. in Boston and discovered they shared an interest in technology and gin. Chalmers, a mid-level FAA manager at the time, was demonstrating an anti-collision device for airplanes under study at MITRE. The senator was among the visiting dignitaries considering more funding for the project. When the president was elected, Masters lobbied hard and successfully on Chalmers' behalf to make him the new head of the FAA.

"Well, it's a miracle so many survived," Chalmers said. "I think it's thirty. We're up to forty-eight casualties, all onboard the plane. No one on the ground was hurt."

"We'll take our good news where we can find it, Bob. Trying to land in a thunderstorm, I hear."

"A sudden storm. They were actually trying to abort the landing when they went in. Both pilots got out, but we haven't been able to talk with them yet. The plane that landed before Coastal reported no turbulence."

Master smoothed a wrinkle in his jacket and nodded knowingly. As a former Navy pilot in Vietnam, he was well versed in the art of slamming an A-6 Intruder onto a rolling carrier deck in the middle of a storm-tossed sea. "Sounds like wind shear. Just like that Delta L-1011 in '85."

"Could be, Dick. Pretty early to say for sure. We don't know whether there was some mechanical failure or the pilots messed up. We haven't found the black box or cockpit voice recorder yet. That'll tell us a lot more. And the pilots, of course."

"Is there any truth to what I'm hearing on CNN about the lack of Doppler radar contributing to the crash?"

The FAA was spending millions of dollars to install Terminal Doppler Weather Radar at forty-seven airports most prone to wind shear. The high-resolution equipment, which provided earlier and more accurate warning of severe storms, typically had run into delays and was operational at only three sites. The reason for the holdup at DFW made Masters uncomfortably warm. He stood and checked the thermostat on the wall.

Chalmers quickly went on the defensive. "That's a premature report. To reiterate, we're not completely sure wind shear brought them down. Assuming it did, the timing of the warning would have had an impact on its usefulness to the crew. We need more information on the storm track, too, before we can positively say how Doppler might have factored into the equation."

"You're talking to me, Bob, not the press. Just give it to me straight. If the tower had Doppler, do you think it might have prevented the crash?"

Chalmers remained silent. He understood the implication behind the question as well as the circumstances that created it. Finally, he let out his breath and said quietly, "Sure, Dick, it might have."

Perspiration began to wilt the starch in Masters' shirt collar. Such was the danger of deal-making on the Hill. An arrangement concerning the new radar at DFW, which seemed to make good sense several months ago, was coming back to haunt him. He adjusted the thermostat to turn up the air conditioning while assessing what could be done to limit the political fallout.

"Please keep me advised on the progress of your investigation. You know my concern about air safety. I want to be sure we're doing all we can to prevent these awful misfortunes."

"I understand, Dick. Give me a few days and I'll get back to you with what should be a significant update."

"I'll look forward to hearing from you. Goodbye, Bob."

Masters pressed the intercom button for his A.A. again. "Laura, is Jeremy out there?"

"Yes, Senator."

"Excellent. Would you both come in here, please."

Jeremy Parker was Masters' chief aide. He was barely twenty-five, but possessed self-assurance and political seasoning well beyond his youth. When he first joined the senator's staff three years ago, fresh out of American University, Masters pegged him as just another idealistic graduate who'd be willing to hustle up position papers until he learned his way around Washington and moved on. Instead, Jeremy had proven himself adroit at handling a wide variety of matters that required discretion and diplomacy. Given the last two phone calls, those qualities would be put to good use again.

The door to Masters' office opened and Jeremy and Laura approached his desk. He motioned them to sit down and loosened his red and gold tie. "We have a couple of issues that need to be handled with the utmost delicacy."

SIX
THE FRONT LINE

J.J. WAS STANDING NEAR THE SUPERVISORS' DESK when Kelly walked into the TRACON and she inspected him with amused interest. Instead of wearing his customary casual shirt and jeans, he sported a ruby cable-knit pullover sweater, gray dress slacks, and black leather shoes. He'd trimmed his hair, too, and the way it fell across his forehead enhanced his rakish appearance.

"How come you're all dolled up today?" she said with a smirk.

Bear heard the comment and swiveled around from his scope, looking Kelly over and chortling. "What's the deal, Rain Main? You finally got a date?"

"Yeah, who are you trying to impress?" Rykowski shouted from across the room.

Kelly held out his hands. "Geez, can't a guy put on nice pants and a sweater without creating a public disturbance around here?"

Despite protesting their reaction, he knew before coming to the airport that they'd notice and make a fuss. He'd dressed up on the theory that the woman from the paper might be inclined to take him more seriously, improving the chances that the *Chronicle* would run a favorable story. After briefly considering a sport coat and tie, he rejected that ensemble as being too over the top. Only the bureaucrats in the front office wore them and he'd never live it down in the TRACON.

Samantha Sanchez pushed her ample body out of the chair at her desk. "Okay, everyone. There's nothing wrong with Ryan trying to raise sartorial standards a bit, especially considering the rest of you have none. I think he's an inspiration to us all."

Kelly bowed deeply. "Thank you, Sam."

"Bear is looking pretty good these days, too." Sanchez felt obliged to compliment him, momentarily forgetting his needling. Losing weight was a constant struggle for her and she respected anyone who fought the battle. "Have you been dieting again?"

Pepperidge proudly patted his belly. "I've taken off thirty pounds in the last two months."

"That's like dropping a deck chair off the Titanic," Kelly deadpanned.

Bear raised a middle finger as J.J. doubled over. Sanchez forced herself not to laugh, peering at Kelly over the desk lamp. "I didn't think you were on the boards today."

"I'm not. Just came into the city to run some errands. I'll be showing a couple of visitors around in awhile. A woman from the *Chronicle* and her kid."

She groaned. "Oh, God. Not another tour."

"Don't worry. I won't pull a Bear."

J.J. looked puzzled. "Am I missing something?"

"You didn't hear about this?" Kelly said.

"I must not have been working that day."

He rubbed his hands gleefully. "Well, you know how Bear hates to give tours. One day last week, he gets off position and Sam asks him to show some nuns around. He tries to get out of it, so Sam starts begging because no one else is available. Finally, Bear agrees. He takes the nuns over to one of the scopes, looks at them with all seriousness and says, 'Sisters, you must be very quiet in here. These people are really busy making life and death decisions.'" He paused for effect and watched Sanchez cringe, waiting for the punch line. "Then he jabs his finger at the scope and says, 'This is fucking Northbrook.' In two seconds, Sam is standing next to them saying, 'Thanks, Bear, I can take over from here.'"

J.J. doubled over again. Sanchez fingered her rosary, praying the transgression would be forgiven. The telephone on the desk rang, interrupting her angst, and she hung up after only a few seconds.

"Your visitors are here, Ryan. Please watch your language."

Kelly was nearing the doorway to the TRACON when J.J. caught up to him and whispered in one ear. "Want to come by my place after work? Let me strip those pretty duds off you nice and slow."

She'd never propositioned him in here before. Boldness brought on by their spat the other day, perhaps. He glanced around and didn't see anyone paying them the least bit of attention, but she'd stepped back to a respectable distance and wore a poker face. There seemed to be a hint of anxiousness in her voice, an appeal to make things right again. Probably just desire. J.J. certainly wasn't the romantic type. He shrugged noncommittally.

"I'll let you know later."

He walked out to the lobby and saw the two visitors standing near a wall of awards commemorating record amounts of traffic at O'Hare. The woman was slender and nearly his height, with shoulder-length auburn hair that gracefully curled around a softly sculpted face. Her son was lanky in that awkward adolescent way, his sweatshirt and baggy jeans hanging loosely on him. He kept moving back and forth to inspect all the photographs and plaques. She saw Kelly approaching and tapped her son on his shoulder.

"You must be Ms. Cochran."

She extended her hand. Piercing round blue eyes held his a fraction of a second too long. "You must be Mr. Kelly. Please call me Christy. This is Jason." Her grip was firm yet delicate. Jason's had the stiffness of a young man still learning how to make an impression.

"Thanks for coming to see what we do. We'll check out the TRACON first—that's where I work. Then I'll take you upstairs to the tower cab." He visually searched her. "No tape recorder? No notebook?"

"I don't write for the *Chronicle*, Mr. Kelly. I just wanted to find out how things work here and pass along any tips to our transportation reporter. So don't be shy. Nothing you say will show up in the paper."

"You needn't worry," he said with a laugh. "I've never met a shy controller. And please call me Ryan."

They followed him down a hallway, their footsteps echoing off the sandy etched cement walls, and through a pair of swinging doors. He stopped just inside the dark room. As their eyes slowly adjusted, Christy and Jason saw with increasing clarity the green radarscopes that lined three of the walls. The scopes were about eighteen inches in diameter and mounted into consoles at a sixty-degree angle. They were framed by various lighted keyboards, telephones, and computer displays. Jutting out into the room from their left was a desk area with several computers and a Teletype machine.

Christy slipped on her glasses. "There's a whole world down here. I thought everything took place in the control tower."

"No, mom," Jason huffed.

"A common misconception," Kelly said charitably. "When you get on an airplane, it's under the direction of the control tower at first. Those people guide it to the runway, clear it for takeoff, and set it up on its initial course heading. Shortly after the flight is airborne, it's handed off to Departure Control, which is here in the TRACON. Departure climbs the flight to thirteen thousand feet, then hands it off to Chicago Center in Aurora. The Center climbs the flight to its cruising altitude and guides it along until handing it off to the next Center—there are twenty of them across the country, plus one in Alaska. This goes on until you're about forty miles from the destination airport. Then the flight contacts Approach Control, which is also in the TRACON. Approach sets up the airplane for landing, then hands it off to the tower."

Nodding at Kelly's explanation, Christy was struck most by the noise, a cacophony of voices, constant clattering, and occasional beeps and alarm bells. It reminded her of a casino. Now that her eyes had fully adjusted, she discovered the clattering came from controllers shuffling plastic strips on racks or tossing them into wastebaskets.

"I thought newsrooms were chaotic. How can you work in all this racket?"

"It gets pretty loud sometimes, but we have a knack for tuning out all the noise and focusing on our traffic. Can you both see okay?"

"RAOIP!"

Christy jerked her head toward the controller who'd shouted. "Is something wrong?"

He answered before Kelly could respond more eloquently. "Rapid ass overtake in progress, ma'am. Nothing to worry about." Then, into his mike, "TWA 317, reduce speed now to two-one-zero knots for separation."

Kelly saw Sanchez glare at him and raised his hands in a gesture of helplessness. He motioned Christy and Jason over to their right, facing a gentle arc of eight radarscopes.

"This is Approach control—the epitome of air traffic. We call it the Front Line. It's the most difficult position and the most popular because it's the most difficult."

Jason struggled to appear nonchalant while Kelly described how different controllers handled airplanes in different quadrants. Smiling to himself,

Kelly watched the kid eagerly take it all in. He turned to their right and pointed.

"Those scopes over there are the Side Line—that's East Departures, North Satellite, and North Departures." He turned to their left. "That's the Foul Line—West and South Departures, and more Satellite positions. We've generally got ten positions open, but we'll go to fourteen if the traffic's heavy."

J.J., who was sitting in front of them on East Arrivals, turned and hollered to Sanchez. "Better get the tower to give us another runway, Sam. Otherwise, I'll have to rack and stack 'em over Kubbs."

"Is she really gonna circle airplanes over Wrigley Field?" Jason asked.

J.J. flashed her dimples at him. "Sure, kid. Give 'em a good view of the game. First-class service, wouldn't you say?"

"She's, ah, pulling your leg," Kelly said. "Kubbs is actually about fifteen miles east of Waukegan over Lake Michigan. It's the northeast navigational fix where we hold airplanes. The southeast fix is called Bears. We just like to use sports terminology."

Jason wrinkled his nose at the back of J.J.'s head, annoyed by her superior attitude. Christy changed the subject.

"Is this really the world's busiest airport?"

"Atlanta handles about a million more passengers a year, but we beat 'em on operations. We're running 2,500 to 2,600 takeoffs and landings a day, plus about 1,200 ops. for the satellite airports. There's more to it than sheer numbers, though. The Bay TRACON in Oakland is very busy. So's Atlanta, Dallas, LAX. The Common IFR Room on Long Island actually runs more ops. than we do because they're dealing with Kennedy, La Guardia, Newark, and MacArthur. All those people work very hard. They'd argue with me, but the difference is that the Common I Room, for instance, is split into five sectors and a controller checks out in just one so he's not handling as much traffic as we do. At DFW and LAX, the runway layouts are pretty simple so they use standard approaches. We have twenty-seven different runway combinations here and our standard approaches end forty miles from the airport. We tend to just fling the airplanes around from there on in."

Jason snickered at the description. "Is the traffic why you have so many runways?"

"And the variable winds. Chicago isn't called the Windy City for nothing. The runway numbers, by the way—like two-seven or one-four—correspond to headings on the compass."

Jason wrinkled his nose again, this time indignantly. "I knew that."

Kelly nodded and directed them to an unoccupied scope. Jason sat down and Christy stood behind him. They both studied the jumble of symbols on the screen while Kelly pointed out different airports and the Lake Michigan shoreline to help orient them.

"What does all this mean?" Jason asked, poking a finger at one of the data blocks.

Christy rested her hands on Jason's shoulders and leaned closer to look. On the scope she saw:

$$B - \quad UAL678$$
$$024 \quad 21T$$

Standing next to her, Kelly discreetly assessed the alluring figure filling out her white blouse and blue jeans.

"That's United flight 678 at twenty-four hundred feet. The B is the position symbol for East Departures—every position here has its own letter so we can tell who's handling it. His ground speed is 210 knots and the T means he's equipped with TCAS. We get all that information from a computer known as ARTS—Automated Radar Terminal System. It works in tandem with the radar."

Kelly twisted a dial alongside the scope and the data blocks for all the targets disappeared. He looked at Christy and caught a faint whiff of—what? Whatever it was, the fragrance appealed to him.

"That's what happened Monday night when the ARTS failed. I can still see the targets, only now I've got to remember who they are. The flight strips help because they repeat some of the data on the scope, but I need to concentrate. See this guy? He's a jet overtaking this prop. If I look away for a second too long, they switch and then I've lost track of who's who. I've just gotta keep the flick."

Christy's head shook, her silky hair swaying. "I don't know how you keep it all straight *with* the data blocks, let alone without them. But I see now how it wasn't quite as dire as we implied in our story."

Jason rested his elbows on the console, inspecting the small keyboard and running his fingers along the compass rose that surrounded the scope. "Can we listen in?"

"Sure."

Kelly rummaged through some drawers at the supervisors' desk and found a pair of Plantronics ultralight headsets with a single earphone and long thin boom mike. Jason slipped his on like an old pro. Kelly led him over to Rykowski on West Arrivals, snared another chair and plugged the jack into the console. Christy shuffled behind them, still fussing with tangled cords. He turned to help, and his senses heightened when one of her arms brushed his chest and warm breath tickled his fingers while he adjusted the mike.

"Need a hand?" J.J., sitting next to Rykowski, grabbed Christy's headset jack and plugged it into her console. Kelly caught her knowing glance and self-consciously moved back half a step.

Christy concentrated on the scratchy cryptic dialogue, grimacing over a high-pitched squeal.

"United 841, intercept the ILS runway two-two right. You're number one. Tower at Ridge is one-two-six-point-niner."

Intercept two-two right, United 841. And you're pretty swell, too, honey.

She turned to Kelly and spoke too loudly, not used to talking over the sound filtering into her ear. "I guess it takes a while to understand it all. There's a lot of static and the pilots get cut off sometimes. That squeal was awful."

"Bad radios are a real headache, but we learn to live with it. The squeal was two pilots trying to talk at the same time."

"Do the pilots joke around a lot?" She motioned at J.J. "One just did with her."

"Some do, but there's not much time for it. By the way, this is Jodi Jenkins. J.J., meet Christy Cochran with the *Chronicle*."

The two women nodded at each other and Kelly could sense J.J. sizing up the visitor. She grinned impishly. "Why don't you tell Christy about that time last winter when I relieved you on position? You know, the pilot who was so interested in snow."

Was it his imagination or was she purposely trying to embarrass him? The story was funny, but not the kind he'd be comfortable telling strangers. Particularly a woman with her kid. And Sanchez would have a fit if she overheard. He gazed levelly at J.J., mulling his response. Christy watched him in anticipation. Finally, he gestured toward Jason.

"Ah, maybe some other time. There's a minor present."

Jason was oblivious, too busy listening to Rykowski and the unseen pilots chattering to each other. He pretended he was the controller. It looked a lot like several of the outer space games he played at the arcade after school. He just had to keep track of all the little blips. Another flashed on the scope and his face twisted in puzzlement. The data block was identical to one for another target. He pointed tentatively.

"How come those two are the same?"

Rykowski had noticed the anomaly, too, and ran a hand through his hair. "What the hell?"

In the northwest quadrant of the scope was a target for Coastal 892, an inbound Boeing 767 level at 5,000 feet. Like a mirror image, the same target suddenly appeared in the southeast quadrant. It was heading directly toward another aircraft at the same altitude. Rykowski turned toward the Side Line and shouted at Greg Webber on East Departures.

"You see Coastal and American? I think it's a ghost, but—"

No one was taking chances. Webber waved a hand and urgently called the flight. "American 304, climb *now* to six thousand, please."

Kelly frowned and stared at the scope. The radar swept past and the two targets jumped perilously close. The Conflict Alert bell began blaring and the targets blinked in unison. The flashing helped Christy spot the problem and she sucked in her breath. American 304's altitude readout increased just before the two blips converged. One sweep later, Coastal's target in the southeast quadrant vanished. The one in the northwest remained.

Christy and Jason traded confused looks. Kelly kept staring at the scope, spotting another data block that displayed CST instead of the usual information.

"Looks like we're coasting and ghosting again," Rykowski spit out disgustedly.

Nodding at Jason, Kelly pointed to the scope. "You're pretty sharp to have seen that. The target up here is real. The one down there was a ghost. It never existed. Something about the electronics in our radar or on the airplane created a false image. We've been getting a lot of these lately. See this target here, the one that says CST? We've also been seeing a bunch of planes go into coast mode. It's like the computer throws up its hands and says, 'I don't know who this guy is so I'm not going to display any information on him.' "

Christy adjusted her headset and Kelly noted the absence of a wedding ring. "You must get confused by all these malfunctions."

"Sometimes. We've been complaining to the agency, but so far they haven't been very responsive."

Christy shivered. She'd never thought much about the fact that controllers were just as responsible for air safety as pilots. It alarmed her to watch them grapple with a system that appeared to be splitting apart at the seams. She swept an arm around the room.

"The radar and everything seems antiquated."

"It belongs in a junkyard," Kelly agreed. "They keep promising us new stuff, but the years drag on and the outages get more frequent."

She nodded gravely and turned her attention back to the radio. He let them listen a few minutes longer before suggesting they go to the tower. Jason reluctantly pulled off his headset and started to give it back, but Kelly held up a hand.

"Keep that for now. You'll want it upstairs."

He put it on again right away, letting it dangle around his neck so he'd look like the controllers.

They rode an elevator to one floor below the tower cab, then climbed a narrow spiral staircase. When Jason ascended into the glassed-in aerie, he could no longer contain himself.

"Wow! This is totally cool."

He and Christy revolved several times to absorb the sweeping view. An imposing bank of billowing storm clouds weighed heavily on the western horizon, masking the late afternoon sun and casting the panorama surrounding them in a soft warm light. Directly below, six black glass tentacles extended from the two main domestic terminals and snaked across acres of concrete. On their right, United Airlines occupied two other oblong terminals capped with curving celadon glass roofs. On their far left, several jumbo jets from around the world were parked at the International Terminal. A spidery web of taxiways on the perimeter led to seven runways that crisscrossed each other seemingly in every conceivable direction.

Gleaming airliners occupied nearly every gate, dwarfing the army of service vehicles swarming beneath them. Many more planes were in motion elsewhere, taxiing, lifting off the ground, settling back to earth. A fairyland of red, blue, amber, and white lights glowed along miles of pavement, and two strings of twinkling pearls sloped toward the airport in the northern sky. To the far southeast, they could make out the skyline of the Loop, framed by the lofty spires of Sears Tower and John Hancock Center.

A muted roar penetrated the thick tinted windows and they turned in unison to see a Boeing 757 leap majestically into the air. The silver American Airlines bird dipped toward them to head west, banking on wings burnished in gold from a temporary sun break in the clouds.

Kelly's mouth curled into an appreciative smile. He never ceased to revel at the sight of a plane taking off, even though he saw it hundreds of times a day when he worked in the tower. A cold scientific equation of physics, but still magical to watch. His gaze shifted to Christy again, to her long legs, willowy arms, and cute pug nose. He found her aura of elegant beauty irresistible and liked that she didn't flaunt it.

Christy caught the stare and appraised him, her eyes holding his with interest. "It's a nice view up here."

He forced his head back toward the window. "You're looking at ten square miles of airport. This was all farmland filled with fruit at one time, which is why they used to call it Orchard Field and why your baggage tag says ORD. O'Hare's the name of a World War II Navy hero. I enjoy it up here. It's like working outdoors, but you don't get cold or wet."

Christy turned and observed the seven people in the cramped pentagonal space. Two appeared to be supervisors, but the others were moving constantly, craning their necks and stretching headset cords around each other as they spoke into their mikes. There were several radarscopes, more racks of flight strips, and batteries of lighted buttons. Rock music blared from a portable radio. She was struck again by the swirl of voices talking simultaneously with the speed of tobacco auctioneers. She tried to tune out the other controllers and decipher the jargon gushing like a fire hose from the one in front of them.

"Coastal 605, cross Bravo behind United from the right side." He paused to listen to the pilot read back the clearance. "American 670, it'll be runway two-seven left. Go out Foxtrot for Mike and follow Coastal from the right side on Mike." Another pause. "Lufthansa 524 heavy, taxi to runway two-seven left via Delta and then through the pad. . . . American 818, runway

two-two left, Bravo, Red Five, and you can monitor the Tower one-two-six-
point-niner."

Suddenly, he waved a hand in the air. "Aw, shit."

He keyed his mike again. "American 670, don't follow Coastal, he fucked
up. Go straight out Fox for Mike and cross Bravo behind United from the
right. Coastal 605, I wanted you to *cross* Bravo, sir. Just go on out Bravo for
Delta now. And show some smoke, Captain. We got a traffic jam."

Christy's eyes widened a fraction, but otherwise she withheld her reaction. Jason grinned and glanced at Kelly, who put his head in his hand.

"That's not supposed to happen—not even at O'Hare." He leaned forward. "Watch your manners, Bob. We have visitors."

The controller swiveled around, looking only slightly embarrassed. "Did
I really say that on the air?"

"Let's hope it's not your time for a tape talk." Every six months, supervisors listened to controllers for an hour and critiqued them.

"Guess I got a little carried away." Noticing Jason, he said, "There's the
Phoenix Suns—that America West plane sitting over there. We call the
airline Cactus."

Jason leaned over the console to glimpse the NBA team's jet.

Christy finally permitted herself a quiet giggle. "So this is rush hour at
the world's busiest airport, eh?"

Kelly moved closer, resisting an impulse to touch her.

"Yep, only ours happen several times throughout the day. Bob is working Outbound Ground. He's getting airplanes from the end of the alley at
each concourse to their runway via taxiways called Alpha, Bravo, Charlie,
and so on. Along the way, he switches them to North or South Local, which
is those two guys over there. They clear everyone to take off and land. This
guy here is working Inbound Ground to get the planes that just arrived to
their gate. And that woman there is working Clearance Delivery. When
pilots first call the tower, she confirms their initial flight plans."

Christy counted eight jets lined up for one runway, eleven for another.
She motioned toward Bob. "He has to talk so much. I'd be hoarse by the
end of my shift."

"The TRACON is harder work than up here," Kelly said. "By that I
mean it's more difficult dealing with the traffic and the winds and getting
everyone spaced correctly. But the guys on ground control work harder

because of all the talking they do. And it's not just a matter of getting everyone to a runway. Bob has to think about where the departures are going. He sends westbounds to one runway, eastbounds to another. He also tries to line up the planes according to different initial course headings. If two planes have the same heading and he sends them to the same runway at the same time, the local controller has to wait longer to launch the second guy because of spacing requirements in the air."

Kelly motioned them over to a black controller who kept looking back and forth between two runways. He took their headset jacks, plugged them in, and got a kick out of the way Jason held the earphone tightly against his head so he wouldn't miss a word.

"Hi Randy. You don't mind if we listen in, do you?"

"Not at all. I even promise not to swear over the air." Randy winked at Christy. "Bob doesn't have the etiquette we Southerners have."

"Randy came from Atlanta Hartsfield," Kelly said. "He's working South Local now. We're on Plan B, so he's landing on one-four right—that's the long runway in front of us—and launching off two-seven left, which is that one over there. See where the runways intersect? Arrivals always turn off one-four before that intersection. Just in case they don't, Randy has to time his departures on two-seven so they're past the intersection before an arrival touches down. Likewise, he has to be sure arrivals will turn off the runway ahead of the intersection before he clears a departure for takeoff."

"People get upset if I put two airplanes there at the same time," Randy interjected in a drawl. "But what they fail to realize is that we're bound to lose a few at an operation this size."

Christy hesitated before laughing. "I'm having a hard time knowing when to take you guys seriously."

"That's easy." Randy flashed a self-deprecating smile. "We never take ourselves seriously."

Kelly pointed at a Lufthansa 747 waiting on the taxiway. "That Frankfurt flight is number one for takeoff."

"I wish I was on it," Jason said.

Randy keyed his mike. "Lufthansa 524 heavy, runway two-seven left, taxi into position and hold. Traffic arriving one-four right will hold short of your runway."

Jason watched the huge Boeing 747 with the blue and yellow tail lumber forward. He listened with rapt attention while his headset crackled again and nudged his mother. "That pilot's accent was weird."

Christy's eyes sparkled warmly at her son, then at Kelly. "He's really enjoying this and so am I. Thanks for inviting us."

Kelly felt a sweet stirring of more than professional interest between them. Motioning at a plane in the air to their right, he said, "Randy will clear Lufthansa to go after he lands."

They all watched the aircraft drift lower toward the other runway. Moments later, the Delta 727 floated across the threshold. A small puff of blue smoke burst from the tires when they scuffed the concrete, then the nose settled onto the ground and the trijet quickly slowed. The plane had barely touched down when Randy keyed his mike again.

"Lufthansa 524 heavy, runway two-seven left, cleared for takeoff. Turn left heading two-two-zero and remain on this frequency for another turn."

Jason could hear the engines spooling up on the radio as the pilot responded. He watched the behemoth jet crawl forward and gather speed. Burdened with fuel for its 4,500-mile journey, the leviathan rolled down the runway interminably and he began to think it would never take off. The distinctive deep-throated whine of its four massive turbofans permeated the tower cab in powerful testament to the departure of the king of airliners. Finally, the nose lifted and the 747 rose deliberately, gracefully banking away to the south. Jason's headset chattered again but he wasn't listening, his eyes transfixed on the jumbo jet pirouetting in the air. He was awed by its beauty and marveled over how something that big ever got off the ground.

Christy watched briefly, then turned to Randy. "You make it look so easy."

"Nothing to it," he said.

"I'm used to pressure in my job, but this would be far too much stress for me."

"It's probably hard for you to believe, but most of us don't think this job is stressful."

Christy stared at him in disbelief.

"Let me clarify that. Moving the traffic is not stressful. It's some of the other things that bother us. Things like equipment breakdowns and management decisions that don't make any sense."

"I'm learning about the breakdowns. What decisions don't make sense?"

Randy thought for a moment. "Changing the taxiway names here, for instance. The one that goes around the perimeter of the gates used to be called the Inner. Now it's called Alpha. The one beyond that was the Outer and now it's called Bravo. That one over there was the North-South and now it's Foxtrot. We had the Cargo, the Stub, the Bridge, the Scenic, Lake Shore Drive, and so on. Well, there's a group called ICAO that wanted us to change the names to the international radio alphabet so we'd be like every other airport in the world."

He looked out the window and keyed his mike. "Lufthansa 524 heavy, turn left heading one-four-zero and contact Departure one-two-seven-point-four. See ya." Plucking Lufthansa's flight strip off a rack, he dropped it into a hole in the console, where it fell 200 feet to the TRACON.

"Now, I'm all for consistency, but hear me out. See that Korean jet over there at the International Terminal? He's parked at Mike seven. There's also a Mike seven taxiway not far from that gate. We've got a Mike Two gate and a Mike Two taxiway, a Foxtrot gate and a Foxtrot taxiway, and on and on. It's confusing. When the weather's bad and we can't see everyone up here, there's the potential for a pilot to misunderstand and be in the wrong place at the wrong time. To minimize the confusion, we came up with predetermined routes, but we don't have one for every contingency."

Randy cleared another plane for takeoff.

"From an outsider's point of view," Christy said, "I can understand why pilots want consistency when they fly to different airports."

Kelly shrugged. "Yeah, but the layout of every airport is different and the taxiways are marked with lighted signs, so how is it better for them because the sign says Alpha instead of Inner? A lot of airports have unique terms. When Seattle traffic is in a south flow, they clear westbound arrivals for the Husky approach because planes turn toward the airport over the University of Washington stadium. Finals to John Wayne Field in Orange County are called Cowboy One and Cowboy Two. One of them crosses Disneyland, so pilots report in over the Mouse House."

"We have this reputation for being renegade cowboys." Randy bit off the last two words with contempt. "Frankly, I felt the same way about O'Hare controllers before I came here. We're not trying to be stubborn or different for the sake of it. We just think we had a system that worked and the FAA made us change for no good reason."

She nodded thoughtfully. "I seem to remember there was a collision out here when I was in grammar school."

"December '72," Kelly said. "Weather was bad that night and the controllers couldn't see anything, plus the ground radar we have isn't very good. One of them told a flight that just landed to 'pull over to the three-two pad' to hold for its gate. The controller meant the three-two *right* pad at the end of the runway the plane landed on, but the pilot thought he meant three-two *left*. On his way there, he crossed another runway when a plane was taking off. Ten people died, I think. That's a perfect example of why we have to be so careful and why we're a little worried about these new names. One word made all the difference."

"Same thing happened on Tenerife in the Canary Islands," Randy said. "It was foggy there, too. A controller and a pilot bollixed up one word and before they knew it, two 747s collided on the runway. Over 500 fried in that one. We take our words very seriously."

"Five hundred eighty-two," Bob clarified over his shoulder. "KLM and Pan Am back in '77." He resumed talking into his mike without looking at them.

Christy shook her head in awe, impressed that Bob had been able to follow their conversation at the same time he was talking to so many pilots. "I see what you mean," she said. Glancing at her watch, she put a hand on Jason's shoulder. "This has really been interesting, but I don't want to take up too much of your time. Perhaps we'd better be going."

Wistful that the tour was ending, Kelly lingered. "Only if you're both ready to leave."

She tugged gently on her son's shoulder. "These people need to get back to work."

Jason was disappointed but he didn't argue. They took the elevator back down to the lobby, and Christy and Kelly waited while Jason used the restroom.

"I really appreciate the time you took to show us around," she said. "It was an education for me and I know Jason was fascinated. He'll be the envy of all his friends."

"Glad to do it. Especially if it helps clear up some misconceptions for a member of the news media." He looked at her directly and lost himself in those round blue eyes. They could melt a man like butter in the microwave.

Christy swallowed and returned his gaze. *There's an attraction here*, she thought. *At least, there's something I haven't felt in a long time. We hardly know each other, but he's easygoing and he's not arrogant like so many men.* She discreetly checked his left hand. *No wedding band. Then again, not all of them wear one. Well, don't just stand there. Say something to keep the conversation going.*

"So what's the story with the woman controller—Jodi, was it?"

He looked surprised. "Uh, we're just friends."

"I meant the story she wanted you to tell me."

"Oh, that." He laughed nervously and stared off into space. "Well, uh, I was talking casually to this pilot one time when the traffic was light. It was gonna snow, so he said, 'I hear you're expecting six inches tonight.' Unbeknownst to the pilot, J.J. had just plugged in to relieve me. When she called another airplane, he realized a woman might have heard his comment. So as soon as there was a break on the frequency, he came back on and said, 'Of snow, that is.' "

She laughed without any hint of prudishness. *He's handsome, too. Definite attraction.* She tried to think of a lively comeback, but none came to mind. *God, I feel like a tongue-tied teenager.* Her stomach fluttered and she sensed the moment slipping by until her practical side came to the rescue and the words tumbled out.

"You said the other day you don't understand what we do at the paper. Perhaps we could clear up some mutual misconceptions over dinner sometime—if you're not married or involved or anything."

The question took him by surprise, even as he acknowledged that he liked the idea. *She was beautiful and seemed intelligent. Not like some of those blow-dried airheads on TV.* The fact that she had a son made him hesitate, but he heard himself agreeing before his mind could stop it.

"Yeah, I'd like that. And I'm not married or anything."

Christy tried not to look too pleased. A decade ago, after the divorce papers were signed, she'd forced herself to go out on a flurry of dates and eventually grown disenchanted with the process. For the past five years or so, she'd tended to shy away from men and her romantic life had withered into nonexistence, resulting in unwarranted insecurity. Something about Kelly, though, made her feel giddy and brash.

"Do you like Japanese food? I know a good place on Clark."

"Sounds delicious."

"I work nights, but I'm off Fridays and Saturdays. If you're free tomorrow evening . . . otherwise, we'll have to wait at least a week."

"I'm off tomorrow, too, so let's do it."

"The restaurant is called Kiyo's. Shall we make it seven o'clock? I can meet you there."

Kelly repressed a smile. She's interested, but she's also cautious. "Seven it is." He turned to Jason, who had just rejoined them. "Nice meeting you, Jason. I hope you enjoyed yourself."

"It was neat." He glanced at Christy to make sure she was listening. "Thanks for letting me see everything."

They all nodded goodbye and Kelly watched them stroll away. He suddenly remembered J.J.'s proposition and debated whether to go back into the TRACON and tell her he'd drop by later. Her invitation had stirred his interest. But now he was preoccupied with tomorrow's dinner. Though he certainly owed Christy no exclusivity, somehow it felt dishonorable to sleep with J.J. the night before their first date. He loitered a few minutes to be sure they were gone and then walked out to his car.

✈   ✈   ✈

"YOU'RE GOING OUT ON A DATE?"

Her sister's astonished tone on the telephone was unmistakable and Christy tried to downplay it. "Carla, you're always telling me I should meet people, so this shouldn't come as a big shock."

"I'd given up. How many years has it been since you and Ron split?"

"Ten."

"Jesus, that long? I can probably count on one hand the number of times you've gone out since then."

"I've dated a lot of men."

"Sure, right after the divorce. Ancient history. I'm talking since you turned thirty. I don't know how you can stand it. I'd be climbing the walls if I hadn't gotten laid for so long."

That was Carla. Though selective about men while the two of them were in college, she'd never hesitated to satisfy her sexual cravings and invariably described her exploits to Christy afterward. Married life hadn't slowed her down. Last Christmas, her husband, Kevin, confided to Christy over a glass of champagne. "I'm not complaining, mind you, but I doubt I could stray even if I wanted to. Carla wears me out." Christy looked around now to make sure Jason was out of earshot and kept her voice low.

"I like sex, too, but that's all most men seem interested in. There's got to be more to it for me. Besides, relationships take time. I don't get to be with Jason much because of my schedule. I'm afraid he'd feel neglected."

"He can handle it. I gather a monk asked you out?"

"Actually, I asked him."

"Excuse me while I drop the phone. You asked him?"

Christy tucked an arm defensively across her chest. "Women are emancipated, you know. We're allowed to do that."

"Yeah, but it's just that you've always been kind of shy around guys. Were you drunk?"

"Thanks for your resounding vote of confidence in me. Will you watch Jason tomorrow night?"

The line clicked. "Hey, that's another call. Hang on a minute?"

"As if I have a choice."

Carla didn't hear, not bothering to wait for the reply. Getting put on hold was a necessary evil in business, but Christy considered it rude on a residential phone. An unwelcome reminder of harried times. She simmered until her sister came back on the line.

"Sorry about that, especially since it was only Don."

Donald Szemasko was Carla's brother-in-law. Failed firefighter turned day trader. After blowing a chance to follow in his brother, Kevin's, footsteps, he'd stumbled into a new vocation and fancied himself a savvy financier. Christy had grown leery of his farfetched schemes.

"Pushing another deal?"

"Coffee futures. I told him I drink the stuff and that's it."

"Good. There's something about him that gives me the creeps."

"Oh, he's okay. Just a little harebrained is all. Oops. Don't tell Kevin I said that. You know how protective he is of Don. Anyway, sure, I'll look after Jason. Kevin will be working, but I'll be home. Just don't make it a real late night. Our flight for Miami leaves early Sunday."

"Thanks, Carla. I'll drop him off about six and be back by eleven."

"Now that's a deal."

Christy hung up and walked into the kitchen to pour herself a glass of wine. Jason was munching on a cookie and watching a small television on the counter. She hoped she wouldn't face the same barrage of questions.

"I'd like you to spend tomorrow evening at Aunt Carla's. That controller and I are having dinner."

He took his time finishing the cookie and avoided looking at her. "Whatever." Then he marched out of the kitchen.

Christy flinched over his reaction. She sipped her wine and stared at the empty doorway. Her little boy was growing up fast and she wished she could somehow slow the process. With just the two of them, she relied on him more than she felt was reasonable for a twelve-year-old, and they'd become more like siblings than mother and son. So it was probably inevitable that he would be jealous or resentful or whatever he was feeling. The television broke through her contemplation.

" . . . crash of the Coastal Airlines jet Monday night and learned more today about the lack of a key piece of equipment in the airport control tower that may have been a contributing factor. John Cambridge in Dallas has the story."

The scene switched to a reporter standing near a fence. Behind him were the approach lights to a runway. It was dusk, and hues of blue and orange streaked the cloudless sky.

"Weather conditions were much different earlier this week when Coastal Airlines flight 1521 attempted to land here at DFW Airport. The DC-9 was flying south through light rain and winds. As it crossed over Grapevine Lake on final approach, the pilot radioed the control tower and was told that conditions were reported smooth. But information gathered from airport sensors and the cockpit voice recorder indicate that within a minute the light rain turned into a torrential downpour and winds began gusting to almost forty miles per hour. That's when the pilot decided to abort his landing. Five seconds later, the plane plunged to the ground and killed forty-eight people.

"Investigators have been focusing on the weather and the lack of any alert to the pilots by the control tower. NBC News has learned that air controllers were unaware of the severity of the rain and winds because the tower is not equipped with high-resolution Doppler radar, which is sophisticated enough to detect very localized storms. At the National Weather Service office just a few miles from here, however, Doppler is considered an essential forecasting tool."

The report cut to a videotaped interview conducted earlier. Cambridge and another man were standing in front of a computer showing a radar depiction of the Dallas-Fort Worth area. "Bill Webster is a meteorologist with the Weather Service in Dallas. He was on duty when Coastal 1521 made its final flight."

Webster pointed stiffly at the computer monitor. "It's impossible to gauge actual wind speed and rainfall from radar, but we can determine the relative severity. At the time of the crash, I could see very clearly that there was a lot of weather activity around the airport. Conditions were ripe for what we call microbursts—sudden and violent changes in wind speed and direction. It's not the kind of weather I'd want to fly in, and I wish I could have spoken to that pilot to tell him what was ahead."

The scene returned live to Cambridge, standing in front of the runway. The roar of a jet swelled in the background.

"More than a decade ago, a Delta Air Lines L-1011 crashed here in similar conditions, killing 137 people. This prompted the Federal Aviation Administration to spend millions of dollars on Doppler radar at selected airports around the nation. While Houston has the new equipment, DFW still does not. FAA officials say this airport is slated to receive Doppler, but that the installation has been delayed. So far, they've refused to tell us why. In Dallas, this is John Cambridge for NBC News."

Christy watched the jet thunder over the reporter and swoop down onto the runway. Then the screen dissolved to black and a commercial for mouthwash appeared. She switched off the set, jarred by the incongruous segue. Gulping her wine, she fretted about the report and the computer glitches she'd seen in the TRACON today. She wished Carla and Kevin weren't flying on Sunday.

Seven

Wind

———

THE SATURDAY MORNING LIGHT, gray and muted beneath an impenetrable sky, matched Senator Richard Masters' mood. He was sitting in the study of his home in Georgetown—one hand holding a telephone to an ear, the other poised over his PalmPilot—trying to snuff out the smoldering brush fire in Dallas. A forgotten cup of coffee on the desk had long since cooled.

"Senator Bond, I dare say we have no choice. We're starting to take a beating from the media. By moving quickly, we can head off any more unnecessary coverage and put a positive spin on our response."

Harrison Bond, a Democrat from Texas, replied dubiously. "Yes, I see your point."

Masters knew he was worried about his constituents, about promises he'd made, about jobs and political quid pro quo. Two months ago, Bond approached him to inquire what influence he might wield at the FAA. The Dallas-area firm of Circuitron, which lost the contract to install Doppler radar at DFW, wanted to lower its bid. At the time, Masters was embroiled in a fight for his bill on foreign timber sales. He saw an opportunity to secure another vote in exchange for persuading the FAA to award the Dallas contract to Circuitron. The two senators reached an understanding and Masters collected another installment of debt from FAA Administrator Robert Chalmers. Subsequently, the FAA agreed to reopen its Request for Proposals. In the wake of the Coastal crash, however, all three men were losing sleep over news media attention on why DFW didn't have Doppler.

"I can fly down there on Monday," Masters persisted. "We'll make an afternoon appearance at the airport and announce that the FAA has agreed to fast-track the installation. I know you wanted the contract to go locally, but with the dynamics of the situation it's unwise to wait any longer."

"Circuitron was counting on it. Buckley says they'd be ready in less than three weeks."

"They should have had their ducks lined up before we got into this. You know we'd be crucified by then. Raytheon's ready now." He grabbed a letter opener off his desk and tapped an impatient beat on some papers. "We're talking one installation, Senator, not a two hundred-million-dollar contract."

Harrison Bond grunted. "Monday at the airport, you say?"

Masters sensed victory and jotted a note in his handheld computer. "Naturally, I'll want to clear all of this with the administrator, but I don't think he'll have a problem. It's really better for everyone. One of my people will fax you my flight and arrival time. I'll handle arrangements with the media from here. See you Monday, Senator."

He hung up, relieved. An afternoon appearance would ensure him coverage on the evening network news shows while depriving the reporters of much time to ask more than a few token questions before they'd have to transmit their videotape to New York. With luck, this might all blow over in a few days. He found the FAA administrator's home number in his Palm and dialed. As he expected, Chalmers readily agreed to the plan.

"Getting this program off the ground has been a nightmare," Chalmers said. "The delays have been unbelievable. If we play this right, it'll be a nice boost. We can fly down together."

"Excellent, Bob. I thought you'd see the merits."

"I'll arrange for the agency's Gulfstream. You can spend some time in the right seat, if you like. We'll leave Andrews at nine. Know where to go?"

Masters didn't get to sit in a cockpit very often but he looked forward to the chance now, salivating like a youngster over a new bicycle. The Gulfstream handled more like a fighter than an executive jet.

"Sure do. Thanks, Bob."

After hanging up, he made a mental note to discuss Tony Martinelli's hotel project in California sometime during the flight.

✈   ✈   ✈

KELLY'S SILVER ACURA LEGEND COUPE whisked along the Northwest Toll-way toward O'Hare, past the clusters of office parks and housing develop-ments that each month crept farther into the countryside. They looked peaceful in the pale early morning light. An hour ago, he'd been slumbering peacefully until one of the TRACON supervisors called unexpectedly and asked him to work the day shift. The wind buffeted his car and he antici-pated a challenging day on Approach. Slowly and subconsciously, he spooled up. His vision sharpened, his muscles tightened and he began looking for holes in the traffic. Near the airport, he spotted planes in the cloudless sky and could tell they were on Plan B again. He felt alert by the time he pulled into the O'Hare parking garage, but he grabbed a double mocha to help kick into high gear on his walk through the Hilton to the TRACON.

He perused the R&I book before checking in with a supe and was in-trigued by the latest entry. The Read and Initial log advised controllers of everything from personnel transfers to procedure changes. The memos were usually routine, but the most recent one signed by facility chief Andrew Hawkins announced a new rule from Washington about TCAS.

"During the Resolution Advisory phase of an event, controllers shall refrain from issuing verbal instructions or otherwise interfering with the cockpit crew. This procedure is being implemented to help ensure that pi-lots are not distracted during a TCAS-to-TCAS coordinated avoidance maneuver."

Bear Pepperidge shuffled up beside him, scanned the memo and sneered. "Another dumb-ass decision from the brass."

"Sounds like they're worried pilots might hesitate before following the RA if we call them."

"They're putting all their faith in technology." Bear keyed an imaginary mike, his voice mocking. "American 518, you're about to climb right through a 767, but excuse me for not saying anything because TCAS is supposed to see it and will tell you what to do."

"Yeah, it doesn't make much sense."

"Doesn't make much sense? It's lunacy. Stop being such an apologist for management."

Kelly tensed. It was too early in the morning for verbal sparring. "I'm not apologizing. I just don't hate them as much as you do."

Bear scratched his shaggy beard and regarded him testily. "I'm proud to be your friend, Rain Man, so I feel I gotta point out a fact of life to you. Right now, you're the star. The best we've got. You like your job and the brass likes you." He jabbed Kelly's chest with a nicotine-stained finger. "But someday that'll change. They'll shit on you like they have the rest of us and you'll find out that the FAA really stands for getting fucked again and again."

Kelly supposed the enmity came from too many years on the scopes. Plus the fact that Bear survived the PATCO strike in '81. Some of those scars ran deep. He looked terrible this morning. His eyes were bloodshot again and his shoulders sagged with exhaustion.

"I didn't think you worked Saturdays."

"Called me in on OT."

"Me, too. Christensen's sick."

Pepperidge slammed the R&I book shut. "You know we're authorized for seventy-eight FPLs? I asked Rykrisp the other day. All we got is fifty-two, plus eleven developmentals. If the goddamned agency would break down and spend some PCS money, we wouldn't have to work so much overtime."

Kelly nodded. The TRACON was chronically short of people primarily due to O'Hare's challenging traffic. But the FAA's paltry pool of Permanent Change of Station money was also a factor. Too often, controllers covered their own moving expenses when they wanted to transfer to another facility rather than wait until the government would pay. Few were willing to spend money coming to Chicago when there was a significant risk they'd wash out during training.

"Look at it this way, at least we're getting rich."

"You and my ex-wives."

Kelly said nothing, unwilling to wallow in Bear's gloom. They sauntered into the TRACON and both snickered at Ray Boskovich standing self-importantly at the supervisors' desk. After being promoted from line controller a few months ago, Boskovich immediately abandoned plaid shirts and jeans in favor of button-down collars and silk ties, consumed by his new status and transparently eager to impress the bosses. Even now, at 7 A.M. on a weekend, Boskovich refused to dress casually. His attitude had changed, too, degenerating into petty criticisms and reprimands. In a caustic reference to his diminutive height, many of the rank-and-file now called him little Lord Fauntleroy.

The Lord consulted his watch to verify they were reporting to work on time and scribbled on a clipboard. "Pepperidge, let's start you out on flight data, shall we?" His upper lip curled condescendingly to indicate he wasn't completely confident Bear could handle the task.

Bear snarled at the veiled insult. Flight data was easy. It primarily entailed ripping apart perforated strips for arrivals and distributing them to controllers on Approach.

Kelly was directed to a Satellite position. Private pilots swarmed the airports in Aurora, DuPage, and DeKalb, but it was one of those days when he created traffic plans almost by intuition. Although he'd had only one day off after working five in a row and should have been fatigued, he was on a high fueled by caffeine and the satisfaction that his plans kept working perfectly. The pilots were in a cooperative mood, too, rarely requiring him to repeat instructions—until a Cessna 150 climbing out of Du Page threatened the streak. He ordered a turn and watched the target inch straight ahead. Long seconds ticked by without a change in heading.

Finally, he muttered, "Well, are you gonna turn, you little S.O.B.?"

He heard the echo in his ears and grimaced. Whoops. The switch on his mike must have stuck open during the last transmission. He jiggled the switch to dislodge it and the sound of an indignant pilot blared over the radio.

"Departure, did you just call Cessna 355 Quebec a son of a bitch?"

Kelly swallowed his laugh and peeked behind him, hoping Boskovich wasn't listening. Fortunately, the Lord's head was buried in paperwork at the supervisors' desk. So, now what should he say?

"Uh, no, sir. That was for another aircraft." Chuckling off the air, he watched the target obediently alter course at last.

"Picking up my bad habits?"

He looked behind him again to see Bear grinning broadly. "I hope not. Here so soon?"

"You've been on position two hours. It's your contractually negotiated break time."

"Oh, all right." Kelly attempted his best imitation of Bosko's upper lip curl. "Sure you can handle it?"

Bear drew himself up to his full 6'2" and imposing bulk. "I used to work four and five hours without a break at Chicago Center. Back in the seventies when we were so short-staffed you couldn't even get off position to piss. One of the guys carried around a coffee can so we could take a leak right at the scopes."

"You're kidding."

"It's the fact, Jack."

"I didn't know that."

"There's a lot of stuff you snot-nosed kids don't know. Now move over, Rain Man, before I get too nostalgic."

After they ran through the transition checklist, Kelly wandered off to the break room. He picked through the *Chronicle* and was pleasantly surprised to find no mistakes in a story about the Coastal crash investigation. He checked the byline. Someone named Ellen Sanders had written it, not the moron who mangled the radar story earlier in the week.

The newspaper reminded him of Christy and their date this evening. In the cold glare of reflection, he wished he hadn't succumbed to those irresistible eyes and agreed to dinner. He knew that Jason was his underlying concern. Coping with the demands of this job was hard enough without the burden of a real relationship. Living with Carol had taught him that. A kid was an unacceptable complication. The sanctuary of peace he embraced at home would be shattered. Then he smiled to himself. Whoa, buddy, aren't you getting a wee bit ahead of yourself? It's just dinner. You're not obligated to propose marriage on the first date. Have a good time and leave it at that.

Back in the TRACON, Boskovich sent Kelly to West Departures. He continued to make all the right moves on the scope and the hourly herds of traffic flowed like a swift-running river. He was so wired by lunchtime that he didn't feel like eating. Standing before a vending machine, he jangled the change in his pocket and repeatedly scanned the unappetizing selections.

"You won't live long on any of that junk."

It was J.J., buying a cup of coffee from another machine. She threw him a look telegraphing her pique for being stood up last night.

Kelly was grateful other controllers were hovering nearby, preventing them from speaking freely. He didn't want to mention his date, thereby inviting a lot of questions, if she was interested in getting together after work. Inserting a couple of quarters in the slot, he pressed the buttons for a Mars bar.

"I know. Break times rarely seem to coincide with when I'm hungry."

"Exercise helps. I run five miles a day." She struck an athletic pose to emphasize the point and remind him what he'd passed up, smiling triumphantly when he glanced down to admire the blue jeans plastered to her firm behind. "Hey, did you hear that Bosko's got an ulcer?"

"No, I hadn't." He affected a tone of concern. "That's too bad."

"Yeah, I'm heartbroken, too. He deserves it now that he's such a chicken-shit supe. Well, afraid I gotta run. I'm due back."

Kelly waved goodbye with his candy bar and watched her sashay down the corridor, the rhythmic clicking of her cowboy boots ricocheting off the walls. So she's pissed. Oh well. About time she suffered some of the frustration I've been feeling. He munched on the Mars bar without giving her another thought and headed for the break room, where he sprawled in a chair to watch a basketball game on TV. Barely cognizant of the players hustling around the court, he let the images wash over him like a salve and felt his mind slow down.

When he returned to the radar room once more, Boskovich told him to take over for Jackson on West Arrivals and he was chagrined to see J.J. working to his left on feeder. He wondered if it was still windy.

"Turn them early," Jackson warned. "It's about fifty knots at altitude."

He slid into the chair and looked up at the surface wind display, which indicated a southeasterly whipping along at a brisk twenty-five knots. "Thanks, Jacko."

Bear sat to his right on East Arrivals. "Two-two is collapsing like crazy," he said. "After I turn them on base, they gain sixty knots by the time I put them on final."

At times like this, Chicago's notorious winds created an accordion effect that made Approach control an art. The airplanes Kelly would handle landed into the wind on runway 14 right, slowing considerably after banking onto final. This dramatically increased the distance between each plane, which is why Jackson advised him to compensate and turn them early to maintain proper separation. Bear's arrivals, landing on 22 right, experienced the opposite effect. Their speed increased as they banked northwest onto their base leg and picked up the tailwind, so he had to delay turning them to maintain the same spacing.

Kelly hooked his feet around the legs of the chair and leaned his elbows on the console. Only five airplanes were in their sector now, but soon they'd be swamped. Befitting his preference for keeping a dark scope, he lowered the video brightness a tad. He could see traffic patterns better if he dimmed the data blocks and range marks until they were barely visible. It made the primary targets blossom like fireworks with each sweep of the radar.

J.J. leaned over and whispered sarcastically in his ear, "Looks very romantic."

He ignored her and focused on the wind, giving it well-deserved attention and respect. She set up the arrivals professionally, handing them off at headings and altitudes that made it easier for him to create gaps, then shoot an airplane in between. An American MD-80 approached from the southwest at 8,100 feet and descending. Kelly intended to slip the plane in on final behind a United DC-10 and in front of a Coastal 737. But when to turn him?

"American 394, what do you show the wind at eight thousand?"

"South at sixty knots."

American's assigned airspeed was 250 knots, which would drop to 190 once it banked into the headwind. Moving the decimal point two places to the left, Kelly decided to vector the plane for final at just less than two miles from the localizer. It was an easy calculation, but variable wind speed and pilot response time could throw the equation out of whack. He waited four sweeps and called the pilot.

The target began turning a few seconds later and the airspeed readout on the data block plummeted. Two-forty . . . 220 . . . 205 . . . 190. After American took its place on final, Kelly executed the splat function, which showed the jet 4.2 miles behind the United heavy and 2.5 ahead of Coastal. He made a mental note of the distances to fine tune his spacing the next time.

Glancing at the arrivals on 22 right, he was dismayed to see four- and five-mile gaps. Come on, Bear, even with the wind you've gotta do better than that. He slewed his cursor onto one of the targets and typed an H next to the data block as if the jet were a heavy.

"Hey, hands off my traffic," Bear snarled.

Kelly smiled in casual reprimand. Bear was a friend, but he wasn't going to allow his work to get too sloppy. He turned back to his scope and out of the corner of his eye saw Bear delete the H. Then he tightened his spacing.

Leaning over, J.J. whispered to him again. "Can't keep your hands to yourself?" She sensually licked her lips.

No one was paying them any attention, but her come-ons were disconcerting. He wasn't sure how he should respond—or whether he wanted to. Pete Rykowski saved him from making a decision when he walked over to relieve Bear. With the traffic picking up, Boskovich was undoubtedly nervous about leaving him on the Front Line. Rykowski raised a pair of fingers.

"Two wrongs don't make a right, but three rights make a left."

Kelly rolled his eyes.

"What the hell is that supposed to mean?" Bear snapped.

"Think about it. It's true."

"Thinking about it is making me dizzy." Bear grumbled through the transition checklist, then yanked his headset jack out of the console and plodded off, muttering to himself.

Kelly watched him, chuckling, then picked up a telephone when the hot line to the tower cab rang.

"We have an official request from several pilots," Randy said. From the tone of his Southern drawl Kelly guessed he was pulling a prank.

"Oh yeah? What's the request?"

"They all want to land on fourteen right."

Pilots occasionally asked for certain runways, but now Kelly was sure this was a prank. "Really? They must know I'm handling that traffic."

Randy laughed, no longer able to play it straight. "Sorry to bruise your ego, Rain Man, but that's not why. American 394 called just after he landed. The pilot says to me, 'Tower, you're not going to believe this, but there's somebody right under the approach lights having, uh, uh, sexual intercourse.' Since then, the frequency's been lighting up and everyone wants that runway."

Kelly tried to visualize the brazen couple who had climbed over the airport's perimeter fence so they could do it to the thunderous accompaniment of jets screaming directly overhead. He hoped Randy hadn't called security so that the adventurous lovers could finish without interruption.

"I'll see what I can do."

He repeated the story to the other controllers on the Front Line and had to endure J.J.'s teasing again when she wriggled suggestively in her chair. Rykowski's face grew into sheepish approval.

"Cheryl and I did that once. Not long before we got married. It was in the back of a pickup truck. We were parked near the end of a runway, watching the airplanes, and when the urge struck we didn't bother to drive home. Boy, talk about the earth moving when those jets roar right over you!"

Kelly wanted to tease Rykrisp, the good Catholic, about engaging in premarital sex, but he had to create another gap. The pace quickened and he felt his adrenaline pumping faster. Talking almost nonstop, his mind leaped two to three transmissions ahead of his voice. He slouched in the chair and his fingers danced a ballet in front of the scope to help him formulate another pattern.

Rykowski picked up the tempo, too, as arrivals poured into the Dump Zone. They reeled them in one after another, playing the wind like expert fiddlers. Kelly spent another half-hour dumping planes into two-mile gaps with the precision of a metronome and again he was disappointed when Greg Webber showed up to relieve him.

Even though his shift was over, his mind still blazed along at maximum cruise speed. He lingered to watch the traffic before finally leaving the TRA-CON, bouncing with each step. While passing the supervisors' desk, he checked the arrival log and whistled.

There was time to kill before his dinner with Christy, but he didn't feel like driving home, then turning around and chasing back into the city. The only thing he could think to do was have a drink in the hotel and catch another game on TV. On his way to the Hilton, J.J. caught up with him and he groaned inwardly.

"Heading home, Rain Man?"

He hesitated for a fraction of a second. "Yeah."

"Well, if you're not in a big hurry"—she paused to let the dig sink in—"how about checking out the approach lights on one-four right?"

They entered the hotel's long atrium lobby and he stopped. Late afternoon sunlight streaming through the tall windows slanted across the left side of J.J.'s face and cast the right side in shadow, accentuating the firm cleft of her jaw and the lines of strain on her forehead. She stared at him intently, discontent in her eyes. Even if he wasn't meeting Christy in a few hours, her taunts were irritating. She was probably just sexually frustrated and disliked losing the upper hand. Which shouldn't be surprising, considering that people in this business were all control freaks to one degree or another.

"I don't think that'd be a good idea. Airport security might catch us."

"Catch us doing what? You mean you're finally interested?"

He doubted she'd planned on risking it, either, probably hoping he'd accept the proposition and agree to go back to her place. Or get a room at the hotel. He frowned, wishing she hadn't forced the issue. "Sorry, J.J. I'm not."

Her thin mouth twitched at the sting of another rejection and she moved closer to grab the front of his black jeans. "Maybe Bear was right. Maybe you can't get it up anymore." She whirled around and stormed across the lobby.

He watched her disappear and angrily stalked toward the Sports Edition bar.

EIGHT

TEA HOUSE

THE DIGITAL CLOCK ON THE DASHBOARD of Kelly's car glowed unforgivingly. He'd lost track of time in the bar while brooding about J.J. and watching the Cubs succumb to the Mets. Now he had barely half an hour to get to the Japanese restaurant on the North Side. He threw on the navy blue sport coat he'd tossed in the back seat, hastily knotted a maroon tie and checked his hair in the rear-view mirror, taming it with a sweep of his hand. Then he noticed the needle on his fuel gauge was nudging empty and swore.

Roaring out of the parking garage, tires squealing, he took the Cumberland exit off the Kennedy Expressway and swerved into a mini-mart two blocks away. A sign on the pump indicated the credit card equipment didn't work, forcing him to use cash. He paced impatiently while gasoline gurgled into the tank and strode inside to pay just as a woman dumped an armful of groceries on the checkout counter. Silently, he fumed while a twenty-something clerk with a vacuous face rang up each item painfully slowly.

"That'll be $22.53, please," the clerk said at last.

The woman fussed with her coin purse and pushed $28.03 across the counter. The clerk counted the bills twice before ringing the amount in the register, but he transposed a couple of numbers and was confused by the change display. Kelly couldn't stand it any longer and stepped forward.

"You owe her $5.50."

The clerk blinked and said nothing.

"Her bill was $22.53 and she gave you $28.03, so you owe her $5.50. My gas on pump four is $17.85. Here's twenty and I'm taking two bucks from her. You can keep the fifteen cents. Got all that?"

Kelly knew he didn't. The clerk stared at him dumbfounded and the woman stifled a giggle. He didn't care. He snatched the singles from her money and sprinted back to his car.

Traffic on the Kennedy was heavy but it moved steadily. The lights of the city swept by in a blur as he looked for holes, gaining a few car lengths here and there. He peeled off the expressway at California, nearly ran three red lights speeding through an industrial district along Diversey, and screeched into the first parking lot he spotted near the restaurant.

He dashed into Kiyo's ten minutes late to find Christy standing patiently near the door. His senses quickened at the sight of her in a teal jacket and skirt and white silk blouse cut low enough to be tastefully suggestive. They were led to one of several tea houses in the back. Snatches of conversation and laughter filtered through the rice paper walls. After removing their shoes, they stepped inside the cozy room and settled onto comfortable benches on each side of a low-set table. A well beneath the table allowed them to stretch their legs normally.

"Sorry to keep you waiting," Kelly said with an embarrassed glance at his watch.

She waved aside the apology. "I just got here myself. No matter how hard I try, I'm perennially five minutes late in life."

He appreciated her casual attitude. Carol used to berate him for being the least bit tardy. "So how do you meet your deadlines?"

"Oh, that's different." She leaned forward and a small sapphire pendant hanging from a thin gold chain drew his attention to her neckline. "Besides, we don't always meet them. Shall we order sake?"

"Never tried it."

"First time for everything. When in Rome, after all. Allow me."

She consulted the menu and skipped over the pricier vintages, pointing to a dry inexpensive selection. Their kimono-clad waitress bowed and backed away, then reappeared shortly with a small carafe of Onigoroshi and two thimble-sized cups. Kelly regarded the cups skeptically.

"It would take dozens of these if I wanted to get you tipsy."

"Be careful. Sake packs a punch." Her cobalt eyes twinkled teasingly with anticipation. "Are you threatening to be dishonorable with me?"

He raised the warm porcelain cup in a toast, aroused by the notion. "It's tempting."

His gaze wandered to her long lips stretched into an enticing smile, down along the contours of her slender neck, down farther still to the cleavage below her pendant. Then he dragged himself back to her eyes, still regarding him with an amused mixture of flirtatious innocence, and told himself that she didn't seem like the one-night stand type. He sipped tentatively from his cup, nodding his approval of the subtle flavor of the sake.

"Your invitation surprised me," he said. "I was rather rude on the phone when I called you at the paper."

"Not really. I appreciated your honesty. You were also very generous to show us around the airport yesterday. It's all Jason's been talking about. Now he wants one of those aviation band radios. Next thing I know he'll decide to be an air traffic controller."

"Or a newspaper editor." He regretted saying it a shade defensively, but she laughed.

"Touché. I'm just afraid he'd get an ulcer—despite what you and Randy said about the stress."

"I know a few who have one. But, contrary to popular opinion, we're not all chain-smoking nervous wrecks who guzzle Maalox for lunch. Randy wasn't kidding when he said we enjoy the traffic. Another controller and I worked 106 airplanes in the last hour we were on position today. That's moving a lot of metal—and we loved it. When the equipment is working and the pilots are listening, when every decision I make is the right one, I'm on top of the world. It's like a high."

She saluted him with her cup. "I can identify with that. Every night at the paper we play a game of beating the clock to get the latest news in before deadline. That's a kick. It's the other issues that stress us out, like when the computers crash or my bosses can't make up their minds about a story. Then the game's not fun anymore. I guess that's what Randy was trying to say."

"Computers." Kelly shook his head and tossed back the rest of his sake. "Our reliance on them worries me."

"It bothers me, too. At least when ours crash we don't have a bunch of airplanes zipping helter-skelter through the sky. To tell you the truth, I got nervous learning about all the things that can go wrong in the TRACON."

"Don't get too alarmed. I gripe about the breakdowns—and I'd be lying if I said some of them aren't serious—but the fact is flying's extremely safe." He thought about the TCAS incident last Monday night and withheld further comment.

They noticed the waitress hovering discreetly and opened their menus. After minimal debate, he ordered teriyaki steak. She slipped on a pair of glasses and carefully studied the entrees, finally choosing shrimp tempura. The glasses quickly disappeared back into her purse.

"So what made you want to become a controller?"

He gave his stock reply. "I didn't have enough education for gentlemen's work or enough nerve for serious crime." Her smile warmed him as much as the sake and he had a sudden urge to kiss those long lips.

"Actually, I wanted to be a pilot. I was for a while. Flew for a small box hauler out of Minneapolis. When Reagan fired all the controllers in '81, a friend showed me a newspaper ad. The FAA was looking for new blood, of course. We got drunk together one night and talked about where we were going. I had all of 307 hours of flight time and the airlines wouldn't look at anyone with less than 1,500. So, I decided to hell with it and took the FAA's introductory tests. They weren't very hard. Then they sent me to the FAA Academy in Oklahoma City for nine weeks. That was the most difficult thing I'd ever done. About forty percent of the class didn't make it. Those who did got sent all over the country. I wound up in the control tower at Salt Lake City airport."

Christy emptied her cup and motioned him to pour some more. Watching his large hand grasp the carafe, she imagined him touching her in places long neglected. She caught her breath over the unexpected fantasy, wondering how much of it was inspired by alcohol, and reminded herself to go easy on the sake.

"Why didn't you join the military? Isn't that where the airlines get most of their pilots?"

"The military and I would not have gotten along very well." He sat back and toyed with his chopsticks. "My dad was ex-Army and loved ordering my mom and I around like a drill sergeant. I moved out the day after high school graduation. The Navy or Air Force would have been great training, but I couldn't stomach submitting to any more mindless obedience."

"Sounds familiar. My dad was a Lutheran pastor. Very strict. Even preached against sex before marriage."

"Did you follow his advice?" He regretted the question the moment he asked it, fearing that she'd consider him too forward.

Her face reddened, but she answered without hesitation. "Yes. That must seem terribly anachronistic."

"I think it shows admirable restraint."

"So much for the rewards of virtue. My sister played the field before she got married and she's still happy. I held out until I finished college and picked a guy who never stopped playing the field. I realized too late I'd fallen in lust, not love."

"Lust is hard to resist. I'm glad you got out."

"I'm glad I got Jason out of it."

Christy didn't know him well enough yet to admit that she more than made up for lost time after the divorce. Satisfying her urge for spousal revenge and parental rebellion, she slept with nearly every man she dated, often on the first night, selfishly using them as they used her. It was a dizzying period of sexual discovery, catharsis, and ultimately emptiness, which is eventually what led her into unintentional celibacy. Guilt washed across her face.

"Sorry to unload on you. That happened a long time ago."

"I'm not sorry." She looked at him quizzically. "Otherwise, you'd have been miserable all these years. You found yourself in a bad situation and you did something about it, which took courage and strength. I admire that. Besides, if you hadn't gotten divorced, I wouldn't be enjoying myself with you tonight."

Flustered, she was grateful the waitress appeared with their miso soup. While they drank it, she vowed not to let unhappy memories put a damper on dinner. She was enjoying herself, too. She watched him drain his bowl, set it aside and look at her with warm understanding.

"A woman I lived with for a while played around on me. I know the hurt and humiliation. Funny thing is I still blame myself, even though I believe what she did is wrong."

"Why do you blame yourself?"

"Carol wanted kids and I didn't."

"That doesn't justify an affair." She hesitated, afraid to ask but wanting to know. "Why no kids?"

He braced for the usual reaction. "I'm too much of a control freak. It's anarchy at every household I see with them."

"Think of it as barely contained chaos."

"Whatever. The truth is I've never had a primal urge to procreate."

Christy knew the feeling all too well. "Then stick to your guns."

Kelly withheld visible reaction, but her response took him aback. He rarely met people who didn't try to debate the issue. Countless friends and acquaintances had told him repeatedly over the years that he'd change his mind. You don't know what you're missing, they'd say. Their insistence amused him at first but then it began to grate. They wouldn't think of being so presumptuous and critical if he'd said he wanted to marry someday or travel or retire early. He suspected that some, disenchanted with their situation, harbored jealousy of the greater freedom he enjoyed.

"I didn't want kids, either," she said. "Ron began pressuring me right after we were married. I kept telling him I was more interested in becoming a brilliant reporter. I guess he succeeded in mind over matter because I got pregnant a few months later, even though I was on the Pill."

She finished her soup and set the bowl down near the end of the table, marshaling her thoughts. "I . . . resented Jason at first. Then I discovered quitting my job was Ron's ulterior motive. He was threatened by the fact that I worked and brought home a paycheck. Knowing that, and getting to know this beautiful helpless human being, made me realize my anger was misdirected." She stared pensively into her sake cup. "If I had it to do all over again, I'm honestly not sure I'd have another child. But I love Jason and can't imagine being without him now."

"It can't be easy raising him alone."

"He certainly keeps me on the go. It would be much harder if I were still a reporter because of the unpredictable hours. Ron and I divorced when Jason was two and I had to go back to newspapers to earn a living. I became an editor so I could count on a regular schedule. A couple of years ago I was put on nights, but luckily my sister volunteered to look after him in the evenings."

"Your parents aren't around?"

"They still live in Peoria, where I grew up."

"My compliments to you and your sister. From what I saw yesterday,

Jason seems like a good kid."

Christy beamed with pride. "Thanks. I think so, too."

"Do you have only the one sister?"

"Yes. Carla's a year younger than I am. She's a travel agent, so she's always finding great deals. She's going to the Caribbean tomorrow."

"A nice relative to have. I hope you get in on some of those trips."

"She's always offering, but it's difficult between my work schedule and Jason's school. We're planning to go to Washington, D.C., this summer. Jason's never been there. What about your family?"

"Just me. Dad wasn't big on kids, either. My folks died several years ago."

"I'm sorry to hear that. Not in a plane crash, I hope."

He grimaced. "Car crash, actually. They lived in a small town outside Saint Cloud, Minnesota, where I grew up. They went into the city to visit friends one night and it got to be pretty late. The friends asked them to stay in their guest room, but my dad was too proud. Insisted he didn't want to be a bother. He fell asleep at the wheel on the way home, rolled the car in a ditch, and killed them both. He wasn't drunk—just tired. And stubborn."

"Oh, Ryan." She didn't know what to say.

He shrugged. The sharp pain when it happened had subsided into a dull ache. "I never lost much sleep over dad, but my mom didn't deserve to go like that." It occurred to him that talking to someone he hardly knew hadn't come this easily in a long time.

Their entrees arrived and they dug in. So far the evening pleasantly surprised Christy, who'd grown weary of the ritual of exchanging personal histories and listening to men who bored her about their work. Kelly made her laugh and managed to talk about his job without condescension. He also seemed genuinely interested in what she had to say. She snared a shrimp with her chopsticks and reached across the table to feed it to him. When his hand held hers for a moment their touch was electric.

"So, uh, have you ever been married?" she asked.

"Nope. Except for Carol, I've never gotten too serious about anyone. I dated a Mormon for a while who tried to persuade me. She also tried to convert me, but I'm not very religious." He grinned, relishing the memory. "One night I took her up to the control tower in Salt Lake to show her around. She got all excited and wanted to talk to an airplane. I guess I wasn't thinking straight because that's strictly *verboten*, but there wasn't much traffic so I figured why not? I told her the call sign to a Beechcraft Bonanza that was coming in to land. She repeated the call sign and the pilot responded, waiting for her to say something else. I swear I wasn't drunk at the time, but I told her to say anything she wanted. So she keyed the mike and said, 'Bonanza 65 Tango, have you accepted Jesus as your personal savior?' I almost died. That poor pilot flying around in the dark must have thought God was calling him."

Christy laughed so hard she nearly dropped her chopsticks. "Did you get in trouble?"

"No. I did get bored and transferred to Seattle a year later. That's where I started working in the TRACON. I missed seeing the airplanes at first, but I liked the challenge of radar. Six years ago, I got bored again and bid for Chicago. I hated to leave the Northwest because it's so beautiful out there, but I wanted to see if I could cut it here." He shook his head. "Man, I thought the Academy was tough. The fourteen months I spent checking out at O'Hare was even harder. It was worth it, though."

"This is the top of the heap for you?"

"Yep. It may not be in a class by itself, but whatever class it's in it doesn't take long to call the roll. We come here for the traffic because the pay is about the same at most other large airports. I'll admit it's an ego trip."

She admired his honesty. "Is that why Randy said you're considered cowboys?"

"Partly. Some of that reputation comes just from the way we talk. We handle so many airplanes we have to be fast and forceful or else the pilots will start questioning us and there's no time for that. We improvise our patterns a lot, too, because of all the runway configurations. The irony is we all have the same scientific technique. At a lot of facilities, each controller does things a little differently, which makes it harder for new controllers to learn."

They lapsed into silence while finishing dinner. As Christy ate the last shrimp and pushed her plate away, a woman's moaning drifted through the wall from the next tea room. The woman giggled and protested mildly. "The waitress might catch us." They heard a door slide shut and then a man's voice. "She can't see us now." The moaning resumed.

Christy and Kelly looked at each other awkwardly before breaking into sly smiles. "I didn't notice that on the dessert menu," he said.

She leaned forward and he was conscious of her breasts straining against the thin fabric of her blouse. "Must be a specialty they don't put on the menu."

They regarded each other with frank sexual interest and he wrestled with his feelings. He'd enjoyed himself far more than he expected and could tell it would be easy to get involved with her. Face it, she's a knockout and a joy to be around. J.J.'s never treated you with such interest. But remember the kid and don't let your libido lead you to do something stupid. Of course, that doesn't mean the evening has to end just yet.

"Shall we take another look at that menu?"

Her eyes twinkled again. They passed on dessert, but lingered over coffee and discovered a mutual passion for old movies, jazz, and photography. The waitress reappeared several times and Christy finally asked for the bill after checking her watch. She was amused when her refusal to let Kelly pay nonplused him.

"I asked you out, remember?"

"Let me retaliate and buy you a nightcap at this jazz club I know in Lincoln Park," he said, fidgeting with his wallet. "It's only a few blocks away."

She bemoaned her curfew. "I'm afraid I can't. Jason's at my sister's and I promised I'd pick him up by eleven."

He hid his frustration. It was true. Once you had kids, they ruled your life.

The night air was cool as they strolled to her car. Couples clogged the sidewalk and she was disappointed each time he moved away from her to dodge around them. Suddenly, he stopped with an exasperated sigh. One of his shoelaces had come undone again.

"These damn things are driving me nuts."

He put one foot up on a fire hydrant and was reaching down when she bent to help. She tried to rationalize that her maternal instincts were taking over, but she knew it was purely a desire to touch him—anywhere. His eyes roamed down the sweeping curve of her back while she deftly retied the laces with just the right amount of tension.

"Thanks. You're pretty good at doing that backwards."

"Comes from having a kid."

Ah, yes. The comment tempered his desire.

When they reached her Honda Civic, she wanted to touch him again, perhaps even hug him, but she sensed his aloofness and was afraid of the reaction. "I had a very nice time tonight." She hoped it sounded genuine.

"Yeah, I enjoyed myself, too. Wish you didn't have to rush home."

"I'll take a rain check on the jazz." She unlocked her car and opened the door.

Kelly nodded, then kissed her lightly on the cheek. "Good night, Christy."

She got in the car and smiled at him, wondering if he'd call. "Good night, Ryan."

✦   ✦   ✦

CARLA LISTENED EAGERLY while Christy described the date and then burst into laughter. "I'm confused. You say you don't like to go out with men because all they want to do is get in your pants, yet now you're disappointed because this guy didn't try. What's with that?"

"I'm glad he didn't make a pass. It's just that we seemed to get along so well I was hoping for a little more than a peck on the cheek." She lowered her voice. "I'm afraid he's not interested in me because of Jason. He doesn't want kids."

Carla smiled sympathetically and studied her sister. Identical in height and hair color, their figures were similar, too. What differentiated them were subtleties in their facial features and mannerisms. Carla's eyes were also blue, but oval rather than round. Where Christy exuded elegance, carrying herself with the refinement of a model, Carla looked like the girl-next-door type. Christy's extensive vocabulary reflected her profession; Carla's was more earthy. Ironically, Christy had always been the less confident one, particularly with men, while Carla the tomboy was more at ease with them.

"Got the hots for this guy, eh?"

Christy blushed. "Well, he is really cute. And funny."

Carla put an arm around her shoulder. "Sounds like you met a gentleman. I bet he's got the hots for you, too. He'll call. Just remember that you'll have to find someone else to watch Jason if Romeo wants to go out with you again anytime soon."

Christy looked at her sister with envy. "Two weeks cruising around the Caribbean. If that's not paradise, I don't know what is. Are you sure you won't get bored?"

"Eat, drink, sleep . . . keep our bed messed up. We'll manage somehow. Kevin made me promise to pack only a couple of bikinis and skimpy dresses. We're both hoping I finally get pregnant."

"Try the conch chowder. I hear it's a great aphrodisiac. Not that you seem to need it."

The ringing of the telephone interrupted their tittering and Carla reached for the receiver hanging on the kitchen wall. "Hello."

"It's Don."

"Hi, Don. How's my favorite brother-in-law?"

Christy made a gagging motion, forcing Carla to choke back another laugh.

"What do you mean by that? I'm your only brother-in-law."

She shook her head. "I know, Don. It was a joke. You don't sound so good. Is something wrong?"

"They fired me today."

"What—again?" This was the third job Szemasko had lost in a year. He'd been working as a cashier at a convenience store only since February. "Sorry, I didn't mean it like that. What happened?"

"The manager said one of us was stealing money. He couldn't figure out who it was, so he said he had to let us all go." Szemasko's voice began bleating. "I swore it wasn't me. All he kept saying was, 'This is just one of those things.' Same as that lawyer told me when I hurt my back."

Several years ago, Szemasko had been helping a friend move furniture into an apartment. While hoisting a couch up a narrow stairway, he slipped and fell. The injury wasn't crippling, but it prevented him from passing the physical exam for the firefighting academy and shattered a dream he'd shared with his brother from boyhood. Szemasko tried to sue the friend, but a lawyer advised him he had no case. Ever since, he'd drifted without direction and lost every job Kevin managed to arrange for him through his contacts.

"I'm sorry to hear that, Don. I'll let Kevin know when he gets home."

"It wasn't my fault. Be sure to tell him." He was blubbering now. "These things just keep happening to me for no good reason."

"I'll tell him. Bye for now." Carla hung up and relayed the news to Christy. "I suppose he'll come live with us again. Kevin will insist on it. Don drives me crazy, though. There's no privacy when he's here." She slumped against the counter and played with the hem of her Chicago Bears T-shirt. "That guy has the worst luck of anyone I know."

"He brings it on himself. Remember when he got fired from that messenger service for mouthing off at the boss?"

"The guy supposedly insulted firefighters and Don took it as a personal affront against Kevin."

"Uh, huh. And then there was that job he had at the stockbroker's office doing data entry on the computer. He blew a great opportunity by hacking into a broker's personal files looking for hot investment tips."

"Yeah, I know. Understands computers, but otherwise he's not too bright."

Christy put a hand on her hip and pointed a finger at Carla. "He loves playing the martyr. Don slipped and fell because he was drunk—and he's never accepted responsibility for that. So now he just plods along, dreaming and scheming about how to get rich quick. Do you suppose he took the cash from the store?"

"I dunno. I hope not." Carla's tone changed from resignation to warning. "And don't ever suggest that to Kevin. He'd never speak to you again."

"I won't, but personally I don't trust him. I think he'd do anything for money."

"Maybe. I'm just glad I won't have to deal with this until we get back from the cruise."

"Well, we'd better get going so you can pack," Christy said.

The two sisters walked out of the kitchen in search of Jason.

NINE
DOPPLER

STANDING INSIDE THE ENTRANCE to a cavernous hangar at Dallas-Fort Worth International Airport, Senator Richard Masters self-consciously adjusted the knot in his copper-colored Armani tie. Wind whistled through the gaping door and he reached one hand up to shelter his carefully coiffed hair, predominantly gray now but lending a distinguished touch to the trim physique that he diligently maintained several times a week at the club. The wind subsided to a whimper and he resumed looking over his notes, prepping for a brief statement to the news media. Behind him were the broken and charred remains of a McDonnell Douglas DC-9 flown by Coastal Airlines. Thousands of pieces of wreckage were scattered across the floor, meticulously positioned by crash investigators trying to reassemble the sixty-ton jetliner and determine why it fell out of the sky.

Masters turned to FAA Administrator Robert Chalmers and Senator Harrison Bond, both of whom were standing next to him at a podium set up an hour earlier. "Are you sure neither of you want to say anything?"

"I'll give you reinforcement during the Q and A," Chalmers said.

Bond shrugged. He still wished he could somehow rescue the radar contract for Circuitron. "It's your show, Dick."

Several television crews and newspaper reporters were assembled in front of them. The print journalists watched with bored amusement while their electronic brethren jockeyed for the best camera angles, adjusted portable lights, and conducted sound checks into their mikes. At length, two of them announced in unison, "We're ready when you are, gentlemen."

Masters spotted Jeremy Parker, his chief aide, hovering on the fringe and cleared his throat. Two men he didn't recognize loitered near the hangar door. One, with flaming red hair, leaned against the wall. The other stood with both arms folded across his chest, chewing an unlit cigar. The TV lights blazed on, bathing the wreckage and the trio at the podium in a bright glow. Masters took a deep breath, his head bobbing slightly as he worked into the rhythm of his speech, leveled on the center of the four cameras—roll tape—and began talking in his commanding voice.

"One week ago, seventy-eight people were flying home to loved ones, to see friends, to complete business appointments. Forty-eight of those dear souls never made it. Their lives ended tragically when the airplane they'd placed their trust in crashed just a few miles from where we stand. Investigators from the National Transportation Safety Board, along with various industry representatives, have been working around the clock since last Monday to determine why."

He motioned to the men on his right. "FAA Administrator Robert Chalmers and I came here today to join Senator Harrison Bond and review their important work. Our mission is to determine whether there's anything we can do to prevent such a disaster from happening again. After carefully analyzing various data, the NTSB tells us they have all but determined that an act of God caused this unfortunate accident. A weather phenomenon known as wind shear pushed the airplane to the ground with such a powerful force that no two pilots in the world would have been capable of pulling out of its grip."

The man with red hair folded his arms and scowled.

Masters raised one of his hands. "Now, having just blamed nature's fury for the lives of forty-eight people, let me hasten to add that we're always striving to make flying safer, to compensate for human error, mechanical failure and the weather's unpredictability. The FAA has been testing state-of-the-art equipment known as Terminal Doppler Weather Radar at selected aviation facilities around the country and agency staff have documented its reliability. Last week, Senator Bond asked me in my capacity as chairman of the Senate Subcommittee on Aviation to help expedite getting Doppler here at DFW. I consulted with the administrator and we agreed the installation should proceed at once. My heart goes out to those who lost loved ones. As a memorial to them, we'll make it a priority that this airport gets the best technology available to make flying as safe as is humanly possible. I'll take questions now."

A *Dallas Morning News* reporter volleyed the first shot. "Senator, is it your contention that the crash might not have happened if Doppler radar had already been installed in the control tower?"

"I don't think anyone can say that with certainty. Wind shears come and go quite suddenly. The point is we need to provide air traffic controllers and pilots with as much information as possible."

The other man near the hangar door chewed his cigar more vigorously.

A reporter from KTVT Channel 11 raised a hand. "Senator, given that Doppler radar is in widespread use by the National Weather Service and my TV station, for that matter, why hasn't it been installed sooner at more airports?"

Masters turned to Chalmers, who stepped to the microphones.

"The Federal Aviation Administration has a comprehensive implementation procedure for new equipment. Specifications must be drawn up, bids submitted and awarded, the device tested in the lab and field. Then there's the installation, which can take a long time because we're invariably dealing with sophisticated electronics. As much as we'd like to hasten the process, we must move with all due caution. The risks are too great to act prematurely."

"But if it's good enough for the Weather Service," a woman from CNN persisted.

Masters leaned forward. He'd been expecting this line of questioning and had formulated a few responses he hoped would make good sound bites.

"The Weather Service has different requirements and responsibilities. The equipment used by air traffic control takes an extraordinary amount of coordination to set up for its mission-critical role. It's not plug-and-play like your average PC."

"Administrator Chalmers, what about other airports that don't have Doppler?" asked a reporter from The Associated Press.

"We have a contract with the Raytheon Company to install forty-seven radar units at airports most prone to wind shear." Chalmers pointed to Jeremy Parker. "The senator's aide can provide you with a list of the sites. I assure you these will proceed as soon as is practical."

They answered a few more questions, mostly relating to the Coastal investigation, before ending the news conference. It went easier than Masters expected. He huddled briefly with Harrison Bond before joining Chalmers and Parker aboard the FAA's Gulfstream jet. Ten minutes later, they were airborne on their way back to Washington, D.C.

✈   ✈   ✈

CHRISTY COCHRAN STEPPED INTO AN ELEVATOR at the *Chicago Chronicle* building and found Ellen Sanders resting against the wall of the car, eyes closed. Her weary appearance contrasted with her customary vitality. Sharon Masters was standing in the car, too.

"Hi, Sharon. Late night, Ellen?"

Sharon smiled and nodded. The transportation reporter roused herself. "Nah. Just chasing around trying to advance this Masters story. Did you catch him on CNN?" Sanders kept her eyes trained on Christy, purposefully avoiding Sharon.

"I heard a radio report driving here. Blaming the Dallas crash on wind shear and touting new radar."

Sanders finally glanced at Sharon, who understood the hesitation. "Go ahead and talk about him. You won't offend me."

"Well, it's too quick," Sanders said with a short nod. "These investigations take as long as a year to finish. Even when it's obvious what went wrong—like the engine falling off that DC-10 climbing out of O'Hare—the reasons why are a lot less clear. He's trying to make it sound noble, but they're hurrying this radar thing for other reasons."

"There's been bad publicity lately about all the breakdowns," Christy pointed out. "An announcement like this helps them look good."

Sanders jabbed the button for the fourth floor. "These elevators are as slow as the FAA. Oh, they're trying to look good, all right, but something else is going on. I have a hunch it has to do with the aviation trust fund."

Sharon nodded knowingly. "You mean the money the government's hoarding for the deficit."

"Yeah, the federal cookie jar. They're supposed to use it on airport improvements, but Congress keeps dipping its paws in it to help balance the books. Current surplus is nine billion dollars. It all comes from people like us paying a tax on our plane tickets, plus other taxes on cargo and fuel."

"So you think Congress or the FAA held back spending some on the new radar," Sharon said, "and now that there's been a crash . . . "

"They have a reputation for taking forever to do something, then rushing in with a quick fix after an accident. I'm just not sure how Masters fits into the picture."

The elevator wheezed to a stop and the three of them got out and strolled past a receptionist toward the newsroom.

"You can be sure of one thing," Sharon said, her soft voice taking on an edge. "Whatever my dad does is for his benefit. If it happens to improve the public good or help a constituent, that's coincidental." She waved a hand. "Because of where I work and for other reasons, I don't exactly have an inside track with him. But if there's any way I can help, Ellen, let me know."

"Thanks." After Sharon walked on ahead, Sanders exchanged looks with Christy and said, "No love lost there."

"From what I gather talking with her, our senator friend isn't exactly a family man—and he's the only family she's got."

"Says a lot about why she won't ride on his coattails."

They sauntered into the city room, alive with ringing telephones, chattering reporters, and the soft clatter of computer keyboards. It was mid-afternoon, the busiest time of day, when the night crew was coming on duty and the day crew was hustling to finish. Christy felt the vortex pulling her into its maw as she turned toward the news desk.

"Good luck with your story, Ellen."

Sanders groaned. "I need it. Masters is out of pocket—not that I'd get much from him—my NTSB source hasn't called back, and I don't have any contacts at DFW."

Christy suddenly thought of Kelly and tried to rationalize that it wasn't just a convenient excuse to call him. "I know someone who may be able to help. I'll ask him."

She went to her desk, logged on to the Atex system, and checked her messages. Then she dialed the number he'd given her last week, admonishing herself to stick to business. If he wanted to see her again, it was up to him to make the first move this time. Someone at the union office told her he was in the TRACON and gave her another number. She redialed and had to wait while a supervisor transferred her call to the phone where he was sitting. When he picked up, she could hear controllers rattling off instructions to pilots in the background.

"Ryan Kelly."

"Hi, it's Christy. Is this a bad time? Are you on position?"

"Yeah, but that's okay. I can multitask. Hang on a sec." He called a pilot, sounding keyed up. "How are you?"

It made her nervous talking to him while he was concentrating on any number of airliners. "I'm fine. How are you?"

"Great." He called another pilot.

"Uh, Ryan, I was wondering if you know any controllers at Dallas-Fort Worth Airport."

"Tower chief. Worked with him in Seattle. United 225 heavy, climb and maintain one-three thousand. He transferred to DFW about the time I came to O'Hare. Why?"

She quickly summarized Sanders' theory.

"Knowing Congress and the agency, that sounds about right."

"What's the chief's name?"

"Lloyd Barker. Not real chummy with the press, so he may not talk."

"Thanks, Ryan." She didn't want to hang up and groped for something else to say, but she suspected it was futile. He's sitting in front of a radar-scope, for God's sake. He's not in the mood to think about asking you out on another date. "So . . . I'll let you get back to work."

"Okay." He called two pilots and Christy was on the brink of hanging up when he spoke to her again. "If you talk to Lloyd, tell him I said hello."

"I will." He's just not interested. Now say goodbye.

"Ah, about that rain check to the Bulls. Can you make it this Friday?"

She was simultaneously thrilled and dejected. "I'd love to, but I can't. Jason's got a science fair that night. Would Saturday work for you?"

"Sure. And I don't mind picking you up."

Christy smiled. Long ago, she'd made a habit of driving herself on the first date so she could leave at any time. That would hardly be a worry now, so she gave him her home address.

"See you at seven," he said. "Gotta go, bye."

She tried to control the grin spreading across her face while dialing Sanders' extension. "Hi, Ellen. I've got a contact for you in Dallas. His name is Lloyd Barker. He's the tower chief."

"Terrific. I assume that's DFW? And is this from a controller stud you picked up at O'Hare the other day?"

Christy had told Ellen about her plans to visit the airport, but hadn't mentioned it since. The reporter had demonstrated her intuition many times, however, so she wasn't surprised that her teasing uncannily hit the mark. Joy seeped through her voice. "Yes and yes."

"Uh, huh. The two of you got something going?"

"Well, we may be getting there. His name's Ryan Kelly, by the way, and he said to tell Barker hello."

"Okay. Hey, thanks a lot."

Sanders hung up and was about to call directory assistance for the number to the DFW control tower when her phone rang again. "Ellen Sanders here."

"Scott Carter here."

Sanders met Carter several years ago while she was covering a USAir 737 that crashed during takeoff in a snowstorm at La Guardia Airport. He was part of the NTSB's Go Team dispatched to accident sites to begin determining what went wrong. His specialty was electronics. What she remembered most was his unruly red hair, thirst for gin and women, and a willingness to speak candidly.

"Hi, Scott. I'm so glad you called back."

"I got your message when I came up to my room to shower. Did you catch Masters' act earlier?"

She opened a file in her computer and poised her fingers on the keyboard. "That's mainly why I'm calling. First, tell me how the investigation is going."

"That's old news. Didn't you listen to the senator and his sidekick?" Carter sounded jaded.

"Sure, I heard him. I want the real story from a reliable source, not some puffery from the politicians."

"Okay, Ellen. Off the record, their dog-and-pony show made me mad. I'd get my ass chewed if my boss knew I was talking to a reporter right now, yet they practically issued a probable cause report on national TV and played fast and loose about the radar. They were here only a few hours, just long enough for the cameras."

"Doesn't surprise me. On the record, is it likely that wind shear caused the crash?"

"It's not official yet and please don't quote me by name, okay? But, yes, we're focusing on that pretty heavily. Information from the black box and the cockpit voice recorder matches the typical wind shear pattern."

Her fingers danced on the keyboard while he recited the technical details, even though she knew that little of it would make the paper. Ellen Sanders took meticulous notes to better understand the issues and pitch stories to her editors with greater confidence. "So is this another knee-jerk response from the FAA or could the tower controllers really have warned the pilots sooner?"

"With Doppler, they would have had more information. We're still looking into the timing, but all the pilots would have needed was about twenty seconds' notice. Off the record, that's why the senator is suddenly pushing the installation here. A controller told me confidentially they were supposed to get Doppler two months ago, but the FAA suddenly delayed the project and reopened the contract. Rumor is they were going to give it to a local bidder."

Sanders stopped typing. "Did I hear you correctly?"

"Your hearing's fine."

"Who's the new bidder? Is the NTSB doing anything about this?"

"A company called Circuitron. And my boss is looking into it. Trouble is, the controller's afraid to make waves by going on the record."

"Anything else you can tell me?"

"Not right now, but give me a call in another day or two."

"Thanks, Scott. You've been a big help as usual."

"I know, and you're welcome. Next time we're in the same city, maybe we can get together. I'm still an available bachelor."

"I'll keep that in mind. Bye, Scott."

She obtained the listing for the DFW control tower and called, but Barker had left for the day and his assistant refused to give her the chief's home number. After she prodded, he agreed to ask his boss to call her. The phone rang less than five minutes later and the voice sounded gruff.

"I appreciate you getting back to me, Mr. Barker."

"You've temporarily given me a reprieve from yard work. My assistant said you're asking about the crash. What do you want to know?"

"I'm interested in the radar you use in the tower. My understanding is that you don't have Doppler."

"That's right."

"I also understand that it was about to be installed two months ago when the project was delayed."

His tone became wary. "Who told you that?"

"I'm sorry, but I'm not at liberty to say. Is it true?"

"I'll be delighted when we finally get Doppler," he said slowly.

Sanders waited, giving him time to say more, but there was only silence. "Why was the installation delayed?"

"I'm not at liberty to say."

She rolled her eyes at his response and pressed gently. "Someone else has given me one version. If you tell me yours and it matches, I can write the story without naming either one of you. But I need confirmation to make sure it's accurate. I won't run anything on the word of one unnamed source."

"I didn't think you people were that choosy about how you got your information." He fell silent again for a few seconds. "How did you get my name?"

"From a controller at O'Hare. Ryan Kelly."

"You talked to Ryan?" He suddenly sounded expansive. "Well, I'll be. How's that peckerwood doing?"

"Uh, fine. He said to say hello."

"He's talked to you about this stuff?"

"Yeah . . . he's given us a tip or two."

"Excuse me while I light my cigar."

She listened to him fire up the stogie, hopeful that anger would overcome his reluctance to talk. Children's voices sounded in the background, suddenly quieted by a woman's reprimand.

"You won't use my name?"

"I give you my word. I'll refer to you as a knowledgeable source in the aviation community." She heard him shifting the phone, as if he was trying to get comfortable, and edged her fingers toward the keyboard again.

"Ryan's a good man. No offense, but he hates the press so I suppose if he trusts you, then maybe I can, too." Barker puffed in her ear. "Ms. Sanders, those forty-seven Doppler units the agency administrator mentioned today were delivered nearly three years ago. So far, the FAA has managed to install them in Houston, Memphis, and St. Louis. O'Hare may become operational this summer. That's about one a year, according to my math, which means we'll be well into the new millennium before they're done. We were all set to get ours earlier this spring when Washington reopened the contract. I was told that our ever-helpful Senator Bond wanted a local company to do the job. I guess they decided it wasn't so important after last week's accident."

Got it. Out of caution and superstition, she pressed the STORE key so the quote wouldn't vanish if the computer crashed.

"Do you suppose payoffs were involved?"

"I have no idea."

"Mr. Barker, the NTSB often runs into a brick wall when it recommends safety improvements to the FAA. It seems ironic to me that here's a case where your agency accepted the advice and has the equipment, but is taking forever to install it. Do you see it that way, too?"

There was a grim laugh on the other end of the line. "You want irony? Our procurement process is so convoluted it takes five to seven years to acquire and install new equipment, which virtually ensures its immediate obsolescence. The situation with Doppler is the tip of the iceberg. Sure, it's silly that we've got a bunch of high-tech radar units collecting dust in a warehouse. What's worse is that facilities across the country suffer from widespread appalling neglect."

He inhaled on his cigar and resumed in earnest.

"The computers at the Center in Fremont, California, failed last Thursday. Maybe you heard about it. Even the backup generator failed so for one hour those guys had *nothing*. That's never happened before. Seattle Center extended its radar as best it could to handle some of the planes and control towers got the rest, but we had a couple of near misses. A few weeks before that, the main computer system at Chicago Center shut down for sixty-five minutes, only in that case the rudimentary backup equipment worked. These outages are happening more and more—all because the FAA won't spend the money to upgrade its facilities."

Her fingers moved furiously and she pressed STORE again, grateful for his willingness to talk frankly.

"These computers are so old they run on vacuum tubes that are a lot like the ones in the TV set your parents had when you were growing up. IBM doesn't make parts for them anymore, so our maintenance people have to go all the way to Czechoslovakia to buy replacements. They shop for other parts at Radio Shack and even pick through junkyards, if you can believe it.

What's frightening is that we're not talking about some little level one tower out in the sticks. In case you don't know, Fremont covers the most airspace of any Center in the country. Chicago is the busiest. It handles three million flights a year."

"You say the backup system worked here in Chicago?"

"Yes, which is important to put in your story. But these shutdowns are bound to happen again and we may not be so lucky next time. By the way, FAA brass will tell you they're planning to upgrade the equipment. Last I heard, Seattle is first on the list and won't get theirs for another three years."

"This is all quite an indictment against your employer."

"Yeah, well, that's the reality. Congress deserves some heat, too. A lot of agency budget requests are turned down because the politicians don't like to spend money on low-profile projects like radar. There's no glory in it for them. No votes."

"The age-old motivation."

"Yep. To be fair, there are plenty of other villains on this Doppler thing. At a lot of airports where it's going in, local landowners are holding up the process by demanding more money for their property than the government will pay. In San Juan, Puerto Rico, there's a historic fort at the preferred site for the antenna. In Tampa, environmentalists are upset because they say it will bother a few turtles. Homeowners near Kennedy and La Guardia are worried about radiation, which, of course, is absurd. The list goes on and on. If the flying public realized all of this, they'd be outraged."

"They'll find out now."

Barker inhaled on his cigar again. "I recall seeing some stuff you've written in the *Morning News*. Are you a Dallas transplant?"

"Never lived there." Given his lack of an accent, she guessed he'd grown up somewhere else, too. "The *News* must have picked up my stories from the wires."

"You seem to know what you're talking about, Ms. Sanders. Give 'em hell."

She smiled at the compliment. On more than a few occasions, she'd scooped a story that the competition missed by distinguishing herself from the pack with an insistence on thorough objective reporting. Now, apparently, her hard-earned reputation had proven once again to be a valuable asset, drawing out an initially reluctant source.

"Thank you, Mr. Barker. My story will be much better because you decided to speak openly."

She hung up, mindful there was plenty to do before deadline. She'd have to confirm what he said about Chicago and Fremont Centers, call Circuitron, and give Senators Bond and Masters the chance to respond. They weren't going to be happy to hear from her.

TEN

THE RATTLER

REMNANTS OF A DEPARTURE RUSH were fading in the TRACON. It was shortly after nine Tuesday night and Plan X was in effect under a light northeasterly wind. Kelly sat on the Foul Line, lobbing westbound departures to Chicago Center. During quiet moments he casually observed Gene Lombardi, who was training on Approach again with Greg Webber at his side. In contrast to that day when he'd nearly lost the flick, Lombardi appeared more confident and creative with his traffic plans. His spacing still needed work, but Kelly could see definite improvement.

Another flight strip clattered onto the console from the tower and he grabbed it. America West 777, an Airbus A320 headed for Las Vegas. It reminded him that J.J. was probably on another winning streak at Caesar's Palace by now and he welcomed the respite from her recent moodiness. She'd left shortly after noon on a FAM flight, riding free while observing the pilots from the cockpit jump seat. Controllers were entitled to six familiarization flights a year, an arrangement the FAA had with the airlines to help teach them how the other half lives. Naturally, they used the fringe benefit on vacations whenever possible. America West's target popped up on the scope after the aircraft gained altitude.

"Chicago Departure, Cactus 777 is with you at twenty-eight hundred."

"Good evening, Cactus 777. Radar contact. Turn left heading two-six-zero. Climb and maintain six thousand."

On the scope, America West joined other flights inching toward the West Departure Corridor, a thirty-mile-wide window delineating one of the TRACON's boundaries with Chicago Center's airspace. Kelly arranged his traffic in two streams climbing to 13,000 feet, six miles side by side and seven miles in trail.

With the rush over, he quickly grew bored. He scanned the other sectors and noticed excessive spacing on the approach for runway nine right. Turning to the West Arrival scope, he wasn't surprised to find Bear. His performance slide seemed to be accelerating. Controller burnout was certainly nothing new but, in this case, it was painful for Kelly to watch because Bear had been one of his primary instructors when he came to O'Hare. They'd formed a special bond and enthusiastically shared the foibles of the Chicago Cubs. He'd even introduced Bear to his second wife, and was relieved when his friend refused to hold a grudge after the marriage soured. It was probably only a matter of time before Bear would be taken off the heavy positions. That would be the first blow. If his careless work continued, Samantha Sanchez would set up an improvement plan that he'd have to complete or forfeit his authority to control airplanes.

Of course, his next annual physical could force him into early retirement. Bear risked losing his medical certification once his vision wasn't correctable to 20/20, his blood pressure couldn't be maintained, he suffered hearing loss or diabetes, and on and on. He also had to take an EKG every four years. Kelly studied the overweight, balding figure hunched in front of the scope, rasping into his mike. Retirement might not be so bad. With twenty-two years, he'd be eligible for forty percent of his pay. Unless a big chunk went to alimony, he'd have enough to live on and be out of the pressure cooker.

"Interesting story about Doppler in this morning's *Chronicle*."

Pete Rykowski interrupted his thoughts and Kelly swiveled back to the scope. A United 757 heading for Denver neared the Corridor. The target began flashing as part of the automated handoff system, indicating the Center was ready to take him, and Kelly told the pilot to switch radio frequencies.

"Sure was. They nailed Masters."

"It's about time someone did," Rykowski said. "Son of a bitch was trying to look like a savior. You have anything to do with it? I saw you showing that fox from the paper around here last Friday."

After reading the story, Kelly also wondered whether his contact with Christy had somehow improved the *Chronicle*'s interest in air traffic control. He doubted it. "I don't think the two are related, but I'll take the credit if you're handing it out."

"I'll bet you'd rather just take her. Nice legs on that one." Rykowski whistled. "If I wasn't married, I'd let her wrap 'em around me anytime." He cackled when Kelly ignored his friend and glared at the scope. Keeping anything private in the brotherhood of the TRACON was nearly impossible. "You *did* have a hard-on. I could tell by the way you were gawking at her."

Bear scooted over on his chair. "Think of it as a noble sacrifice, Rain Man. Stick it in her and maybe the paper will keep sticking it to the agency."

Their brutal banter, which Kelly usually engaged in with the same reckless abandon, suddenly offended him. He bored into his friend's tired brown eyes, his voice soft but firm.

"Watch your spacing, Bear. Slowdowns are illegal."

Pepperidge jolted at the slap. In the brotherhood, the basest, most perverted remark will simply provoke an equally coarse response. But ridicule someone's ability to separate airplanes and you've personally affronted their very essence. He laughed nervously and rolled the chair back to his scope.

Rykowski watched Kelly warily and noted the way he clenched his mike switch. "Have we offended thee?"

Kelly hissed under his breath. "We can't afford a weak stick in here."

"Something else is bothering you. What's up with this woman?"

"Nothing." He called a pilot and felt the stare.

"You two seeing each other?"

Kelly knew Rykowski would keep needling until he'd pried it out of him. He detected concern rather than crass curiosity and so he relented, speaking quietly to prevent the others from hearing. "We had dinner, that's all."

"Well, well, well. She's got a son. I thought you didn't want—"

"I don't!" Kelly swallowed hard to regain control. "Christy's . . . a nice person. She's not just some piece of ass."

"She is gorgeous. And if she's nice, too." He shrugged. "That's an irresistible combo, Rain Man."

Kelly called another pilot. "I know. We're going out again." He hadn't planned to ask, but the sweet sound of her voice on the telephone yesterday reminded him of those mesmerizing blue eyes that reached right into his soul. He couldn't resist.

Rykowski whistled again, ever so softly. Wait till Cheryl hears about this.

She's been trying to set him up with one of her friends for years. "That's great. I take it her kid's the problem?"

"Besides the fact that this job doesn't mix well with relationships."

"Nonsense. Look, you've got no family, all your friends are controllers and you live in a big house by yourself."

"I have Rudy."

"Sorry, I forgot about the cat." Rykowski said it with exaggerated contrition. "I'm not suggesting you do anything rash, Rain Man. All I'm saying is there's a lot more to life than moving metal. I think you're missing the big flick."

Kelly grunted and called another plane. More to life, indeed, but this job demands such a high degree of commitment and intensity it tends to crowd out everything else. He was afraid the distraction of a relationship would take the edge off his finely tuned skills. He also knew his lifestyle didn't mesh well with others.

"It was a disaster when I lived with Carol. I'd get off work racing a hundred miles an hour, so when I got home I'd drink and channel surf to come down to her speed. By the time I went to bed, she'd be asleep. Or at work because of my schedule."

Rykowski racked his flight strips. "The Rattler can be a bitch."

Controllers used the term to describe the rotating shifts that bounced them between day and night like a baby's toy. At the time, Kelly was working the Iron Man—two evenings, two days, and a midnight shift. His days off changed every other week, too. Recently, management instituted permanent days off, which everyone bid on by seniority and kept for a year. He'd managed to avoid the midnight shift and was working three evenings followed by two days. Tuesday nights were a killer because his head didn't hit the pillow until about 1 A.M., then the alarm screeched at 5:30 so he'd arrive back at the airport by 7. Although he enjoyed a long weekend from Thursday afternoon to midday Sunday, the punishing rotation was taking its toll.

On position, he made a decision every other second and each one had to be right. During heavy traffic or bad weather, the mental effort was exhausting. His commute was tiresome and the overtime insistent. The cumulative effect left him sapped of energy on his days off and occasionally unsure of how long he could gut it out. In return for all of this, the FAA classified him as a GS-14. With OT, extra money for training developmentals, and the twenty percent demonstration pay given to controllers at selected busy facilities, he was earning about $100,000 a year. And it was no small matter of pride that he knew he could fling tin with the best of them.

Kelly's eyes wandered about the room, at the dingy carpet, creaky chairs, and radarscopes that belonged in the Smithsonian. This was his home, where he felt comfortable and secure, where others respected and admired him. But Pete was right—something was missing. He'd been lulled into complacency by the great easy sex with J.J. that wasn't so great or easy anymore. When you got down to it, the two of them were just trying to fill voids in their lives with empty shovels. At least he could admit it to himself. He'd lost patience with J.J.'s insistence on bending him to her will. Fleetingly, he questioned whether his interest in Christy was motivated by spite. Then he smiled shyly. Admit it. You can't wait to see her again.

"Want to stop for a drink later?" Rykowski asked. "I won't hound you about her."

Kelly suspected his friend was being less than truthful and he didn't want to explore any more of his feelings publicly tonight. "I'd better not. The Rattler's got me on a quick turn."

$$\text{✈} \qquad\qquad \text{✈} \qquad\qquad \text{✈}$$

JASON ANSWERED THE DOOR the following Saturday evening when Kelly arrived at Christy's home, a cozy red brick Tudor in Oak Park. The youngster mumbled an invitation to enter while staring at the hardwood floor. Kelly eased past and stepped into a living room twenty degrees cooler than outside. They stared awkwardly at each other until Jason jerked a thumb toward a staircase leading to the second floor.

"She's still getting ready."

"Okay. Thanks."

Kelly surveyed the room, uncomfortably aware that although he talked for a living he found himself at a loss for something to say right now. Several candid pictures of Jason were perched on different pieces of furniture and a portrait of a woman with a striking resemblance to Christy hung on a wall. Must be the sister. Above the fireplace was a copy of Ansel Adams'

Winter Sunrise. The shot was one of his favorites. He liked the pastoral beauty of the grazing horse against the majestic backdrop of the Sierra Nevada mountains. He spied a baseball trophy on the mantel below.

"Pretty warm today. You get out to play ball?"

Jason shook his head.

It was so quiet they could hear the hum of the refrigerator in the kitchen.

"So . . . you're in the sixth grade?"

"Seventh."

He winced inwardly at the error and was about to ask what school when Christy's happy voice floated down the stairs. "I'll be just another minute or two, Ryan. Jason, why don't you show him how you make music on the computer?"

The suggestion came as a relief for Kelly and he looked expectantly at the silent boy. They shuffled into a small den, where Jason sat in front of a PC on the desk and clicked the mouse button a few times. New wave music played for several seconds. When it stopped, he stared resolutely at the monitor. Kelly felt ill-equipped to deal with the situation. He wondered if the kid was simply having a bad day or unhappy that his mother had a date. He decided to make one more stab at conversation.

"Your screen looks different than mine at home. What—"

"I'm running Linux," Jason said, his eyes glimmering. "It's a technically superior operating system to Windows. Free, too. You know much about PCs?"

"A little. They're everywhere so I guess we all need to know something about them."

"That's what my mom keeps telling me. My friend's dad is a programmer and helped me install Linux."

The glimmer went out and the room was quiet again until a soft meow from a chair in the corner beckoned Kelly. For the first time he saw the cat, completely black except for a few wisps of white hair on its throat. Grateful for the distraction, he cautiously approached and tentatively stroked its fur. The feline stretched and rubbed his head against Kelly's hand. Jason watched with interest but said nothing.

"So you've met Shadow." Christy stood at the door, looking fresh and vibrant in a tailored blue dress. "Have you got your backpack ready, Jason?"

"Yeah, I'll get it." He marched out of the room.

"Jason's going to a friend's. He's too old to suffer the ignominy of a baby sitter." She reached down to caress Shadow. "I'm impressed. He usually bites the head off strangers who try to be friendly."

Kelly was tempted to ask if she meant Shadow or Jason. "He probably smells Rudy. That's my cat. Fat and affectionate. Follows me around the house like a loyal puppy. I really miss him when I go out of town."

She was touched by the way he talked lovingly about his pet. "Does he sleep with you?"

"Every night."

"You didn't warn me about your unconventional sexual preferences."

"I never bring it up on the first date. Tends to scare women away."

Jason walked back into the den looking surprised and indignant when he found them both laughing. Christy sensed it was best to leave right away and they headed out of the house. When they stopped at Kelly's car in the driveway, she admonished her son in motherly fashion.

"Don't cause any trouble at Dave's."

"No, mom. Later."

He strode along the sidewalk and she shook her head, embarrassed. "Aren't you going to tell Ryan goodbye?" He waved a hand without turning around and continued to the fourth house down the block, then ran up the steps and disappeared inside.

Kelly opened the car door, fending off anger. The brat had been so polite at the airport. Of course, it had been in his best interests then. Christy touched his arm and resentment melted away.

"Sorry about that. It's been a long time since I've gone out with anyone and he's become kind of protective. It's sweet, really, how he tries to look after me."

Kelly grinned. "So he's miffed that I'm moving in on his girl?"

"I know it sounds silly. He's just a little jealous."

And worried that you'll try to rule his life because he's been through that before with other men, she thought. Most of them didn't want the extra baggage of a child. The few who seemed willing invariably disagreed with Christy's philosophy on raising him. It's what drove a stake through several budding relationships.

"I don't blame him. I'd be jealous, too." She heard more than politeness in the comment and laughed shyly.

He walked around the car and settled behind the wheel. "I like your taste in photography. Those pictures of Jason are great, too."

"Thanks. I took them myself."

"How did you get to be so good?"

"I'm not that good. I took a class in college—at the University of Illinois here in the city. I shot for the student newspaper and thought about sticking with it, but decided I was better at words than pictures."

"What else do you shoot?"

"Candids of other people. Some landscapes. If you're interested, I'll show them to you sometime."

"I am. Any nudes?"

She was startled until she caught him grinning again. "Women *or men?*"

"How about both in the same picture?"

"Sorry, you're out of luck." She turned her head away, then cast him a sideways glance, trying not to smile. "Lecher."

He chuckled, already glad to be with her and enjoying their penchant for teasing each other without forced humor or ridicule. As he steered the car onto the Eisenhower Expressway and streaked toward the glittering skyscrapers of the Loop, his irritation with Jason faded away.

"I'd like to read some stories you've written."

"That was years ago. It feels like I've been an editor forever."

"Do you miss writing?"

Christy stared out the window and mused. "I miss meeting people and seeing new things all the time. I don't miss being away from Jason. I get my creative fix by taking pictures now."

"You could get pretty creative with nudes."

Even though she knew he was kidding—wasn't he?—she'd already fantasized about what Kelly might be like in bed. The big bear type didn't interest her. His slender build and handsome face attracted her and she watched his large strong hands as he deftly worked the gear shift to pass a few cars.

"I'd need a model. Are you offering to audition?"

He smiled mischievously and changed the radio from a rock station to jazz.

Luxuriating in the leather seat, she envied the roominess of his car compared to hers. The fact that he didn't brag about it pleased her. Too many men substituted possessions for personality in their misguided attempt to impress. She commented on the music and their conversation started flowing so naturally that they hardly noticed the drive to Lincoln Park. It was a short walk from the parking lot to the nightclub, where they navigated down a narrow staircase before snaring one of the last tables.

It didn't surprise him when she asked for a scotch on the rocks. Frothy drinks with umbrellas didn't seem her style. They listened contentedly to a female pianist whose buttery voice harmonized with a saxophonist and ordered hors d'oeuvres along with their second round. The music was at once mellow and sensual, and matched their mood. When Kelly suggested a third round, she opted for Irish coffee. After the waitress served them, she took one sip and frowned.

"Either this is peppermint schnapps and hot chocolate or they brew a strange blend of coffee here."

He immediately summoned the waitress, brushing aside Christy's protests that schnapps was fine. "This is not Irish coffee. Can we get what we ordered, please?"

The proper drink was served in less than a minute and she nodded with satisfaction. "You didn't have to do that."

"It's my nature. I deliver perfection and therefore I expect perfection. When I don't get it, I'm unhappy."

Christy noted his tone of finality. "You get that way from the job, I presume?"

"And my dad."

"The drill sergeant?"

"Yeah."

She studied him in profile as he swayed to the beat of the music. The tightly coiled energy and emotion that occasionally burst through his calm exterior intrigued her. Despite his laid-back attitude, he spoke succinctly and moved with a fluid economy that reflected little wasted effort. When his eyes casually swept the room to keep tabs on the activity, he did so without making her feel ignored. She liked that he was open-minded, yet old-fashioned enough to open doors for her. He was patient and unassuming, but she suspected that under the right conditions his energy could mushroom into a mighty temper.

The musicians took a break and Kelly suggested they walk to another club in Old Town. Along the way, the crowds jostled them and he was acutely aware of their bodies touching. It seemed too distant when they moved apart, so he reached for her hand and found it open, waiting for his. She smiled contentedly and motioned at the other people.

"There are times when I still get claustrophobic in the city. Since I didn't have a car in college, I used to go to the top of the John Hancock building just to get away and find some breathing room."

"I guess that's the urban equivalent of a drive in the country." He pointed at the skyscraper with its crisscross bracing and crowning band of light, soaring into the night sky a mile and a half away. "I've never been up there."

"How long have you lived here?"

"Six years."

"Then it's about time you went. The view will be beautiful on a clear night like this."

"The car's the other way."

She squeezed his hand. "The walk will do us good."

Half an hour later, they emerged from an elevator into the softly lit observation deck, 1,030 feet above ground, facing east toward the black void of Lake Michigan. The vista of Chicago unfolded when they rounded a corner. Kelly found it surreal to look at the city stretching into the distant horizon without hearing its ever-present hum. The grid pattern of streets was immediately recognizable and he identified the red and white luminous rivers of the Dan Ryan Expressway to the south, the Eisenhower to the west and the Kennedy to the northwest, culminating in the brilliant cluster of O'Hare. Anti-collision lights on a few airplanes blinked in the sky.

Christy shivered and he snaked an arm around her waist. She laid her head on his shoulder, and the warmth that flowed between them more than counteracted the air conditioning. Wordlessly, they admired the panorama for a long time. Neither wanted to move, unwilling to break the intimacy of the moment and uncertain about what should happen next.

At length, Kelly coughed. "Are you hungry? We can grab a bite somewhere on the way back to the car."

"Let's just go back to my place." She whispered it without looking at him.

They hailed a cab to his car and spoke little during the drive to Oak Park. Christy enjoyed the music playing low on the radio, but as their silence grew she felt obliged to make conversation lest he think she was bored.

"Thanks for helping the paper the other day with the name of your friend in Dallas. He turned out to be a good source."

"That was a good story. I wish the same reporter had covered our beacon outage the other week."

"Ellen was busy with the rapid transit hearings. She's one of our best writers and she's very thorough. I'm sure she'll have a hard time getting anything out of Senator Masters for a while—until he needs her to leak something favorable to him, that is."

The meandering tenor of a saxophone sounded erotic. Kelly peeked sideways at Christy's face, rhythmically highlighted by the passing street lights. The crass comments from Bear and Rykowski echoed distantly when his gaze shifted to the hem of her dress riding midway up her thighs. His fingers tapped the steering wheel while he struggled over how to phrase what he wanted to say. Too soon, they were pulling into her driveway and he was still searching for the right words when they approached the front door. She faced him expectantly.

"To be honest, Christy, I haven't been out on a date in a long time, either." Not a real one, anyway. He shuffled and began again. "What I'm trying to say is I think you're very nice to be with. Actually, more than just nice . . . ah . . . "

Soft and yielding, her mouth closed on his and their arms wrapped around each other. His tongue found hers and the kiss deepened with urgency. She moaned as he ran his fingers through her silky hair. When their kiss broke, she looked at him directly.

"Jason's spending the night with his friend." Her voice quivered slightly.

Kelly reveled in the fullness of her breasts against his chest and knew she must be feeling his response. He wanted to stay. It would be so very easy, but he lectured himself that she was too decent to sleep with simply out of lust. He kept worrying about balancing work with a relationship—and dreaded the thought of trying to get along with Jason. He breathed deeply.

"What I failed miserably at saying a moment ago was that I think you're pretty special." He wistfully caressed her backside and felt her pressing against him. "But . . . I'd better go. I don't want to do anything before I'm sure we're both ready. And I can't believe I just turned you down."

Christy laughed gently. She took his face in her hands and they kissed again, tenderly, longingly, and with promise. When they reluctantly broke apart, she was pleased that his eyes mirrored the disappointment and relief she felt. It was probably smart to wait. Ruefully, she remembered a couple of other romances that ignited like a rocket, then crashed and burned.

"Since you insist on being a gentleman, when can I see you again?"

Despite his angst, despite Jason, he knew it was impossible to ignore his burning desire for her and he regretted their work schedules. "I'm afraid I can't make it till next Friday."

"It just so happens that I'm free. I'll make you a proposition that'll save us both some money. If you bring a movie for the VCR, I'll make us dinner."

He kissed her lightly on the lips, anticipating the inevitable. "It's a date."

ELEVEN
EDCT

S LUMPED IN A SEAT at one of O'Hare's gates for the Friday afternoon flight to Washington, D.C., Sharon Masters fumed about her father. His phone call had come late yesterday. A hearing on something or other had been scheduled and he'd gotten embroiled in a problem with his bill on fruit exports or lumber or whatever the hell it was. As soon as she detected an excuse, she'd tuned him out. Bottom line: He wouldn't make it to Chicago for her birthday. Surprise. "But I've cleared my calendar for you tomorrow night, Pumpkin." Sharon glumly surmised he had no idea how impersonal that sounded. He promised a swing through the National Gallery of Art on Saturday and said he'd already arranged for her flight.

Her fingers picked at a tear in the black leather armrest of the chair. Anger had flared when he mentioned the ticket. Of course he'd bought it before consulting with her, wrecking plans for a celebration here with friends Saturday night. Cavalier presumption bred by too many years inside the Beltway. He irked her even more with a veiled insult about the *Chronicle*'s coverage of his appearance at Dallas-Fort Worth Airport. "These issues are very complicated and your colleagues insist on oversimplifying them."

She nearly told him to go to hell, but bit her tongue at the sudden memory of her mother's gentle patience and fierce loyalty. Her mother had always been so generous with love, always taking the time when her father wouldn't. Now that he was the only family she had, Sharon grudgingly acknowledged she wasn't prepared to turn her back on him just yet. And so she hadn't argued, sullenly agreeing to fly to the capital for the weekend.

The shrill persistent beep of an electric cart gliding through the bustle along the concourse dimly penetrated her gloom. Sitting next to her, a man in a rumpled brown suit spoke wearily into a wireless phone, explaining how the client declined his latest offer and decided to buy elsewhere. She gazed into the cockpit of a jet parked on the other side of the terminal window in front of her. Only one pilot was seated inside. She wondered whether he was married and how often he left his family to ferry others to their loved ones. Or to broken promises.

Enough. Sharon stretched and fluffed her short blonde hair, trying to shake off melancholy.

The public address system clicked on with a loud chirp and a woman's artificially cheerful voice reverberated through the gate area.

"Good afternoon, ladies and gentlemen. Coastal Airlines flight 276, nonstop service to Reagan Washington National Airport, is now ready for boarding."

Her father had paid for a first class ticket—she suspected it was his way of trying to smooth things over—so she was among the first to walk down the Jetway. She settled into a wide leather seat—1C on the aisle—buckled her safety belt and leaned over to stare out the window at another pilot walking across the concrete apron below.

✈   ✈   ✈

FIRST OFFICER JERRY PEARSON squatted to inspect the right main tricycle gear of the Boeing 757 while conducting the customary preflight walk-around. Plenty of tread remained on the Goodrich tires. He couldn't see any cracks or other damage to the gear struts, nor any hydraulic fluid leaking from the wheel well. He lingered to examine everything more closely than usual because the logbook indicated the plane had landed excessively hard an hour ago.

The log also noted the auto throttles failed during the flight from Phoenix, which helped Pearson visualize the landing. Auto throttles maintained speed within a precise range and were usually kept on until the aircraft was just a few hundred feet off the ground. The pilot may not have had much experience flying without them. While fighting the gusty winds earlier, he probably slowed too much, then sank and crunched onto the runway. One of the flight attendants told him on her way off the plane that the touchdown jarred open several overhead bins, spilling passengers' coats and bags into the aisle. Even though Maintenance declared the plane airworthy after a hard-landing inspection, Pearson took his time to scrutinize everything again. He stood and finished his walk-around, then trotted up the steps of the Jetway.

"The gear looks fine," he said, squeezing into the right seat of the cockpit.

Captain Craig McKenzie nodded while testing the weather radar. "Thanks, Jerry. Maintenance is deferring repairs on the auto throttles till this bird is back at the base in San Fran tomorrow."

"Figures. They make flying a lot easier. I wish Maintenance considered them a no-go item instead of a luxury."

But Pearson knew the decision made sense. Although the auto throttles helped conserve fuel, canceling the flight to fix them would cost far more in lost revenue and complications. Coastal didn't have a replacement 757 it could simply trot out of the hangar. He slipped on his headset and tuned in the Automated Terminal Information Service, a continuous loop tape of current conditions that controllers in the tower recorded at least once an hour. As he listened, Pearson adjusted the altimeter to the current setting and made mental notes of several other details. Then he called for their flight clearance.

"Coastal 276, you're cleared to Washington National via O'Hare nine to Giper, then as filed. Maintain five thousand. Squawk three-one-two-four. Uh, stand by 276."

O'Hare nine was a standard departure route. Their first radio fix, Giper, would take them over the Michigan-Indiana border near South Bend, and was so named to honor Notre Dame's famed football star George Gipp. From there, they'd follow their usual flight plan, crossing to the north of Columbus, Ohio, then across the Virginias, and on into D.C. While waiting for Clearance Delivery to call back, Pearson dialed in their assigned squawk code, a unique number that identified their plane when its Mode C transponder relayed altitude information to be displayed on controllers' radarscopes.

"Coastal 276, National has just instituted flow control because of the weather there, so your EDCT is now two-two-three-zero Zulu."

Both pilots grunted. It was nearly five o'clock local time and they were scheduled to leave. If they did, they'd wind up circling over Wash-

ington, waiting to land. For efficiency and to save fuel, ATC delayed
their expected departure clearance time until there was a slot for them
in National's arrival flow.

Pearson consulted his watch and craned his neck, looking out the side
window at an ominous wall of storm clouds approaching from the southwest. "If we don't get out of here soon, that front will close the door on us."

Captain McKenzie's leathery face crinkled in frustration, but he preferred this to the old days. When he was a green first officer in the 1960s,
flights departed as close to their scheduled times as possible. Then they
stacked up over busy airports at 1,000-foot intervals and slowly spiraled
their way down single file.

"It'll be close, but I'd rather hold for the weather here than wait over
National. Ever hear of Black Friday?"

Pearson shook his head.

"You're too young. It was in July '68 and I was flying for Eastern. ATC
got backed up with more than two thousand flights in the New York area
alone, mostly because of bad weather. Delays here at O'Hare were just as
bad. I spent the day on a milk run up the Atlantic seaboard and never made
the last leg from La Guardia to Logan. It was the worst anyone had ever
seen and got people to thinking about flow control."

Two years later, the Central Flow Control Facility, also known as CF
Squared, was created as an integral part of the air traffic system. At an FAA
building in Herndon, Virginia, a computer digested every flight plan in the
nation, then calculated when planes should cross each radio fix to minimize
holding in the air. Controllers at the Centers issued speed restrictions and
ordered minor course changes, when necessary, to hand off flights to the
TRACONs as close to their flow times as possible. Once the crush of airplanes backed up thirty minutes or more, Flow Control held flights at their
departure airports.

Pearson glanced at his watch again. Coastal boasted in newspaper and
television ads about its excellent on-time record, and management repeatedly reminded its crews to maintain it. In the cutthroat climate of today's
airline business, he knew Coastal's survival—and his own—depended on
it. He also knew ATC overreacted sometimes. He'd twice been held for an
hour while flying the Chicago-San Francisco run the month before. In both
cases, the delay was needless because restrictions into SFO were canceled

during the four-hour trip. A flight was considered late if it pushed back from the gate more than fifteen minutes after its published departure time.

"Even if that front holds off, we're not gonna make it outta here on time," he said.

McKenzie grinned slyly. "Unless they need the gate earlier, let's wait until ten after. Then we'll ask to push."

The first officer nodded. Legally, they'd be leaving on time even though their flight wouldn't take off until 5:30 anyway. Behind them through the open cockpit door, Pearson could hear passengers jostling down the aisle.

✈   ✈   ✈

"HIT ME AGAIN, HARRY." Slouched over the horseshoe bar, the stout man waved his empty glass.

Harry eyed his customer with concern while beer streamed into a clean glass that he tilted beneath the tap. He placed it in front of him just as the rising head of foam stopped perfectly at the rim. "For someone's who starting off the weekend right, Mr. G, you don't look so happy."

Günther Schwartz sipped his second Miller of the afternoon and licked the froth from his upper lip. The roar of a jetliner thundered overhead, rattling bottles behind the bar. Schwartz uttered an obscenity, but it was drowned out by the departing flight so he was forced to repeat it, this time with more vigor and elaboration.

"Those fucking airplanes are ruining everything."

"Tell me about it," Harry said, placing a small bowl of mixed nuts on the polished worn bar. "Can't hear the game on TV whenever one of 'em takes off."

Schwartz leaned his head on a hand. "I just dropped the price on my house another ten grand. At this rate, I won't be able to pay off the bank."

Günther Schwartz had been a regular at the 6511 Club for as long as Harry could remember. Four nights out of five, the graying pear-shaped machinist would pit stop at the bar on 55th Street across from Midway Airport after finishing his shift at a small die-casting shop in Cicero. Then he'd waddle around the corner to his home on Luna Avenue for dinner. Now that two of his three children had graduated college and moved out— the middle son hadn't finished yet, which was a touchy subject with

Schwartz—he'd been trying in vain to sell his house and retire early. He dreamed of traveling around the country with his wife in the enormous motor home parked in their driveway.

Harry replenished another customer's drink and sauntered back to Schwartz. "You've lived in that house since your kids were rug rats. Your mortgage can't be that big."

"I took out a second to pay for their college. Plus I still owe a lot on my Winnebago. If I can't pay off everything when I sell the house, I won't be able to quit my job." Schwartz swallowed the last of his beer and Harry automatically poured another.

"Had any offers lately?"

"Only that lowball one a coupla weeks ago. Every buyer who comes through loses interest as soon as they hear those goddamned jets."

Harry placed both hands on the bar and adopted his most sympathetic demeanor. He resisted the urge to ask Schwartz why he bought a house next to an airport in the first place. That would be bad for business. Another airplane rumbled overhead and its deafening roar intensified when the front door to the bar swung open. A lanky kid in his early twenties stepped from the bright light pouring through the doorway, glanced around the tavern and sat on a nearby stool when he spotted Schwartz. Harry could not recall the face.

"Heineken."

Harry didn't budge. "I'll need to see your ID."

"It's okay," Schwartz said. "This is my son, Bradley. He's twenty-three."

A bottle of Heineken and a glass quickly appeared on the bar. Bradley's black hair was cropped short on top and shaved around the sides. A small silver ring pierced his left ear. Remnants of acne speckled his face and dark circles rimmed his eyes. He slurped beer from the bottle and gyrated to a silent beat, surveying the bar with a sneer. Then he turned to his father, smirking at the belly straining against the buttons of his plaid polyester shirt.

"How's it hangin', pops?"

Schwartz unconsciously straightened up on his stool. "End of a hard week at work, son. That's how it is in the real world."

"Yeah, yeah. I'm working hard, too—at school." He swigged more beer and gobbled a handful of nuts.

"How much more money is it going to cost me before you get your diploma?"

"Get off my case, will ya? You wouldn't send me to that flight academy so I could become a pilot. I've had to change my major a coupla times. Gotta find my *niche*." Brad emphasized the last word to remind his father that he'd counseled all three children to select their lifelong occupation with care. He slapped him on the back. "I've only got another thirty credit hours to go."

Schwartz nodded somberly. Another year, minimum, because the kid had a habit of skipping class as well as changing majors. "It didn't take Elizabeth and Kenneth forever to finish college. Your sister even graduated a semester early and now she's making good money at the hospital. Why can't you be more like her?"

"Because I'm not her—I'm me! Why can't you accept that?" Brad slammed his Heineken bottle on the bar, prompting a warning glance from Harry.

Schwartz decided not to pursue it, loath to provoke another fight. He hadn't intended to bring up the issue, but it just popped out after Bradley's comment. He sipped his beer and took another tack. "I didn't think you drank here. Not your kind of crowd."

Brad looked around again. No one else in the joint was under thirty. "Yeah, well, mom said you'd be here. We gotta talk. Since you mentioned money, I need some."

"I've already paid your tuition for this semester."

"It's for my car."

"What's wrong. I thought it was running fine." Schwartz studied his son with suspicion.

Embarrassed, Brad looked away. "I got a few parking tickets."

Schwartz turned back to his beer, both hands curling into fists. "You pay those yourself, Bradley. I will not waste my hard-earned money on your irresponsible driving behavior." His irate tone conveyed the finality of a bartender's last call.

"Gimme a break. The cops put the Denver Boot on my car. They won't take it off till I fork over."

Schwartz began to chuckle. "So, the big man on campus has too many parking tickets and the police have Booted his car. Ho, ho, that's funny! How many?"

"I dunno." He gulped his beer, stalling. "Fifteen hundred dollars' worth."

"Jesus Christ, Bradley! What the hell have you been doing? Didn't you think this would all catch up with you?"

Brad said nothing, inwardly amused by the outburst. If pops was going to freak over a few parking tickets, he'd shit his pants finding out about the pot smoking. And the shoplifting. And the time he and Stan liberated six PCs from the university's computer sciences lab. The outer casings were stenciled with school identification codes, but they'd bought new ones from a mail-order catalog and then sold the repackaged systems to unsuspecting students. That slick little operation scored them several thousand dollars.

"Well, tough luck, kiddo," Schwartz said. "I hope you haven't been spending all the money you earn at the mall on drinking." He slapped his son on the back, suddenly enjoying a moment of payback. "Tell you what. Don't worry about the beer. It's on me."

Brad's eyes pleaded and his voice whined as he played his last card. "Come on, pops. How am I gonna get to campus?" How am I gonna get to see my girlfriend. Come on, you fucking tight-fisted geezer. I haven't had any pussy in a week.

Schwartz smiled serenely at Harry and signaled for another beer.

✈   ✈   ✈

AT PRECISELY TEN AFTER FIVE, Jerry Pearson called Coastal's Ramp Control and received permission for the flight to push back from the gate. Captain McKenzie pressed the tops of both rudder pedals.

"Brakes released," he said to Pearson. Then he keyed his mike. "Ground, brakes are released and we're ready to push."

"Okay."

The response from the ground service chief standing on the concrete below was nearly drowned out by the shrieking of nearby jets. The chief held up a closed fist at the driver of a tug tethered to the nose gear, then opened his hand and pointed toward the plane's tail. A third man standing behind the gleaming blue and white 757 checked for taxiing aircraft and ground vehicles before waving luminescent orange wands to direct the tug driver. Slowly, the 155-foot-long twinjet rolled backward and swung around so that it was pointed toward the end of the wide alleyway.

"Start two," McKenzie said.

Pearson engaged the start switch and watched the RPM gauge, listening to the starboard engine spool up. McKenzie waited until RPMs reached forty-five percent a few seconds later. "Start one."

Pearson repeated the process and both pilots monitored the instruments, hearing and feeling the Boeing jet come to life. The Pratt & Whitney engines were humming steadily now and everything in the cockpit appeared normal. In the cabin, flight attendants performed their safety demonstration to a largely indifferent audience. McKenzie set the brakes again and called to disconnect the tug as Pearson switched to a tower frequency to let them know they were ready to taxi.

"Coastal 276, it'll be two-two left via Bravo and Delta. You've got another fifteen minutes before your EDCT so pull into the two-seven left run-up pad. Monitor the tower one-two-zero-point-seven-five when you get there."

Pearson repeated their clearance while McKenzie nudged the throttles forward. He used the tiller to steer the aircraft out of the alleyway and along the maze of taxiways, parking on an expanse of concrete near the end of runways 27 left and 22 left. He grabbed the final takeoff checklist, announced each item, and waited for Pearson's response.

When they were done, they sat restlessly and watched a constant procession of airplanes taxi past them onto both runways and take off. The jets shimmered in the early summer heat before scampering away with a vibrating roar. The approaching squall line edged forebodingly across the southwestern sky. It would be over the field in minutes. Finally came the call from the tower.

"Coastal 276, runway two-two left, taxi into position and hold."

McKenzie nodded toward the storm. "We're getting out just in time."

Pearson reached up and pushed an alert button to ring a chime in the cabin three times, warning the flight attendants that takeoff was imminent. McKenzie steered the jet onto the rubber-scarred concrete and centered it on the embedded string of green lights stretching into the distance.

"Coastal 276, turn left heading one-four-zero, runway two-two left, cleared for takeoff."

"We're rolling, Coastal 276," Pearson replied.

McKenzie pushed the throttles forward and sank back into his seat from the whining turbofan engines that were blasting 80,000 pounds of thrust.

The lights at the edge of the runway whizzed past in an ever-quickening blur, changing from red to amber, then to white. Pearson monitored the instruments and called out advisories.

"Eighty knots." The airspeed indicator rose steadily. "V-one."

Decision speed. They were hurtling along at 120 knots now and had to take off or abort immediately, otherwise there wouldn't be enough room to stop before reaching the end of the runway. McKenzie scanned the instruments as he'd done thousands of times before. The myriad gauges and dials appeared precisely as they should. The jet surged forward.

"VR," Pearson said. "Rotate."

The ground quickly fell away when McKenzie pulled back on the control yoke. Although business travelers heading home for the weekend usually packed the flight, the plane was only half full this evening and leaped into the sky. He watched the vertical speed indicator, waiting for a steady climb.

"Positive rate. Gear up."

Pearson flicked the lever and hydraulic lines groaned, pulling and folding the heavy gear into the fuselage. They leveled off at 1,000 feet and allowed the airplane time to gain speed for maneuvering.

"V-two. . . . V-two plus ten," Pearson announced.

They were now flying ten knots faster than their climb-out speed. McKenzie pulled back on the yoke again. "Flaps five."

Pearson reached forward and retracted the flaps to five degrees. They passed through 1,500 feet and the captain banked the aircraft left toward their assigned southeasterly heading. The Tri-State Tollway slid below them and the Chicago skyline swung around, looming ahead.

"Coastal 276, contact Departure on one-two-seven-point-four."

The deep Southern voice of the Local controller was familiar to Pearson, who'd been based in Chicago for three years. There were several controllers he knew solely by the metallic tone of their voices, a detached camaraderie they maintained exclusively through the radio. He keyed his mike.

"So long."

TWELVE

PLAN WEIRD

K ELLY FANNED HIS CARDS ON THE TABLE in the TRACON break room and beamed. "Full house sure looks good right now. Can you top that, Bear?"

His friend threw down his cards with a frustrated flick of the wrist. "It's always the little things. If I hadn't dumped that deuce . . . "

Gene Lombardi, who'd been allowed to join the poker game thanks to Kelly's gentle prodding, tossed in his hand, too. "Little things mean a lot. They add up one by one until eventually they're overwhelming."

Pete Rykowski shook his head in awe. "Some days you're unbeatable, Rain Man."

Kelly scooped up the cards and shuffled them into a tidy stack. "Looked like a nasty storm heading for us on the radar earlier. Anyone been outside lately to see if it's raining?" He hoped the front would bring cooler weather. Today was only the fifth of May, but the city had baked under a weeklong heat wave that he feared would stretch into another sweltering summer.

Rykowski raised an index finger and offered his philosophical platitude for the day. "Either it will or it won't."

"That's not profound," Bear said with a snort. "That's stupid."

Rykowski affected an offended look.

"Hate to win and run, but I gotta get back," Kelly said.

"I'll be there in a minute, too," Bear grumbled.

Lombardi was spending another day training with Kelly and walked beside him as he jauntily strolled down the corridor, past the mailboxes and vending machines crammed with junk food. The candy bars and assorted bags of greasy snacks reminded Kelly of the home-cooked dinner he was

supposed to have enjoyed with Christy this evening and he frowned. He'd
been hauled in on overtime yet again and had to cancel their date. Days had
dragged since last Saturday night, which told him how much he wanted to
see her. She'd been understanding on the phone, but there was no mistak-
ing the disappointment in her voice. They immediately rescheduled for the
following night, and the sensual way Christy said she was looking forward
to it quickened his senses as he pushed through the door to the TRACON.
He checked in with Boskovich, who forced a tight smile.

"Take over for Jackson on East Departures. Oh, and watch your phraseology. I noticed you didn't say 'runway' when you cleared some arrivals to
the ILS before your break. Just a small thing, Kelly, but we've got to stay
sharp here, don't we?"

Most of the managers left them pretty much alone so long as they moved
the traffic. Boskoprick was shaping up to be an irritating exception. Sum-
moning his best imitation of a chain gang inmate, Kelly drawled, "Yes sir,
boss." He shuffled over to the Side Line as if hobbled by leg irons. Lombardi
trailed him, grinning. Out of the corner of his eye, Kelly gleefully caught
Bosko glaring. Samantha Sanchez was smiling faintly at her desk, which he
took as confirmation that she disliked the new supe, too. He plugged in his
headset jack and counted nine flight strips on the console.

Although Kelly served as Lombardi's primary instructor, the developmental was supposed to observe other controllers as part of the process of
checking out on Approach. But he revered Rain Man and wanted to hang
around him for a while longer. He always learned something. "Mind if I
watch?"

"Feel free, but be prepared for little Lord Fauntleroy to yank you back to
the Front Line. You can let me know if I do something stupid."

Lombardi couldn't imagine that possibility.

"We've just switched to Plan Weird," Jackson said.

"Okay. Know why we call it that, Pizza Man?"

Lombardi had never heard that particular bit of lore when he checked
out on Departures several months ago. He pondered the runway configura-
tion. "Well, let's see. I suppose it's because east and north departures go to
different headings instead of the same one and they're handled by different
controllers."

Kelly nodded. The kid knew how to think and that was important in here, where you couldn't do the job effectively by rote. "Exactly. A distinctive aspect of that for yours truly is I'll be working traffic from O'Hare *and* Midway. I'm getting thirsty for beer already."

Midway traffic added a layer of complexity. After taking off from the airport on Chicago's South Side, the flights contacted a Satellite position in the O'Hare TRACON and climbed to 4,000 feet. Then they switched to the East Departures controller, who set them up for handoff to the Center. It had to be done quickly. There was only about fifteen miles in which to get them on the right heading and climbing to 13,000 before they reached the East Corridor, a line over Lake Michigan that extended from abeam of Northbrook to south of the Museum of Science and Industry.

Jackson looked up at the Systems Atlanta, a nine-inch black-and-white TV mounted above the radarscope that displayed the weather, radio frequencies, airport diagrams, and other information. He punched a code and the transition checklist appeared. "Equipment status is normal, but the weather's about to crap out. Those storms will be here any minute."

Kelly perused the weather radar display, which showed a cluster of green and a few spots of red just southwest of the field. "I can't wait."

"No special activities." Jackson tapped the rack of flight strips with his pen. "We're expecting Kiwi and Simmons next from Midway. Otherwise, the boys upstairs are trying to launch as many as they can before we have to close the door."

Kelly scanned the scope again, letting the flick settle into his head. Note American 1286 nearing the ten-mile ring. "Okay, I've got it." He signed the log as Jackson stood, then slipped into the chair and keyed his mike, instructing the MD-80 to turn east at 6,000 feet.

Jackson sauntered off and Kelly hunched forward on the console, dimming the video as usual. A flight strip rumbled down the tube from the tower and clattered onto the console. Northwest 391 to Detroit's Wayne County Airport. He placed it on the rack with the others. Kiwi Air Lines 004 started blinking on the scope as it roared away from Midway. The flight strip told him the departure was going to Newark. He slewed on the target and pressed ENTER to accept the handoff from South Satellite. One of the pilots called a moment later.

"Chicago Departure, Kiwi flight four is with you at thirty-nine hundred."

The data tag indicated 38, which didn't surprise Kelly. Mode C transponders often lagged behind actual altitudes, particularly when airplanes were climbing or descending. It changed to 39 while he instructed the pilot to head east at 5,000 feet. He warned Kiwi and American of each other's proximity, then watched the two targets merge and separate when Kiwi flew below the MD-80 headed for Boston.

In the lower right quadrant of the scope, arrivals streamed westward across the lake while descending to 7,000 feet. One by one, they turned right at the twenty-five-mile ring around O'Hare and followed the Lake Michigan shoreline north for final vectoring. Kelly had to keep his departures below the arrivals until they passed each other, then he could climb them for handoff to the Center.

In the lower left quadrant, Northwest 391 would reach the ten-mile ring soon and have to turn east to head out over the lake, a standard departure route. A nearby target for Simmons 4009, the name used for American Eagle, began blinking after leaving Midway while another flight strip rumbled down the tube. Coastal 276 to Washington National.

As he scanned the traffic and tried to work into a rhythm, the anticipation of a pleasurable evening with Christy—perhaps the entire night—stirred his loins. Reluctantly, he pushed it away when Simmons 4009 checked in on the frequency and he cleared the flight to a right turn toward the lake. Traffic was thickening now and he was on the brink of talking constantly.

"Chicago, Coastal 276 is at three thousand."

Get to you in a second, pal. Gotta turn Northwest 391 first. The pilot barely finished the readback before Kelly keyed his mike again. "Coastal 276, Chicago Departure. Radar contact. Present heading, climb and maintain five thousand."

"We're going to five, Coastal 276."

His eyes darted to each of his targets in order. Note American and Kiwi beyond the shoreline and arrival flow. Time to kick 'em upstairs for the Center. "American 1286, climb and maintain one-three thousand."

There was no response. The target inched along, level at 6,000.

He tried again.

No response. *I don't have time for this.* Those planes will be at the East gate soon and they'd better be at the right altitude or the Center will scream.

"Kiwi four, climb and maintain one-three thousand."

No response and suddenly Kelly sensed he wasn't talking to anyone. He reached up and switched over to the standby radio, but had to wait several seconds for the relay to kick in before he could repeat his transmission to American.

"Cleared to thirteen, American 1286."

Kelly sighed and immediately called Kiwi. As the pilot acknowledged, he heard Lombardi tell Bosko that their primary radio had failed. It was a momentary fright that happened once in a while. J.J. got bitten on East Arrivals last week when two airplanes were pointing toward each other on their base legs before turning onto final for the 27 parallels. They were at the same altitude and if it had taken her a few more seconds to switch to the standby radio, she would have kissed separation goodbye. Kelly thanked Lombardi and studied another flight strip that was placed on his console. Prairie 1411, an ATR-72 turboprop out of Midway bound for Indianapolis.

The brief delay had interrupted his tempo and put him behind. Note Simmons and Northwest beyond the shoreline, ready for more altitude. Note Coastal has to turn east before he sails over Midway. Also note Prairie climbing out, which means Coastal has to go to six to top the prop and I'll have to issue traffic because they'll be at separation minimums. He hooked his feet around the legs of the chair and felt his stomach coil.

"Coastal 276, turn left heading zero-niner-zero. Climb and maintain six thousand. Traffic one o'clock, two miles eastbound, climbing to four."

"Left to zero-nine-zero and we're going to six thousand, Coastal 276. Traffic in sight."

Kelly sent Simmons and Northwest to their handoff altitude. Coastal caught his eye while the pilots responded. The target's altitude readout leaped to 58, then dropped to 52 within one sweep. He tapped the glass scope with his forefinger a few times, knowing this had no real effect but reassuring himself that somehow he was corralling the data bits back into order.

Note American's ready for handoff and Kiwi's clawing for altitude because it's hot out there. The data tag indicated Kiwi was a Boeing 727, a thirty-year-old plane some flight crews called the Jurassic jet. He issued instructions for the start of an S-turn to give it more time to climb before reaching the Corridor. Then the target for American disappeared when Chicago Center bought the handoff. Kelly glanced up at the weather display again to see that the storms were over the airport. The radar glowed green and red, meaning departures would cease anytime now.

"Prairie 1411 is coming up on four thousand."

Lombardi bent over Kelly's shoulder as he keyed his mike. "You see Coastal's altitude jumping around?"

"Prairie 1411, turn left heading zero-seven-zero. Climb and maintain five thousand. Traffic two o'clock, three miles eastbound at six." His eyes flicked back to Coastal. The data tag now showed 54. "Yeah. Thanks, Gene." He waited for Prairie's readback, then called the flight to D.C. "Coastal 276, say your altitude."

"Two seventy-six is climbing through fifty-five hundred, on our way to six."

"Thanks, 276."

With the next sweep, Coastal's readout showed 57. *Well, that's probably right.*

Kelly switched Northwest 391 and Simmons 4009 to the Center's frequency and turned Kiwi 004 back northeast, grateful it was approaching handoff altitude. Another flight strip from the tower dropped in front of him. USAir 1246 to Pittsburgh. He added it to the stack as his eyes registered what his brain took another second to comprehend while running through the sequence on the scope. Coastal's altitude was now showing 62. One of the arrivals—Atlantic Airlines 59—was at 7,000, turning north just off the shoreline on a path that would take him right in front of Coastal. Suddenly, the altitude readouts flashed 63 for Coastal and 69 for Atlantic.

Lombardi leaned on the console. "What's Coastal doing?"

Kelly spun around to determine who was handling Atlantic and saw Bear sitting on East Arrivals. The targets started blinking and the CA alarm began beeping.

"Coastal 276, say your altitude."

No response. What the hell?

"Coastal 276 has an RA and we're climbing."

Okay, they were busy watching TCAS, but never mind that because this is not the time to bust altitude. He keyed the mike, his voice low but urgent. "Coastal 276, *do not* climb. There's traffic above you. Two o'clock position. A two-seven."

No response and the CA kept blaring and the readouts flashed again. Sixty-five for Coastal, 67 for Atlantic. Kelly broke into a sweat.

"Hey, Rain Man! Bear! You got those two?" The shout came from Greg Webber on North Satellite. Several other controllers watched the conflict on their scopes and grimaced. Behind them, Boskovich marched over to Pepperidge on the Front Line.

"He's following TCAS," Kelly yelled, his eyes glued to the scope.

The radar swept by and the targets merged and Kelly closed his eyes.

Oh, fuck. He subconsciously heard another pilot on the radio and told him to stand by. All he cared about right now was Coastal 276 and Atlantic 59. The readouts flashed again, but they were hard to decipher because the information was overprinting. He squinted and thought they both showed 66. The radar swept around again with agonizing slowness and the readouts changed to CST.

Coast status. The computer had lost track of them.

He filtered out all the noise in the TRACON and riveted on the jumble of targets, rotating sweep, and clutter of other video that he usually ignored. Now he was seeing it all one pixel at a time.

With a detached sense of calm, he slewed on the targets and shut off the CA alarm, wishing irrationally that silencing the beep would magically keep the two airliners apart. He wondered how many people were onboard. It was something he scarcely thought about, couldn't allow himself to think about, because he'd told himself time and again that this was only a game. He moved little green blips around on a screen and the only difference between a Cessna 172 and a Boeing 747 was speed and wake turbulence.

The targets jumped apart after the next sweep and there were only two blips.

Kelly closed his eyes again. He considered himself an agnostic, but the only thing he could think of doing was thank God.

Lombardi slumped beside him. "Mother have mercy on us."

"Chicago Departure, USAir 1246 is still level at four thousand, heading one-four-zero."

Get it together, my friend. You can't put everyone on hold and let them listen to elevator music. He started to speak and nothing came out, so he tried again and found his voice, somehow imbuing it with confidence and authority.

"USAir 1246, I'm sorry. Radar contact. Present heading, climb and maintain five thousand."

The pilot was responding and Kelly was trying to breathe normally again when the target for Atlantic 59 disintegrated into three blips.

THIRTEEN
THE POND

THE SCATTERED FLUFFY CLOUDS, infused with pastel shades of lavender and pink from the setting sun behind them, reminded Captain McKenzie of a painting by Monet. The control yoke vibrated slightly in his hands as the 757 sliced into one of the clouds, masking the windshield in translucent white, then broke out the other side and headed for another. While climbing to their assigned altitude of 6,000 feet, McKenzie allowed himself a moment to admire the natural beauty that had made him yearn for the skies ever since he was a boy in Montana. Through the side window he glimpsed Soldier Field, its colossal orange, yellow, and blue stands empty now, and the green expanse of Grant Park as they passed overhead along the Lake Michigan shoreline.

"*Traffic, traffic.*"

The synthetic voice of the computer snapped him out of his reverie and drew both pilots' attention to the TCAS displays on each of the two horizontal situation indicators. A small white airplane near the center of the fish-finders denoted their aircraft. Higher and to the right was an amber circle with +12↓ printed next to it. This was the intruder—1,200 feet above and descending from the south—that set off the Traffic Alert. If the two planes continued on their present paths, TCAS calculated they would collide in forty-five seconds.

In the nose of the 757, a transponder sent a signal containing information about Coastal's altitude, bearing, and speed to a similar transponder in the nose of the intruder. Four miles away, a Boeing 727 flying as Atlantic Airlines flight 59 from Miami relayed back a signal with similar data. Now that the two transponders had locked onto each other and were coordinating a possible maneuver, the exchange occurred once every second.

Pearson cocked his head to the right and anxiously searched the sky. "These clouds aren't gonna make it easy to see him." Nor was their closing speed, which he estimated at 550 knots.

McKenzie scanned the other instruments and peered out the window, one eye continuously flicking to the fish-finder. Previous Traffic Alerts he'd been involved in usually ended without incident. The airplanes leveled off or turned before a Resolution Advisory was necessary. He'd responded to an RA twice, his heart rate spiking significantly while he religiously followed the computer's dictates. ATC insisted the evasive maneuver had been unnecessary both times, but McKenzie wasn't convinced. He liked the traffic display and felt more secure having the computer as a backup to controllers.

The amber circle edged toward their white airplane and changed to a red square. The accompanying data tag flashed +07↓.

"Climb, crossing climb." The synthetic voice rang out as red and green lights illuminated around the vertical speed indicator.

McKenzie pulled back further on the control yoke to increase their rate of ascent from 1,000 to 1,500 feet per minute, his throat tightening. He thought it made more sense to level off or descend since the intruder was above them, but the matrices of the encounter and surrounding traffic must be such that the computer determined a climb would be more appropriate.

Pearson's nose almost touched the windshield. "I still don't see him. I probably won't with these clouds."

"Keep looking." McKenzie monitored the VSI needle, continuing their ascent to move it from the red back into the green. A lock of iron gray hair fell across his forehead and he impatiently brushed it away, expecting to hear TCAS announce "clear of conflict" any moment.

"Increase climb—increase climb!"

The voice was louder and more insistent and the first breath of fear stirred the hairs on the back of his neck. He pulled harder on the yoke and the VSI needle swung to 2,500 feet per minute. He heard ATC calling them and Pearson say they were responding to the RA. McKenzie's hands grew sweaty and the corner of his mouth twitched. I know there's traffic above us. TCAS is going nuts about it.

The red square dogged them relentlessly on the fish-finder.

Pearson stole another look at the display. "This doesn't seem right, Captain."

McKenzie struggled with the urge to change course. He didn't like putting all his faith in a computer and deviating from an ATC clearance, but legally they had no choice. FAA regulations and Coastal Airlines policy required them to do whatever TCAS ordered. Besides, he knew the machine could calculate bearings and altitudes that would lead them to safety in the blink of an eye. He watched the altimeter spin through 6,500 feet, eager to level off as soon as TCAS alerted them they were out of harm's way. He checked the fish-finder again, then frantically searched the violet sky. His hands turned white gripping the control yoke and he considered leveling off, remembering the echo of the controller's warning.

Pearson muttered as they streaked through the flock of clouds. He barely had time to scan before his view was blocked again. They broke into the clear once more and he instinctively yanked his head back from the nose of the 727 mushrooming off their right side. It was so close he could see the pilots sitting in the cockpit.

"Holy shit! Traffic three o'clock—*our altitude!*"

✈   ✈   ✈

SITTING IN THE MAIN CABIN of Atlantic Airlines flight 59, a small boy wearing a cowboy shirt and jeans repeatedly flipped a baseball into his mitt. Suddenly, the plane lurched into a steep dive and the ball tumbled out of his glove, rolling against the foot of a passenger in the row ahead. The man scooped up the ball and twisted against his safety belt to turn around.

"Here you are."

"Thanks, mister. My name's Matt. What's yours?"

The man smiled kindly and shook the boy's hand. He wished he had a son like Matt. "I'm Kevin. Nice to meet you, Matt. Better hang on to that."

Matt tucked the ball securely in his mitt and Kevin turned back around.

Forward in the cockpit, the first officer saw the Coastal 757 burst out of the clouds from the left. He yanked on the control yoke and jammed one rudder pedal to the floor in a desperate attempt to steer above and behind the other plane. The 727 was starting to respond when the outboard edge of its port wing grazed the top of the 757's starboard wing. Then the Jurassic jet shook violently from a sickening crunch of metal as the wing slashed through the vertical stabilizer on Coastal's tail, ripping half of it away.

The horrendous jolt back in the cabin shook Carla Szemasko to the bone and pulled her painfully against the seat belt. Horrified, she watched a flight attendant who'd been collecting cups and napkins catapult off her feet and thud against the overhead bins. The woman hung briefly in the air before falling backward across the lap of a startled passenger. She spilled over the armrest of his seat in a twisted heap, her head bent against the floor at an unnatural angle.

The airliner shuddered and plunged to the left.

Carla and everyone else in window seats on that side of the plane slammed against the cabin wall. With her face plastered to the cold Plexiglas, she peered out and caught her breath. Half the wing was gone in a jagged tear. She flailed an arm across the empty seat between them and managed to grab her husband's wrist, but it was torn away when the plane spiraled and they were suspended upside down, held only by their safety belts. The flight attendant's body was flung against the ceiling of the cabin like a rag doll, then back to the floor again as the plane kept rotating. Kevin managed to smile at Carla while clutching the armrests of his seat.

"Hang on, baby. The pilots will pull out of this."

She longed to believe him, but obviously he hadn't seen the missing wing. When she opened her mouth to tell him, only a whimper trickled out. Terrified of looking outside, she was unable to resist. Vertigo quickly consumed her from the water and clouds and city skyline that spun dizzyingly into view as if she were riding on a Ferris wheel gone berserk.

Several overhead bins broke open and carry-on bags pummeled disoriented passengers unable to protect themselves with their hands and arms. Galleys fore and aft erupted in a din of clanging metal and shattering glass. Matt cried hysterically and clung to his mother's arm, too scared to notice when the ball and mitt sailed out of his hand. More and more panic-stricken people screamed as it became clear they were powerless to do anything except sit and hang on and wait for the inevitable as their mortally wounded airliner plummeted out of the sky.

Carla forced herself to ignore the maelstrom and focus on a small patch of blue and gold fabric in the seat in front of her. *Think of something else, anything but what's really happening.* That secluded beach came to mind, a

silver crescent moon hanging overhead amid twinkling stars. The undulat-
ing sand had been soft and warm beneath their blanket with Kevin on top,
his tender whispers hot on her neck. She let out a soft cry, remembering the
night they'd left the ship for a few romantic hours ashore during an idyllic
twelve-day cruise in which she'd lost count of the number of times they'd
made love.

Tears dribbled down her cheeks over the sweet memory clashing with
the macabre reality of the present. She saw Jason's cute dimples and Christy's
warm smile when they were at the house the other weekend, and remembered telling her sister that she finally hoped to get pregnant on this trip.
Now she'd never know.

Carla turned to Kevin and their eyes met in a haunting exchange of fear
and affection. "I love you," she whispered.

"I love you, too, baby." Then he looked beyond her, wide-eyed, past the
window.

Flames were fanning the ragged edges of the wing stump.

Color drained from Kevin's face. He grabbed her hand and squeezed so
hard it hurt. His mouth began moving, but his halting utterances were
incoherent. Carla could tell he knew now that they weren't going to make
it. She breathed heavily, wanting to scream, desperately wanting to *do something* other than just sit here, waiting, watching it happen.

Oh, gentle Jesus, there's so much more of life to live. *Please don't let
me die.*

✈   ✈   ✈

KELLY'S EARPHONE CRACKLED ALIVE while he stared at the scope in aston-
ishment. The pilot's voice was controlled, but laced with fear.

*"Mayday, mayday. Coastal 276 is declaring an emergency. We're losing alti-
tude and we've got no hydraulic power."*

He whirled in his chair—"Bosko!"—and fixed his eyes on Bear, who was
turned in his direction. Pepperidge ran a hand through the few strands of
hair on his head, looking confused and shocked. Kelly felt cold and nauseous, and wanted to run from the scope. Leadenly, he turned back.

"Coastal 276, do you want the equipment?"

"Yes . . . uh, stand by." The copilot kept his mike keyed and Kelly could

hear the captain shouting orders over the blaring of an alarm bell.

"They won't want to land here." It was Boskovich. Sneering and puffing his chest in vindication over catching something the star had missed.

Kelly glanced up at the Systems Atlanta. The storm had cut the runway visual range to minimums. Good point. He should have noticed that before making the call. Don't lose it. *Not now.*

"Coastal 276, the RVR here is four hundred feet. Midway is eight miles directly behind. Do you want to go there?"

While they waited for a response, Boskovich nervously studied the scope. "What happened?"

Kelly struggled, unable to find the willpower to say what he couldn't imagine saying. He saw Sanchez hovering behind Boskovich and J.J. walking into the TRACON. When he finally spoke, he sounded disembodied.

"I just ran a couple together over the pond."

"What do you mean?"

On reflection, he supposed it was natural that others would find it hard to accept the nightmare they strove every second to avoid. But right now, he was taken aback by the question. It was perfectly, appallingly clear to him. He turned to the haughty supe with a carefully knotted silk tie in his button-down collar and stared at him contemptuously.

"Are you fucking blind?" He jabbed his finger at the data block for Atlantic 59. When the radar swept past, the three blips fragmented into five.

✈   ✈   ✈

LARRY LINDSTRAND EASED THE WHEEL BACK TO CENTER, aiming the bow of his thirty-five-foot Beneteau at a skyscraper along the shoreline. It felt great to be sailing again after hibernating through another insufferable Chicago winter. As the owner of Lindstrand Motors, he didn't have to ask for permission to take the afternoon off when the urge struck and he decided to put *No Wheel Drive* through its first sea trial of the year. Cindy, the blonde receptionist he'd hired for reasons beyond her telephone skills, squealed in delight when he asked her along. The wind whipped up her dress again while she clung to the lifeline on the bow and he caught a generous flash of thigh before she matted it down. Cindy didn't appear too embarrassed.

"This is great, Larry. Thanks for inviting me."

Lindstrand grinned lewdly. You can thank me later, honey. "We'd better get back. That storm'll be here soon."

Cindy looked up at the clouds, which were whiter and more scattered than the thunderheads clustered threateningly over the city skyline. She heard the whine of a jet and cocked her head, searching for it. Something odd about the sound piqued her senses. Suddenly, the Atlantic Airlines 727 plunged out of the clouds upside down and rolling clockwise.

Cindy gasped and a hand flew to her mouth. Lindstrand followed her gaze and stared in stunned silence at the fire burning furiously on what remained of the left wing. The silver and blue T-tailed jet spiraled several times more before a series of blasts rippled across to the other wing and in both directions along the fuselage.

Screaming, Cindy scurried along the deck to Lindstrand. He hugged her briefly, then jumped below to fetch a camera. Scrambling back on deck, he madly jabbed his finger on the shutter while pointing the camera at sections of the cabin that broke away in flaming pyres and tumbled toward them, bathing the sky and water in an eerie orange glow. Pieces of wreckage began raining on the lake and a sizable section of wing crashed off the port bow, rocking the boat.

"Shit! Get below!"

They scampered down the companionway and Lindstrand prayed the boat wouldn't take a direct hit, but there were several thumps on deck. Each one made him duck and wrenched another shriek from Cindy. Through the companionway, he saw the nose and cockpit falling, and he raised his camera again to click a few more shots. Splintered from the rest of the fuselage with entrails of wiring and cables dangling out the open end, the wreckage splashed down barely ten yards away and threw a wave over the stern before sinking. The torrent of debris slowly subsided and Lindstrand crept unsteadily back on deck.

The sky above was strangely serene again. The only sound came from the familiar slapping of waves against the hull and this unnerved him. Wreckage bobbed in the water, some of it still alive with flames, and the acrid odor of burning jet fuel saturated the air. Lindstrand surveyed the debris and gave himself time to comprehend what he'd just seen.

"C'mere, Cindy. It's all over," he said soothingly, more to reassure himself than his companion.

Several pieces of aluminum with torn jagged edges littered the cockpit deck—he hadn't bothered putting up the bimini before today's sail. Near the wheel was something else that appeared sickeningly familiar. He refused to believe it at first and tried not to look again. Unable to contain his curiosity, he turned back and edged closer until he could no longer deny that it was definitely the bloodied and charred stump of a human arm. He heard Cindy cry out. Then his stomach roiled and he lunged for the lifeline, vomiting over the side.

✈   ✈   ✈

THE IMPACT PUSHED DOWN what was left of Coastal's tail and slowed the 757 almost instantly by fifty knots. Captain McKenzie gripped the yoke and concentrated on the feel of the airplane, trying to ascertain what control he had left. The rudder was gone and the instruments indicated they'd lost all three hydraulic systems, confirming what his senses told him. He moved a lever for the Ram Air Turbine, which activated a wind-driven pump that was supposed to return pressure to the flight controls. He pushed the yoke forward to regain speed and the twinjet nosed over too far. Gingerly, he pulled back and gradually brought them level again.

"The RAT's given us some control. Tell Departure we're declaring an emergency."

Pearson dazedly keyed his mike and made the call. When the controller suggested Midway because of poor visibility at O'Hare, McKenzie shook his head. Despite his eagerness to get back on the ground, he didn't like MDW. It was a cramped airport with stubby runways that may have been fine for propeller planes flying in the 1940s and '50s, but was barely adequate for even the smallest of today's jets.

"Ask about Gary or Indianapolis, even Detroit or Milwaukee. Anywhere but Midway."

Pearson pointed at the instrument panel. "We're losing fuel, Captain. I'd say eight thousand pounds or so since we hit."

McKenzie had been too busy flying to notice. He looked at the gauges and winced. The levels dropped as he watched. The other plane must have torn holes in the wing tanks. "Christ, I guess it's Midway, like it or not. Tell 'em I'm starting a right turn and advise our fuel situation."

As Pearson relayed the message, McKenzie discovered they had little aileron control. Delicately, he manipulated the engine thrust to try banking the 757. It worked, just like the United DC-10 crew had done before making an emergency landing in Sioux City, Iowa, after losing hydraulics. Images of the jet exploding on the runway came to mind and he blinked them away, trying to focus on the flight controls.

"Coastal 276, if able, turn right heading one-eight-zero and maintain five thousand for now."

"We're trying," Pearson said. "Please have the equipment standing by."

"Roger, 276. Attention all aircraft, please report any sightings of other aircraft, ah, any wreckage that you see."

The drone of a turboprop filled their headsets. *"Chicago, this is Prairie 1411. We saw an explosion in our twelve o'clock position a few moments ago. . . . Looked like an aircraft breaking up. It fell right into the lake."*

McKenzie shivered. No one could have survived. He deemed it nothing short of a miracle that his craft remained aloft. A check on their fuel situation drew him back to the task at hand. There was plenty to do before landing. The time to agonize was later. He keyed the intercom and punched the code for the first flight attendant, fervently hoping she was still sitting in her jump seat on the other side of the cockpit bulkhead since they hadn't reached 10,000 feet.

"Debbie, are you okay?"

"Yes, captain," she replied tentatively, betraying her brave front. During their layover, Debbie had confided that she'd just gotten engaged. "What happened?"

"We hit another airplane." McKenzie hesitated, astounded at hearing himself say the words. "We've lost our hydraulics and will land at Midway in five minutes. Tell the passengers to brace. You know the drill. I'll warn 'em one minute from touchdown. Keep things together for me back there, Deb. I'm counting on you."

Debbie Donatello grasped the edge of her jump seat to stop shaking and tried to compose herself. McKenzie treated the cabin crew with respect and dignity, which she viewed as a natural extension of his professionalism as a pilot. If anyone can get this thing down, he's the one.

"Yes, Captain."

After McKenzie clicked off the intercom, Donatello rang the other flight attendants and advised them. Then she switched to the main cabin PA system. She paused, unsure how much to say. In order to lessen the potential for panic, she decided to reveal as little as possible. Taking a deep breath, she squeezed the transmit button.

"Ladies and gentlemen, we're experiencing some difficulty and will be landing shortly. Please stay in your seats, keep your seat belts fastened, and remain calm. The captain will give you a warning when we're about ready to touch down." She paused again, willing herself to sound matter-of-fact. "When he does, for your protection, please bend forward and place your arms over your head. We'll be on the ground in a few minutes. Thank you."

Donatello replaced the intercom mike in its holder and noted with perverse satisfaction that the man in seat 3C, who'd been leering at her ever since boarding, now looked subdued and nervous. She smiled reassuringly at the young woman two rows forward.

Sharon Masters summoned a weak smile in return. Despite the flight attendant's confident manner, she was frightened and wanted to know what so-called difficulty was prompting the emergency landing. She'd flown through turbulence before, but the jolt a few minutes ago was the worst she'd ever felt on an airplane. She tugged her seat belt tighter and looked out the window. The sight of the shoreline returning into view did little to reassure her.

FOURTEEN

MDW

T HE TRACON WAS IN PANDEMONIUM. Pete Rykowski, Steve Christensen, and a supervisor crowded behind the East Arrival scope, where Bear sat dumbfounded. He'd been handling the traffic just fine. Even his spacing was respectable until Atlantic suddenly disregarded his descent clearance and broke through 7,000 feet. Bear's shoulders sagged and his hands lay limp on the arms of the chair. The feeder man had taken over both positions and was coordinating the transition to Christensen now.

J.J. joined Sanchez, Boskovich, and Lombardi behind Kelly. She'd returned from Las Vegas only the day before. Different surroundings had sown a fresh perspective and she felt remorseful for treating Rain Man badly of late. But there'd been no chance to apologize and now her heart went out to him as he grappled with the unthinkable. Boskovich flicked a switch to put the frequency on a speaker and they heard the pilot's decision to land at Midway.

Sanchez shouted across the room to the Satellite positions on the Foul Line. "Get everyone out of three-one center!" The controllers immediately began diverting arrivals from the approach path for Midway's longest runway.

Boskovich grabbed the hot line phone and punched the button for the airport. "Shut off departures. You're gonna get Coastal 276 in a few minutes. A five-seven coming from over the lake. Total hydraulic failure. We'll give you fuel and souls when we know it." He hung up and leaned over Kelly. "J.J. will take over."

"Have her handle everyone else, but let me get this guy down first."

Boskovich shook his head and started to say something when Sanchez cut him off. "Let Ryan do this." Sanchez motioned J.J. forward and Lombardi moved aside so she could plug in to direct the other four planes Kelly was working.

"Coastal 276, proceed direct to Midway," he said. "You're cleared to land on any available runway. Equipment will be standing by. If you get a chance, give me fuel and number of souls on board."

The copilot chuckled grimly. *"Fuel when we land is uncertain. We've got nine thousand pounds right now, but it's dropping fast. SOBs holding steady at 114."*

Kelly welcomed the sense of humor. Someone had to keep hope alive. That his own voice stayed calm surprised him, given the chemistry experiment churning in his gut. "Thanks, 276. Remain on this frequency."

Boskovich called Midway again with the information, which would be relayed to the Fire Department. As soon as he hung up, Kelly swiped the phone and rang Chicago Center. "Forget about Coastal 276. He's going to Midway."

"We'll need a down time," said the person who answered.

Always the paperwork. The bureaucrats would get upset if the Center's log failed to note when the flight landed. "I'll get back to you," he said tersely and banged the receiver back on its hook.

Then there wasn't much to do except track Coastal's target as it swung clockwise in a wide arc toward the airport. Kelly sat immobile, holding a swirl of questions and fears at bay until flight 276 touched down. J.J. calmly called several planes while glancing at him sympathetically. Boskovich shifted behind the two, restless without any orders to give. Sanchez crossed her arms and watched the scope. Elsewhere around the room, controllers kept one eye on the crisis in between talking to their traffic. Lombardi succumbed to the urge to distance himself from it and drifted over to the flight data desk, where several others had gathered. They were joined by more controllers who rushed back from the break room after hearing about the midair. Jackson looked at the scope he'd left not fifteen minutes before and shuddered.

"Are we clean?" he asked softly.

No one answered.

✈   ✈   ✈

IN THE COCKPIT OF FLIGHT 276, Captain McKenzie agonized over the fuel gauges. Six thousand pounds remained. *That means more than a thousand pounds a minute are gushing out of the tanks and we won't land for another five, so it's going to be close. Of course, that prediction is based on the gigantic assumption that no spark from the engines catches the fuel on fire and blows us all to hell.* He pushed the nightmare out of his mind and turned his attention to their landing.

"We'll have to execute alternate flap and gear extension, Jerry. Let's start with the non-normal checklist."

Pearson flipped to the proper section in the manual and began reciting two pages of items. They used an electric motor to extend the flaps as far as possible. Pearson rotated a crank in the floor to open the gear doors and they heard a resounding thunk when the wheels fell into position by gravity. They'd barely finished all the checklist items when Midway came into view on their right. McKenzie glanced at the fuel gauges again.

Twenty-five hundred pounds remaining.

He adjusted the throttles to ease out of their gentle turn and the nose settled on the airport, tiny in comparison to O'Hare. The plane kept rocking and he struggled with the yoke, using what little aileron control they had trying to steady it. Storm clouds loomed on the horizon while they completed the landing checklist.

Pearson reached up to press the cabin alert button again. "Landing gear?"

"Down and three green," McKenzie said.

"Auto brakes?"

The captain grunted. "Armed on max." *We'll need them. I hate Midway.*

"Speed brake?"

"Armed."

"Flaps?"

"Select twenty. In transit."

McKenzie made yet another fuel check. *Only 1,900 pounds left. So very close.* "Better warn them back there."

Pearson keyed the cabin PA. "Ladies and gentlemen, please take your brace positions. Thank you."

McKenzie thought of all the frightened passengers bending forward. *If we can just get this bucket down, it'll be a good scare and nothing more. A story to tell the grandkids.* Three-one center sliced diagonally across the one-square-mile airport ahead and he frowned in anguish at their minuscule salvation.

"How long's that runway?"

Pearson checked the Jeppesen chart. "Six thousand five twenty-two, fifty-eight twenty-six available."

McKenzie would have preferred much more. There's never enough concrete in an emergency. Midway's cramped location, with homes and businesses directly across the street from the airport, forced him to maintain a higher glide slope and land farther down the runway. He pursed his lips and checked their fuel one last time.

Eight hundred pounds.

They were practically on fumes and he expected to hear the engines cut out any second. Gliding was out of the question at this speed and altitude. They'd simply drop like an anvil onto the rows of brick bungalows passing below.

"Call ATC and let them know our position." McKenzie didn't know why he issued the order. It wasn't necessary.

Pearson obediently keyed his mike. "Departure, Coastal 276 has three-one center in sight. Fuel is minimal, but the engines are still cranking."

"Godspeed."

The one simple word reminded McKenzie they could all be safe in another minute. It made him realize he'd only wanted to hear a reassuring voice. He sat up straighter and concentrated on their final approach, slowing another ten knots. Too much speed bled off and he tickled the throttles forward, visualizing the pumps suck out what little fuel was still sloshing in the tanks. Ford City mall disappeared off to their left.

The plane dipped right and he heard muffled cries from the cabin and braced for the inevitable, but the steady whine of the engines persisted. Keep it level—we don't want to cartwheel at the last minute like that DC-10. He mentally saluted the United crew with newfound respect for their impossible task. The 757 passed through the gust of wind and McKenzie kept nudging one throttle or the other, wobbling down the glide slope. They swept over a large railroad yard, more brick bungalows, and the airport boundary. Painted markings at the end of the runway slid below in a blur. Flare-out was normal, but the seconds ticked by interminably until he finally felt the main gear settle onto the ground with a few reassuring thumps.

He let out his breath in a long sigh. This wasn't going to be another

Sioux City.

Pearson cheered. "Nice landing, Captain!"

Watching their speed as they hurtled down the runway, McKenzie realized the auto brakes weren't working. When he pressed the tops of both rudder pedals to apply the brakes manually, the pedals went all the way to the floor.

✈   ✈   ✈

EFFORTS TO LOCATE SURVIVORS from Atlantic flight 59 were in full motion. The first phone call to the Chicago Police Marine Unit came in at 5:44 P.M. Lt. Dan Brenecke shoved aside a half-eaten ham sandwich on his desk and scribbled notes while the woman who identified herself as Sanchez from the FAA outlined the scope of the disaster. Brenecke had seen his share of boat collisions, fires, drownings, a few private plane crashes, and even the occasional homicide. This was bigger than anything he'd responded to in seventeen years on the force. The last time an airliner dropped into the lake, he vaguely recalled, he was a young boy learning to swim at a YMCA on the South Side.

Sanchez was succinct and professional. "Number of souls on board is unknown, but we estimate two hundred. I'll call back when I find out. Last known position two miles offshore, roughly abeam of Meigs Field."

Even while he was still on the phone, Brenecke stood and yelled at others in the office to dispatch all the available patrol boats. No sooner had he hung up than a second alert came in from the emergency operator.

"I just got a call from a distraught pleasure boater who says a civilian jet crashed into the lake. Estimated location about a mile offshore of Meigs."

Brenecke was heartened by this small piece of good fortune. If the boater had estimated correctly, it would take them only five or ten minutes to get to the scene from their location along the locks south of Navy Pier. He and two other officers jumped aboard one of the station's forty-five-foot boats and pulled away from the dock. More officers followed in two smaller boats. As they heaved southeasterly, Brenecke planted himself inside the wheelhouse and radioed the Fire Department's Air and Sea Rescue detail at Meigs. He watched with satisfaction when two helicopters rose from the field a few minutes later.

He dialed another frequency to radio the Coast Guard and was informed they'd already received a call from the FAA and dispatched two forty-one-foot utility boats. But it would be at least forty minutes before they converged on the scene because one was coming from Station Wilmette, twelve miles north of downtown, and the other from Station Calumet Harbor far to the south. Five helicopters were en route and could be expected much sooner, however.

Finally, Brenecke called the Illinois Department of Conservation Police to send whatever boats they could spare. He snatched a pair of binoculars and scanned the choppy waters ahead.

"How long before that storm reaches us, Bill?"

"Less than an hour, lieutenant," said the officer at the wheel. "The forecast is for westerly winds to thirty-five knots and seas up to four feet."

Brenecke frowned and squinted through the binoculars again. Contrary to the pleasure boater's estimate, they were nearly two miles offshore before they saw the first pieces of wreckage. On closer inspection, it appeared to be fragments of the fuselage. He checked the Loran-C display and wrote the latitude and longitude in a notebook.

The voice of an officer on one of the other boats squawked from the radio speaker. "We're seeing stuff, lieutenant. Mostly pieces from the plane. A few body parts. No sign of survivors yet."

"Keep looking. We've only got about forty-five minutes to sunset."

The deep drone of a white and orange Coast Guard HH65A chopper throbbed overhead and its searchlights strafed the surface of the lake. Brenecke switched radio frequencies again to ask the pilots for a report.

"The wreckage site covers approximately two square miles, sir. There are three pleasure boats in the area that you'll want to escort out and the news media have arrived. A Channel 5 'copter started circling a few minutes ago."

Brenecke knew it would be a frenzy in no time. The media and private citizens would come sniffing like maggots. They'd have to form a security line around the perimeter and broadcast a notice to mariners on one of the VHF-FM bands that the area was now restricted. He picked up the radio mike and began making a flurry of calls.

✈   ✈   ✈

No FLUID. No BRAKES. *Shit.* Captain McKenzie gritted his teeth.

He yanked the throttles back to idle, raised the reverse thrust levers and slammed the throttles to the firewall. The jet whizzed along at more than 100 knots past a pair of intersecting runways. Reverse thrust from the screaming engines slowed them, but not nearly fast enough. McKenzie stomped vainly on the rudder pedals as 200,000 pounds of metal and plastic and hopes and dreams hurtled toward a six-foot-high blast wall at the end of the runway. A chain-link fence stood a few hundred feet beyond. Through the fence he could see cars and trucks moving along the two streets that bordered the northwest corner of the airport.

Pearson pressed against the back of his seat in an involuntary reaction to looming disaster. "We're not gonna stop in time."

McKenzie knew it. "I'll have to veer off the runway. I don't want to hit that blast wall."

Both pilots studied the area beyond with dread, finding no suitable escape route. Homes lined the street to the left. On the right was a small vacant lot next to what looked like a tavern and more houses. McKenzie decided to aim for the vacant lot, uncomfortably aware that their wing span stretched nearly 125 feet. As for the cars and trucks, well, there wasn't a horn they could honk. He bemoaned their loss of fuel. But for that, they could have diverted to another airport and wouldn't be staring at the blast wall that was blossoming in the windshield. They'd survived a midair collision and limped back on the ground—only to be cheated of the earth's safe embrace at the last minute.

"I'm going for the right," he warned Pearson. "Hang on."

McKenzie turned the nose wheel and the mighty jet thundered off the runway, across a stretch of taxiway, and onto the grass. He struggled to maintain steering control, but the nose gear collapsed and the two pilots were thrown forward when the front of the plane dropped to the ground. Both engines slung from the wings plowed up turf. The starboard engine broke from its mounts as the wing ripped into the side of a red and white checkerboard shack housing navigational equipment. The airplane dipped, tearing away part of the wing, and swung to the right toward the tavern.

Pearson swore.

The nose mowed down the fence and the fuselage careened across the street, sparks flying in a piercing screech of aluminum scraping against pavement. Glass shattered as the plane slammed a CTA bus sideways before smashing into the small frame building. A fraction of a second before the cockpit rammed the front wall of the tavern, McKenzie forgot about his passengers, the plane, and everything else. He thought only of his wife, Helen, who was probably at their home in Reston, Virginia, right now and how much he loved her.

"Damn."

✈   ✈   ✈

GÜNTHER SCHWARTZ SHUFFLED UP LUNA AVENUE slower than usual, unsteadied by the four beers he'd consumed. Even when sober, his portly build and short legs contributed to a penguin's gait that was the object of frequent insults from his middle son. Schwartz burped and mumbled clever comebacks that he knew he'd forget the next time Bradley provoked an argument. He muttered more caustic comments while walking past his son's red Camaro, immobilized on the street in front of their home by the orange device locked onto the left front wheel. Irritation faded when he turned his attention to the motor home parked in their driveway.

The thirty-four-foot Winnebago Vectra was Schwartz's pride and joy. A stretch financially, he'd spent countless evenings pleading to Edith that they'd done the right thing. Finally, during last summer's three-week adventure through the Badlands, Yellowstone, and Arches National Park in Utah, his wife had agreed. One evening over dinner, Edith confessed that she loved the luxury and freedom it gave them to tour a nation so rich in natural beauty. Neither of them said so, but they both knew it also provided a fresh mutual interest in their thirty-year marriage.

Schwartz admired the beige vehicle whose twisting rose and teal stripes fluttered along its sides like streamers in the wind. The Chevy 454 big block engine purred smoothly, even when they'd nudged 12,000 feet traversing Loveland Pass west of Denver. Edith deferred to her husband on the mechanical merits of their traveling home but she bubbled with excitement about the convection microwave oven and bedroom TV hooked up to a small-dish satellite.

As Schwartz savored vacation memories, the familiar roar of a jet mushroomed behind him. Angrily, he turned around to shake his fist at the persistent din that stood between him and the carefree life of retirement. Suddenly, he staggered backward, startled to see a plane crashing through the fence that bordered the airport along 55ᵗʰ Street. He watched agape as the jet hit a CTA bus and several cars before disappearing behind the Franklins' house on the corner of the block. A deafening explosion launched boiling clouds of fire and smoke from the location of the 6511 Club he'd left only moments ago, propelling Schwartz back farther still until his feet stumbled over the curb and he fell onto the grass across the street from his house.

Billowing flames rapidly engulfed the Franklins' bungalow, causing more explosions that spewed glass, bricks, and splintered wood down the block. Two houses away, Edith appeared at their front door and Schwartz waved frantically.

"Get out! Get out *now!*"

The frumpish woman tentatively stepped outside, cringed from the boom of another blast, and scurried across the street. She clutched Schwartz's arm as he struggled to his feet.

"Where's Bradley?" she asked frantically. "I thought he was with you in the bar."

"He left in a huff awhile ago. Didn't he come back home?"

Schwartz started toward their house, but Edith restrained him. "No. He must have gone to see some friends."

Trembling with fear, they watched the fire leap to the Dobsons' roof and race down a screened-in porch framed with wood. Their beige brick bungalow was next in line. More debris showered the street and a piece of plane wreckage flattened the "For Sale" sign that had been a fixture in their front yard for the past year. Schwartz sagged at the first blow. Then a sudden notion occurred to him. The irony was sweet and he chuckled. It was perfect.

"Take my house, too! If I can't sell it, let the damn thing burn! It's insured." He laughed with glee, then the smile faded from his face.

Just steer clear of my Winnebago. He lamented the fact that the keys were hanging on a hook in the kitchen right now. He studied the fire and assessed the risk. Sweat broke out on his face and he stumbled unsteadily before abandoning the idea.

Edith looked askance at her husband, convinced he was drunk. Yet another explosion assaulted her ears and she shrank away from what looked like part of a jetliner's tail sailing through the air. The jagged metal piece glinted in the sunlight before pitching down and slamming against the motor home, shattering the side window near where they sat when eating at a small dinette set.

"No!"

Schwartz's anguished cry was drowned out by the blaring horn of a fire truck charging onto their block. Crews spilled from the rig and hustled toward the two burning homes. They doused splotches of flames scrabbling for a foothold on the roof of Schwartz's house, but lacked the manpower to contain a blaze consuming the towering oak tree in his neighbor's front yard. Günther and Edith watched helplessly as the top third of the tree groaned, then tilted in the direction of the Winnebago.

"No. No! *No!*"

Edith had to restrain her husband again as the massive burning limb snapped off from its trunk with a resounding crack and smashed squarely onto their retirement dream. The Winnebago swayed under the impact, its roof crumpling. The satellite dish flew off its mountings and rolled across their front lawn. Through the front windshield, they could see flames licking at the interior. Schwartz held the sides of his head in disbelief while firefighters drove back the blaze at the Dobsons' house, leaving his home undamaged except for a few scorched shingles. Even Bradley's goddamned car survived without a scratch. At last, a crew trained a hose on the motor home, but it was useless. Within minutes, all that remained was a burned out shell.

Schwartz slumped against Edith with a whimper.

FIFTEEN
SOBs

———

ON BOARD *NO WHEEL DRIVE*, Larry Lindstrand gratefully accepted a towel and glass of water from Cindy. She'd gotten over her initial shock, swallowing the urge to vomit, and periodically looked out at the debris surrounding the boat, shaking her head in disbelief.

"Are you okay, Larry? That was awful."

He wiped his face and swirled some water in his mouth to wash away the bitter taste of bile, spitting over the side. "I'm fine, thanks."

Carefully averting the patch of deck where the stump lay, he steadied himself and noticed that she'd placed the pieces of wreckage on a seat in the cockpit. It occurred to him that they'd make good souvenirs and might even be valuable enough to sell to curiosity seekers. Off the bow, he heard a growing rumble and counted five police boats converging on them. Three helicopters hovered overhead. Hastily, he collected the wreckage and stowed it out of sight below deck, winking conspiratorially at Cindy. When one of the boats drew alongside, an officer appeared on deck and shouted.

"This is a restricted area now, sir, and there's a storm approaching. You need to get back to shore."

"Yes, officer. I'm the one who reported this," Lindstrand said. "I was just waiting for you to get here. What about . . . that?"

Cindy pointed gingerly at the charred limb, a blackened watch still encircling the wrist. Blood oozed from the ragged end where it had been ripped from the shoulder of a male passenger. The officer grimaced and ducked inside the wheelhouse. He reappeared with a camera, hopped aboard the Beneteau, and took photographs from various angles. Lindstrand and Cindy looked away as he pulled on latex gloves and slipped the arm inside a rubber body bag, dripping a trail of blood on the wooden slats covering the deck. They turned back when they heard the comforting sound of the zipper sliding shut. The officer took a notebook out of his shirt pocket and jotted down their names and addresses. With a quick nod, he hopped back aboard the police boat, which motored farther out into the lake.

Too weary to sail, Lindstrand started the engine on *No Wheel Drive* and steered the other way to his mooring at Burnham Park Harbor. He tied up at the dock and was hosing the deck when Cindy whispered that a news crew from Channel 7 was approaching them. The clean-cut reporter in a navy blue suit spoke first.

"Hey, you two were just out on the lake, right? Did you happen to see that plane crash?"

Lindstrand recognized his face from the newscast. "Yeah. We were there right when it happened, in fact. Even got some pictures."

The reporter eagerly motioned his cameraman forward. "Would you tell us what you saw?"

Lindstrand turned off the hose and fought back a smile. The chance to be on television and potentially garner free publicity for his car dealership delighted him. But this was a tragedy so he'd better show the appropriate emotions. As he nodded in studied seriousness, bright lights blazed on and the reporter moved closer with a microphone.

"Don't worry about the camera. Just relax and say what happened."

Drawing on his experience making commercials, Lindstrand easily and vividly recounted the event, ending with his discovery of the arm. "It really shook us up. We were afraid we might get hurt or even die if a big piece of wreckage hit the boat."

Cindy nodded, wide-eyed. "Some of it did."

The camera swung to her as the reporter asked, "You say some wreckage actually fell on your sailboat?"

Cindy hesitated, realizing she shouldn't have mentioned it. Glancing sharply at her, Lindstrand recovered and cut in smoothly.

"Ah, she means the arm. A few pieces of the plane came pretty close. I thought we were a goner when I saw that cockpit heading toward us. We caught a wave over the stern when it splashed down."

The rest of the interview proceeded without any other gaffes, including Cindy's comments on their front-row seat to the disaster. In response to a

question about Lindstrand's occupation, he mentioned the name and location of his showroom and hoped they wouldn't cut it out when the tape was
broadcast. The news crew offered to buy Lindstrand's roll of film, but he
politely refused. No sense selling to the first prospect when he might be
able to create a bidding war after contacting several other TV stations and
newspapers.

✈   ✈   ✈

KELLY GRIPPED THE PHONE while a tower controller at Midway narrated
Coastal's landing, culminating with the crash. "Man, I was having drinks at
the Club this same time yesterday. Sorry, guess you're not too interested in
hearing that right now."

"That's okay," Kelly croaked. "Thanks."

He hung up the receiver with exaggerated gentleness. The usual buzz of
controllers talking to airplanes was strangely out of place compared with
the horrific scene he pictured. Slowly, he turned to Sanchez and Boskovich
and repeated what the controller had told him.

Sanchez hung her head, cursing softly. "Let's go talk about this at my
desk."

Kelly signed the log and stood. He felt disjointed and light-headed. Without being told, he knew he was decertified at this moment and wondered if
he'd ever again sit at a radarscope. His eyes fell heavily on J.J.

"Would you call the Center and tell them Coastal's down time—and I
mean that in the most literal sense—is 2251?"

J.J. nodded silently and looked like she was bidding him farewell.

Lombardi observed Kelly walking like a zombie over to the supervisors' desk with Sanchez, Boskovich, and Pepperidge. Sam motioned to
him and he swallowed hard. "Come on over, Gene. I'll want to hear
what you saw, too."

She gestured at Bear. "Okay, Frank. Let's have it from the top."

Bear folded his arms firmly against his chest. "I asked Atlantic if he was
ready to come right down." He cleared his throat to steady his raspy voice.
"I told him he'd be number five if he was ready and he said yes. So I cleared
him to seven and turned him north and he confirmed the clearance. Next
thing I know he's busting altitude. I never heard from him again."

Sanchez turned to Kelly. "What happened on Departures?"

He leaned against a file cabinet and closed his eyes, reliving the fateful moment with chilling clarity. His stomach tightened around a gnawing emptiness that reached up and squeezed his throat. It was scary to be so out of control. His natural tendency was to take complete command of a situation. Now, he felt like the unwilling star of a tragic play. He opened his eyes and saw Sam waiting patiently. Where to begin? How to explain what he didn't understand?

Boskovich stared at him disdainfully. Bear and Lombardi tried to appear supportive, but their eyes betrayed fear. Watching the controllers on position, Kelly fervently wished he was one of them. He rubbed a hand across his face in a futile attempt to wipe away this ghastliness. Finally, he coughed and the words started tumbling out.

"I cleared Coastal to six thousand on a zero-niner-zero heading. I was busy with the traffic and handed off Simmons to the Center. Then I saw Coastal bust through sixty-two hundred and keep on going. After the next sweep, I saw Atlantic drop through sixty-eight right into Coastal. That's when Coastal radioed they had an RA. I think I told them 'don't climb' and issued traffic. The targets co-located a few seconds later."

Boskovich curled his upper lip. "You should not have called Coastal after they reported the RA. Didn't you read the memo that was posted two weeks ago?"

It had been a reflex. When it was obvious Coastal and Atlantic might run into each other, he didn't stop to think. "Yeah, I read it, Bosko. I couldn't just sit there on my hands and let 'em smack."

"The memo clearly states you are not to interfere during a TCAS event."

Even though he was right, Boskoprick's snide tone offended Kelly. "Fuck the memo! You think the fact that I issued traffic made any difference?"

Raymond Boskovich drew himself up to his full height, still a head shorter than Kelly, and placed both hands on his hips. Sanchez raised a hand, but Bear cut in before she could say anything.

"Goddamn it, Sam, sounds like TCAS ran 'em together!"

"Let's not jump to conclusions," she said. "I want to hear the tape, but apparently you had the traffic separated and they acknowledged the clearances. So they were responding to their RAs and hit. How? That's not supposed to happen."

Boskovich scowled at no one in particular. "Maybe Kelly confused the Coastal pilots when he told them not to climb."

Sanchez shook her head, hoping one of her people hadn't done something wrong. Technically, Rain Man should not have made the call, though she understood all too well why he did. But if he or Bear had seriously screwed up, she was afraid TRACON chief Jeff Richardson or Andrew Hawkins, who ran the whole show at O'Hare, might hold her responsible. She knew they'd been lukewarm to promoting a woman into management and suspected they'd jump at the chance to demote her. Even Bosko was probably sizing up the opportunities—or was that paranoia? He looks like he's ready for blood. Maybe he's just scared like the rest of us. She held up her hands in a cautionary gesture.

"Let's all try to calm down. Gene, do you have anything to add?"

"Rain Man's primary radio crapped out, but that was a few minutes before . . . "

Kelly pitied Lombardi, his face ashen. He had nothing to worry about. In no way could he be blamed. But it would take a long time coming to terms with what they'd just been through. Maybe forever.

"I switched to the standby right away," Kelly said. "It didn't have anything to do with this."

Sanchez nodded. "Ray, go run the tape and pull the DARC. I've got phone calls to make."

Immediately after seeing the target for Atlantic 59 break up on the scope, Sanchez contacted the Coast Guard and Chicago Police Marine Unit so they could start searching the lake. Now she had to alert Hawkins, Richardson, the FAA's Regional Office, and Washington. Someone at the R.O. would make the unpleasant calls to Atlantic and Coastal.

Bear stared pointedly at Boskovich. "We're okay, Rain Man. We didn't do a damn thing wrong."

Kelly wished he shared his friend's bravado. He suspected it was just whistling in the dark. "So what if we didn't? There's still a bunch of dead people out there. I don't think it matters to them."

Bear didn't answer.

"Let's go," Boskovich said.

Kelly ignored his overbearing tone. He was suddenly eager to get away from the TRACON. Listening to the Coastal pilot and watching the target inch around to Midway raised his hopes that at least one airplane would survive this madness. He pictured the disaster at the airport and winced. Everything had sounded routine as Coastal headed toward the lake. What was he missing? Guiltily, he recalled thinking about Christy after his break. Had she distracted him?

The three men walked out into the corridor, squinting from the harsh glare of the overhead lights. Rykowski joined them in his official union capacity as facility representative of the NATCA local. Silently, they marched single file past the administrative offices and into a room where a data systems specialist sat in front of a PC near a row of ancient Sperry Univac 8300s. The Univacs ran most of the electronics in the TRACON and control tower as well as the Direct Access Radar Channel that tracked every flight handled at O'Hare. A rack of six tape recorders stood along one wall of the room, enclosed by a glass door with a small lock. The FAA was legally required to maintain a record of every word spoken on the air.

Boskovich talked to the man at the PC, then inserted a key in the lock and opened the door. After switching on one of the standby recorders, he turned off the one above it and removed the reel that contained the fateful words spoken by Kelly, Bear, and the pilots. He placed the reel in a playback-only machine and pushed REWIND. The inch-wide tape accommodated twenty channels, enough to cover every position in the TRACON and tower. It took a few minutes to find the right frequency and transmission. When he did, there wasn't much to hear.

"Atlantic 59, you're number five if you're ready for the slam dunk." Bear's deep voice echoed tinnily in the room.

"Atlantic 59 is ready to come down."

"Atlantic 59, turn right heading three-six-zero. Expedite descent and maintain seven thousand. Traffic ten o'clock, three miles eastbound, climbing to six."

The traffic was Coastal 276.

"Three-six-zero and seven for Atlantic 59, and we're looking."

Kelly shivered at the sound of the pilot's voice, one he knew he'd never forget. That pilot had been alive not thirty minutes ago. The tape rolled through several more transmissions with other flights before the Conflict Alert warning beeped. There was nothing more of interest. Boskovich rewound the tape and switched frequencies and they heard the sequence on East Departures, including Kelly's request for Coastal's altitude.

He smacked a fist against his other palm. "That's right, I forgot. Coastal's Mode C was acting strangely. The readouts were jumping all over."

Boskovich switched off the recorder. "Did you verify altitude?"

"Yes." Kelly closed his eyes and concentrated. "It dropped before I asked them. Afterward, it seemed okay."

"There's no telling whether their Mode C was working or not," Rykowski said. "If it wasn't, that might help explain things."

Boskovich nodded dubiously and turned to the man using the PC at the desk. "The DARC will give us a good read on that. How much longer, Ed?"

Data systems specialist Ed Stewart was creating a profile of the accident. When he finished, they'd have a color printout of both flights' precise speeds, bearings, and altitudes at all times.

"At least another hour, Ray. These things take some time to reconstruct."

"Give us a call as soon as you're done."

"You got it."

✈   ✈   ✈

ATLANTIC AIRLINES PASSENGER RELATIONS AGENT Michelle Woods had been locking up her desk to leave work for the weekend, looking forward to curling up with a glass of wine and the latest novel by her favorite mystery author. Instead, she was now shepherding two dozen relatives and friends of passengers aboard flight 59 through a crowded concourse at O'Hare and into a secluded room used by the airline's Sterling Club members. She remained standing while they settled into chairs and sofas far more plush than the utilitarian seats at the gate. The thick maroon pile carpet muffled their footsteps. When the oak-paneled door to the concourse swung shut with a decisive click, sealing off the room from the commotion outside, Woods envisioned a coffin lid closing.

Soft-spoken and barely twenty-seven years old, she'd never suffered the loss of a loved one. She didn't want to do this alone, but there wasn't any choice. Atlantic had a small base in Chicago and the station manager was ill. A vice president at corporate headquarters in Miami told her to handle the situation until several executives could fly up later that evening. Clenching her hands, she braved the anxious audience.

"I, uh, I'm afraid I have an unfortunate announcement to make." Clearing her throat, she looked around the room but avoided direct eye contact with anyone. "Flight 59 experienced some trouble on its arrival in the Chicago area. I mean, uh . . . there's been an accident. I'm sorry. I don't have many details."

Woods blushed, embarrassed by her clumsy explanation. Of all days for Henderson to call in sick. A young mother holding a cooing infant swaddled in a gaily colored jumpsuit caught her eye as the woman's mouth fell open. Nearby, a man dropped his bouquet of red roses to the floor and stared blankly.

"What happened, exactly?" he asked.

Woods smoothed her skirt and cleared her throat again, forcing out the words. "Flight 59 hit another airplane and . . . crashed into Lake Michigan."

There was a collective cry, then silence. A muffled flight announcement filtered through the oak-paneled door. Sitting on the edge of a sofa, a middle-aged woman held both hands to her face and sobbed. "Dear God. Please tell us they didn't all die."

Woods cringed and put an arm around her. "I'm very sorry, ma'am. Authorities are still searching the lake but . . . at this time it appears there were no survivors."

Based on the call she'd received from the FAA, she knew the chances of finding anyone alive were virtually nil. The woman started crying, babbling into Woods' shoulder, and she picked out the words "daughter" and "honeymoon."

A heavyset man pacing near the back of the room shoved both hands into the pockets of his tweed sport jacket. He stopped and stared menacingly at her, his florid face contorted into a snarl. "My brother and his wife were on that plane. He was a good firefighter—the best. You'll be hearing from my lawyer. This is going to cost you big time." He stormed out of the room and slammed the door shut.

No one else spoke. Woods tried to avert everyone's eyes but she felt them weighing on her from all directions, some glaring, others disbelieving, still more haunted with shock. Unsure what to do, she consoled the woman on the sofa again. The door to the concourse opened and she fully expected to see the irate man stomp through. Instead, an airport chaplain stepped into the room. With great effort, she refrained from running to hug him.

At Atlantic Airlines' arrival gate for flight 59, the ticket agent on duty tapped a few keys on his computer. Throughout the terminal, electronic displays changed from "Delayed" to "Canceled." It crossed the agent's mind that Atlantic would establish a new flight number for its daily afternoon service from Miami to Chicago, perhaps by tomorrow.

✈   ✈   ✈

LIKE MOST PEOPLE THAT EVENING, Christy and Jason heard about the crash on television. They were eating dinner in their kitchen and the small set on the counter was tuned to the news on Channel 2. The story about an airliner smashing into homes across the street from Midway Airport immediately caught their attention. Details were sketchy and there was no video because a camera crew was mired in rush-hour traffic, but it was enough for Christy to call the *Chronicle* and tell them she'd come in. The assistant news editor who handled the desk on her days off sounded distinctly relieved. She hung up and looked at Jason.

He knew what she was thinking. "I'll be all right alone. I am twelve, you know."

The forced maturity in his voice made her smile. "I'm sure you would be all right alone. But since I worry enough for the both of us, why don't you call Dave and see whether you can spend the evening with him?"

Jason's eyes lit up at this unconsidered possibility. He dialed the number and Christy spoke with the friend's mother to confirm it would be all right. The two of them left the house ten minutes after hearing the report.

While driving to the paper, she tuned in several radio stations that were devoting all their news coverage to the crash, even though little information was available yet. With a start, she realized Carla and Kevin were flying home this weekend from Miami. She berated herself for not bothering to ask about their airline and flight number. She wasn't even sure what day they were returning and prayed it wasn't tonight. After a commercial ended, the newscaster came back on.

"We've just learned the plane that crashed was Coastal Airlines flight 276 from Chicago to Washington, D.C." Christy sighed with relief. "The pilots apparently experienced difficulty after taking off from O'Hare and were attempting to make an emergency landing at Midway. Our reporter is on the scene and we'll give you more information as soon as we receive it."

The *Chronicle* newsroom was bustling when she strode in. Reporters who were normally gone by now had returned. Mark Shepherd, the typically bored night city editor, talked animatedly to several of them clustered around his desk. Tony Wilson on the Picture Desk held a phone to each ear and was speaking rapidly into the two-way radio to a photographer in his car. Christy walked up to the news desk, where Managing Editor Ralph Metcalf greeted her exuberantly.

"Thanks for coming in, Christy. This is one helluva story. We've got two reporters and a couple of shooters down at Midway and another crew at the lakefront. We're going up four pages, maybe more if we can fill them. I just talked with Circulation and we'll bump the run by twenty thousand. Have you eaten, by the way? We're sending out for pizzas."

"What's going on at the lakefront?"

"Haven't you heard? The jet that crashed at Midway was trying to land after hitting another plane over the lake. The second plane exploded and fell into the drink."

The thought of Carla and Kevin came to the fore again, but it was interrupted when the assistant news editor asked if she'd take over the layout for page one. Metcalf answered.

"Yes. She'll do the front and the two of you can work out the inside crash pages. Lisa will handle the rest of main news. Now that you're here, Christy, I'd like to have a short meeting." He cupped both hands and shouted, his voice booming across the room. "Shepherd! Wilson! In the bullpen as soon as you're free."

They gathered in the conference room where a few hours earlier section editors pitched their top stories in hopes of getting them on the front page. Cityside didn't have much to offer then. Shepherd now ticked off a litany of possibilities. Christy jotted notes on a legal pad.

"Ellen will write the main piece. We've budgeted forty inches. She's on the phone with the FAA right now and will take feeds from our people at Midway and the lakefront. Davis and Meyer are at the media center the Marine Police set up in the terminal at Meigs Field. We don't expect survivors from that one and there's not much to see from the shore, so whatever they turn may fold into the main. I've got Duncan and Chesterfield getting color for a definite sidebar from Midway. They'll follow up at hospitals in the area if anyone got out alive. We'll give you another sider on a Boeing 727 that crashed in the lake in 1965 when the pilots misread their altimeter, plus some previous midairs."

Photo Editor Tony Wilson tossed a dog-eared print from United Press International on the table. The crumpled tail of a United Airlines jet lay incongruously in the middle of a city intersection. "I had the library dig this out of the files. Happened in 1960 when United and TWA hit over Brooklyn. Expect similar stuff from Midway. We also got a call from a free-lancer who's bringing in some film he shot from a sailboat on the lake."

Metcalf whistled and pushed the UPI picture toward Christy. "Be sure to run that with the sidebar. Bob, can you give us a map showing the flight paths?"

Artist Robert Gabelli was drawing on a pad. His rough sketch showed the long finger of Lake Michigan, bordered on the left by Chicago. Cross-hatched lines denoting runways pinpointed O'Hare on the Northwest Side and Midway on the South. "Working on it. I need information."

"Ellen's getting that," Shepherd said. "I just found out the other plane was an Atlantic Airlines 727 coming in to land at O'Hare. I don't know from where yet."

"Get someone to hammer on both airlines for lists of passengers," Metcalf urged. "They'll say they've gotta notify next of kin first, but I want those names to run tomorrow, if at all possible. Christy, are you feeling okay?"

Atlantic flew to Miami, didn't it? *Oh, my God.* "I'll be back. I'm sorry— I have to check something." She bolted from the room and sprinted toward Ellen Sanders' desk. The transportation reporter was still on the phone and Christy paced impatiently until she put a hand over the mouthpiece.

"You need me?"

"Where was that Atlantic flight coming from?"

"Miami. Why?"

Christy sucked in her breath and started to ask about the passenger list when the assistant news editor hollered at her from the desk, waving a telephone. "Someone named Szemasko. Says it's urgent."

She ran, leaving a confused Sanders in her wake, and grabbed the receiver. "Carla?"

"It's Don." His voice was slurred and a jukebox blared in the background. "They're dead, Christy. Kevin and your sister. That fucking airline killed them."

He kept ranting, but she wasn't listening. Stunned, she dropped into a chair, loosely cradling the phone in her hand. Carla dead. *Sweet Jesus, why?* She was so vibrant and full of life. And Kevin, such a kind and gentle man who made her sister happier than she'd ever been. Don's irrelevant tirade poured from the receiver and she stared at it dumbfounded. Then she softly set the receiver back on the phone, cutting off the high-pitched voice, and gazed into space, her eyes welling up with tears.

Metcalf approached tentatively. "What's the matter, Christy?"

Without looking at him or the others around the desk, she struggled to find her voice and said dully, "My sister was on that flight. The one that crashed in the lake. My sister and her husband."

Shepherd barged into the group before anyone could respond. "You're not gonna believe this, but Sharon Masters was on that Coastal plane. The senator just called to tell us and ask what we knew so far."

Metcalf blanched, his earlier excitement tempered now that the story had struck home. "Damn. Duncan's at Midway, right?"

"And Chesterfield. I called Duncan on his cell phone and told him to look for her. Get this. Masters said his wife was killed in that Aeromexico collision over California back in '86. Talk about a bizarre coincidence."

Metcalf gestured at Christy. "John, her—"

"By the way, the Marine Police and Coast Guard called off their search for the night. They say there's nothing but body parts and wreckage out there."

Metcalf winced as Christy put her head down on the desk and sobbed in labored breaths.

✈   ✈   ✈

THE NORMALLY NONDESCRIPT INTERSECTION of 55th Street and Central Avenue at the northwest corner of Midway Airport was a war zone. Plane wreckage and rubble from the demolished tavern and homes smoldered now beneath a steady downpour, starkly illuminated by several powerful lights mounted on metal stands. What was left of the once sleek and gleaming 757 lay broken in three large sections. Huge gashes had been ripped open on the left side of the cockpit. Aft of the wings, a dump truck that collided with the plane had severed the tail section from the rest of the fuselage, much of which was melted down to the framework beneath its aluminum skin. Ironically, the bottom half of the tail, which sported part of a stylized globe similar to Pan Am's emblem, was unscathed except where fire singed the edges. Nearby, the charred carcass of the CTA bus lay on its side. Its photogenic location next to the tail would be broadcast repeatedly on television throughout the evening.

The 6511 Club no longer existed. A 2,000-degree inferno incinerated the modest red frame tavern, Harry the bartender, and six patrons who'd toasted farewell to Günther Schwartz moments before the jet smashed through the front wall. Several other people burned to death inside their cars after they crashed into the airliner that suddenly materialized on the street in front of them.

Police barricaded 55th and Central in all directions and positioned squad cars at side streets along 54th. Schwartz and his wife, Edith, along with several neighbors, were evacuated and spent a few uneasy hours milling behind the barricades before they were allowed to go back home. Several camera crews managed to slip through the police line and filmed the chaos unchecked by authorities too busy to stop them. News photographers in three helicopters hovering overhead also shot videotape but the red, white, and blue flashing lights from emergency vehicles turned the footage into a confusing kaleidoscope. That didn't stop the TV stations from running it repeatedly.

As a triage team fanned through the area, ambulances and aid cars shuttled survivors to five hospitals, their sirens repeatedly swelling and fading in the wet windy night. Dodging hoses that snaked across the waterlogged streets like twisted strands of spaghetti, medics placed color-coded tags on the wrists of victims. Green went to the lucky ones who could walk. Yellow and red tags were placed on those with more severe injuries. But in most cases, rescuers sadly shook their heads and slipped on black tags. They found some passengers wandering in shock. Others were still strapped in seats thrown from the aircraft when it broke apart. A pilot with four stripes on his torn and soiled jacket was lifted into an aid car, his head swathed in bandages.

Remnants of personal belongings littered the ground in poignant testament to the cataclysm. A polished black penny loafer lay next to a melted purse with a charred tube of lipstick and a hairbrush poking through the tatters of one side. Shreds of clothing were strewn everywhere. Draped over the curb was part of a flight attendant's uniform with a scorched nametag still attached that read "Debbie."

A young woman lay on her back in the street, one leg crushed by a utility truck that tipped over after its driver swerved to avoid the jet. Rain poured in torrents, and a paramedic from Rescue Squad 5 wiped away water dribbling down his forehead as he knelt beside the woman. He didn't need to see her red tag to know she was critically hurt. Warm breath tickled his cheek when he bent to her face. He held two fingers against her neck, located the carotid artery, and consulted his watch.

"One twenty," he told his partner.

Her cheeks felt cold. After getting a blood pressure reading of ninety over sixty, he knew the shock was well developed. Ignoring legalities, his partner set up a saline IV in each of her arms without bothering to call a hospital.

"She qualifies for trauma criteria," said the paramedic leaning over her. "This one goes to Christ Community. Can you hear me, ma'am?"

She moaned and moved a hand to shield her face from the rain. The paramedic thought it was a beautiful face beneath the smudges and streaks of soot. He adjusted the blanket over her.

"What's your name, young lady?"

"Sharon," she gasped.

Behind them, several firefighters maneuvered pneumatic air bags into position to lift the truck off her leg.

"Okay, Sharon. We're going to get you out of here just as fast as we can."

Sixteen

Valhalla

S *wish—swish.* Kelly stared unseeing at the two-lane road disappearing into the blackness ahead through wiper blades flopping across the windshield. They reminded him of the radar sweep, the sweep he couldn't get out of his mind now nor the nightmare that replayed with insistent cruelty.

Coastal 276, do not climb. There's traffic above you.

And the tiny green blip that represented all of the humanity on board Atlantic 59 disintegrating into three fragments. The image was engraved into his memory. He squeezed his eyes shut, willing it to disappear, but the image intensified and so he reopened them, finding it safer to focus on the barren fields passing by outside the window.

Swish—swish.

He'd endured several more difficult hours at the airport before getting permission to go home. Facility chief Andrew Hawkins, whom Sanchez reached on his car phone, had arrived in the TRACON by the time Kelly and the others returned from listening to the voice tape. Tall and angular, Hawkins stood ramrod straight with both arms crossed in front of his chest, nodding tight-lipped at something Boskovich had just said. When Hawkins turned to Sam, Kelly overheard his flat nasal voice.

"Neither of them leaves till they piss."

Controllers underwent random drug tests every year or so and it was mandatory when there was a crash. Kelly bristled. Take all you want because you won't find anything incriminating.

"I've called Upjohn," she said, referring to the company hired to conduct the tests.

Hawkins granted her a look of faint admiration for being so thorough. Maybe Sanchez was okay after all, he thought. Maybe. He still wondered how much he could count on her in a clutch. He noticed the controllers approaching and faced them with a sympathetic smile. "How are you two?"

"TCAS did this," Bear hissed.

Hawkins coolly studied the aging controller, his steely eyes narrowing. The agency had subjected TCAS to extensive testing before imposing the billion-dollar system on the airlines. Despite hearing oft-voiced concerns from Bear and others, he believed in it. Politically, he knew he had to. Stretching his neck, he said levelly, "We'll see about that, Frank."

Kelly shrugged. He didn't know what to say.

"It's a very difficult day for all of us," the chief said. He looked down at the floor, his arms still folded across his chest, then back at the two controllers. "I'll do whatever I can to help you through this but, as I'm sure you know, you're both decertified until we complete our internal investigation. Of course, the NTSB will be here shortly to conduct its own inquiry. If we determine that you acted in accordance with the regulations, you'll be permitted back to work after you successfully complete a written test and pass a check ride on position."

A small cynical smile crept across Kelly's lips. Thanks for your generous support, pal. That speech was straight out of the manual. The lack of compassion didn't surprise him. Hawkins was a bureaucrat recently transplanted from Minneapolis, marking time at O'Hare before moving up the management hierarchy. He'd never been a line controller and therefore couldn't really understand who they were and what they did. No doubt he was already sizing up a host of consequences beyond the several hundred deaths, not the least of which Kelly suspected concerned the significant blot that would stain his record here now.

Hawkins turned a page in the manual. "Samantha has summarized what happened, but I'd like you to fill out your statements this evening. I'll need them for Washington."

"What's the rush," asked Rykowski.

"It's easier while the events are still fresh in their minds," Hawkins said.

"Their statements will be more accurate once they've had a chance to think about what really happened. If they fill out anything tonight, consider it preliminary and subject to revision."

Hawkins tipped his head in agreement and turned to Kelly and Bear. "Also, by law, we'll have to take urine samples from you."

The two controllers stood silent. They knew the drill. Pre-established steps that took on new meaning tonight.

Hawkins' face and voice softened. "Then go home and get some rest. We can talk again when you feel up to it. You've just been through a very traumatic experience. We've taught you to block out any thought of the people on board those airplanes, but at some point reality will hit home. You'll benefit from professional counseling. A peer debriefer from our Critical Incident Stress Management program will contact you in a day or two. And I hope you both already know that my door is always open."

He patted them on their backs in a stilted motion, uncomfortable with such camaraderie among the rank-and-file. Sanchez fished out two accident report packets from a file cabinet and hesitated before handing them over, as if this somehow rendered a verdict of culpability.

"Make your statements factual. Don't second-guess yourselves. It's up to the investigators to analyze everything."

The representative from Upjohn arrived moments later, a young man looking as if he just as easily could have been delivering pizzas. In turn, he escorted Kelly and Bear to the restroom, where they filled a small plastic vial and wordlessly gave it to him. Then they accompanied Rykowski to the union's office, a small windowless room that always stank of stale cigarette smoke, to fill out their reports. Kelly collapsed into a chair. The laces on one shoe were loose again and he irritably kicked it off before tipping his head back against the wall. Pepperidge lit a Marlboro, fed one of the forms into an old IBM Selectric typewriter, and stared at it.

Rykowski perched on the edge of a dented and scuffed gray metal desk, slowly rubbing his palms together. "We're pretty clean. I just wish you hadn't issued traffic to Coastal when he said they had the RA. That's the new rule, Rain Man. No interference."

"The rule is absurd."

"Agreed. But it exists and you broke it. That gives the FAA an opening, if they want to make a case about this."

Kelly fingered the blank Personnel Statement and Midair Collision Report. *Did I confuse the pilots by making that call? If so, the agency will crucify me. If so, a lot of people died tonight because I fucked up.* These past fourteen years have been a good ride and I'd hate for it to end. But, God, if they died because of me, how will I ever live with myself? He shuddered.

Bear dragged on his cigarette and started pecking at the keyboard, his halting percussion magnified in the cramped quiet room. Kelly knew Bear was going to take forever, so he swiped a clipboard from a hook on the wall, uncapped a pen, and began printing in his neat slanted handwriting.

"My name is Ryan Kelly. At approximately 1735 CDT, I was working the East Departure position in the ORD TRACON. . . . " He spent about twenty minutes completing both forms. Heeding Rykowski's warning to Hawkins and knowing that his memory could play tricks when he was upset—the erratic altitude readouts flew out of his head, didn't they?—he finished with the caveat, "I reserve the right to amend this statement based on a review of the tapes and any other data involved."

Pepperidge was still plunking away when Kelly trudged back to the radar room. TRACON chief Jeff Richardson had joined Hawkins, Sanchez, and Rykowski, all of whom were talking with two men he'd never seen before. The younger one inspired images of a clown with his unruly bush of red hair. The other had slicked back thinning blond hair, a chunky face with a prominent chin, and blue eyes behind wire-rimmed glasses that took in everything slowly and thoughtfully. Rykrisp reached for Kelly's paperwork as Sam motioned to the older of the strangers.

"Frederic Esterhaus, this is Ryan Kelly. Mr. Esterhaus is the NTSB's investigator-in-charge of the accident." They shook hands and Kelly liked the firm friendly grip. Sam nodded at the redhead. "This is Scott Carter, another member of the Go Team."

He grasped Carter's hand. "It didn't take you guys long."

As soon as Esterhaus and Carter heard about the accident, they'd dashed to Reagan Washington National Airport just in time to catch a flight from D.C. to Chicago. Seven other members of the Go Team planned to follow them on a later flight. The investigators would spend several days swarming over the wreckage, sifting for clues, and questioning everyone involved to build the foundation for their probable cause report.

"We just arrived," Esterhaus said. "Mr. Hawkins and Ms. Sanchez have been apprising us of the events. If you don't mind, I'd like to chat for a few minutes."

Kelly nodded wearily. "Okay."

"Let's do it in my office," Hawkins said, holding out an arm to show the way.

They all walked to the administrative wing. The interview didn't take long. Kelly repeated what he'd told Sanchez, this time more calmly. To his surprise, he was already adjusting to the nightmare. Esterhaus and Carter asked only a few questions, all of them relating to the altitude readouts.

"I know these things are complicated," Rykowski said when they appeared to be finished, "but it seems to me that something went wrong with TCAS."

Hawkins leaned forward in his tan leather executive chair and folded both hands on the desk, clasping them tightly to help him maintain control. "That's premature, Pete. It's much too early to speculate. Besides, TCAS has proven itself to be extremely reliable."

Esterhaus removed his glasses and wiped the lenses with a handkerchief. He studied Rykowski, Hawkins, and Kelly, then spoke deliberately. "With few exceptions, these accidents occur as the result of a lot of factors. Each one is relatively minor, but becomes significant in combination with others. There are many, many questions to be answered before we can determine what happened with any certainty."

"Of course." Hawkins said it a shade too harshly as he leaned back in his chair and forced himself to smile pleasantly at Esterhaus.

"We're done for now," the investigator said. "Thank you very much, Mr. Kelly."

Hawkins inclined his head. "Ryan, you're free to go."

Swish—swish.

The monotonous drone of the windshield wipers started to reverberate inside the car, inside Kelly's head, even when he closed his eyes. The rain had tapered to a drizzle, so he finally reached over and turned them off, slumping deeper into the passenger seat.

J.J. glanced at the dark figure next to her. She'd volunteered to take him home so he wouldn't have to spend the night alone. Rykowski was doing the same for Bear. The lights of Woodstock glowed on the horizon as they sped north through the shallow hills of farmland along Route 47.

"Where do I turn?" Her low voice broke the silence of the hour-long drive.

"Right to zero-niner-zero on Bull Valley Road. Up ahead."

"Zero-niner-zero on Bull Valley," she repeated, trying too hard for a relaxed effect.

They rolled into town a few minutes later and he mumbled only a few more straightforward directions to his wooded driveway. She parked in front of the house, not realizing there was an attached garage in back. He led the way along a covered rock path with granite stepping stones to the wide front door. J.J. lingered to admire the cedar-sided house with its broad overhang and multi-pitched roof. An Oriental garden with several Japanese maple trees, assorted ornamental grasses and other low-lying plants, and more rocks faded into the darkness beyond pools of light from low-level lanterns on each side of the path.

Her cowboy boots clicked loudly on the slate entryway inside. The house was open and airy. It naturally drew her eyes up to the two-story vaulted cedar ceiling, framed by massive beams. A spiral staircase on her right led to a long hallway with a wood and glass banister that overlooked the great room. To the left was a sunken area with sofas and chairs clustered around a two-sided fireplace. There was another room beyond, where she glimpsed a television and shelves lined with books. She moved to a wall of windows at the back of the room and saw a wooden deck with several levels terraced around a spa. Beyond there was only darkness.

Whistling her approval, she said, "This is a really nice pad, Rain Man."

He was splashing scotch into a glass at a bar near the kitchen. *A nice house, yes, but I don't deserve to live here. Not after tonight, when so many others won't ever go home again.* He emptied half his drink in one gulp, its burning warmth stretching his lips tight.

"I'd forgotten you hadn't seen it." Because of her never-sleep-over rule, they'd always gotten together at her condo in Schaumburg.

She continued looking around, absorbing this glimpse into his character. It almost felt too personal being here. "I always wondered how you put up with the commute. Now I understand. I don't see any neighbors."

"I like privacy and breathing room." Under the circumstances, he felt too ostentatious to mention the five acres. He sat on a stool and motioned at the bar. "I'm not feeling much like a host. Help yourself."

J.J. poured a shot of Laphroig from the open bottle and checked out the generously stocked liquor cabinet. She was struck by the comfortable elegance of Kelly's home contrasted with his often bawdy personality in the

TRACON. She'd worked with him for four years—slept with him for two—but was discovering how little she really knew about this man. He hadn't opened up, J.J. realized, because she'd never expressed much interest. She eased onto a stool next to him and placed a hand on his arm.

"Ryan, I did some thinking in Vegas. I owe you an apology. I've been kind of a bitch lately."

He wasn't going to argue the point, but her timing intrigued him. He took another long pull on his scotch. "Dispensing sympathy as a sop to my conscience for running two together?"

She vigorously shook her head. "No way. I've been thinking, that's all. I know you want more than sex from me." Her drink disappeared with a twist of the wrist. "I'm not sure if I have it to give you but I'm willing to try. I wanted to tell you sooner. There just hasn't been a chance since I got back."

"Yeah, well, I appreciate all that. I'm a little preoccupied right now."

He didn't know what to make of her new attitude and figured he should tell her about Christy, but he wasn't in the mood. He stood and shifted restlessly. He didn't want to go near the television, unwilling to face the news reports yet. Mostly, he felt like crawling into a hole.

"Look, I don't mean to be rude, but I just want to go to bed." He motioned behind her. "The guest room's off to the left. A bathroom's in there, too."

J.J. slipped off the stool and hugged him. For the first time in their relationship, her embrace felt maternal rather than sexual. She smoothed his hair and searched his hollow brown eyes.

"I understand. Selfish of me to bring it up now, but I had to get it out. Would you like me to join you?" She trailed off. "We could just snuggle. A warm body might make you feel better."

There'd been so many times when Kelly longed for the comfort of falling asleep in each other's arms after lovemaking. That it took until now to draw out her sensitive side struck him as sadly ironic. He squeezed her shoulders.

"Thanks. I'm glad you're staying over, but I need some time . . . alone."

He left J.J. standing at the bar and plodded up the stairs. Without bothering to undress or pull down the comforter, he fell heavily across the bed. Almost immediately, Rudy emerged from the shadows and leaped up to him. The cat molded himself against Kelly's side and purred softly under his gentle stroking. It was surprisingly easy to drift off, but he woke an hour later and couldn't fall asleep again.

At length, he stepped onto the deck outside the master bedroom and leaned his arms on a wooden railing, shivering in the chilly air. J.J. must have turned off the lights downstairs and retired because it was pitch black all around him. The roof of the sky was laden with stars now that the clouds had cleared. Occasionally, jet engines whined faintly and interrupted the stillness. Each time, he ruefully looked up at the blinking red and white lights crossing overhead on their way to O'Hare, wondering how the pilot of Coastal 276 reacted when he told him not to climb. His words echoed hauntingly and he wished he could somehow rewind the tape for a second take.

When the sky began to brighten with the first hues of dawn, he finally went back inside. Sleep came fitfully.

✈   ✈   ✈

J.J. WAS WATCHING TELEVISION when the telephone jangled shortly after nine. It was already the second call of the morning. Greg Webber rang earlier to check on Kelly and say he'd drive out to ferry J.J. back to the airport. She grabbed the cordless unit from a marble and glass coffee table, hoping to shield Kelly from the barrage she knew was brewing. The female caller seemed startled to hear J.J.'s voice.

"Hi. May I speak to Ryan, please?"

"I'm sorry. He can't come to the phone right now. May I take a message?"

"This is Christy Cochran. I—"

"You work for the *Chronicle*, don't you?" J.J. remembered meeting her in the TRACON.

Christy's tone sounded off-guard. "Yes."

"Mr. Kelly has nothing to say to the press right now. I suggest you contact our Public Affairs office in Des Plaines."

J.J. started to hang up but Christy spoke again, distressed. "Wait—you don't understand. I'm not a reporter. I'm calling as a friend. We're supposed to see each other tonight, but I need to break our date. I'm sorry, I thought Ryan lived alone. Who are you and how do you know me?"

"Oh."

J.J. had suspected Kelly's interest when he kept fawning over the woman during the tour. Apparently, she'd been right and he didn't have the balls to tell her last night. Two-timing bastard. With effort, she remained polite.

"Sorry, Christy. This is Jodi Jenkins. We met in the TRACON. I thought the press was starting to badger him about the crash."

"I remember. Hi. What do you mean about the crash?"

"I thought you were going to question him about his part in the accident."

"You mean Ryan was *involved?*"

She took perverse satisfaction in delivering the news. "One of two controllers who were directly involved."

"Oh, God. Was he—what happened?" J.J. said nothing, and Christy misinterpreted jealousy for professional confidentiality. "I know these things take time to figure out, but do you have any idea? I'm asking as a friend, not as a member of the news media."

You mean lover, don't you? "We're still sorting it out," she said frostily. "Ryan's been pulled off the scopes pending the investigation." Let her stew over that till she finds out it's standard procedure.

There was prolonged silence. When Christy finally spoke, an odd edge tinged her voice. "I've got to go now." A sob caught in her throat. "Please ask him to call me."

"Sure. Something wrong?" She felt like cackling.

"My . . . uh . . . my sister and her husband were on the Atlantic Airlines flight." Her voice cracked again.

J.J. nearly swore out loud. "I'm very sorry for you, Christy."

"I'd better go now. This is all happening too fast. I don't know what to think."

The line clicked and J.J. heard a rustling behind her as she switched off the phone. Kelly had come into the room and was watching the TV, tuned to a local station running continuous reports about the crash. Aerial images on the screen showed the broken carcass of the Coastal 757 amid several demolished buildings. The cloudless blue sky seemed to mock the devastation below. If only the weather had been like this last night, the pilots might have seen each other, he mused. Or Coastal would have returned to O'Hare instead of going to Midway. If only . . .

The scene dissolved to a slightly blurry photograph of the Atlantic Air-lines cockpit, violently torn from the body of the plane, plunging into Lake Michigan. "This dramatic picture was taken by a man in a sailboat just a few yards away," the narrator said. "Car dealer Larry Lindstrand told News Channel 5 that he feared for his life while he and a companion helplessly watched parts of the doomed jetliner fall all around them."

A videotaped interview of Lindstrand appeared on the screen. "We were afraid we might get hurt or even die if a big piece of wreckage hit the boat," he said. A woman standing next to him made a comment Kelly couldn't hear, then a reporter asked whether anything fell on board. Kelly caught a look passing between them before Lindstrand said, "Ah, she means the arm. A few pieces of the plane came pretty close. I thought we were a goner when I saw that cockpit heading toward us. We caught a wave over the stern when it splashed down."

The screen switched again to an anchorman in the studio.

"That was the horrible scene on the lake yesterday evening. In a few minutes, we'll take you back to the lake live on our News Chopper 5 with coverage of Coast Guard divers retrieving the wreckage. But first, here's an update on the terrible toll of this tragedy. As we've reported, all 182 people aboard the Atlantic jet perished. We've just received an update from Coastal. Airline officials now tell us that forty-eight of the 114 on board managed to survive. Several of those are listed in critical condition at area hospitals. At this time, there are also twenty known bystanders on the ground who were killed when the jet crashed at Midway."

A running total appeared next to the anchorman's head, and it struck Kelly that they could have been summarizing the city budget. It added up to 268 deaths. He grew pale and put his hands on the back of a beige sofa to steady himself. Noticing J.J. was off the phone, he pointed at the receiver, still in her hand.

"Who was that?"

She carelessly tossed it on the sofa and seethed. "Your girlfriend. When were you planning to tell me about her?"

"I'd have gotten around to it. I wasn't trying to hide anything."

"You had the perfect opportunity when I was spilling my guts last night. Conveniently, you didn't say a word. Are you fucking her?"

His hands fell to his sides and curled into fists. "We've had dinner and drinks. That's all."

"Right. Like, do I have 'naive' written on my forehead? If you want out of our relationship, say so. Don't go sneaking around behind my back picking up new snatch."

"Why you self-centered insensitive little bitch! I've just been involved in a midair, for Christ's sake, and all you can think about are your silly ass feelings." He moved closer until his face was inches from hers, breathing heavily. "I'm starting to get the flick. Until last night, you couldn't care less about me unless you were horny. Then you cozy up trying to be manipulative. I should have known you're a control freak."

The doorbell rang and she was grateful for the interruption. He was partially correct. She didn't really want to get more involved—just felt sorry for him. But she wasn't willing to let him dump her.

"It's probably Greg. He's here to take me back to the airport."

He jerked his head. "Good. Get out!"

She brushed past him, stopping at the entrance to the room and smirking primly. "Oh, I almost forgot. Your little tart's sister and brother-in-law were on Atlantic 59. Something tells me from the way she hung up that you won't be getting any from her again. Better get used to being hard up, Rain Man, because that makes two of us. You certainly won't be getting any more from me, either." She stomped out and slammed the front door.

Kelly slumped against the back of the sofa as if she'd kicked him in the gut, sucking the air out of his lungs. No longer could he hold the anonymous deaths at bay. Suddenly, they'd become obscenely personal. He recalled the picture of Christy's sister on a wall in her home and fought to breathe. Speechless, he stared at the TV and felt the tears. Jesus, of all the people.

SEVENTEEN
PAINTED DESERT

THE DIM LIGHT GRADUALLY INTENSIFIED, accompanied by a soft beeping. She felt something covering part of her face and one arm throbbed with a dull ache. Blinking, Sharon Masters struggled to focus through the haze and realized she couldn't muster the strength to do anything more than slowly move her head back and forth. A young man she didn't recognize sprawled in a chair across the room, watching basketball on a TV mounted from the ceiling. Smooth metal bars framed the sides of the bed and an IV bag hung from a stand. Nearby, a heart monitor hiccuped steadily.

Images drifted back. A heart-rending jolt, the flight attendant's reassuring smile, an emergency landing. Then nothing except for a dim recollection of raindrops stinging her eyes, flashing lights, and an oppressive weight pinning her to the ground. Gripped by the terrifying memory, she sat up on her elbows with a start and gulped for air. Her mouth felt cottony. Reaching for a water pitcher and glass on the bedside table, the IV needle in her arm tugged painfully against the bandage holding it in place and she moaned.

"Oh, you're awake." The young man sprang out of the chair, a gold tie dangling loosely from his unbuttoned shirt collar. A dark blue sport coat was folded neatly over the back of the chair. "How do you feel?"

"My mouth is so dry," she croaked.

"Here, let me get that for you."

He hurriedly poured water into the plastic glass and held a straw to her lips. She sucked the liquid gratefully, savoring its refreshing coolness.

"Who are you?"

"Jeremy Parker, ma'am. I'm one of the senator's assistants. I flew in with him last night after we heard about the . . . accident."

He didn't appear much older than she was, but he conveyed an air of polish that she attributed to working in D.C. "Where's my dad?"

"The senator stepped away for a moment. I'll go let him know you're awake."

Sharon watched him hustle out of the room. She felt stiff and leaden and there was a tingling in her left leg. She used her one free arm to shift on the bed and try to scratch it, but couldn't reach. The TV emitted a muted cheer from the crowd at the basketball game. Searching for the remote control, she spied it on a table across the room and sighed. She detested sports. The action on TV ended and she heard a newscaster announce highlights from other games the previous night. After a commercial, an anchorman began talking about the collision. Parker had kept the volume low so as not to disturb her and she strained to hear.

" . . . joins us live at Christ Community Hospital in Oak Lawn, where Senator Richard Masters is maintaining a vigil for his daughter. Twenty-two-year-old Karen Masters was a passenger on board the plane that crash-landed at Midway."

"My name's Sharon, you buffoon," she muttered. Her father's telegenic image flashed on the screen. A hive of reporters surrounded him, thrusting microphones in his face and shouting questions.

"What's the situation, Senator?"

The tingling in Sharon's leg intensified. Grasping one of the metal bars, she managed to haul herself up into a sitting position.

"The situation is we have almost fifty people at this and other hospitals in the area who are bravely trying to recover from injuries they suffered in last night's tragedy. I can honestly say I share the grief and pain of the survivors and their families because my daughter was one of the victims."

"How is she, Senator?"

Sharon reached down again to scratch her leg. She patted the blanket and drew in her breath. There was nothing from just below her left knee. Frantically, she pounded the bed, vainly trying to find what was obviously gone.

" . . . gravely hurt. The doctors had to amputate a leg. There was no choice because of blood loss and damage to the bone and tissue. But she's lucky to have survived. Nearly 270 other poor souls were not as fortunate."

Masters' voice subsided to a faint echo as Sharon's vision blurred and a wave of heat suddenly drenched her with sweat. Her chest heaved spasmodically and the heart monitor erupted in a frenzied stutter. Hysterically, her mind searched for a way to somehow change the unthinkable.

"How is she handling it?"

The senator held up a hand and adroitly sidestepped the question. "It's too soon to tell. What we need to be asking is how this could have happened. How could two airliners collide while flying within the supposedly safe cocoon of a sophisticated air traffic control system the taxpayers have spent hundreds of millions of dollars to establish and maintain? As chairman of the Senate Subcommittee on Aviation and the concerned father of a victim, I will be taking a close personal interest in the accident investigation. Once we determine what went wrong, I can assure you I'll work to implement the appropriate safeguards."

Light-headed, Sharon fell back onto the pillow and clutched the blanket. They should have asked before chopping off her leg. This was unbelievable! She placed a hand over her face and yearned for the remote control to tune out her father's platitudes. Finally, he stopped talking. Several minutes later, he strode into the room, followed closely by Parker. He lowered one of the metal bars and sat on the edge of her bed, his face registering poised concern.

"How are you feeling, Pumpkin? Sorry, I mean Sharon." Masters glanced at Parker, laughing awkwardly. "I've called her that since she was a little girl, but she hates it."

One of her hands beat the bed and he leaned back involuntarily, afraid she'd hit him. "You bastard. You selfish, egotistical, power-hungry bastard! Goddamn it, why do you always put your precious politics before everything else?"

Masters clenched his jaw and suppressed the urge to yell back, conscious of Parker, whose face betrayed shock tinged with understanding. When the senator resumed, he spoke quickly and pleadingly. "Pumpkin, I'm so sorry about what happened. I can't tell you how much I wish I'd come to Chicago as we planned. But surely you can't blame me. No one could have predicted all of this. I know the trauma of the accident and finding out your leg is gone must be a shock, but you'll be fine. They have wonderful prostheses nowadays and I'll make sure you get the best care."

She disgustedly shook her head, bitterly recalling the midair collision that killed her mother on a trip home from Mexico. Sharon was nine and devastated. She admired her father's brave front when he wept only briefly, but later discovered his true sentiments. A freshman senator at the time, Masters manipulated the death into a *cause célèbre* and became a familiar face on network news programs that portrayed him as the grieving widower waging a noble fight to implement TCAS in the U.S. airline fleet.

What the cameras didn't record were private moments of smug satisfaction over a tragedy he successfully parlayed to launch his career into the national spotlight. Sharon remembered the night he enjoyed brandy and cigars with another groveling aide, a Young Turk much like Parker. Watching TV in a nearby room, she overheard them gloating about the senator's skyrocketing public approval rating. "My sex life's improved, too," he'd admitted with inebriated carelessness. "Women have been throwing themselves at me and who am I to refuse them?" Hurt and scared by the comment, she'd lain awake in bed wondering whether he'd try to get rid of her. Now, the memory enraged her.

"You just don't get it, do you?" Her rising voice pushed him off the bed. "I'm flat on my back in the hospital—after losing a leg, for God's sake— and you hold a fucking news conference! All you care about is using me as an excuse to get on TV. You were the same way with mom." Tears streamed down her face. "I want you to leave."

"Sharon—"

"I said get out of here!" Screaming now, her fist banged the bed again and her face flushed with anger. "Just leave me alone."

A nurse rushed into the room, alarmed by the commotion. Masters stared at the floor, peeved and embarrassed. "My daughter's a little upset. It's understandable after what she's been through."

"Get him out."

The nurse touched Masters' arm. "Perhaps you'd better wait outside for a few minutes, Senator. I'll get something to sedate her."

"I don't need any sedation. I'll be fine as soon as this asshole leaves."

The nurse checked the IV and cast Sharon a stern look. "You should be more respectful, young lady. He is your father, not to mention a United States senator."

"He's my father in name only. And you should learn to mind your own business. If you knew him like I do, you'd never vote for him."

The nurse sniffed her disapproval before retreating into the corridor with Masters and Parker. Sharon threw a box of tissues after them at the open doorway. *I almost died and he acted like he couldn't care less. He didn't even try to hug me.* She used her gown to wipe the tears from her face.

She was still fuming when an orderly appeared with a lunch tray. He retrieved the box of tissues from the floor and made a show of placing it on the bedside table. The meal was sparse and tasteless, fueling her despondency. She skewered a thin slice of dried turkey with her fork and was listlessly chewing on it when Robert Duncan walked into the room.

"Hi, Sharon." The reporter held up a bouquet of daffodils and lilacs as he took in her matted hair, bandaged face, and red-rimmed eyes. "These are for you."

She smiled for the first time since the accident. "Oh, Bob. That's sweet of you. Thanks."

"Actually, they're from the paper." He brought a hand from behind his back and presented her with a long-stemmed yellow rose. "This is from me." He was pleased to see her face light up.

She accepted the rose and inhaled its sweet aroma. Duncan moved around the bed to place the bouquet on the windowsill and turned back to her, uncertain what to do next.

Sharon tentatively held out her arms. "Would you mind giving me a hug?"

Duncan happily complied. He'd fantasized about it many times, but today's circumstances turned the reality of the moment awkward and he held her stiffly. Sharon sobbed and he stroked the back of her head.

"The nurses told me about your, uh, surgery. That's a tough break."

Another sob unleashed a full-fledged cry. Words dribbled out, swelling into a torrent about her leg and her father. Duncan tried to ignore the stirrings he felt from her soft body pressing against him through the flimsy hospital gown. He murmured a few consoling words, but mostly he just fed her tissues and listened to the venting. At length, she subsided.

"I've sure given you an earful, haven't I?"

"No problem. You need to get it out. Look, I'll be honest. I came here to see how you were, but the paper hoped I could interview you." He hesitated. "Maybe I should come back another time."

Duncan's sensitivity touched her. She remembered Christy's warning about his reputation as an uncaring Lothario—was it only a few weeks ago? It seemed like an eternity now.

"A first-person account of the crash would make a good story," she said with growing excitement. "Something the *Trib* might not have."

"Shepherd figured he'd pitch it for page one tomorrow." Duncan's eyes twinkled. "You'd get a byline, too."

Sharon looked at him gratefully for this professional courtesy. She pressed a button and a motor whirred while the head of the bed elevated so she could sit comfortably. "Get out your notebook."

✈   ✈   ✈

RIDING IN A FRIEND'S CAR, Brad Schwartz snickered when they turned onto Luna Avenue and he spotted the burned-out carcass of the Winnebago in his parents' driveway. After they parked on the street and got out, Stan pulled the driver's seat forward and his family's yellow Labrador hopped from the back. Wagging his tail with interest, Moose followed Stan and Brad as they surveyed the charred rubble of the first two houses on the block and the blackened tree limb that had smashed onto the roof of the motor home.

"Looks like the blimp took a direct hit," Brad said gleefully.

Stan burst into laughter. "Blimp. That's choice." Moose jumped up on his hind legs, sharing in the fun. "Nothing but a piece of crap now. Ready for the junkyard."

Brad had used the term several times with his parents, much to their indignation. From his perspective, the taunt was well-deserved. Due payback for frequent needling that he finish college and move out so they could get on with their retirement. Brad couldn't say in general whether there was any substance to the middle child theory, but it certainly held true in his family. For as long as he could remember, it seemed as though his siblings were doted on while he existed on scraps of affection and recognition. Where the 'rents nurtured and counseled his older sister and younger brother, he usually had to sort through problems and decisions on his own. They were raised with care. He was simply left to grow up by himself. Brad was born just eleven months after his sister. He was eleven when he discovered the pregnancy was unplanned, and since then had convinced himself that was the reason for both real and imagined resentment from mom and pops. That his current leisurely pace to graduate frustrated them gave him a sweet sense of satisfaction.

"Maybe you should call it the Hindenburg," Stan suggested.

Laughing shrilly, they circled Brad's Camaro and checked for damage. They found nothing wrong, except for the orange Boot still locked in place.

"What are you gonna do about that?" Stan asked.

"I dunno." Brad kicked it and groaned, grasping his foot in pain. "If my old man won't give me the money, I'll figure out something. Maybe another midnight raid on the computer lab." He smiled slyly at Stan, who nodded knowingly, and slapped his friend's hand in a high-five. "Hey, man, thanks for driving me downtown last night and picking me up this morning. Mission accomplished."

After storming out of the 6511 Club, Brad had hiked over to Stan's house to ask for a lift to the University of Illinois campus west of the Loop. They drank several beers at a favorite hangout before Stan left and Brad walked to a pizzeria. He ordered a large pepperoni and sausage to go, then took it to his girlfriend's apartment, where they watched news coverage about the crash while eating. He was unnerved to learn that he'd left pops in the bar minutes before the disaster, and called home to find out whether his folks were all right and the house was still standing. He had to try several times before they answered and nearly bagged the effort after his initial concern faded. But he persisted when he realized the effect it had on Gina. Between each call, she preoccupied him in the bedroom with eager expressions of relief that he'd survived.

Stan grinned wolfishly. "Anything to help a guy score."

Moose suddenly stood still, perking his ears and looking at two coeds walking along the other side of the street. One was blonde and stood a few inches shorter than the other, an Asian woman with long straight black hair. Both wore snug-fitting tops and jeans, and carried backpacks. Wagging his tail, Moose scampered across to them. He rolled onto his side when they set down their backpacks and squatted to pet him.

"Oh, he's so cute," the blonde gushed. She looked across the street. "Hi, Brad. Is this your dog?"

"No, he's mine. His name's Moose," Stan hollered. Under his breath, he said, "You know these girls?"

"Just the blonde. Sarah lives down the street."

"He's real friendly," she said, standing up.

"I think he wants you to walk with us," Stan said.

"We're in a hurry right now." She flashed a bright smile. "Maybe another time. Brad knows where I live. Bye, guys." She slung her backpack over one shoulder and started to move on.

"See you, ladies. Here, Moose." Stan clapped his hands. The Lab circled the coeds once more, basking in their attention, before running across the street. The women waved and Brad and Stan waved back.

"He's a handy little guy to have around," Brad remarked.

Stan rubbed Moose's head. "Don't you know why dogs are man's best friend? Moose is a babe magnet. He's helped me get laid a lotta times. Lemme know if you ever want to borrow him." He winked at Brad.

"Thanks, man. I might take you up on that."

"Actually, Moose is pretty special." Stan reached down and scratched behind the Lab's ears. "He was supposed to be a Seeing Eye dog, but my uncle gave him to us when we had to put Jupiter down." Stan's uncle was a canine behavior specialist who ran a renowned training academy. One specialty involved training dogs to help the disabled. "Man, this guy can't speak English, but he sure understands it. Don't ya, boy?" Moose wagged his tail and rubbed against Stan's leg. "Well, I gotta book, too. Later, dude."

Brad watched his friend peel away from the curb and turned toward the house. Strutting around the Winnebago, he chuckled over pops' likely reaction—God, he wished he'd seen that! As he inspected the piece of plane wreckage sticking partway through a broken window, an overweight cop ambled down the sidewalk from 55ᵗʰ Street and stopped in front of the house.

"Good day," he said, touching the visor of his hat.

"How's it going?"

"Do you live here?"

Brad nodded.

"Too bad about your motor home."

"Yeah, too bad." Brad suppressed a grin.

The cop pointed to the wreckage. "Be sure not to touch that, son. It's part of the investigation. The Feds will get it today or tomorrow."

"Gotcha."

The cop waved a hand and sauntered off. Brad turned back to the Winnebago, taking in the demolished interior, melted tires, and water trickling from the undercarriage onto the driveway. The water drew his attention to something sticking out from beneath the vehicle. He nudged it into view with a foot. Swiveling around, he saw that the cop was still walking back toward 55th.

✈   ✈   ✈

JOHN SHEPHERD FINISHED EDITING Duncan's interview with Sharon and closed the file on his computer screen.

"It's a good read, Bob, even though she can't remember much about the landing." After the plane's nose gear collapsed in the grass at Midway, Sharon said she'd blacked out. "The belly slide into the bar is bad enough. Can you imagine being on the one that dropped in the lake?"

"I'd die of fright on the way down. I hope I would." Duncan paused and grimaced. "Otherwise, it'd be a helluva wait."

Shepherd nodded toward the news desk across the room. "Christy's sister died in that one. Metcalf sent her home last night, but she's here now. Showed up an hour ago with her son."

Both men watched her poke half-heartedly on a keyboard. Jason sat two desks away, idly turning pages of a newspaper. "They probably need the distraction," Duncan said. "Better than sitting around at home." He shifted impatiently. "You gonna read my other story? It's the historical sider."

Once again, the paper planned to run several extra pages on the collision in its Sunday editions. Duncan's burst of energy mildly surprised Shepherd.

"Why all the effort?" he asked. "We don't pay you by the word."

"Just trying to cover different angles."

"Duly noted." Shepherd pressed a few keys on his computer terminal and the file appeared. "Here it is."

▲UFBYLINE▲
By Robert Duncan
Chronicle Staff Writer
"See and be seen."

This antiquated concept of air traffic control proved tragically inadequate on June 30, 1956, when two airliners collided over the vast expanse of the Grand Canyon. All 128 people aboard both planes were killed.

After the TWA Constellation and United DC-7 tangled at 21,000 feet near a radio fix known as Painted Desert, an intense public furor erupted. Sweeping changes eventually resulted, transforming ATC from a limited manual system into today's sophisticated computerized one in which all commercial and many private flights are under constant radar control and radio contact.

It may be hard for us to fathom in an age of wireless telephones and laptop PCs, but in 1956 airliners routinely flew through great swatches of U.S. airspace that were beyond the range of air traffic controllers and their radarscopes. Along with see and be seen, the aviation community relied upon the dubious principle of "big sky, little airplanes" to keep everyone safely apart.

Most of the time it worked.

Shepherd continued reading and frowned. "Don't quote from reports so much. What does this mean?"

Duncan bent forward, following his editor's finger. "The Civil Aeronautics Board said Grand Canyon happened because the pilots couldn't see each other. Duh. But they basically blamed that on limitations in the traffic control system."

Shepherd tapped on the keyboard. "Then say so. Cut the bureaucratic jargon." He read some more. "Geez, same two airlines whacked again over New York City four years later."

When the planes hit each other at 5,200 feet, the United DC-8's No. 4 engine tore into the TWA Constellation. The whirling turbofan blades ingested a passenger before smashing out the other side of the fuselage and plunging into a playground at a housing project. The force of the collision broke the "Connie" aircraft into three pieces and it immediately crashed near Miller's

Field on Staten Island.

The United jet hurtled to the ground in Brooklyn, narrowly missing a school before it crashed at the intersection of Seventh Avenue and Sterling Place [note to citdsk: pix of this ran in sat. editions]. Most of the fuselage and the right wing then slammed into the Pillar of Fire Church and destroyed it in a raging inferno.

Six people on the ground were killed, as well as 128 passengers and crew members aboard both planes. Miraculously, an 11-year-old boy sitting in the rear of the United jet survived for a day, long enough to tell doctors valiantly trying to save him that snow-laden New York "looked like a picture out of a fairy book" before the crash.

Shepherd pressed the H&J key to get an inch count for the story. "We may have to dump some of the descriptions. I like 'em, but this is long, even for a Sunday piece."

"Don't lose the next part," Duncan cautioned. "These two accidents are why the government made the airlines install Mode C transponders. That's how controllers identify the planes on their scopes. Take out the stuff about their lousy ground radar, if you have to. It's just another example of how slowly the FAA responds to equipment needs."

Shepherd skimmed the copy. "Agreed. You got the '81 strike in here?"

"After the next few graphs about mechanical breakdowns and low staffing. They walked out on August third, demanding a $10,000 a year pay raise, shorter hours, and better equipment."

"I remember Reagan told them to take a hike. He fired thousands."

"Yeah, like two-thirds of all controllers—the 11,560 who wouldn't come back when he ordered them to."

"He had no choice. It's illegal for government employees to strike."

"I know." Duncan sighed. "But the sad part is many of the issues that led to the strike still exist. A lot of control towers and radar rooms are plagued by equipment breakdowns and excessive overtime."

Shepherd listened with half an ear while reading more of the story.

On Aug. 31, 1986, an Aeromexico DC-9 en route from Mexico City to Los Angeles collided with a private Piper aircraft over

Cerritos, Calif. Eighty-two people were killed, including 15 on the ground. The disaster arguably spurred as much change in air traffic control as the Grand Canyon crash three decades earlier.

The National Transportation Safety Board's investigation of the accident urged the FAA to expedite its development of a traffic alert/collision avoidance system, versions of which had been under study since before Grand Canyon. "Had a TCAS alert been provided to the DC-9 pilots," the NTSB wrote in its report, "the probability of (seeing the Piper) would have increased from 30 percent to 95 percent."

One of the accident victims was the wife of Sen. Richard Masters, a member of the Senate Subcommittee on Aviation who was later elected its chairman. Masters, R-Calif., became a leading advocate of TCAS in Congress and is credited with helping to bring the system online after years of bureaucratic and technical delays.

The Air Line Pilots Association, Air Transport Association and other industry groups have lauded TCAS as a much-needed safety improvement, but controllers steadfastly warn that the system has serious technical flaws.

"TCAS is susceptible to frequent false alerts," said Peter Rykowski, Local C-90 facility representative of the National Air Traffic Controllers Association. "In many cases, pilots responding to TCAS have flown closer to each other than if they'd continued to follow instructions from the controller who was already providing safe and legal separation."

ALPA President Dennis Montgomery takes a different view. "We have documented cases where TCAS has saved the day," he said. "It's an extremely valuable backup for controllers who too often are overworked."

Although TCAS could not have prevented a 1991 runway collision at Los Angeles International Airport that killed 35 people, controller fatigue was a factor.

"That's the one where a jet landed on top of a commuter plane waiting to take off," Shepherd said. "The controller screwed up."

Duncan turned defensive. "Yeah, but the NTSB also blasted the FAA. The probable cause report reamed management for lapses that led to the controller's mistake. Tower supervisors didn't have proper backup procedures and top management was accused of neglecting problems at LAX. That's the overall point of my story."

> The NTSB report illustrates a disturbing theme in air traffic control spanning the four decades since Grand Canyon. Despite numerous technological advances, accidents continue to occur partly because of fundamental systemic problems.
> "TCAS can be useful when it works properly," Rykowski said. "But don't miss the big picture. In its report about LAX, the NTSB talked about bad management and inadequate equipment. It's what they've been harping about—and we've been harping about—for years."

Shepherd pressed the STORE key as Christy Cochran and Ellen Sanders converged on his desk. Christy's eyes were puffy and bloodshot. "When will you have an update to your budget?" she asked.

He motioned at Duncan. "Besides his interview with Sharon, he's got a nice history piece, but it needs trimming."

"I've got a *great* story—I think," Sanders interjected. The other three swung toward her. "One of my sources at the FAA tells me they've traced several problems with TCAS to a particular unit made by Circuitron."

"Isn't that the company Senator Masters did a favor for?" Shepherd said.

Sanders' head bobbed. "Through his influence, the FAA was all set to give the Dallas contract for Doppler radar to Circuitron, after they'd already awarded it to another company. He had to back pedal after the crash there. Circuitron makes TCAS units that cause ghost targets on radarscopes and stop working if there are more than a hundred planes in the area. All the information on the scopes gets wiped out and the controllers just see CST. Happens a lot at O'Hare, Kennedy, LAX."

Christy remembered such an incident when she and Jason visited the TRACON. "Did Circuitron make the TCAS computers that were on our two planes?"

"I'm checking that. Several manufacturers do. If these were from Circuitron, we may have a scoop on what caused the collision."

Christy thought the theory was interesting but unlikely. She suspected a human was to blame. That a computer glitch might have killed Carla, as it might miscalculate a telephone bill, was too impersonal and ironic. Something of this magnitude had to involve more than a faulty silicon chip. Besides, it seemed apparent that a controller was to blame. The comment from Kelly's friend when she called his house this morning indicated he was at least partially responsible. Otherwise, why would they take him off the job? Even worse, Jodi's reticent tone seemed to transcend a purely professional relationship. He'd claimed he wasn't involved with anyone. If that was true, then why was Jenkins there so early on a Saturday? Slimeball. He's just like all the others.

"Can you get in touch with your friend at O'Hare?" Sanders asked.

Christy snapped back to reality. "What?"

"I'd love to talk to the controllers who were involved last night, but the FAA is stonewalling me. Do you suppose your friend might help us again? You told me his name, but I've forgotten it."

She'd held off mentioning him to the city desk, reluctant to breach a personal trust. That consideration was swept aside now by simmering anger from her phone call. *To hell with him.* If he really isn't to blame, it'll be his chance to say so. If he did screw up, well, he'll have to face the consequences sooner or later.

"My so-called friend's name is Ryan Kelly and he was directly involved. I'll message you with his home phone number."

Sanders' eyes widened. "I thought you two—never mind. Why didn't you tell me this sooner?"

Without responding, Christy turned around and walked back to her desk.

EIGHTEEN
MODE C

THE PHONE CALL ROUSED KELLY out of a troubled sleep, bringing a welcome end to his nightmare. "Hello."

"Hi, Ryan, it's Sam. Sorry I woke you. How's it going?"

He rubbed his face to wipe away the horrific image. Tumbling bodies cartwheeled in slow motion from the stricken airliner, falling one by one toward their cold watery grave. The aluminum tube spit its victims into the yawning void with the relentless rhythm of a machine gun.

"Okay, I guess. What time is it?"

"Ten-thirty Sunday morning."

Rudy meowed in mild protest as Kelly shifted on the bed, his slumber disturbed. "What's going on?"

"The NTSB is back and wants to talk with you some more."

"I told them all I know Friday night."

"This is standard. They always do a preliminary interview and come back in a few days figuring people will remember something else. Gives you a chance to settle down and think more clearly. Uh, they're also concerned about the Mode C readouts you say you got from Coastal."

"Why?"

Sanchez's voice stayed level and quiet. "They don't see anything unusual on the DARC printout. It shows a normal climb from the time Coastal took off until the accident."

Rudy meowed louder when Kelly shot up in bed. "What the hell? I saw them go crazy for a minute."

"I've known you for a long time, Ryan, and if you say they were dancing in circles, I believe you. But I'd better warn you that certain other people aren't so convinced."

"Bosko?"

"How did you guess?"

"He's a candy ass."

"Hawkins seems skeptical, too. I haven't talked to Richardson yet."

Kelly fell back onto the pillow, consumed with anger and gnawing fear. Fourteen years as a controller with a first-class record didn't seem to count for much right now. Was it too much to ask to expect their trust in him? Then the butterflies churned again. Had he really seen what he thought?

"It's nice to know I have management's full confidence and support."

"For what it's worth, you have mine."

The comment did little to console him. Sanchez wielded influence as an area manager and he knew she was honest. She didn't play political games like some of the others. But she reported to Richardson, who had final say in the TRACON. Richardson, in turn, answered to Hawkins, who was the FAA's top gun at O'Hare.

"I appreciate that, Sam. When do they want to see me?"

"As soon as possible."

"I'll be there by noon."

He replaced the phone and padded into the shower, ignoring Rudy's plea for breakfast. As the cascading hot water washed away remnants of sleep, the scene on the scope coalesced once more. He could see Coastal's altitude readout fluctuate just as clearly as he could see Rudy pacing on the other side of the glass shower door. He heard himself hand off an American flight to the Center and tell Kiwi to turn, then watched as Coastal's altitude seemed to settle down. What else? He was missing an obvious detail. Something important. His mind struggled to latch onto it, but the memory danced beyond reach. A dull ache built in his head from the effort to remember. He toweled himself dry, pulled on jeans and a sweater, and swallowed two Advil capsules.

The red light on his answering machine was blinking when he walked downstairs. He pressed PLAY and poured some cat mix into Rudy's bowl while the metallic voice reverberated through the kitchen.

"Mr. Kelly, my name is Ellen Sanders and I'm a reporter for the *Chronicle*. I understand you had some involvement in Friday night's midair collision and I was hoping you'd be willing to discuss it with me. I'm sure this is a difficult time for you, but your cooperation would help me write a more complete and accurate story. You can reach me—"

He punched the STOP button. He had no interest in talking to a reporter and wondered how she obtained his non-published telephone number. Then it occurred to him. He'd given his number to Christy before their second date and she must have passed it along, a violation of trust that annoyed him.

✈   ✈   ✈

KELLY JOGGED DOWN THE STAIRS to the atrium lobby for the TRACON and control tower, one level below ground between Terminal Two and the Hilton. Another controller heading up the stairs looked away. Partly out of embarrassment. Partly out of superstition. The gesture made Kelly feel like an outcast, reminding him that he'd broken the golden rule.

He'd run two together.

"They're waiting for you in Hawkins' lair," the other man said in passing.

The comment encouraged Kelly. At least he hadn't been completely ostracized yet. Wondering what else people knew, he anxiously strode to the facility chief's office. Hawkins was chatting with Richardson, Sanchez, Boskovich, Rykowski, and the two NTSB investigators he'd spoken with Friday night. The chief sat behind his desk, swiveling casually in his leather chair. The others were assembled on two sofas. Hawkins politely tipped his head when he saw Kelly at the door.

"Come in, Ryan. Nice of you to make it here so quickly. Have a seat."

Someone quietly shut the door behind him. He eased into the open chair and nodded to everyone. The conversation grew stilted, then hushed, making him more uncomfortable.

"How are you doing?" Hawkins asked.

"I wish we didn't have to be here right now."

"We need to go over an inconsistency in your statement," Boskovich interjected.

Hawkins smiled thinly at the impetuous supervisor. Bosko lacked class, but they were of like minds on this. Kelly had opened a can of worms that provoked an onslaught of frantic calls from Washington. Hawkins was exhausted from placating the brass and filling out reports that could stall his career in mid-flight. Unless he handled this right, he'd never make it to headquarters in D.C. He sat back and said nothing.

Kelly cocked his head at Bosko. "I meant I wish all this had never happened."

Esterhaus pulled a miniature tape recorder out of the breast pocket of his sport coat and placed it on Hawkins' desk. "We have just a few questions. Do you mind?"

"Be my guest."

The senior investigator switched it on. "For the record, this is Sunday, May seventh, in Chicago, Illinois. My name is Frederic Esterhaus. With me is my associate, Scott Carter. Also present are Andrew Hawkins, Jeff Richardson, Samantha Sanchez, and Ray Boskovich of the FAA, as well as Peter Rykowski, NATCA facility representative. We are speaking with Ryan Kelly, an FPL controller at the O'Hare Airport TRACON. Mr. Kelly, would you please tell us again about the altitude readouts you received from Coastal flight 276 prior to the accident."

Kelly sat back with his arms dangling on the chair, trying to appear confident. "It's like I said the other night. I cleared Coastal to climb and maintain five thousand. Then Prairie departed Midway and I told Coastal to go to six. As I worked the other traffic, I noticed his data tag showed fifty-eight, then fifty-two. A few seconds later it showed fifty-four. That's when I called to verify altitude and he told me he was actually at fifty-five."

Esterhaus wrote on his pad. "So, to the best of your recollection, there was only the one oddity. By that I mean the apparent change from 5,800 feet to 5,200 when, in fact, the aircraft was supposed to be climbing."

"That's the only one I noticed. I wasn't monitoring Coastal exclusively so there may have been other fluctuations I didn't see."

"I understand," Esterhaus said, nodding thoughtfully and reviewing his notes. He looked up with a disarming smile. "Forgive me, Mr. Kelly, but we're a bit mystified. We have printouts from the Direct Access Radar Channel. As you know, it provides a very thorough and precise readout of an aircraft's flight profile. It shows Coastal 276 climbing normally at 1,000 feet per minute. There's no indication its Mode C was transmitting faulty readings."

Kelly swallowed, conscious of everyone staring at him. "I know what I saw. That readout wasn't normal."

Boskovich cleared his throat. "Maybe you misread the data tag."

Kelly noted the Lord was impeccably dressed as usual, including a blue sweater vest that he'd added to his ensemble. It accentuated his supercilious attitude. "I considered that. I've also spent a lot of time thinking about what happened." He stared earnestly at the two investigators. "I am absolutely certain, as surely as I'm sitting in this chair, that my memory is accurate."

Carter, the red-haired one, leaned forward. "We're not trying to imply anything. We were just a little surprised when the DARC didn't corroborate your statement. We're still searching for Coastal's flight data recorder, which we presume will bear out what you're saying."

Boskovich enjoyed watching Kelly squirm. He always acted so cool and indifferent in the TRACON, as if he never sweated like the rest of them. Well, no controller is invincible, and now the star was getting his comeuppance. He straightened his tie and stuck in another needle.

"It's not uncommon for the mind to play tricks after you've been through a traumatic experience."

"Back off, Bosko," Rykowski said. "Ryan's one of the best controllers in the house. He deserves a little more respect and consideration."

Kelly noticed Hawkins studying him intently, almost accusingly.

"Gentlemen," Esterhaus cut in, "we look forward to analyzing the aircraft's black box. That should certainly clarify matters. You needn't worry about this unduly, Mr. Kelly. I've no reason to disbelieve your statement."

"I wouldn't make it up."

"No one's suggesting you did, sir. One more question, please. Are you aware of the controller's responsibilities during the Resolution Advisory phase of a TCAS event?"

"I'm aware of the agency's rule prohibiting me from saying anything to the pilots involved." He searched their faces for understanding. Sanchez smiled sympathetically, but Hawkins and Richardson sat impassively. Boskovich curled his lip. "When it happened—when I saw the two targets about to co-locate—I couldn't just sit there. I had to issue traffic." He was afraid to ask but needed to know. He leaned forward and rested his elbows on his knees. "Does the DARC indicate the pilots reacted to my call?"

Esterhaus set the pad aside. "We don't know because we haven't time-matched it with the audio tape yet. Once again, the aircraft's black box and cockpit voice recorder will give us a precise answer. Is there anything else, anything at all, that you'd like to add to your statement?"

There really wasn't. He'd already told them about the radio failure, but that didn't have a direct bearing on the accident because he'd quickly fired up the backup system. He raised his hands in supplication.

"Find the black box."

Esterhaus switched off the tape recorder. "We intend to, Mr. Kelly. Don't try to read anything into our questions. We're merely attempting to ascertain what happened, not hang anyone from the cross. I thank you for talking with us today." He pulled a business card from a flap pocket of his coat. "Please call me if something else comes to mind."

Kelly took the card and grasped the offered hand, then nodded to the others. Hawkins, Richardson, and Boskovich avoided direct eye contact. Sanchez stood and held his arm.

"Thanks for coming in. Get some more rest and I'll touch base with you in a few days."

He was heading out the door with Rykowski when Hawkins called to him. "Just so you know, Ryan, we're releasing your name to the press today. Frank's, too. They've been leaning on us and I don't see how we can hold off any longer."

Kelly shrugged. "That's your call, Andy."

He and Rykowski walked along the corridor without saying anything. When Kelly paused outside the TRACON, Rykowski nodded with understanding and went on in to give his friend a moment alone.

Management's distrustful attitude was troubling, though Kelly had to admit not too surprising. He was heartened by Sam's support, but wondered how long she'd stand by him in the face of pressure from her bosses. What sent chills down his spine, however, was the lack of corroboration from the DARC. He couldn't explain the discrepancy and it shook a deep-seated belief in his abilities. He suspected the other controllers were aware of this development and it spawned doubts about the reception he'd get inside the radar room.

Taking a deep breath, he pushed into the darkness. No one noticed him while he stood near the door and allowed his eyes to adjust, the familiar surroundings slowly coming into focus. It was strange being here, listening to them spit out their terse instructions when he knew he was legally prohibited from joining in.

Never mind legalities, I couldn't hack it right now.

"Hey, it's Rain Man!" Webber had spotted him. "Back to work so soon?"

Other heads turned and hands motioned him over to the Front Line. He passed J.J. on East Departures, sitting at *that* scope. She fixed him with an icy stare and went back to racking her flight strips. Webber sat behind Lombardi, apparently training Pizza Man on East Arrivals. The warm sound of their voices made Kelly realize he needn't have worried. The doors to the TRACON demarcated a line of death between management and controllers. In here, he'd find strong and unwavering support—except, apparently, from J.J. Webber slapped him on the arm.

"How's it going, buddy?"

"Holding my own."

"What brings you here?"

"The NTSB missed me."

"You didn't say anything stupid, did you?"

"I told them the truth, of course."

"What did they ask about?"

"The Mode C readouts," Rykowski said. "Bosko had the gall to imply that Rain Man misread the scope."

"What kind of shit is that?" Lombardi protested. "I saw it, too."

Kelly hit his head with the palm of a hand. "That's right. I knew there was something I'd forgotten. They didn't find anything unusual on the DARC printout for some reason. Bosko's convinced I lost it. This'll flatten the son of a bitch."

"I'll tell Hawkins when I go on break."

"Thanks. The two guys from the safety board seem to be keeping an open mind, but Hawkins acted real non-committal. Richardson didn't say a word the whole time I was in there."

Rykowski looked at him and Kelly prepared for one of his dime store philosophies. "I could have predicted it. This might be the first midair caused by TCAS. The agency is hardly gonna want to admit that."

Lombardi finished calling an airplane. "Did you read the *Chronicle* this morning? One of their stories mentioned some bad TCAS units that cause coasting and ghosting. Maybe that's what screwed up, Rain Man."

"Maybe. Otherwise, I'd better hope the NTSB stays objective. I don't think they play politics like the FAA. How's Bear?"

Webber shook his head. "Drunk. He's been hitting the bottle pretty hard."

"He'd better sober up because they're giving our names to the press. We'll be on *Hard Copy* soon."

"I'll get some information together on you to hand out when they call," Rykowski said. "This is gonna get ugly."

A wave of helplessness washed over Kelly. Events that he had no control over were unraveling his secure familiar world. He mumbled a few parting words and ambled toward the door, catching Webber look at J.J., then at him. He wondered what she'd told Greg after rushing out of his house yesterday.

✈   ✈   ✈

KELLY SPRAWLED ACROSS HIS SOFA, sipping scotch on the rocks and petting Rudy while he gazed at the TV. When the movie credits rolled, he realized he couldn't remember what the film was about. A vacuous story that took his mind off reality and nothing more. He tapped the remote control to change stations and stumbled onto CNN. Next to the newscaster's head was the all-too-familiar photograph of Coastal's tail beside the bus.

"—*Chronicle* reported today that the government is investigating defective TCAS units made by Circuitron Corporation of Dallas. FAA officials have acknowledged that these anti-collision computers fail to work under certain conditions and create false targets on controllers' radarscopes. The FAA, which requires TCAS on all U.S. airliners, says it plans to order the defective devices removed for repair. TCAS is a major focus in the investigation of last Friday's midair collision over Lake Michigan. A spokesman for Circuitron, one of four companies that makes TCAS units, revealed that its equipment was installed on the Coastal Airlines jet involved in the tragedy. However, he insisted the unit was manufactured more than a year after problems with earlier models were identified and corrected."

Kelly emptied his scotch. So much for that, assuming the company was telling the truth. It was hardly a given these days. He waited, hoping the next story would say investigators had found Coastal's black box. Instead, the newscaster changed topics. Kelly surfed some more and flinched at a report about the crash on a local station.

"—number of deaths has risen to 269." The reporter stood outside a two-story brick Georgian house next to an older woman whose face was stricken with grief. "The Norton family was among them. With me is Mrs. Elizabeth Norton of suburban Park Ridge. Mrs. Norton's son, daughter-in-law, and five-year-old grandson all perished aboard Atlantic Airlines flight 59."

The camera zoomed in on a snapshot Norton held that showed the little boy happily waving a baseball mitt over a birthday cake.

"I can't believe they're gone." Norton said. She paused, overcome by grief. "This picture . . . a few other pictures . . . they're all I have of them now." She choked off a sob. "They were so young. Matt was just a baby. It's not right—kids shouldn't die before you." Her grieving voice swelled with indignation. "I can't understand it. Don't they have ways of making sure air controllers are competent? The system warned the pilots in time, but that one controller told them to ignore it. My family would still be alive if he hadn't interfered." She sobbed again. "Now everyone is dead."

The reporter clutched his microphone and looked seriously into the camera. "Mrs. Norton is referring to TCAS, a computer intended to prevent midair collisions. FAA officials revealed today that one of the controllers disregarded regulations and countermanded avoidance maneuver instructions issued by TCAS to the pilot of Coastal flight 276. The controller, Ryan Kelly, has been placed on leave pending the investigation."

Kelly snapped off the set and fled to the deck outside, his heart pounding in his ears. The magnitude of the tragedy and the swath of life cut down appalled him. A routine climb and a routine descent. They happened thousands of times a day in the skies over Chicago. Until two of them ran together. On his scope.

Do not climb. There's traffic above you.

And now the agency was using his well-intentioned warning to hang him. Of course, that was easier than admitting their sacred system could have failed. Blame the equipment and implications for air safety quickly became expensive.

The shrill jangle of the telephone through the open door to the house jarred his frazzled nerves. It had started ringing off the hook today. He knew who it was. The *Chronicle* reporter kept calling and had been joined by half a dozen more. He had no desire to speak with any of them. Besides, what would he say? The answering machine picked up again.

"How does it feel to be a murderer?"

Kelly jerked around and stared at the machine hanging on the kitchen wall above the counter.

"I know you're there, listening like a coward. You can try to hide, but you can't escape. I'm watching. You made a mistake—a big mistake—and now you're going to have to pay for it." A sinister laugh rippled out onto the deck. "Cowards deserve to die."

Click.

Dial tone blared momentarily from the broken connection and the machine's blinking red light held him in a trance.

NINETEEN
WAKE TURBULENCE

HUNCHED OVER THE CEDAR RAILING of the deck behind his house, Kelly sipped a cup of coffee to the accompaniment of robins chirping in the woods bordering the small backyard. Despite the cool shade—this side of the house faced west so he could enjoy the sky's evening masterpieces—perspiration dampened his skin. He'd tried to dismiss last night's crank call as just a creep playing a sick joke, but apprehension persisted. If the jerk had his phone number, he might know his address.

Gathering his wits after the call, he'd methodically locked all the doors and windows. Then he'd armed the security system, a precaution he usually skipped while at home. He'd installed the system primarily for burglary and fire protection when he was away. Now, as the threatening voice replayed in his mind, the chirping robins that normally sounded so soothing underscored the isolation of his once cozy sanctuary.

Footsteps crunching on gravel from the right startled him. He realized he'd neglected to close the gate at the end of his driveway, though it hardly mattered because anyone could easily climb over the post-and-beam fence surrounding his property. Before he could decide what to do, a short brunette in a khaki shirtwaist dress rounded the corner on the path running alongside the house. She waved and tentatively walked across the deck to him.

"Good morning. I'm Ellen Sanders of the *Chronicle*. Are you Ryan Kelly?" He nodded reluctantly and took the business card she held out. "I rang the doorbell and knocked, but no one answered. Sorry, I wouldn't have barged in here if I'd been able to reach you on the phone. I've been trying for two days."

"It's been ringing constantly with you press people."

The competitive streak in her couldn't resist. "Have you talked to them?"

"I don't have a comment for any of you."

Sanders stepped back to lean an arm on the railing and looked at him casually. "My stories are only as good as my information. I need your help to make them accurate." Her tone was earnest, but understated.

"Anything I said right now would be trite and inconsequential." And twisted against him somehow. He'd read too many stories marred by too many mistakes.

"May I at least quote you on that?"

Her polite perseverance chipped a sliver off his armor of resistance. "Okay, but nothing else," he said warily.

Sanders pulled a reporter's notebook out of her purse and briefly scribbled in it. She regarded the haunted eyes, sad twist of his mouth, and resigned voice, subconsciously filing away details for the article she was determined to write. With his trim physique and handsome face, she could see why Christy was attracted to him. Something told her she'd get her interview, but now was not the time to push too hard. Part of her goal driving all the way out here had been simply to establish personal contact. Some sources took time to develop. Few responded to pressure. They talked because they wanted to or had ulterior motives for answering her questions. Kelly was the key player in a major running story, however, so she decided to make one last attempt.

"My sources keep saying you broke policy. They're practically blaming you for the collision. I'd really like to hear your side, Mr. Kelly. Believe it or not, I can help. Are you sure you won't reconsider?"

"Sorry." She didn't seem as overbearing as other reporters he'd seen on television. Though persistent, she sounded sincere. But his mistrust of journalists ran deep. He watched her tuck the notebook back in her purse. "How did you find me?"

"Your driver's license showed up in an online records search."

He shook his head over that long lost commodity called privacy. "There's no getting away from you people, is there?"

She didn't appear the least bit offended. "If you change your mind, please give me a call. I'm genuinely interested in the truth."

"Okay, but it's an active investigation. Basically, my hands are tied."

"You can phone me day or night," she said with a pleasant smile. "Good bye."

Sanders turned and disappeared around the corner of the house. He gave her a few minutes before strolling to the gate to make sure she'd left and that no one else was there. The two-lane road was reassuringly deserted. He pulled the *Chronicle* out of its blue box and trudged back up the driveway to close the gate, which was electrically controlled from the house or by a device in his car.

The day's headlines screamed at him: "Honeymoon ends tragically," "Black box eludes investigators," "Controller's actions questioned." His name leaped off the page from the last story, tingling his face with a hot flush.

Kelly tossed the paper in the kitchen trash and his stomach growled as a parting comment. He'd eaten little in the past few days, unable to summon an appetite. Now he was ravenous. After finding nothing of interest in the cupboards or fridge, he hesitated, worrying about last night's call. It could have been a prank—or someone deranged might be out there determined to harm him. His stomach growled again and he snatched his car keys off the counter, refusing to become a prisoner in his own home.

At the Jewel in town, he absently dropped groceries in a cart and automatically wheeled up to his favorite checker. He didn't feel like talking and considered moving to a different line, but it was already too late. Rita saw him and grinned.

"Hey, handsome, where have you been hiding? I can only hold out so long, you know, before I shamelessly throw myself at some other stud."

Rita was married, talked constantly about her four kids, and loved to flirt. Kelly always responded in kind, but today he couldn't muster the spirit. "Hi, Rita."

She swept his items past the scanner and cast him a sideways glance. "Pretty awful about that crash, huh?"

He barely nodded.

"That'll be $38.97." She leaned across the counter while he fished several bills out of his wallet. "The news keeps talking about that guy who messed up. Will he lose his job?"

Rita knew Kelly was a controller at O'Hare, but he'd never told her his name. "I don't know."

She took his money. "Well, no offense, but he ought to. I mean—if he did screw up. That's criminal with all those people dead."

Kelly's lips stretched tight while he accepted his change. "I hope you accept food stamps," he said softly. Rita's eyes suddenly widened and she bit her lip sheepishly as he stepped away.

Fucking public. Fucking reporters. They didn't understand all the complications. They couldn't be bothered. It was far easier to blame him. Christ, my own bosses are ready to make me the fall guy. And, deep down, he worried that all of them were right. Despite his brave front at the meeting in Hawkins' office, he agonized over his final call to Coastal, a reflexive move that might have backfired big time. He marched to his car, threw the bag of groceries on the passenger seat, and jammed the gear shift into first. Tires squealed when he rounded a corner too quickly, bearing down on a mother and daughter walking across the parking lot.

Shit!

The two women froze in his path and Kelly stomped on the brake pedal. His Acura screeched to a halt inches from tragedy and stalled. Groceries flew out of the bag and tumbled onto the floor.

The women stared at him for a few stunned seconds and then the mother yelled something he couldn't hear. Mortified, he sank back in the seat as she stormed off, pulling her daughter by the arm. He gripped the steering wheel to stop his hands from shaking and breathed deeply. The sound of a horn snapped him back to reality. Quickly, he started the car and eased out of the lot.

When he crested the hill half a mile down the road from his house, he could see two vans from TV stations parked in front of the gate. Several people milled about and a couple of them shouldered minicams. He slowed at his gate, determined to drive through, but someone dodged in front of the car and forced him to brake. The minicam lenses bored in on his window and a microphone was thrust between them.

"You're Ryan Kelly, aren't you? Will you comment on the crash?"

He inched the car forward. "Sorry, but I have nothing to say."

"How do you feel about the people who died? Are you sorry about that?"

Kelly gripped the steering wheel again and forced himself to stay calm. Don't answer. No matter what you say, it'll come out wrong. With supreme effort, he kept his voice under control. "I have no comment. Please let me through to my own home."

"Has the FAA said anything to you about keeping your job?"

"Why didn't you follow the rules?"

"Do you feel responsible for killing all those people?"

Bastards.

He kept his foot on the gas and the person standing in the driveway finally jumped aside. Okay, now just close the gate so they can't follow. He pressed the device on his visor. Blinking back tears, he watched the wooden gate swing shut in the rearview mirror.

✈   ✈   ✈

KELLY BUTTONED HIS SPORT COAT and nervously felt his tie before opening the heavy wooden door to Saint James Lutheran Church along West Foster on Chicago's Northwest Side. He cautiously walked inside and mumbled thanks to a polite man in a black suit who handed him a printed program.

Six days after the midair, Kelly still hadn't worked up the courage to call Christy, but he felt obligated to pay his respects at this memorial for Carla and Kevin Szemasko. He'd spotted the notice in the previous morning's *Chronicle*. Slowly pacing up the main aisle, he saw firefighters dressed in black and gold uniforms sitting bolt upright along two rows of pews. Another three dozen or so mourners were spread out around them, speaking softly, some dabbing tissues to their eyes. Melancholy organ music filtered through the nave. Kelly eased onto one of the hard wooden benches several rows behind everyone, and picked out Christy and Jason sitting in front. Two older couples he guessed were parents huddled next to them.

A pastor stepped behind the pulpit and the organ dwindled into silence. In a gentle measured cadence, he spoke eloquently of life's unfairness and the premature passing of a vibrant young couple. Christy took his place when he was done. She looked elegant in her black wraparound dress and he realized how much he longed to take her in his arms.

"One of Carla's greatest gifts was the zest for life she shared with those around her," she said in a trembling voice. "You were never just her sister or friend. Instead, you were an accomplice giggling through her latest adventure."

Kelly was too distracted to pay attention. He groaned inwardly over the pain etched in her beautiful face and his heart ached with guilt every time she paused to fight back a sob. He glanced at the mourners, many of whom had bowed their heads in sadness and reflection. Jason put an arm around one of the elderly women in front who was shaking spasmodically. Kelly slunk down in the pew, feeling like an intruder on the grief all around him. He hoped Christy wouldn't see him, fearful of her reaction. But when she paused again and gazed across the audience, her eyes met his and she nodded in acknowledgement.

"Carla always made it fun when you were with her. I'll forever miss her *joie de vivre.*"

Christy walked slowly back to her seat and received a consoling hug from Jason. Several firefighters paid their respects to Kevin and then the pastor returned for a final prayer. It was a simple service that moved Kelly. Poignant words from family and friends about two innocent victims with so much promise. He imagined the hundred other memorials that had been held across the city in the past few days and his mind reeled over all the shattered lives.

When everyone began filing out of the church, Christy maneuvered toward him through the crowd. He stood hesitantly, not ready for the moment of reckoning he'd been dreading.

"It was nice of you to come. I didn't expect to see you here." Her tone was cool.

"I'm very sorry about your sister—your family." It sounded so inadequate, but how else to express his remorse?

"You had it right in the paper. Anything you said right now would be trite and inconsequential." He winced. "I'm trying to keep an open mind, Ryan, but it sounds like you screwed up. All I've heard is that you disregarded protocol."

"Don't believe everything you read. Your friends haven't been doing me any favors with their incomplete and unsubstantiated stories."

She crossed her arms. "You were pulled off the scopes. They wouldn't do that if—"

"It's standard procedure, whether I screwed up or not."

"Then what really happened? If you have nothing to hide, then why won't you comment?" Her cobalt eyes blazed. "You sounded guilty as hell on the news."

"Why should I comment when I have no assurance you'll get it right?"

"We can't get it right unless you talk to us!"

"I don't trust you people!"

He glanced around to see if anyone was watching them and noticed a heavyset man looking in their direction. Maybe coming here wasn't such a good idea. He breathed deeply to regain his composure. "Your paper in particular doesn't have a great track record. Remember the beacon story?"

"Of course I do. You called me up to bitch about it." Her face softened. "That's how we met. Remember?"

He thought about the first time he saw Christy and yearned again to hug her. To somehow undo everything.

"I—I'm sorry. Whether you believe me or not, I didn't do anything wrong. At least I hope I didn't. When the computer told Coastal's pilot to climb, I broke a rule by warning him he was heading into the other plane. That's all. I had a moral obligation. TCAS was running them together." He looked at the ground, then off into space, anywhere but at those piercing blue eyes. "The pilot may have listened to me and ignored the computer. Or he may have followed the computer and ignored me. One of us told him wrong."

"How can you be so sure about all this? I thought these accidents take time to solve."

"It's gonna turn out to be me or TCAS. I don't think it was me because I saw the scope flip out. Besides, pilots love the computer. People trust machines. They don't trust each other anymore." His voice drifted lower and he began mumbling to himself. " . . . other things . . . the radio. I could have climbed Coastal sooner if it hadn't gone out . . . I could have climbed him to six thousand right away instead of five."

Christy shook her head impatiently and frowned. "What are you talking about?"

"Little things, that's all. They might have made a difference. Put Coastal somewhere else when it happened."

"What things?"

He shrugged. They were nuances he didn't have the energy to explain right now. An awkward silence settled over them.

The heavyset man in the tweed jacket broke away from the crowd. Christy saw him approaching and held out an arm. "This is Don Szemasko, my brother-in-law. Don, this is Ryan Kelly."

They politely clasped hands.

"Do you work at the paper?" Szemasko asked.

"No. . . . I'm an air traffic controller," he said quietly.

Szemasko dropped his hand and motioned at the mourners. "My brother was a respected firefighter. A lot of his crew would be upset if they knew you were here." His expression hardened. "Are you the one I heard about on the news? The one who fucked up?"

Definitely not a good idea being here. He resisted an urge to run. "I'm the controller, but I take issue with some of the reports."

"They say you interfered. You killed all those people!"

Kelly's neck reddened. "Look, I was just doing my job."

"You lying son of a bitch!" Szemasko loomed closer, ready to throw a punch, but Christy placed a hand on his chest.

"Don't start."

"I'm not starting anything. He's got a lot of nerve coming here."

"I came to pay my respects," Kelly said evenly.

Szemasko moved to take another step, but Christy pressed her hand harder against his chest. "I don't want a scene here. So stop it, right now! Do you think Kevin would want this?"

Szemasko glared at Kelly, breathing heavily and taking his measure. "I'll see you in court, asshole," he said finally and stalked off.

"Mom, we're waiting for you." Jason's summons drifted across the pews. He was shuffling next to the two elderly couples.

Christy waved a hand and turned back to Kelly. "Sorry about Don. He doesn't have much class." She wrapped her arms across her chest and looked down, tracing the tip of one shoe back and forth across the wooden floor. "I don't know whether to believe you or not, Ryan. What I do know is that two people I loved are dead. Someone's responsible for that and you're not saying much." Her eyes glistened with tears. "Thanks for paying your respects."

Before he could respond, she strode away.

✈   ✈   ✈

THE CHURCH WAS NEAR BEAR'S APARTMENT in Franklin Park. Still queasy from the emotional scene at the memorial service, Kelly decided on impulse to visit him. They'd talked by phone several times since last Friday, but hadn't seen each other. And right now, Kelly figured both of them could use the companionship of a friend.

As traffic crawled south through the lights along Harlem Avenue, he opened the sliding glass moon-roof. In contrast to the hot noon sun blazing into the car, a song with an ominous beat pulsed from the radio. At the next red light, hairs on the back of his neck stirred. He studied the rearview mirror. Was that second crank phone call the other day making him paranoid or was he being followed? It was impossible to tell in this traffic.

He turned right on Belmont, drove another three miles, and pulled up in front of a red brick six-flat set back from the street behind a shallow manicured lawn and perfectly trimmed, waist-high hedges. He walked along the sidewalk to the entrance and scouted the neighborhood. Everything seemed normal. He didn't see any suspicious vehicles and shook off his unease. The music must have sent his imagination into overdrive. He climbed to the second floor and knocked on one of the doors. Bear appeared, looking haggard and unshaven. Deep circles rimmed his eyes. One was puffy and bruised.

Kelly laughed. "Is the other guy better or worse off?"

Bear gingerly touched a finger to his swollen eyelid. "I was minding my own business having a beer at Charlie's. Then the news comes on and this prick sitting next to me starts blaming controllers for all the flight delays. I couldn't make the dumb ass understand we don't schedule the traffic—the airlines do. It was a fair exchange of blows, I'd say."

"You're making this harder than it already is, Bear."

"Yeah, I know. It was a stupid thing to do, but I'm tired of getting dumped on. You'd like to come in, I suppose?"

"Unless you've got a woman stashed in there."

"I wish. Excuse the lack of furnishings, but I just moved in a few weeks ago and Donna's got most of our stuff."

The apartment was depressingly sparse. A small television was perched atop a box in the living room in front of a solitary lawn chair and a desk lamp on the floor. In the kitchen there was a cheap table and two vinyl chairs. Kelly peeked out the window above the sink and saw Bear's black Corvette in the parking lot below.

"You want a beer?"

Bear stood by the open refrigerator door and Kelly noted the standard bachelor fare: two six packs, carry-out boxes of leftover Chinese food, and a few jars of condiments whose contents would be congealed solid if his friend hadn't moved in only recently. He didn't feel like drinking, but he wanted to break the ice.

"Sure."

The Budweiser was tasteless but cold. As they sat down at the table, Bear scooped up a stack of unopened mail and threw it on the counter. Then he guzzled half his beer in several long swallows.

"The guy at the bar sent me over the edge, that's all. Have you been following the shit they're saying about us?"

"The usual half-truths and sensationalism. Several reporters came to my house."

"I suppose the only reason they haven't bothered me yet is that few people know I live here."

"Gotten any crank calls?"

"No." Bear looked sideways at him. "Have you?"

"Last Sunday and another on Tuesday."

"Jesus, that's nuts. You called the police?"

"What would they do?"

Bear nodded and finished his beer. Without getting up, he reached to the fridge and snared another one.

"The news is sure worked up about your last radio call to Coastal. Yesterday, some TV dickhead made a big deal about me being on sick leave just before the accident, as if that had anything to do with it. I took two weeks off trying to fix things with Donna and they make it sound like I'm a mental case. If the FAA can't pin it on the pilots, you can bet your balls they're gonna come after you and me."

"I think you're right."

"Of course I am. I'm old and therefore wise. Did you go back and tell them Pizza Man saw the Mode C jumping around, too?"

"Lombardi did."

"What'd they say?" He looked at Kelly knowingly, anticipating the answer.

"The NTSB guys are holding out for empirical corroboration. I'm hoping it shows up on the black box."

Bear pulled out a Marlboro and lit it, jabbing the tip across the table. "Hope like hell, my friend, because the NTSB lives by empirical evidence. If they don't find it, Hawkins is gonna figure you're crazy or making it up to hide something. Either way, your career is trashed. He'll figure out a way to take me down, too."

"The union wouldn't let them get away with it."

"It would be an interesting fight to watch, but NATCA would lose. Oh, I'm a proud member and I know about all the good things they do, but I also know they have their limits. There's too much riding on this. No way the agency is gonna admit its billion-dollar baby is flawed. They'd much rather blame us."

"Even if they let me come back, I'm not so sure I could hack it anymore."

"Time heals a lot of wounds. I'm sure you'd do fine. Just don't hold your breath waiting for the chance."

Kelly nodded, furrowing his brow in thought and sipping beer. "There's something I want to run by you. Something I've been thinking about."

"I've got lots of time to listen."

Kelly hesitated, wrestling with a sense of foolishness. He toyed with his beer bottle and took another sip. "Well, it's been almost a week, you know, since the crash and they still haven't found Coastal's flight recorder."

"It'll turn up."

"You'd think it would have by now."

Bear shrugged.

"So I got to thinking. The box might have gotten ripped from the tail during the midair and fallen into the lake."

"I suppose. But if it did, the salvage people should have picked up the pinger signal by now. Those boxes are built to withstand that kind of impact into water."

"Yeah, unless . . . " Kelly hesitated again. "I know this is gonna sound weird, but did you see that interview on TV with the guy on the boat?"

Bear laughed, amused by the macabre irony. "Yeah. Poor schmuck's out sailing with his babe and all of a sudden they're at ground zero of a plane crash. That's what I call being in the wrong place at the wrong time."

"Did you notice anything unusual about the interview?"

"No."

"I've been running it over in my head a lot and there was a point when the woman said something. I couldn't hear it, but I caught a look." Kelly stared at his beer bottle, fearful of the reaction he expected. "It's just a hunch, but I think the guy's dirty. I bet he took some pieces of wreckage and it's possible he's got the black box."

Bear grunted and reached into the fridge again. "Sounds to me like you're grasping at straws, Rain Man."

Kelly's eyes pleaded for affirmation, even a token acknowledgement that he could be right. "I know it's a stretch, but that box is proof I'm telling the truth. It's gotta be found."

Bear lit another cigarette and smoked it, looking at Kelly impassively and considering the possibilities. With a long sigh, he said finally, "Okay, for the sake of an interesting discussion, let's say your guy does have the box. I know there's some sick fucks out there who like to scam that stuff as souvenirs. Let's say it dropped near his boat and he scooped it out of the water. Had to have happened like that because if the box hit the deck it would have punched a hole right through the boat. I'm willing to be charitable and agree that your scenario is conceivable. Now what? You don't even know who he is."

"Yeah, I do." Kelly thought back to the interview, closing his eyes and picturing the TV screen with the man's name printed across the bottom. "Larry . . . Lunt? No, Lundgren. Or Lundstrom. Something like that. They said he was a car dealer. Not a salesman, but a dealer. Like he owns the place. You got a phone book? Preferably the Yellow Pages."

With a snort, Bear opened a cabinet, pulled out the hefty directory, and tossed it on the table with a thud. "You're on a wild goose chase, my friend."

Kelly ignored him and flipped through the pages, running a finger down the listings for auto dealers. He suddenly stopped and poked excitedly at the book, beaming at Bear in vindication.

"Here he is! Lindstrand Motors. Sixty-five hundred North Western. He's right in the city."

"Uh, huh. Great. So now that you know his name, what's your next move, Sherlock? If you go to the cops, they'll say they can't do anything. No probable cause."

Kelly sat back in the chair, his face turning glum. "Yeah, I'd considered that. I don't know what to do."

"Nothing, if you're smart. Tell anyone else what you just told me and they'll think you're crazy. I'm the one who's supposed to play that part in our little duet."

The telephone rang and Bear grabbed the receiver off the counter. "Yeah." He swigged his beer and listened. Then his face darkened and he gripped the bottle so hard the veins on his forearm stood out. "Donna, I don't give a goddamn what you say to the press. If you think you can threaten me, then you're the one with the serious mental health problem who needs attention."

He slammed the receiver back on the phone and studied the smoke curling from his cigarette until it burned down to the filter. Kelly said nothing, waiting for him to explain.

"My not-soon-enough ex-wife thinks she can get a bigger property settlement by threatening to tell reporters we're divorcing because I'm whacked out in the head. Donna knows this would come at a rather inconvenient time, so the bitch figures she's got me by the balls."

He used his thumb to flick one of the bottle caps on the table into a wastebasket against the far wall. The shot went wide and the cap clattered onto the floor.

Twenty
Black Box

FREDERIC ESTERHAUS STOOD NEAR A TAXIWAY at Meigs Field along the lakefront, arms folded across his stocky chest and his hair rippling in a stiff breeze. A large yellow crane near the shore occupied his attention. Smoke belched from an exhaust pipe when the crane hoisted thick metal chains tethered to a jagged section of fuselage. He counted seven windows along the dented aluminum fragment, eerily vacant now but once the vantage for terrified passengers witnessing their plunge into the abyss. As the crane lifted the scrap from an offshore barge and swiveled toward a long flatbed truck, the wind surged and several blue letters of the airline's name twisted into view. Workers standing on the truck reached out to steady the piece of wreckage before it was carefully lowered and laid flat.

Esterhaus pursed his lips, impatient with the tedious pace of recovering the Atlantic Airlines Boeing 727. Two miles offshore, he could see a flotilla of Navy and Coast Guard cutters that had dropped anchor a day after the collision. During the past week, divers repeatedly slipped thirty to forty feet beneath the surface of the cold water, hovering inches above the bottom while casting their flashlights across the murky lakebed. Scattered amid the broken bottles, rusted tin cans, and other detritus from mankind were thousands of metal and plastic remnants from the jet, along with hands, limbs, torsos, and skulls. Some of the human remains were grotesquely disfigured or burned. Others were unscathed except for their bluish-white skin tone.

Divers scooped them all into nylon bags and hauled them to the surface, where they were logged and taken to the Cook County Morgue. The plane wreckage was transferred from the barge to trucks that drove to Midway Airport. In a hangar along the West Ramp, investigators painstakingly labored to reconstruct the pieces into the airliner they once belonged to.

Esterhaus took only partial comfort in knowing that progress was proceeding much faster on the Coastal Airlines Boeing 757. The wreckage had been moved from the intersection of 55th Street and Central Avenue to a second hangar at Midway. Its cockpit voice recorder was found three days after the crash and sent to the NTSB lab in Washington, D.C. The day before, divers retrieved Atlantic's flight data recorder from the lake and investigators shipped it along, too. The inability to locate Coastal's flight recorder, however, had bedeviled everyone involved.

Esterhaus noticed a car approaching. He saw Scott Carter behind the wheel and his spirits lifted with the possibility of good news. The electronics expert rolled to a stop next to him and stepped out of the rented gray sedan, the wind whipping his wild red hair into a frenzy.

"Tell me what I want to hear, Scotty."

"You aren't going to like this, but we still can't find the friggin' black box," Carter said. He leaned against the front hood, observing the crane swing back and forth between barge and truck. "I can't imagine how we've missed it. We've triple-checked the dump truck that ran into the tail and keep picking through other rubble at the site."

"It's conceivable the force of impact ripped it from its mounting and threw it into the fire at the tavern. When the truck broke open the tail and the plane suddenly decelerated, that's the logical place it would have gotten tossed. But those boxes can survive hell."

"Doesn't it figure? The one that's missing crashed on land."

Esterhaus nodded. Every flight recorder contained a pinger encased in a cylinder bolted to the front of the box. Workers often used the cylinder as a carrying handle when removing the box for maintenance. The pinger emitted a low audible tone, but only when immersed in water. Brushing his hair back, he said, "We need that box to answer at least two key questions—whether the pilot responded to TCAS or the controller and what altitude readings his Mode C was transmitting."

"Do you suppose someone walked off with it?"

"Unlikely. We've had the area well-secured."

"Well, it's driving me nuts. Have you been watching the news? They're serving up the controllers at the stake."

"I know, damn it!" Esterhaus pounded the hood of the car. "The sooner we find that box the better."

"By the way, the lab in Washington called me an hour ago. They time-matched the DARC printout to the TRACON audio tape as best they could. But they still can't really tell whether Captain McKenzie followed TCAS properly."

Technicians compared the DARC's profile of the flight—showing speed, bearing, and altitude—with the audio tape containing dialogue between Kelly and Coastal's copilot, Jerry Pearson. Unfortunately, the tape wasn't linked to a clock like the DARC. That made it nearly impossible to coordinate the two records closer than several seconds because the technicians had to estimate the time lag between Kelly's instructions and McKenzie's response. Only with information from the flight data recorder could they know exactly what happened when.

A wireless phone chirped and they both reached inside their sport jackets. The call was for Esterhaus.

"Hi, this is Doctor Conrad at Christ Community Hospital."

"Good morning, Doctor."

"Mr. Esterhaus, you asked me to advise you if there was a change in the pilot's condition. I regret to say that Captain McKenzie died a little while ago—at nine-twenty, to be exact. As you know, he had a serious concussion. A blood vessel burst and he suffered massive hemorrhaging."

Esterhaus groaned. Pearson hadn't survived either. "I'm sorry to hear that, Doctor. Thank you for letting me know."

He hung up and told Carter the news while he fished a cigarette and lighter out of his pocket. "Now we need that box more than ever. Washington's been getting a lot of heat from the FAA. They're panicked because of the TCAS issue."

Carter tented his hands around the flickering flame of the lighter until the cigarette tip finally glowed. "I've been thinking about Kelly's statement. TCAS gets its altitude information from Mode C. I know there's a redundant system to verify that info, but what if it wasn't working? In that case, Coastal's Mode C could have given TCAS bad altitudes and told McKenzie to fly right into Atlantic 59."

"An interesting theory, Scotty." Esterhaus put a foot up on the bumper of the car and contemplated it. "But you're forgetting that in a coordinated maneuver the two TCAS units are talking to each other constantly. Atlantic would have caught the error. Besides, we'd have seen it on the DARC."

"It wouldn't take much with a closing speed of five hundred knots or so. Just a few seconds at a critical time and—wham—they're toast."

Esterhaus held up his cigarette and watched the ash blow away. "I'm not convinced the Mode C was jumping around," he said tentatively. "My guess is the pilot reacted to Kelly's warning instead of following TCAS. If I were him, I'd be nervous about deviating too much with all that traffic around me. Kelly said he saw only one fluctuation. I bet he's just confused."

"Another controller saw it, too."

"Yeah." He took his foot off the bumper and kicked a piece of gravel on the service road into the grass. "He might just be protecting a colleague. He's trying to certify in the TRACON, you know. This would buy him a lot of support from guys on the line. I'm afraid I don't consider him an unbiased witness."

His phone chirped again and he pulled it out of his pocket. "Esterhaus here."

"Good morning, this is Ryan Kelly."

"Hello, Mr. Kelly. How are you?" Esterhaus traded glances with Carter.

"Oh, slowly going insane. I wanted to ask about Coastal's black box."

"What a coincidence. Mr. Carter and I were just discussing it."

"You mean you've found it?"

"I'm afraid not. And I can tell you that we're just as anxious to locate it as I'm sure you are."

"Well, I figured I'd hear about it on the news, but I wanted to check. Sorry to bother you."

"Not at all. Is there anything else?"

"Nope, but thanks." He paused for a second. "Good bye."

"Call me anytime. Good day, sir."

The chief investigator tucked the phone back in his pocket and glanced at Carter, who nodded with understanding. Turning toward the distant skyline of the Loop, past the Field Museum and beyond Grant Park's broad expanse, Esterhaus picked out the imposing terra-cotta façade of the Hilton hotel along Michigan Avenue. The Go Team would stay there for a few more days until they wrapped up their initial probe and flew back to Washington. Several of them would return in a month or two, most likely to the same hotel, for public hearings on the accident. They needed to know a lot more before then.

Scattered clouds glided across the turbulent sky, and he watched them as if they could impart some wisdom about what happened up there last Friday. Every investigation followed the same pattern, yet each one presented its own peculiarities and unique obstacles. Each one challenged him to be open-minded and resist passing up a particular path of inquiry because of manpower limitations, prejudice, outside influences, or any of a hundred other factors. But the path to resolution was necessarily paved with all available information. He turned back to Carter, his voice insistent.

"Keep looking for that box, Scotty. It's the only way we'll get our answers now."

✈   ✈   ✈

KELLY HUNG UP THE PHONE and paced in his kitchen. He was stir crazy from sitting helplessly on the sidelines. For the past week, he'd seldom slept for more than a few hours at a time and ate only sporadically. Now, the urge to take control gripped him like gnawing hunger pangs. Despite Bear's skepticism, Kelly clung to the hope that the car dealer would prove to be his salvation. But he agreed with Bear about the police. They weren't likely to question Lindstrand or search his house based on the word of someone widely regarded as the chief culprit in the midair. He was in danger of losing his job and reputation, and therefore someone who could be characterized as desperate. If Lindstrand had, indeed, stolen some wreckage, Kelly would have to ferret him out alone.

He thought about his plan. At first, the idea appeared to be nothing more than a far-fetched heroic fantasy. But the more he considered it, the less crazy it seemed. In the end, he decided there was nothing to lose.

He consulted the Yellow Pages again to confirm the address of the dealership and jotted the phone number on a slip of paper. With Rudy following, he ran upstairs to his bedroom, rummaged through the closet, and pulled out a small pair of binoculars and a camera. He grabbed his wallet from the armoire, plucked a wireless phone from its recharging unit, and then stood still for a moment, considering what else he might need. The plan's simplicity was stark, even naïve were he pressed to admit it. Nothing else came to mind. Back downstairs, he poured cat chow in Rudy's bowl to overflowing, armed the security system, and strode through the connecting door to the garage.

The drive to the dealership in Rogers Park on Chicago's North Side took nearly an hour and a half. After an effortless run into the city via the tollway, Kelly exited the Kennedy Expressway at Nagle, headed north to Devon, then slogged his way east through the Edgebrook business district and a collection of stately homes in Lincolnwood. He turned left onto Western and pulled over one block later beside a tall wrought iron fence that bordered Warren State Park.

Lindstrand Motors stood across the street, a one-story, brown brick structure that covered most of the block. A blue sign above the long showroom window identified the dealership. Several vehicles were parked inside at odd angles, partially obscured by large white painted letters on the window trumpeting a sale. Lindstrand specialized in used foreign models. Kelly picked out a sporty MG convertible, low-slung Jaguar XKE, and a Mercedes coupe. At the south end of the building, directly across the street from him, a chain-link fence surrounded a lot filled with more cars.

He slumped in his seat and slowly scanned the showroom through the binoculars. At the far end, a salesman sitting behind a desk held a document in front of a middle-aged couple, his pen dancing across the paper as if he were explaining its terms. At this end, another man stood talking with a blonde woman seated at a reception desk. A service window and three glassed-in offices lined the rear of the showroom. A third man speaking into a telephone occupied the largest of the cubicles. Was that Lindstrand? Kelly couldn't tell. The man's face was hidden by one of the letters on the window outside.

The man hung up the phone, then stood and stretched. He reached behind his office door and retrieved a suit coat, slipping it on while sauntering into the showroom. The man who'd been talking with the blonde drifted away and she smiled at the newcomer when he approached. They exchanged a few words, then she stood and the two went out a side door into the fenced lot. Kelly could see them more clearly in the bright glare of the midday sun and he adjusted the focus of his binoculars.

Lindstrand was taller than Kelly would have guessed from the interview on TV. The camera had held him in a tight head and shoulders shot. And unlike the other day when he was dressed casually, today he wore a gray pinstripe suit. But it was definitely him. Kelly remembered the curly brown hair, narrow eyes, and slightly crooked smile. The blonde looked familiar, too, in her ivory silk blouse and short black skirt.

He slumped further in the seat to minimize his risk of being seen as they passed through a large gate that opened onto the street and strolled north along the sidewalk in front of the dealership. He sat up again and was about to pull into traffic and follow when he saw them enter a small Italian restaurant in the next block.

Satisfied that his quarry would be occupied for an hour or so, Kelly pulled away from the curb to check out the rest of the dealership. He turned left at the corner onto Albion, then left again into an alley behind the building. On the other side of the alley were a couple of three-story brick tenements, one facing north onto Albion and the other facing south onto the next street. Another alley that separated the rear of the apartment buildings formed a T intersection near the fenced car lot. Wooden porches and stairs covered in dirty, peeling white paint hung off the back of each tenement. Kelly idled past the single door on the back side of the dealership and noted that the only access to the fenced lot was through the gate in front.

He swung around onto Western and parked in between several other cars near the north end of the showroom. After checking his line of sight through the rear window to make sure he could still see Lindstrand's office, he sank down in the seat once more. With nothing to do but wait, he had plenty of time for reflection. Shaking his head sheepishly, he hoped his gambit wouldn't be a foolish waste of time. He was trained as an air traffic controller, not some detective savvy in the art of stakeouts. Chiding himself that he had no business being here, another part of him argued that at least he wasn't just hitting the bottle and indulging in self-pity.

Shortly after one, Lindstrand and the blonde emerged from the Italian place and walked back to the showroom. Kelly gave them a few minutes to get situated and summoned his nerve. Taking a deep breath, he powered up his phone and dialed the number on the slip of paper he pulled from his pocket. He twisted around in the seat and aimed the binoculars through the rear window again. Peering through them, he had a clear view of the receptionist and Lindstrand, sitting in his office behind her. The phone rang twice before her perky voice came on the line.

"Lindstrand Motors, this is Cindy. How may I help you?"

"Get me Larry."

"Who's calling, please?"

"Just tell him it's personal."

"One moment, sir."

He heard a click and saw Lindstrand reach for the phone on his desk. Several seconds later, the line clicked again.

"This is Larry Lindstrand. Who am I talking to?"

Kelly lowered his voice. "Someone who has an interest in airplanes—like yourself." He kept his eyes glued to the binoculars, on the alert for any visual cues that Lindstrand might offer.

"I'm not sure I understand. We sell cars here."

"Forget the cars. I know you deal in plane wreckage, too."

Lindstrand stood and closed the door to his office. Kelly watched closely, his heart beating faster. He was winging it now, waiting to see how Lindstrand reacted. If he admitted he had anything from the crash, Kelly could pretend he wanted to buy it. Otherwise, he'd have to bluff him with the threat of exposure.

"I'm still not following you."

The guy was playing it cool, but Kelly surmised he wouldn't have closed his office door if he had nothing to hide. "Don't be coy. I know you've got some stuff from the plane that dropped in the lake last week."

Lindstrand perched on the edge of his desk, smoothing the hair on the back of his head. At length, he said warily, "I don't know what you're talking about."

He moved to hang up the phone and Kelly barked, "I know you stole some wreckage, you fucking maggot." Lindstrand froze. "Turn it in to the police or I'll make sure they check out your house. I know where you live and I'll be watching—"

Lindstrand slammed down the receiver, and Kelly saw Cindy turn her head toward his office. Lindstrand eased onto the chair, running a hand through his hair again.

Kelly sighed with satisfaction. So far so good. He felt certain that Lindstrand was dirty. He'd just have to keep a close watch now and hope the car dealer would lead him to the booty. Kelly figured that Lindstrand wouldn't dare contact the authorities for fear of incriminating himself. More likely, if the call had truly shaken him, he'd simply ditch the stuff somewhere. Which was fine, so long as Kelly got his hands on it.

Lindstrand emerged from his office a few minutes later, apparently having regained his composure. Kelly observed him chat casually with Cindy and the two salesmen. Then he went back into his office and used the phone again to make several calls. Kelly longed to hear the conversations, praying that he wasn't telling an accomplice to get rid of the wreckage.

The afternoon dragged interminably. His spirits slowly faded as he imagined a variety of dead-end scenarios. Lindstrand might simply decide to ignore the call. He could have stashed the wreckage in a storage locker somewhere, content to leave it there for weeks, even months. Perhaps he'd already sold it to another scavenger. And Kelly couldn't dog Lindstrand forever. Once he ended surveillance, even temporarily, the dealer could act with impunity.

Shadows gradually sloped farther across the street and Kelly grew stiff from his contorted position. Staring through the binoculars made his eyes tired and he rubbed them repeatedly. Wearily, he realized the absurdity of his actions. A wild goose chase, indeed. He'd succumbed to the tension of the past week and deluded himself into believing that Lindstrand was somehow involved, a notion that seemed ridiculous now.

Traffic along Western steadily increased, signaling the evening rush hour. He was massaging a painful spasm in his neck when Cindy walked out of the showroom. During a momentary gap between vehicles, she scurried across the four lanes. With growing concern, he watched her approach his car. He turned around to face forward and followed her short black skirt as it loomed in his side view mirror. Suddenly, she stopped and unlocked the door of the car parked behind him. Across the street, the lighted sign above the showroom window blinked off. Kelly consulted his watch and saw that it was six o'clock.

Switching to his rearview mirror, he watched Cindy glance backward to check the traffic as her car lurched forward. His Acura rocked and he heard a thud, followed by the tinkling sound of breaking glass. Cindy said something and got out of her car, slamming the door.

Kelly cringed, realizing he'd have to talk with her but concerned that she might recognize him. Every time the TV stations broadcast a story about the crash, they flashed his personnel picture released by the agency. The *Chronicle* had published it in several editions, too. He grabbed his sunglasses off the dashboard and slipped them on. Fearful of what might happen next yet grateful for the chance to stretch his aching body, he stepped onto the street.

"I'm so sorry. I thought I had enough room to get by." Cindy wrung her hands and inspected the damage. "It's not too bad."

Kelly nodded. Her green Ford Escort was angled partway into the street. The bumper had ridden over his and the right edge had smashed his left taillight.

Cindy paced back and forth. "Oh geez, now my insurance company's gonna cancel me. I just had an accident last year."

Kelly noticed the two salesmen standing outside the dealership, watching them. Where was Lindstrand? Cindy's dimpled face clouded, recognition dawning.

"Say, don't I know you?"

The salesmen assessed the traffic, looking as if they would cross the street at the next break. Kelly shuffled nervously. *Christ, this is unraveling in a hurry.* He kept one eye on the dealership and said charitably, "You're right. The damage is minor. Let's just forget about it"

"That's really nice of you, mister." Cindy perked up, still trying to connect his face with a name, then glanced at the broken taillight. "Are you sure?"

The salesmen stepped off the curb.

Kelly smiled broadly and waved a hand. "No big deal. It's the perils of parking in the city."

"Well, you're saving me a big headache. Thanks again." She batted her eyes. "Have a nice day."

The salesmen paused when they saw Cindy get in her car and pull away, the right rear tire crunching over shards of glass on the street. Kelly scrambled back into his car, contemplating the next move. In his peripheral vision, he could see the salesmen still standing on the sidewalk. If he didn't drive away, they'd wonder what he was doing. They might even come over to inquire. He wiped the perspiration off his brow with the back of a hand. A few seconds later, he saw them head for separate cars parked in the fenced lot.

Kelly sighed again and grabbed the binoculars, frantically searching for Lindstrand. The showroom was dark now. Damn it! The twit helped him escape. He watched the salesmen leave the lot and merge into traffic. With a growing sense of futility, he kept scanning the empty showroom. Then he noticed another car moving in the lot. It stopped and Lindstrand got out, disappearing from view next to the building.

There he is. But what the hell is he doing?

Kelly turned on the ignition, swore impatiently at a few passing cars, then sped down the street. He squealed onto Albion, turned his Acura around, and parked facing Western.

Snatching his binoculars and camera off the passenger seat, he sprinted down the alley and crouched near the bottom of the wooden stairs behind one of the apartment buildings. While catching his breath, he spotted Lindstrand placing something inside the open trunk of the silver Mercedes coupe that he'd just moved. Lindstrand straightened and turned to the open trunk of a red BMW parked nearby. Moving quickly, he lifted a scrap of metal and transferred it to the Mercedes. Kelly's heart leaped.

The stuff was here all the time!

He peered through the camera viewfinder and memorized the license plate on the Mercedes. Looking at the plate on the Beemer, which read "Larry1," Kelly realized that Lindstrand was removing the wreckage from his own car.

"Hey, what are you doing?"

The voice from above startled him. He looked up to see a big-bellied man in a white T-shirt and baggy plaid pants leaning over the second story porch of the apartment building across the alley. Kelly smiled inanely and put a finger to his lips. Lindstrand was moving another piece of wreckage and hadn't heard the tenant. Kelly raised his camera and pressed the shutter release, but nothing incriminating appeared in the shot.

"I said what the hell are you doing down there? I'm calling the police!"

This time Lindstrand jerked his head up. He searched for a moment and then saw the man on the porch. Hurriedly, he slammed the trunks of both cars and jumped into the Mercedes. Kelly heard the engine crank up over more shouts from the tenant. He grabbed the wooden banister to haul himself up and dashed down the alley toward his car. He dropped the keys while opening the door and scraped his knuckles scooping them up. Throwing the binoculars and camera on the passenger seat, he started his car and pulled forward to the intersection just in time to see the silver Mercedes turn out of the lot and head south.

Kelly jammed the gas pedal down and darted onto Western in front of an approaching bus, its driver leaning angrily on his horn. He craned his head from side to side, trying to pick out the Mercedes. Several blocks ahead at the traffic light for Peterson, he saw it peel off to the right. Kelly whizzed past several slow-moving vehicles on the right and turned at the intersection from the left lane, provoking more honks.

With the silver coupe in sight several cars ahead, he licked the blood off his skinned knuckles and wiped the sweat from his brow. Traffic flowed steadily along Peterson, making it easier to follow the Mercedes. But Lindstrand crossed Pulaski on the yellow and by the time Kelly sailed through the intersection the signal had changed to red. Moments later, patrol car lights flashed in his rearview mirror.

Fuck!

Kelly briefly considered not stopping, but he knew that would only aggravate matters. This wasn't some Hollywood action movie. He pulled over in front of several stores near Cicero and pounded the steering wheel as the Mercedes proceeded through the lights. While he watched the car angle onto the northbound ramp for the Edens Expressway, a policeman appeared beside his window. His black leather belt bristled with a billy club, service revolver, and shiny silver handcuffs. Kelly pressed a button to open the window.

"May I see your driver's license and vehicle registration, sir?"

Kelly looked up dejectedly at the impassive face, knowing it was useless. "Officer, I'm following a guy who stole some wreckage from the plane that crashed in the lake last week. I'm . . . involved in the investigation and he's getting away."

"You ran a red light back there, sir." The policeman curled his fingers impatiently. "Just give me your license and registration."

Kelly fumbled with his wallet and handed over the documents. "I have his plate number," he pleaded. "Could you at least get on your radio and have him stopped?"

"Turn off your engine and relax, sir. This won't take long. By the way, did you know your left taillight is broken? I'll have to cite you for that, too."

Kelly leaned back against the headrest in despair. Then a thought occurred to him. He powered up his phone and reached in a pocket for Frederic Esterhaus' business card. Quickly, he punched in the number. *Please be there and answer.* After three rings, the investigator's slow deliberate voice came on the line. Kelly closed his eyes in relief.

"Esterhaus here."

"Hi, this is Ryan Kelly again."

"I'm having dinner, Mr. Kelly. Can this wait?"

"Oh, sorry to interrupt. Actually, no, it can't wait. Look, this is going to sound really wild, but you've gotta believe me. I had a hunch about this guy I saw on TV the day after the crash, a hunch that he took some wreckage that fell in Lake Michigan. I just saw him with some of it. He put it in the trunk of his car and he's taking it somewhere."

Kelly shook his head. He felt like a blithering idiot.

"These were pieces of wreckage from last week's collision?" Esterhaus sounded dubious.

"That's right. He's got them now and he's going somewhere. I was following him, but I got stopped for running a red light. Now he's getting away."

There was a gentle chuckle on the other end of the line. "Never an officer around when you need one, but when you don't . . . "

"I know it must sound crazy, but it's for real. He could have the black box. If you can get the police to find this guy, we may be able to get it back. I know his license plate number."

"How did you find this man and catch him?"

Kelly wiped his brow again. "It's too involved to explain right now. Please trust me. I wouldn't lead you astray."

"No, I don't think you would. I must say this is definitely a first for me." Esterhaus spoke in a maddeningly slow pace, but he sounded increasingly convinced. "I'm not the commander-in-chief, so I don't know how much pull I'll have. But I can try. What's the license number?"

Kelly repeated it from memory. "His name is Larry Lindstrand. Last I saw him, he was heading north on the Edens Expressway."

"Got it."

"Could you call me if they find him?"

"Certainly. What's your number."

Kelly gave it to him and sighed deeply. "Thank you for believing me."

"I doubt you'd make this up. I'll be in touch."

There was a click as the connection broke. The leather belt reappeared outside the window and the officer handed him his license, car registration, and a citation.

"Watch those traffic signals, sir. And get that taillight fixed."

Kelly behaved like a model driver on the way home. He was in no mood for another ticket and disconsolate that he'd let Lindstrand slip away. Esterhaus' response had been encouraging. At least he'd believed him. But Kelly remained pessimistic that the police would find Lindstrand before he threw the wreckage down a sewer, in a river, or wherever he'd been taking it. He was approaching the tollway exit for Route 47, which would take him home to Woodstock, when his phone rang. He answered hopefully.

"This is Ryan Kelly."

"Esterhaus here. I owe you a debt of gratitude for your quick thinking. Sheriff's deputies picked up Mr. Lindstrand in Lake County not long after he left several pieces of wreckage in a field outside Wauconda. I gather he was very surprised when deputies pulled him over a few minutes later. He denied everything at first, but once the officers mentioned a witness had seen him put the items in his trunk, he directed them to the field."

Kelly gripped the phone with mounting excitement. He was almost afraid to ask. "What did the deputies find?"

"Metal parts. I haven't seen them yet, but from the description I was given it sounds like one was a section of wing flap. Sorry, Mr. Kelly, there was no black box. But your intuition served you well and I thank you. Every piece of wreckage is important. I have to make a few other calls now. Perhaps some other time you'll tell me the whole story."

He held the phone limply now, only half-listening to Esterhaus. *Yeah, great intuition. But they still didn't have the box.*

✈   ✈   ✈

KELLY STROKED THE FUR along Rudy's back while watching the late news on Channel 2. Purring contentedly, the cat ensconced himself deeper in Kelly's lap and he wondered whether Tubbo had gained more weight. Rudy's bowl was nearly devoid of the mix he'd left this morning, which should have lasted several days. The little pig had no restraint around food.

The newscast led with Lindstrand, breathlessly reporting on this bizarre twist in a story that still dominated the city's attention. Kelly was only mildly curious. His interest had waned considerably after hearing that Lindstrand didn't have the box. Bear was right. He'd been grasping at straws. He pictured his friend watching this report and smiling triumphantly on having been proven correct. The screen switched from the anchorman to a live interview with Esterhaus, speaking in what appeared to be a hotel lobby.

"The NTSB is extremely grateful for the role that Mr. Ryan Kelly played in retrieving this important evidence. Airline accidents have been caused by something as seemingly insignificant as a single bolt. It's imperative for the investigation team to be able to assess every last piece from the two planes."

Kelly grunted. It was the first positive publicity about him since the collision.

"How did he know that Lindstrand stole the wreckage?" asked the reporter standing next to him.

Esterhaus smiled inscrutably. "I received a phone call from Mr. Kelly earlier this evening alerting me to the theft and the approximate whereabouts of the suspect. That's all I know. You'll have to ask him for the details."

They'd been trying. During the past hour, his answering machine recorded a steady string of inquisitive reporters urging him to call back as soon as possible. The phone rang yet again as Kelly walked to the bar to refill his drink. Christy's warm voice filtering across the room stopped him.

"Hello, Ryan. I was hoping you'd be there. We need to talk. There's some things I'd like to say, but I don't want to do it in a message."

She still sounded depressed but her anger, which paralyzed him yesterday, had dissipated. An element bordering on tenderness had replaced it and something else, almost a touch of contrition. Her voice beckoned him into the kitchen and he grabbed the receiver off the wall.

"I'm here, Christy. I've just been screening my calls."

"Oh, hi. I'm sorry to bother you so late."

"It's no bother."

"Ryan, I've been thinking a lot since we talked at the church. And I just saw you on the news."

He laughed nervously. "Yeah, must be another slow day since they're still preoccupied with me."

"Sounds like you've been busy. What's all that about?"

"I'll tell you sometime. Right now I'm pretty tired."

"I understand. That's not why I called, anyway. I'm not working on a story. I wanted to apologize—and hear your side of the story. Don made me realize I was jumping to conclusions like everyone else. You didn't do anything wrong last Friday, did you?"

Kelly put a hand against the counter for support and closed his eyes. "No. And you have no idea how much what you just said means to me."

"You were trying to tell me things yesterday, but I wasn't in the right frame of mind to listen. I want to hear about them." She paused. "There's something I need to ask first, though. I thought you said you weren't involved with anyone."

Her change of tack threw him for a second. "I—I'm not."

"Then how come that woman answered your phone Saturday morning?"

"I was too shaken up Friday night to drive, so J.J. took me home. She slept in my guest room. Look, she and I used to have a relationship but we don't anymore. Not since I met you."

He heard a soft sigh on the line. "Why didn't you call me?" Her voice conveyed mild hurt, but not reproach.

"I wanted to." He looked down at the kitchen floor. "I should have."

"Well, a lot's happened and it's going to take awhile for all of us to get through it. I'd rather not discuss it on the phone, though. Why don't you come to the house tomorrow night for that dinner we never had?"

"I'd like that. I want to tell you about everything."

"I want to hear. Is six o'clock okay?"

"See you then."

✈   ✈   ✈

CHRISTY ANSWERED THE DOOR when Kelly arrived. Her flowered sundress coordinated with the bouquet of irises and white carnations he handed her. She fingered the single red rose in the center and kissed him on the cheek.

"Thank you, they're beautiful. Come in."

Kelly saw no sign of Jason and was relieved. Lingering emotions from the midair, its consequences for Christy, and the effect on their relationship swirled threateningly just below the surface, ready to shatter his fragile exterior of self-assurance. Dealing with a hostile kid was the last thing he needed right now.

"Would you care for some wine?" she asked. "It's a young Chianti with promise."

"I'd love it."

He followed her into the kitchen, feeling more comfortable yet still unsure of what to say. She held up the bottle in a model's pose, trying to lighten the atmosphere. When he nodded approvingly, she uncorked it, filled two glasses, and handed him one.

"Here's to a new beginning." Lines of fatigue etched her pale drawn face. Despite the dark circles under her eyes, though, she looked at him without accusation and he relaxed some more.

"Arghh!" An audible groan sounded from down the hall.

Christy giggled. "For us, anyway. Jason's tearing his hair out over the computer."

"I know the feeling," Kelly said with a grin. "What's his problem?"

"Don't ask me. He put in a new sound card the other day and now his music program won't work. He's been fussing with it all afternoon. Why don't we pop our head in to say hello and then leave him alone to sulk?"

Kelly preferred to stay in the kitchen where he felt safe, but he couldn't think of a polite way to refuse. Bracing himself, he followed her to the den and saw the cover of the PC propped against the side of the desk. Jason was peering inside the computer at a forest of circuit boards and cables.

"How's it going?" she asked.

"I still can't get the sound card to work right. It must be an IRQ conflict."

The diagnosis meant nothing to her. "Ryan just got here."

Jason barely glanced up. "Hi." He resumed inspecting the PC.

"Hello." Kelly looked at the model airplanes hanging from the ceiling and several photographs of old steam engines on the walls. He recognized the Great Northern 2-6-6-2 Mikado steaming across a wooden trestle. "I've had my share of IRQ hassles. They're a real pain."

"No kidding. I made sure everything has a different setting, but the midi port won't work."

Rykowski had asked Kelly for help one time when he was installing a sound card for his kids. Success came after a frustrating evening of swearing over cryptic manuals and fiddling with settings, accompanied by copious amounts of beer. He was grateful for the experience now.

"Have you checked the I/O addresses? There should be three for your treble, bass, and midi. They'd be in your autoexec-dot-bat file."

Jason sat down and tapped on the keyboard. Like IRQ levels, each device in the PC had an input/output address in memory. No two could be shared.

"I bet that's it," he murmured. "The midi on the sound card is using 220 and so's the game card." He changed one of the settings and rebooted the computer. Music surged from two speakers on the desk.

"Thanks," he said grudgingly.

Christy slipped a hand through Kelly's arm, grateful the ice seemed to be melting. "He's trying not to show it," she whispered, "but I think you've just made his day."

"Do you make backups, Jason?"

"Nah."

"You should. Then you'd have copies of all your programs and files if something goes wrong. Makes it easier to fix problems."

Jason looked away and Christy retracted her arm. "I don't appreciate you telling him what to do."

"Hey, it was just a suggestion."

"That's not how it sounded."

She whirled around and left. Kelly followed her into the living room, where she was staring out the front window. "My son and I have gotten along fine for ten years now without being told how to run our lives," she said without facing him.

He gulped his wine and wondered how things could have gone to hell so suddenly. "You're the expert on parenting. Not me. I'll admit that any day of the week." He raised his glass in another toast. "Can we start over here?"

Christy huffed and walked to some shelves near the fireplace, pulling out a CD and banging the plastic case shut. She dropped the disc into a player and punched the ON button. Then she plopped onto the sofa and sipped her wine in silence, listening to a female vocalist harmonize with a muted trumpet. Kelly eased onto the other end. At length, she relaxed.

"Sorry I snapped. Baggage from an old relationship. And I guess the accident has me on edge."

"Like you said, it's gonna take awhile."

She studied his face. "Yeah. This is one hell of a way to start a romance." They both laughed, the tension dissipating again. "So how are you?"

"I haven't been sleeping well. My apologies if I nod off."

"Thanks for the warning. I'd hate to think it was my company." She shifted toward him and rested a hand on his shoulder, sending tingles along his arm. "It would be all right if you did. I've been so caught up with my own problems that I hadn't considered what you've been dealing with. You've been through a lot. There's something to be said for just letting your body take over the healing process."

"How's Jason taking this?"

"We had a little chat the other night." It had been a long talk and his maturity impressed her. "He seems to understand more about the accident than I do. He thinks it'll turn out to be the result of a lot of little things."

"He's right. I keep thinking about things I might have done differently. If I had, maybe Coastal wouldn't have been in the wrong place at the wrong time."

"Is that what you were trying to tell me at the church?"

"Yeah. It's not like I did anything wrong, but if I'd climbed Coastal sooner or turned him toward the lake sooner, he would have been somewhere else. Rykrisp—our union rep—told me they would have missed each other if they'd had just another half second."

She shook her head sadly. Too often, mere fractions separated life and death. An image of Carla formed, her face stricken with terror as the plane plunged toward the lake. Shivering, Christy banished the vision to a small compartment in her mind that she resolved to keep firmly closed.

Watching the light reflecting off the ruby wine in his glass, Kelly said, "I'm afraid the agency's gonna blame me, whether I screwed up or not."

"So what really happened? I need to know."

"It's complicated, but I'm convinced TCAS ran them together. Coastal's altitude was jumping around on my scope, which must have affected the computer's instructions to the pilots. When I saw those two planes heading for each other . . . I just reacted and warned Coastal."

"Sounds prudent to me."

"But the pilots may have hesitated as a result. I don't think they did, but the agency would like nothing better than to blame it on me. Otherwise, they'd have to admit their fancy system is at fault."

"Isn't there something you can do?"

"Got any suggestions? I'm at the mercy of the NTSB and whatever evidence they find."

She tucked both legs underneath her to get more comfortable. "You've certainly been helping them on that score. How did you learn about the car dealer?"

He recounted his interpretation of the TV interview, his phone call to Lindstrand, and the stakeout. Christy listened intently and stifled a chuckle as he described Lindstrand taking off in a panic after the tenant bellowed from above. When he mentioned the red light, she laughed.

"Based on your luck, I'd avoid espionage as a career."

"It's a lot trickier than they make it look in the movies."

"Well, on the bright side, that little episode has helped your image. I know the news media aren't your favorite people, but maybe you should capitalize on it and talk to them. Let the public hear your side of the story about the accident."

"I'm afraid I'd come off as a shrill whiner. And the public would have a hard time understanding it all."

"Don't underestimate them. They're not as dumb as the politicians and some of us in the media make them out to be. Besides, you have a very believable face."

She was about to say something else when Jason charged down the stairs from the second floor, wearing a backpack. "I'll be at Dave's." He stood for inspection before his mother, then turned to Kelly. "Thanks again. That PC was driving me nuts."

"Sure. I noticed you're into trains."

"Yeah, they're cool. My mom took me to the railway museum in Union once. They've got some great old cars and engines there."

"I live nearby. You'll have to come to my house sometime and see my model railroad. It takes up most of the basement. I suppose your mom could come, too." Christy frowned, trying to look offended. "And call me Ryan. Or Rain Man. That's what I go by in the TRACON."

"Okay." Jason regarded him with growing appreciation. "Rain Man."

Christy stood and tried to kiss him but he wriggled away, embarrassed by such affection in front of another guy. "Later."

Kelly watched Jason hustle out the door. Maybe they'd get along after all. His mind reeled at the possibility. It was a complicated issue he was too overwhelmed to consider right now. He turned to Christy as she settled back on the sofa.

"Like I was saying, the public doesn't want to understand something like this. They can't identify with a computer chip. They need a human to blame."

She nodded knowingly and he saw a flicker of guilt cross her face.

"There's something else I need to say. I'm deeply sorry about Carla and Kevin. God, Christy, of all the people to be on those planes. And all the others, too." He rubbed his eyes, sagging under the weight of the catastrophe. "It's something I haven't come to grips with yet. Maybe I never will."

"Thank you for saying that." She blinked back tears. "I haven't really accepted Carla and Kevin being gone yet, but I know I'll have to in time. You'll get through this, too. Perhaps we can together." Sipping her wine, she held a finger to his lips. "Let's not talk about the accident anymore tonight. We both deserve a break." Her sensual mouth curled into a shy smile and she looked at him directly. "I meant what I said about your believable face. It's one of your best features. I enjoy being with you a lot, Ryan."

Her comment momentarily swept away his worries. He was happy and tongue-tied and hesitantly leaned forward to kiss her. When the oven buzzer went off, she giggled.

"Saved by the bell."

She hurried off to silence it, leaving Kelly to scold himself for making a move too quickly. The appetizing aroma of dinner lured him into the kitchen, where she was bending over a dish of lasagna baking in the oven. He feasted on her enticing figure and she caught him staring after closing the door and turning off the oven. She sauntered over and wrapped her arms around his neck. He reached for her waist with anticipation.

"I like being with you, too, Christy. A lot."

She tilted her head at the oven. "Dinner's ready, but what do you think about having dessert first?"

He didn't have to think. He pulled her against him and their lips met in a long glorious kiss that left them panting when they finally broke for air. Their hands ravenously explored each other as they kissed again. His fingers slipped beneath the straps of her sundress and eased them off her smooth shoulders. He caught his breath when the dress fell in a heap around her ankles. Christy stood before him naked, her eyes smoldering with desire. Her forethought fueled his lust, and he nibbled on one of her breasts while she attacked the buttons of his shirt. Then she groped with the zipper on his black jeans until her fingers completed their eager search.

Christy's bedroom seemed miles away and she didn't want to wait another second, but the fear that Jason might return unexpectedly tempered her passion. Gathering up their clothes, she smiled salaciously and reached for him again.

They scampered upstairs and she kicked her bedroom door shut behind them. Tumbling onto the covers, her moans soon intensified into euphoric gasps from his gentle and adept ministrations that resurrected feelings she'd gone too long without. Kelly elatedly discovered that her ardency to satisfy him was accompanied by a playful yen to tease. Swelling waves of pleasure washed over them, cresting in blissful release when neither could hold back any longer.

They decided to eat dinner in bed, both wanting to nestle within the intimate cocoon of her room. She threw on a blue silk robe and loosely tied it with the sash before disappearing to the kitchen. When she returned carrying plates of lasagna, he relished her aura of glowing contentment. The robe fell open when she sat facing him cross-legged on the bed and the sight of her stirred his hunger anew. Without trying to compare, he knew that it had never been this good with J.J., Carol, or anyone else for that matter. His emotional involvement with Christy was obviously a factor, but she was different in many other ways. After clearing his plate, he set it on the nightstand and reached out to trace the back of his fingers around her breasts.

"Is this what you meant when you said to let your body take over?"

"Not specifically." She smiled dreamily as her nipples stiffened over the delicious sensations he was creating. "But it's just what the doctor ordered."

His hand fanned out over the flare of her hips. "I've heard therapy is effective only if it's administered regularly."

She stacked her plate on top of his and beckoned him. "Then we'd better have another session."

They laid beside each other and he kissed the tip of her nose. Suddenly, he raised up on one elbow. "What time is Jason due back?"

"Don't worry." She covered his mouth with a deep kiss and her hand moved beneath the sheet, finding, enveloping him. "Jason's spending the night at Dave's and we'll have time for breakfast before he even thinks about coming home."

Later, Kelly and Christy basked in an exhilarating afterglow that was as fulfilling as their lovemaking itself, and they talked until drifting asleep in a tangle of arms and legs. Thirds came sometime during the night and when their insistent cravings ignited again the next morning, they devoured each other for breakfast in the shower.

Once downstairs, Christy purposely kept the TV in the kitchen turned off while brewing some coffee to shield Kelly from any reports on the crash. She forgot about the *Chronicle*, which they both saw on the front porch when he opened the door to leave. A headline yanked his soaring heart back to earth.

"Missing black box holds key to controller's fate."

✈   ✈   ✈

GUZZLING ORANGE JUICE FROM A CARTON, Brad Schwartz read the same headline with keen interest. After perusing the story, he put the juice container back in the refrigerator and swaggered downstairs to the basement. Mom and pops were gone, checking out RV dealers to find a replacement blimp, so he decided to take advantage of the opportunity. Circling underneath the stairs, he reached up to the rafters and moved a piece of scrap wood aside to uncover his bong and stash.

He inhaled a hit and held it, looking at the metal object temporarily sharing space in the rafters. It was about the size of a shoebox and painted orange with black letters printed on a white background in English on one side, French on the other: "Flight Recorder. Do Not Open." The sides were scratched and dented in a few places, but otherwise it appeared undamaged. The orange color had caught Brad's eye when he'd spotted it on their driveway beneath the Hindenburg the day after the collision.

He walked over to a small window and pulled it open, exhaling into the outside air. He'd known that taking Coastal's black box was a federal offense, but he'd brushed the thought aside as the vague notion of a scheme took shape while he stood on the driveway. The box could provide him with a way to have some fun, maybe even get back at pops.

As the days passed, temptation grew strong to somehow implicate the old man with the theft. The cheap bastard had steadfastly refused to pay his parking tickets. He'd even turned down the plea of a loan, forcing Brad to endure riding on CTA buses and the "El" to commute to classes and his job at Ford City mall. Last night, the fucker had the gall to broach the subject of rent. You're an adult now, he'd lectured in his condescending way, droning on about accepting responsibility. Then came the ultimatum. Brad would have to fork over every month starting this fall.

And so, a new possibility coalesced in his devious mind. An unthinkable one that was too radical to ignore.

He'd also known, of course, that stealing the box would confound investigators, a consequence that gave him juvenile satisfaction. What he couldn't have anticipated was how much that would affect one man, an air traffic controller he'd been reading and hearing more and more about during the past week. Today's article said the NTSB was skeptical of his claims about a radar glitch and that information from the flight recorder was the only means of resolving the dispute.

Other fragments about the controller came to mind. He'd read that this Kelly guy raked in something like a hundred grand a year. One of the TV stations said he lived in a fancy house on five acres. Posh—that was the word they used. The equation added up. Brad needed money and it sounded like Kelly had plenty. If he and the NTSB wanted this box so badly, well, he'd be happy to let them have it. Only first, Kelly would have to hand over a suitcase full of cash.

Brad took another hit off the bong and leaned against the stairs, pleasantly floating with his high. He felt no remorse for the theft nor his mercenary plan. It was a dog-eat-dog world and you had to seize opportunities whenever they presented themselves. Did the high rollers on Wall Street play by Robert's rules of order? Of course not. Even pops wasn't so lily-white. When their house was robbed a few years ago, he'd inflated the claim by several thousand dollars and used his ill-gotten gains as a down payment on the blimp. He'd rationalized it as compensation for pain and suffering. *Yeah, right.* Here was a chance to bag a substantial payoff, one too irresistible to pass up. And, after all, wasn't the old man always harping about the importance of money?

Brad laughed giddily, debating how much to demand. Fuck the parking tickets. A deal like this could help set him up for life.

But he'd have to be careful. The stakes were high and he had no illusions. Losing meant he'd go to prison. He'd have to find out more about Kelly. Follow him, take his measure. He'd also have to plan the exchange with *beaucoup* precautions because that would be the riskiest part of this venture. His first order of business was to acquire some wheels. The TV said Kelly lived in Woodstock, way the hell out in the sticks. Stan would never drive him there. Besides, even if the dude agreed, involving him would dilute the profits. No, he'd figure out his own transportation.

He breathed deeply to steady himself, then replaced his bong and stash in the rafters.

TWENTY-ONE
SQUEEZE PLAY

S ENATOR RICHARD MASTERS swept into the reception area of his Capitol Hill office and snatched a pile of telephone messages off his administrative assistant's desk.

"Your daughter called," Laura said.

While hastily sorting through the pink slips, he asked distractedly, "How is she?"

"Feeling a lot of phantom pain." Masters glanced at Laura, then continued shuffling through the messages. "It'll be another week or so before the hospital lets her go home. They're fitting her with a temporary prosthesis and starting physical therapy already. Except for the pain, Sharon sounded okay, like she's beginning to accept what happened. Would you like me to get her on the phone for you?"

He plucked out a slip containing the FAA administrator's name and dropped it on Laura's desk. After checking his watch, he sheepishly shook his head and moved toward his office. A vote was scheduled on the floor of the chamber in fifteen minutes.

"Not now. Send her flowers. Sign the card 'thinking of you' or something—whatever sounds good. But ring Bob Chalmers first."

"Yes, Senator."

Laura dialed Chalmers' number as he closed the door behind him. Then she wadded his message into a tight little ball before flinging it in a wastebasket. She flipped through her Rolodex for the florist's number while waiting for the call to connect and decided to order an even larger bouquet than usual. She was always generous with Sharon. Knowing that the senator's daughter received scant affection from her father, Laura figured she deserved small acts of kindness whenever possible. Masters' assistant didn't worry about the gesture being misinterpreted. Long ago, Sharon suspected who actually made arrangements with the florist and had called Laura to thank her. Masters was oblivious to their secret understanding.

In his office, the senator perched on the edge of his leather chair and was scribbling a note to Laura on one of the phone slips when she buzzed him over the intercom. "Administrator Chalmers is on line one, Senator." He hastily finished writing, reached for the receiver and settled comfortably in his chair.

"Hi, Bob. I've been looking forward to your update."

"I just got one from the NTSB chairman an hour ago. Wreckage recovery is proceeding steadily, but they still can't find Coastal's flight recorder. That's the plane the controller says was giving out bad altitude information."

"Is this the same controller who ignored regulations?"

"Yes." Chalmers cleared his throat. "Ryan Kelly countermanded the Resolution Advisory, which is forbidden by a new agency regulation. We implemented the rule after an incident in Chicago last month. The chairman told me today they can't be sure whether Kelly's warning had any effect on the cockpit crew's response. Frankly, I doubt it. When TCAS tells pilots to do something, they do it."

"Anything else?"

"At least one investigator believes that faulty altitude readouts may really be a factor. His theory is that TCAS could have issued an erroneous RA if Mode C was transmitting bad information."

Masters stopped fiddling with his tie and sat up straighter in the chair. "What evidence is available that Mode C wasn't working properly?"

"Well, right now there's only Kelly's word and a developmental who claims he saw it. Both pilots died and the NTSB didn't find anything unusual on the radar printout. They're desperate to get their hands on the black box."

"Kelly's obviously shaken up by what he saw. The other controller is just a trainee, as I recall." Masters leaned his elbows on the desk, struggling to stay calm. "And yet the NTSB is taking them seriously? They think TCAS may have told the two planes to fly into each other?"

"That's one of their theories, Senator."

After decades of development, thousands of hours of flight testing, and several years of service in the U.S. airline fleet, it was inconceivable to Richard Masters that TCAS could have caused the very disaster it had been designed to avoid. He massaged his right temple with his free hand.

"What's Kelly's status?"

"Other than issuing traffic during the RA, his performance on position that night was satisfactory. In fact, the air traffic manager at O'Hare says they're almost done with their inquiry. They have no reason to prevent him from returning to work. Once he feels mentally ready, of course."

"Before we find out what really happened? I'm uncomfortable with allowing a controller who may be responsible for one of the worst aviation disasters in history back on the line."

Chalmers cleared his throat again. "Well, practically speaking, our people here in Washington won't finish reviewing the case for another few weeks. And Kelly may not want to come back right away."

"I'd tread very carefully on this one, Bob." Masters wagged a finger at his unseen listener. "TCAS is big. There are a lot of lives, jobs, reputations, and money riding on this."

"I understand, Senator."

Masters sank back in the chair again and massaged his temple some more. The airlines wouldn't appreciate hearing they'd invested millions in a flawed system. That sort of news boded ill for the people like himself who'd promoted it. His personal fortune was at risk, too. Since before TCAS was implemented, Masters quietly started acquiring Circuitron stock. The company's booming production of TCAS units, Doppler radar, and other avionics pleased investment analysts. Their reports often referred to Circuitron's GPS devices as a cash cow. The stock had split several times and climbed steadily, closing last Friday at $82 a share. He made a quick mental calculation—his holdings were worth $1 million or so. There'd been a dip earlier last week after the story broke about defective TCAS units the company manufactured several years ago, but the share price was already rebounding. If the NTSB determined that a Circuitron component caused the collision, resulting in staggering company liability, the price would plummet into free fall.

He switched the receiver in his hands so he could rub his left temple. When he continued speaking, his voice was low and terse.

"We need to be very clear on this. Computers may run the world, but they're programmed and operated by humans. They do what we tell them. I know your controllers are highly trained and proficient. Naturally, you're protective of them. But Ryan Kelly messed up. So, before anyone rushes to assume that TCAS did something, let's be sure we review all the possibilities." A thought occurred to him. "Perhaps I spoke too quickly about Kelly going back to work. You'd have another chance to monitor his performance. Give us more ammunition at the public hearings."

"If Kelly's not ready, we can't force him."

"I've read his file and it sounds like he lives for the job. Besides, you're always whining about staffing needs in Chicago. Use that to help persuade him. I don't care what it takes—just do it. And be sure someone watches every move he makes. If Kelly so much as scratches his nose wrong, I want it fully documented."

The phone line hissed softly with prolonged silence from Chalmers.

"Are we together on this, Bob? It isn't going to be a TCAS failure."

Seconds ticked by before Chalmers finally spoke, his tone heavy with resignation. "I read you crystal clear, Senator." He paused again. "By the way, you contacted me several weeks ago about a new hotel near John Wayne Field. I had someone here look into the case and we discovered the paperwork got mixed up. The safety waiver has been approved. We haven't notified our Los Angeles field office, but I thought you'd like to know in case you speak with Mr. Martinelli before he gets the news from us."

Masters beamed. "Thanks, Bob. I appreciate the heads-up."

✢   ✢   ✢

THE NEWS BLITZ ABOUT THE COLLISION raged unremittingly during the next few weeks, fueled by the public's unquenchable thirst and the media's headlong rush to slake it. The frenzy mystified Kelly as much as it irritated him. Several hundred people died on the nation's highways every two days with hardly a one-column headline. When the same number flamed out in a plane crash, reporters couldn't say enough. Endless repetition of what happened and ill-informed analysis on the talk show circuit sparked overheard conversations that hounded him at the supermarket, in gas stations, restaurants, stores—wherever he went.

Several new items raised the volume of babble. The FAA leaked information from its employment files, prompting intense scrutiny of three-and-a-half decades he and Bear had spent on the job. A few minor infractions were dusted off and hyped into significance. Subsequently, several TV hosts and newspaper columnists questioned why the two hadn't been fired long ago. Unsafe condition reports they'd written about TCAS problems also drew attention. All the news accounts mentioned controller displeasure with the system. A radio show host renowned for his conservatism implied that they deliberately undermined it.

One story Kelly longed to hear was the discovery of Coastal's black box. But his disappointment grew increasingly bitter with each passing day. Exasperated, he stopped reading the paper and turned off the TV or changed the channel when a crash segment began. While surfing now on a Thursday afternoon, he stumbled across yet another talk show. This one claimed to probe the personal life of air controllers. His finger hovered on the remote control before he froze.

"We've been speaking with Donna Pepperidge, who recently separated from one of the controllers involved in the collision over Lake Michigan," the host announced. "Before the break, Donna, you were describing some of the incredible pressure controllers endure on the job. Could you tell us how that affects them at home?"

He hadn't seen her in months. After the wedding, she rarely associated with Bear's friends. A gold bracelet glittered as she brushed a stray lock of otherwise carefully coifed hair behind an ear. Jewelry, makeup, and designer clothes had made a sweeping transformation. Donna had looked distinctly more working class when she met Bear, tending bar and itching to leave her blue-collar neighborhood south of O'Hare.

"Well, Ted, I quickly learned that living with a controller is not a democracy." Chuckles rippled through the audience. "They spend their whole day telling people what to do, so I guess it's hard for them to stop when they walk through the front door. They're very quick to make decisions and take action. I suppose that's good, but I often got left out of the process. Oh, and they're rubbernecks." Widespread snickering erupted, which made her reconsider. "Actually, I can't say they're all like that. I just know about Frank."

The camera zoomed in on Ted's earnest face. "We'll hear from the wives of other controllers in a minute. What else can you share with us about

Frank?"

Donna hesitated, and to Kelly it seemed more for effect than concern about Bear or qualms over being indiscreet.

"Even though things didn't work out between us, I'm worried about him. He has some real problems I hope he can resolve. It's not just his drinking. Near the end, he wasn't himself. I had a feeling something bad would happen. I knew he was burning out from the job, so I encouraged him to take sick leave. He did, but only for a couple of weeks. Then he went back to work. I guess O'Hare meant more to him than us. That's when I realized it was futile and we split up."

The camera held them in a tight two-shot while Ted frowned. "When did this happen?"

Glistening tears welled up on cue. "A few weeks before the collision."

Ted paused long enough to let the inevitable conclusion form, then said somberly, "We'll take phone calls from wives of other controllers after this commercial break. Stay with us."

Kelly had heard more than enough. He clicked off the set and paced in front of the sofa. So the bitch came through on her threat. He figured it was idle talk that day she called Bear at his apartment. She'd pulled it off nicely, too, with just the right touch of feigned pity and concern. In the process, she painted a perfect portrait of an unstable controller. It wouldn't sway the NTSB, whose investigators relied on careful analysis of incontrovertible facts. But he knew that someone as politically motivated as Hawkins would seize on Donna's characterizations as further validation of Bear's perceived incompetence. One more log in the fire that was sending his friend's career up in smoke. He grabbed the cordless phone on the coffee table and dialed Bear's number, praying he hadn't seen the show. The ringing went unanswered.

He'd barely switched off the phone when it jangled in his hand. Out of habit, he waited for the machine to pick up. He wondered whether it was the crank, who persistently left variations of the same chilling message two or three times a week. Instead, the upbeat voice of Samantha Sanchez blared from the speaker in the kitchen. He pressed a button on the cordless.

"I'm here, Sam. Live, not Memorex."

"Oh, hi Ryan. I hope you're sitting down. Hawkins just gave me the word from Washington. You've been cleared to return to work."

Kelly eased onto the sofa. "Before the accident hearings even start? That seems unusual."

"I thought so, too, but the brass can't find a reason to keep you off the boards. Their only concern was your final call to Coastal and the consensus is that it didn't make any difference. Personally, I'm looking forward to having you back. If you're ready, that is."

Anticipation of sitting in front of a scope again thrilled him, pushing aside his indignation with Donna. Even so, he resented the limitations that work would impose on his ability to spend time with Christy, a realization he found revealing. And was he ready? It seemed as though his frayed nerves had mellowed since the collision and that he'd gradually shaken off the body blow to his confidence. Management's tacit support was encouraging. But, already, his gut churned with apprehension. Could he still handle the job? There was only one way to find out.

"I'm going crazy sitting around the house. I'd like to give it a try."

"That's great to hear, Ryan. You'll have to recertify, of course."

Written exam and a check ride on position. Kelly hoped that Sam would jack in with him. He could use the support of a trusted colleague.

"No sweat. How about if I start next Monday? That'll give me a few days to spool up."

"Fine. Since your medical certificate was lifted, you'll have to take a physical. I'll tell the flight surgeon at the Regional Office to expect you at nine. Assuming you pass, which I'm sure you will, come on over to the airport. If you decide Monday's too soon, just let me know. I don't want to rush you."

"Thanks, I appreciate the latitude. What about Bear?"

Sanchez paused. "Washington hasn't cleared him yet."

"What's the holdup? If anyone should go back, it's Bear. He didn't do anything wrong."

Her reply was hushed against a background of controllers talking to airplanes and he realized Sanchez was calling from the TRACON. "Hawkins doesn't think he's capable. I have to agree with him this time. You know Bear's been sliding lately. His drinking since the accident doesn't help matters. I'd be uncomfortable with him on the Front Line. I hope you understand my position."

"He's not as bad as people are making him out to be. The stuff in the papers and on TV is a lot of crap and you know it."

"Yes, I do, but you have to admit he's in no shape to control airplanes right now."

Kelly sighed heavily. "Yeah, I know. I'm just afraid the agency will never take him back."

"His behavior has a lot to do with that. You're one of his closest friends. Maybe it'll help if you talk to him."

"I intend to."

"Good luck, Ryan. See you Monday."

"Bye, Sam."

He switched off the phone and was setting it back on the table when it rang again. She must have forgotten something. "Yeah."

"Ryan?" That voice. Deep, soft, and deliberate. Not Sam's. The crank's. "What a treat to get you and not your answering machine."

He clutched the phone, barely breathing, saying nothing. This was far more personal than listening to a message.

"What's wrong? Cat got your tongue? That's not all you're gonna lose."

"Who is this? Why do you keep calling me?"

"I don't want you to forget about what you did. All those lives are on your hands. I can't let you get away with it."

He laughed grimly. "No worries, pal. The FAA will make sure I don't."

"And do what? Put a letter in your file? You deserve more than that. An eye for an eye. It's my duty. Your time is coming . . . you miserable piece of shit."

Despite the repetitive threats, the calls had bred impatience and contempt. Kelly finally lost his temper. Being out of control did that to him.

"Go fuck yourself, asshole!" He punched the OFF button and tossed the phone on the sofa.

✈   ✈   ✈

CHRISTY AND JASON DROVE TO KELLY'S HOME on Sunday afternoon. She was looking forward to a steak barbecue and walk through the woods to top off a rare three-day weekend for having worked so much overtime during the initial aftermath of the collision. Jason was keen to see the model railroad. Both were intrigued by his house and spacious property. When Christy noticed the hot tub sunken in the deck out back, she expressed regret for not bringing her swimsuit.

Wistfully, Kelly imagined the two of them naked in the spa, which inspired other fantasies. He fleetingly wished Jason hadn't come along until he reminded himself that both mother and son were enjoyable to be around.

"Where's the train?" Jason asked impatiently.

"We'll get to that in a minute." Kelly ducked into the kitchen and reappeared with a small gift-wrapped package he handed to Jason, who immediately ripped it open. His eyes gleamed at the aviation band radio.

"You can listen to airplanes like that day you came to the airport," Kelly said. He watched with delight as Jason eagerly slipped the batteries in their compartment so he could switch it on.

"You didn't have to do that," Christy said. She punctuated the comment with a kiss.

"Try the frequency one-two-eight-point-four-five. That's West Arrivals."

Jason punched in the numbers. "*—descend and maintain seven thousand.*" "*Down to seven, United 623.*"

"Radio contact established," Kelly said with a thumbs-up.

"Awesome! Thanks, Rain Man."

"Now we can see the train."

He led them downstairs to a daylight basement with one glass wall that faced the woods. His HO-scale layout stood chest high and spanned two other walls, with several peninsulas extending into the center of the room. He manipulated a hand-held control unit, and a highly detailed steam engine pulling 1930s-era boxcars slowly edged away from an industrial area. The train snaked through rugged mountains that soared from floor to ceiling before it chugged past a painted backdrop along the walls.

"I make the mountains by soaking paper towels in plaster and draping them over crumpled-up newspapers," Kelly explained.

"I'm glad you have some use for the *Chronicle*," Christy teased.

Jason shunted around the room, losing himself in the miniature world. "It looks so real."

"Here, you be the engineer." Kelly offered him the control unit. "Twist that dial for speed. The button applies the brakes."

Jason watched with fascination as the model engine responded to his adjustments. Speed and braking action even simulated the momentum of a real train weighing thousands of tons. A long cord tethered the control unit to a power supply, allowing him to walk alongside the moving cars. Kelly sent a second train cruising halfway around the mainline and into a siding as Jason's glided by in the opposite direction.

"Let's see how organized you are." He pointed to a pair of cars parked on a siding at an oil refinery. "In the fewest moves possible, pick up the two tankers and then drop off the last three cars that are already on the train at the logging mill over there. Use this to undo the cars. Just slip it between the couplers and twist." He handed Jason a tool that looked like a jeweler's screwdriver.

Jason furrowed his brow. "I'm not sure I know how to do that."

"Think of all the angles."

He put his hands on his hips, pondering the puzzle. "I'm not getting it."

"Concentrate. You can do it." Kelly's encouragement inspired a determined nod from Jason, but summoned a glare from Christy.

"Stop pressuring him! He's not a pilot who has to do everything you say."

He cringed, realizing too late he'd stumbled over an invisible line and provoked the lioness protecting her cub. Unlike the other times, though, Jason defended him.

"Mom, it's okay. He's not pressuring me. It's just a challenge. Look."

It had dawned on him how to complete the maneuver. He nudged the dial on the control unit and attached the tankers to the engine's front coupler before continuing on to the logging mill. He uncoupled the tankers just beyond a switch to the siding, backed up and pulled in next to the mill to drop off the last three cars. Then he moved the engine forward out of the siding and eased it into reverse to recouple the tankers to the back of the train.

"See? I did it."

Christy's face reddened with conflicting emotions. After several seconds of awkward silence, she fled upstairs. Kelly and Jason exchanged looks of understanding.

"I know you weren't telling me what to do, Rain Man."

"I'm glad. I'd better tend to her. You okay here?"

Jason nodded and winked, a knowing wink between friends commiserating over a lovers' quarrel.

Kelly found Christy leaning on the deck railing out back, her face still flushed and taut. He took her hand. "Let's go for that walk."

She followed him wordlessly. They crossed a small backyard smelling of freshly mown grass toward woods that were lush with foliage in full bloom. A small parting in the trees led them down a narrow meandering trail carpeted with leaves from stands of oaks and maples. Fallen logs scattered amid ferns and blackberry bushes sprouted with new growth. Christy sensed movement several times and turned her head to glimpse squirrels scampering away from the fringes of the path or scurrying up the sides of trees. She heard the soothing sound of gurgling water and they soon strolled up to a wooden footbridge spanning the stream that cut through his property.

They stopped to watch the clear shallow water running over rocks, carrying occasional leaves and twigs downstream. With relief, Kelly sensed she was relaxing and slipped an arm around her waist.

"Why did you get upset back at the house?" he asked quietly.

"Because every guy I've gotten involved with has taken that as a license to run Jason's life. Now you're doing it."

"No I wasn't. He said so himself. What's really the matter?"

"I just told you."

Sunlight filtering through the trees dappled her pouting lips and he briefly covered them with his. She kissed back half-heartedly.

"Let me tell you something," Kelly said. "A month ago, I'd never have dreamed that Jason and I would become friends. Kids scare the daylights out of me." He shook his head. "But we're getting along really well. I know what it's like to live under a dictator and I'm determined not to be one myself."

She sniffed. "He does look up to you."

"I can't believe how much I enjoy watching him learn things."

"You're very patient with him."

"So what's the deal?"

Christy squeezed his hand and sighed. "It's me, I suppose. I've been happier in the past month than for as long as I can remember. The three of us have spent a lot of time together and it's been wonderful. When I'm that happy, I get scared something will mess it up. So when you and Jason bump heads, I overreact and push you away. I'm afraid history will repeat itself."

"Don't judge me by other men you've known."

He tightened his arm around her waist and she let her head fall against his shoulder. The heat from her body stirred desire and his hand strayed down over her backside. Beyond his sexual yearnings, he was comforted by a warm contentment more satisfying and secure than he'd experienced with any other woman. Dawning awareness of this deeper intimacy filled him with awe and gratitude.

"The past month has been terrific for me, too. It's funny. For years, I've resisted getting involved with someone because of my work. Now that my job's in the toilet, I'm walking on air because of you. You're very special, Christy. You've given me something else to care about. There was a time when I didn't think that was possible."

A shy smile spread across her face. "Sorry I acted foolish."

They kissed again, tenderly, and resumed walking. She wouldn't say it in so many words, but Carla's death created a void she was thankful Kelly filled so well. She wondered how their relationship might change when he was working at the airport again, whether his concern about balancing both worlds was well-founded or simply misplaced insecurity.

"The accident hearings are in another week," she said. "Do you suppose you'll get to go back to work after they're over?"

"I've been meaning to tell you. I'm starting on Monday."

She glanced at him in surprise. "So your bosses finally came to their senses?"

"Maybe. They haven't exactly rallied to my defense in the press, which makes me wonder whether they've got something up their sleeve."

"That sounds like paranoia. I'm sure the union's pressuring them. You didn't do anything wrong, so how can the FAA prevent you from working?"

He grunted. "The agency's riddled with politics. They'd figure out a way."

She nodded knowingly. "So wait awhile. Get through the hearings first."

"I've considered that. But I'm bored and I figure it's like falling off a horse. If I don't try now, when they're giving me the chance, maybe I won't have the nerve later on."

"Are you sure you're ready?"

"To tell you the truth, part of me can't wait and part of me is terrified."

She squeezed his hand. "It's probably just stage fright. I bet you'll do fine."

"Thanks for your confidence in me."

"Thanks for inviting us to your home."

Up ahead, blackberry bushes rustled and a white-tailed deer hopped lithely onto the trail. Christy gripped Kelly's arm and marveled at the elegant creature warily watching them. No one moved for several seconds. Then the buck slowly stepped away and bolted into the woods on the other side of the path.

"He was so beautiful," Christy said. "Do you see them very often?"

"Not as often as I'd like. I love living so close to the wildlife."

"I love how peaceful it is here."

"It's about time you saw the place. Say, why don't you two spend the night? Jason's certainly enjoying himself." He didn't want to, but offered a concession. "We can sleep in different rooms if you feel weird about him."

"I don't think I could trust myself."

"Excuse me?"

She glanced around to make sure they were alone, mindful that the deer might be watching from behind the cover of brush. Caressing the front of his jeans, she smiled wantonly when he responded. Their lips met and their tongues danced. Moaning, she shimmied against him.

"I want you, Ryan. If I stayed, we'd wind up in the same bed and it wouldn't look right with Jason here."

"He must know we're sleeping together," Kelly said gently.

"I admit I'm being old-fashioned. Someday—soon—I'll talk to him about sex between us." She brushed the hair from his forehead. "He thinks you're a gentleman."

"Uh, huh." Kelly was thinking about his libido. "Is there no way I can dissuade you of your high moral standards?"

Christy looked behind them toward the house, which was well hidden from view. Satisfied, she took his hand and placed it on her left breast. "No, but kiss me some more before we go back."

Standing on the path, they indulged themselves until there was a danger they wouldn't be able to stop. With effort, they reluctantly disengaged from their breathless embrace and retraced their steps through the woods. Back at the house, Christy uncorked a bottle of merlot she'd brought while Kelly went into the garage to get charcoal for the barbecue. He returned to the kitchen empty-handed, scratching his head.

"I could have sworn I had another bag," he muttered.

Christy shrugged at the oversight and handed him a wineglass. "Here, drink this. It'll soothe your nerves while I buy some at the supermarket."

"I'll go. You stay here and relax."

"It's no bother. I saw the Jewel when I turned onto your road." She kissed him. "That's energy to get the steaks ready. I expect them to be marinated by the time I get back."

Kelly listened to the sound of her car fade down the driveway as he took three filets out of the refrigerator. Whistling happily, he spread his favorite sauce over them and set the table in the dining room. While he was carrying ears of corn out to the grill, Rudy scampered across the deck and rubbed himself against his leg.

"Hey, Tubbo, you've been ignoring our guests. What the hell?"

He noticed a black plastic film container attached to his cat's collar by a thin chain. Rudy batted at the container while Kelly removed it. Inside was a folded sheet of paper with individual letters pasted together from various magazines. His face grew hot with rage and fear as he read it.

> "Haven't you taught this guy to avoid strangers? You know what they say about curiosity and the cat. Curious about the black box from Coastal 276? You can have it for 50 grand in cash. A small price for saving your career. You can save your life, too, by keeping the cops out of this. I'm watching and I'll know if you do something stupid. When you have the money, put a classified ad in the *Chronicle* about losing a three-legged cat named Phoenix. List your cell phone #. Don't make me wait long. Your cat will lose a leg for real and I won't stop with him."

Kelly's hands shook as he reread the note.

He shoved it in his pocket and gathered Rudy in his arms, petting him protectively. Shivering from a sudden cold sweat, he surveyed the yard and woods. Was someone out there, watching him now? He carried Rudy to the kitchen and poured some mix into his bowl.

Remembering Jason, he ran downstairs to find him still absorbed with the model train pike. He barely noticed Kelly lock the sliding glass door. He quickly searched the rest of the house and secured all the windows and doors. There was no sign of anything unusual. His mind reeled over what to do next when he heard Christy's car pull up outside. He went to open the front door and took the bag of charcoal she was carrying, latching the deadbolt behind them.

Her face was pale as she followed him into the kitchen. She swiped her wineglass off the counter and swallowed several gulps.

"Whew! That was close. I was about to turn into your driveway when this car suddenly appeared out of nowhere. It swerved across the center line and forced me off the road. The driver didn't even stop. He just kept on going the other way, toward town."

"Are you all right?"

"A little shaken is all. It was weird—I had the impression he shot out from behind the bushes alongside your house. Could it have been your neighbor?"

An eerie sensation of dread took Kelly's breath away. Rudy had gone outside just before Christy and Jason arrived. He slipped a hand in his pocket, fingering the note. "What kind of car was it?"

"Let me think. . . . Uh, gray sedan. Dodge or Plymouth, something like that."

"Nick and Ellie drive a Jeep Cherokee." He took her in his arms and hugged so tightly she protested mildly in pain.

"Hey, not so hard. I'm okay. Probably just some joyriding kids who lost control." She held a hand to his cheek and studied his face, seeing anxiety and confusion. "What's wrong, Ryan?"

He didn't want to alarm her. And it was hard to overcome years of handling everything alone. "I'm just relieved you're not hurt."

She appraised him skeptically. "Come on, now. I know you better than that. Something else is bothering you. Keeping secrets from me?"

He wasn't sure how to put it, wasn't sure he believed it yet himself. The idea that some lunatic would have the audacity to demand money for a critical piece of plane wreckage was reprehensible. Were the crank calls merely a warm-up? A sinister ploy to break down his resolve? Or was another asshole responsible? Christy was looking at him intently and he decided to hedge, irrationally reasoning that hiding part of the truth would somehow ensure her safety.

"Some crank has been calling me. But I think he knows where I live. . . . He could be the one who almost ran into you."

Her eyes widened and she gulped more wine. "You mean he's been spying on you? On us?"

"Maybe. He says he is, but I don't know that for sure."

She glanced nervously out the window and back at Kelly. "How long has this been going on?"

"The calls started the Sunday after the crash."

"All this time? Why didn't you tell me?"

"I figured he was just trying to rattle me. I didn't want to scare you."

"Well, I am scared." Christy's face registered momentary pique over his lack of trust in her. "Who do you think is doing this?"

"I wish I knew. It may be a relative of someone on one of the planes or possibly a survivor."

"Can't the police do anything?"

"I haven't told them. So far, it's only been crank calls."

"It could be a lot more, Ryan. This nut sounds dangerous. You should call the police."

"I will. As soon as you and Jason go home."

They left after a subdued dinner. He walked them out the front door to Christy's car, admonishing her to use her wireless phone if anything suspicious happened during the drive back to Oak Park. She leaned against the car and cast him a stern look.

"Promise you'll call the police?"

"Scout's honor." He pulled her to him and held his cheek against hers, then spoke softly into her ear. "I've been thinking about something. I hate to say it, but maybe it'd be safer if we don't see each other for a week or two. Let things shake out a little. If this guy *is* following me, I don't want him to find out where you live." He closed his eyes, fearful that the crank or the extortionist—one in the same or both—might already know.

Christy said nothing for a moment, considering, worrying about Jason. "I don't like it, but I suppose you're right. We'll miss seeing you." Their mouths met in a lingering kiss and then she got into her car.

Kelly bent over and waved at them through the open door. "Drive carefully. And I'll call you. Bye Jason." He waited until her taillights trailed off down his driveway before he plodded back inside the house.

Perversely, Kelly was relieved. No longer did he have to speak ambiguously about his outrage and trepidation. He slouched in an easy chair in the great room and memorized the wrinkled note after reading it so many times.

He flirted with the idea of handling the extortionist on his own, but dismissed it almost immediately. The authorities, of course, were far better equipped to deal with crime.

He retrieved the phone book from a drawer in the kitchen and was looking up the number for the FBI's field office in Chicago when the note's warning came to mind. Gazing through the kitchen window, into the black void of the woods beyond and all that could be lurking out there, he slowly closed the phone book. His line might somehow be bugged. He'd wait and call from the privacy of the NATCA office at O'Hare.

Kelly trudged upstairs, looking behind him to make sure Rudy was following, and pressed a button on the security console near his bed to arm the system. After crawling under the covers, he cradled Rudy in his arms and lay in the darkness for a long time before dozing off fitfully.

Twenty-two
Check Ride

K ELLY'S FINGERS KNEADED THE STEERING WHEEL during Monday morning's drive down the Northwest Tollway for his first day back at work. He weaved through the traffic on autopilot, a swirl of competing emotions crowding his thoughts. Excitement and uncertainty about doing the job. Suspicions over the brass and their unknown motivations. And anticipation of the phone call he'd make to the FBI as soon as he arrived at O'Hare.

He was so preoccupied that he almost forgot about his physical at the FAA's Regional Office near the airport and had to swerve onto the exit for Devon at the last moment. While impatiently enduring the flight surgeon's methodical examination, he hoped his blood pressure wouldn't surge above acceptable limits. At last, the doctor nodded approvingly.

"Everyone at the agency should be so fortunate, Mr. Kelly. You're perfectly healthy. I'll call Sanchez and let her know the results."

Ten minutes later, Kelly screeched into the parking garage at O'Hare. He bypassed his customary stop for a mocha at the latte stand in the Hilton and marched directly to the NATCA office. No controllers were in the room and he sighed with relief. Despite rehearsing what to say, he sounded disjointed on the phone to the FBI. The agent listened politely, asked a few questions, and said she'd meet him at the airport in an hour.

Next he called Esterhaus, who had returned to NTSB headquarters in Washington several weeks ago. He accepted the news with resignation.

"I've worked on a number of investigations where scavengers walked away with wreckage, but no one's ever demanded money in return. At least that explains why we haven't been able to find the damn thing. If a speaker phone is available when the FBI talks to you, please call me back so I can listen in."

Kelly promised to do so and walked into the TRACON to inform Sanchez. She beamed when she saw him and firmly grasped his hand.

"Welcome back, Ryan. It's really good to see you."

"Thanks, Sam."

He looked at the Front Line, where Jackson was feeding flight strips to Christensen. On the Side Line, Webber sat joking with J.J. Across the room on the Foul Line, Lombardi stood behind Rykrisp, jacking in to take over on West Departures. The clatter of the strips and chatter at the scopes all came back in a rush and he resented his distraction with the FBI. He turned back to Sam. Dim light reflecting from a low-level desk lamp washed across her face, highlighting the fatigue around her eyes, and he noticed that she'd gained more weight.

"Can we talk somewhere else?" he asked.

"Sure." She followed him through the doors out into the hall. Two controllers walked past and greeted Kelly on their way inside. One slapped his palm with a high-five. As he watched them enter the TRACON, Sanchez smiled sympathetically. "It's too soon, isn't it? You'd like more time off."

"No, that's not it." He waited for the doors to swing shut and checked the hall to make sure no one else was nearby before speaking softly. "You're not going to believe this, Sam, but some moron claims he's stolen Coastal's black box." Sanchez's eyes widened. "And he wants fifty thousand dollars from me before he'll give it back."

Her jaw dropped. "You're right, I don't believe it! What kind of fucking asshole would dream up a stunt like that?"

He shrugged and suppressed a smile at her slip of tongue. Sam rarely swore.

"Have you contacted the FBI?"

"They'll be here soon. I won't be able to start work for a few hours, I imagine."

"Don't worry about that. We'd better tell Hawkins."

They walked quickly to his office, where the chief received Kelly with uncharacteristic warmth and shook his head in amazement when he heard.

"Someone's got *cojones* of steel, I'll give 'em that much. The FBI can interview you here. My phone has a speaker." He called Judy, the receptionist in the lobby, and told her to direct the visitors to his office when they arrived.

Two agents showed up within the promised hour. After passing through the security doors behind Judy's desk, they flashed their badges to Kelly and Sanchez, who were waiting in the hall. The woman had short black hair and wore a navy blue pantsuit that hugged her compact athletic figure.

"I'm Special Agent Andretti. We spoke on the phone."

"Ryan Kelly. This is Samantha Sanchez, my immediate supervisor."

They shook hands and Andretti motioned to her partner, who had a swarthy complexion and muscular build. "This is Special Agent Rodriguez."

After more hand-shaking, Sanchez led the way to Hawkins' office and they went through another round of introductions while settling onto the sofa and chairs. Andretti unzipped a black portfolio and pulled out a pen to take notes. Kelly dialed the number for Esterhaus, identified everyone in the room and sat down. Without further preliminaries, he then answered a thorough series of questions about the note, his recent activities, and—once he mentioned them—the crank telephone calls. He'd had the presence of mind to preserve the note in a Ziploc bag, and everyone gathered around to read it when he placed it on the desk.

"We'll check for fingerprints," Andretti said, "but I doubt we'll find any except yours, Mr. Kelly. I presume the FAA has them on file?"

"Yes."

"Interesting touch telling you to use the name Phoenix for the ad," Rodriguez said. "Legendary bird that burned itself to death, then rose from the ashes to live again. Perp has a sense of humor."

"Or at least a knowledge of mythology," Andretti said.

She tucked the note in her portfolio and studied Kelly with steady probing eyes. "Why didn't you contact us right away?"

"I, uh, was worried about him watching me, maybe even tapping my phone line." Embarrassed, he avoided her gaze. "I suppose that seems neurotic."

Andretti kept watching him, evaluating his demeanor. At length, she smiled, apparently satisfied. "I appreciate your desire to be cautious. Who else knows about this?"

"No one outside this room. Our receptionist is obviously aware that you're here, but she doesn't know why. I can't imagine anyone in the facility—"

"You'd be surprised," Andretti cut in. "Don't let the circle get wider. That includes people you think you can trust and especially the lady friend you mentioned who works for the *Chronicle*. If the media gets wind of this, it'll turn into a circus and there's no predicting what the perp would do then."

A groan emanated from the speaker on the desk. "I don't even want to think about that," Esterhaus said.

"Try not to be overly concerned about his threats," Rodriguez said. "His primary goal is to get the money. It's unlikely that he wants to complicate this any more than is necessary."

"We'll arrange for the cash," Andretti continued in her businesslike manner. "We'll also coordinate with the McHenry County Sheriff's Department to beef up patrols around your house, but not so much that the perp would notice if he keeps you under surveillance. I say 'he' because it's likely that a male is doing this. And we'll monitor your phone line. The crank calls may or may not be related. Either way, I gather you wouldn't mind if we catch the caller and put a stop to them."

Kelly nodded slowly, still struggling to accept that he was at the center of this bizarre affair.

"Go ahead and place the classified ad in the paper. Call me as soon as he contacts you again." She handed him a business card. "I'm available at that number twenty-four hours a day. Use a land line where you have privacy. If he's dumb enough to call you on his cell phone, we'll find him through your billing records. If not, we'll see how it goes. Who's your service provider?"

"Ameritech."

Andretti scribbled in her portfolio. "All right, then. That's it for now— unless Mr. Esterhaus has something to add." She looked at the speaker.

"No. I don't see that we have any choice but to play along. Please keep me advised."

"We'll certainly do that, sir. And thank you for your cooperation, Mr. Kelly. We'll be in touch," Andretti said. The two agents stood and Kelly moved to escort them out, but she waved him off. "We know the way."

As they retreated down the hall, Hawkins hung up the phone and laid his hands flat on the desk. "Well, this is all rather unheard of, I'd say. But you seem to be handling it with your usual aplomb, Ryan." He leaned back in the chair and folded both arms across his chest, looking expectantly at Kelly. "Are you still feeling up to going back on the line?"

"Under the circumstances, I think that's a bad idea," Sanchez interrupted. "You've got a lot on your mind right now, Ryan. Perhaps you should wait until this FBI business is resolved."

Kelly smiled confidently, unwilling to betray any misgivings. Sam's suggestion made a lot of sense. If he abided by it, he knew his decision would be understood and accepted by some of the controllers. However, it bothered him that others, including Hawkins, would view his reluctance as a sign of weakness. Perhaps the chief had been hoping he'd decline when Sam called the other day. Emboldened with a growing cockiness, he wanted to prove he could still keep his shit together despite everything that had happened.

An inner voice cautioned him not to let ego override good judgment. He liked to call his work a game, but that was an oxymoron and he knew it. The night of May fifth certainly taught him that, as if the previous fourteen years hadn't. *Are you sure you're still the star you once were? Is it worth the risk of finding out?*

Sanchez and Hawkins were watching him closely. He glanced at each of them in turn and nodded decisively, rubbing his hands together. "It's all right, Sam. Let me at those scopes. It'll take my mind off this and everything else."

Sanchez frowned but Hawkins smiled broadly. He stood and walked around his desk to put a hand on Kelly's shoulder. "I didn't think you'd let this side issue get you down. Good luck on your check ride, Ryan. I'm sure you'll do fine."

Sanchez and Kelly shuffled wordlessly down the hall and parted ways near the doors behind Judy's desk. He stopped briefly in the union office to call the *Chronicle* and place the ad before rejoining her in the TRACON. Tapping a folder on her desk, she regarded him with concern.

"This is the written exam. Are you sure you really want to go through with this now?"

"Absolutely, Sam." Being in here, where he belonged, strengthened his resolve. No way would he let any nonsense about the box deter him. If Hawkins hoped he'd wimp out, that was too damn bad. And if the chief wanted to catch him doing something wrong, he'd be out of luck. Kelly intended to go strictly by the book.

He sat down, opened the folder and completed the test in an hour. The question about responsibilities during a TCAS event perversely amused him, but he answered it with the same solemnity as the rest of his responses. The exam wasn't difficult and he needn't have casually browsed through several manuals before Christy and Jason arrived at the house yesterday afternoon. He finished and handed it with a flourish to Sanchez, who began reading immediately.

Looking around the room, he noticed that Rykrisp and Lombardi had switched to East Arrivals. The developmental was talking on the radio, gaining more experience to check out on the Front Line. Kelly couldn't resist sauntering over and slipping on his headset to listen in.

"American 893, descend and maintain seven thousand," Lombardi said.

"American 893, disregard," Rykowski countered abruptly. "If you can expedite down to four thousand, you're number two."

Lombardi glanced at Rykowski and shrugged, then made another call. "United 487, turn left heading two-four-zero and maintain two-one-zero knots."

Rykowski keyed his mike again. "United 487, make that heading two-*five*-zero please."

Lombardi rapped United's flight strip against the console in irritation. "I was going to shoot him into that hole you gave to American. Now you're turning him wider than I want. What gives?"

Rykowski poked a finger at the scope. "I got American to slam dunk for us to make more room for Delta coming in over here. He can be number two and United cruises in behind."

"If I'd dumped United first, then American and Delta would have fallen into place with no delay anyway."

Kelly saw the merits of both plans. Clashes between instructors and developmentals weren't uncommon because of differences in technique. But Rykrisp seemed unusually edgy. He wondered why. Lombardi sighed loudly and called another pilot. Several transmissions later, Rykowski modified his clearance once again.

"Slowing to one-eight-zero knots instead, Coastal 290. Hey, Approach, did you bring your dad to work with you today?"

Lombardi swallowed an urge to laugh. Kelly unplugged and chuckled. "Nice to see you're still in top form, Rykrisp."

He looked up with hardened eyes. "Watch yourself in here, Rain Man. There's only so much we can do for you."

The veiled warning made Kelly uneasy, reminding him of Andretti's caution against trusting people. She'd been referring to the extortionist's plot, of course, but Rykrisp's comment raised anew his suspicions over management's unexpected about-face. Was the union chief aware of some hidden agenda? Kelly edged away from the Front Line without further comment and walked back to Sanchez.

"You passed, of course," she said.

He bowed graciously.

"Why don't you just hang out for a while. Get the feel again. Have I mentioned that I'm concerned about you rushing into this?"

Kelly grinned. Forget Rykrisp. It felt good to be here. "I'm feeling fine, Sam. But I won't turn down the chance to sit around at government expense. They do it to me all the time."

He moved from one position to the next, acknowledging greetings from each controller and absorbing the flick. He tested himself several times by memorizing targets, turning away to silently recite them, then looking back for confirmation. As the Noon Balloon traffic rush gained momentum, everyone began talking constantly. Watching the frenetic ballet in motion was exhilarating. It helped him work up enough courage to swing by *that* scope, where Jackson was handling East Departures. Just as he'd been doing before Kelly took over on the night that still took his breath away.

"Northwest 388, turn left heading zero-niner-zero. Climb and maintain six thousand."

Kelly could hear himself saying the same thing to Coastal 276. A few minutes later, he drifted away and noticed Boskovich speaking to J.J. at the supervisors' desk. They both glanced in his direction and she stared coldly. Kelly sensed they were discussing him and a vague feeling of dread settled like a dense fog. Sanchez joined them and motioned him over. As Kelly approached, J.J. broke away from the group and walked toward him. He hadn't seen her since that Sunday after the crash when he came in to answer questions about the Mode C readouts.

"So, back in the saddle again?" She sounded scornful.

"I can't let you have all the fun."

"Think you can handle the bucking Bosko?"

"No sweat."

There was an edge to her laugh. "Yeah, I'll bet. Must have had great inspiration during your leave."

J.J. brushed past him and walked out of the TRACON. Breathing deeply to clear his mind, he stepped over to Sanchez, who gestured at Bosko.

"Ray will plug in whenever you're ready for your check ride."

"Anytime, Sam."

"Let's go," said the diminutive supe.

As they moved toward the Front Line, Kelly glared at Sanchez behind Bosko's back. She raised her hands and mouthed the words, "Hawkins made me."

They took over for Rykowski and Lombardi. Seven airplanes were on final and four impending arrivals appeared on the Tab list. Despite his veneer of assurance, Kelly spent an extra twenty seconds studying the scope and had to jigger with his microphone jack before he successfully plugged it into the socket.

"Okay, I've got the flick." His voice sounded more confident than he felt.

Lombardi stood and gripped his arm. "Good luck, Rain Man."

Kelly sat down and ran his fingers along the wooden shelf that was built in at each console to provide space for the flight strips. Strangely, the scope seemed larger than before. He dimmed the video, cleared his throat, and squeezed the mike switch.

"Delta—ah, correction—United 611, descend and maintain seven thousand."

"We're out of eleven for seven, United 611."

Bosko's presence sent tingles across the back of his neck. He sensed Rykrisp standing behind him, watching, too. Ignore. There's a gap you can shoot in front of United. Check the wind first so you'll know when to turn Air Canada. One-eight-zero at fifteen. He spit out the clearance and the pilot read it back. As the jumble of targets swarmed on the scope, his vision blurred momentarily. *Jesus, am I really ready to do this?*

The beam swept around, the targets flashed, and suddenly he lost the flick.

He couldn't remember his plan and stared uncomprehendingly at the data tags, unable to grasp their information. He didn't breathe and clamped his mouth shut to hold in a scream. The nightmare replayed, bodies tumbling out of the airliner one after another. *Not now.* His eyes narrowed on the green blips. *Move them around so they don't hit each other, that's all. But there's hundreds of people on board and those planes are all converging.* Focus. *You've done this once or twice before. Should I turn United or American first? Shit, man, I'm lost!* Stop whining, make a decision, and call an airplane.

Panic passed with the next sweep.

Kelly blinked and the flick reappeared. His plan coalesced again and he calmly turned United 611 onto final. He glanced at Boskovich to see whether he'd detected anything wrong. The supe fingered his tie and stared back defensively. Kelly swiveled around to the scope again and breathed deeply. For the next hour, he hurled airplanes in the sky like he'd done it only yesterday.

Break a leg, pal. Just a touch of stage fright.

Boskovich finally unplugged his headset and stood. "You seem to be taking your work more seriously. Your phraseology has improved. I'll sign off on recertification." It was said nearly devoid of emotion before he walked away.

Kelly tossed off Bosko's attitude with a snort. Never mind him. I'm back in the trenches. Back on the glorious Front Line.

Rykowski, who was still standing behind Kelly, flipped the bird to Bosko. "Hey, everybody," he shouted. "Rain Man's in the pool again. Send him your airplanes."

A chorus of cheers erupted and then Kelly felt a hand on his shoulder. He looked up at Sanchez's smiling face. "Nice going," she said. "You okay on the position for another hour?"

"All day, Sam."

✈   ✈   ✈

SHARON MASTERS GRIMACED in determination and scuffed her left foot along the white linoleum floor of the outpatient clinic at Northwestern Memorial Hospital on the Near North Side. For the first time since acquiring her artificial limb, she was attempting to walk unaided by crutches or the parallel bars.

"Very good," the physical therapist exhorted. She stood several feet away with outstretched arms, waving Sharon on and ready to catch her if she stumbled. "You can do it. Now the other foot."

Sharon clenched her jaw and swung her right leg forward, then the left again. Haltingly, clumsily, she paced the length of the room before collapsing into the therapist's arms in a fit of laughter and tears. She heard clapping and saw Christy Cochran applauding in the doorway. Placing a hand on the therapist's shoulder for balance, Sharon turned and awkwardly shuffled over to her. The two women embraced warmly before Christy helped Sharon to a chair, sitting beside her.

"You'll be running the four-minute mile in no time. Duncan told me you'd be here, so I dropped by to see how you're doing. I'm impressed."

"She's making excellent progress," the therapist said, easing toward the door. "I'll leave you two alone to chat and be back in a little while, Sharon."

Christy studied her face. Some of the innocence was gone, replaced by firm resolve. But Sharon's short blonde hair was still styled in that adorable bob and she exuded the perkiness Christy remembered from the *Chronicle*.

"I'm coming back to work next week," Sharon said brightly. "Metcalf told me I could help cover the crash hearings."

"Are you sure you want to?"

"I wouldn't miss them for the world."

"How are you otherwise?"

"Duncan visits every day and helps keep my spirits up. We've even gone out a few times." Sharon nudged Christy's arm. "My sources tell me you've been in good spirits lately. They say you and that controller are really hitting it off."

Christy smiled sheepishly and speculated on who supplied the information. Gossip spread like wildfire in a newsroom. "We're getting along great. Jason even likes him."

"That helps. It can be hard on kids when their parents develop new relationships."

"It took them awhile to get to know each other, but now they act like best buddies. I think it's sweet. Ryan gave Jason an aviation band radio and he spends hours listening to the pilots and controllers talk. Now Jason wants me to take him to a hobby shop so he can buy Ryan a present for his model train."

"Sounds like it's getting serious. Are you falling in love?"

Christy smiled again. "Well, it's a little too soon to know. He's preoccupied about a lot of stuff and I don't want to push."

"I'm sure it's a very stressful time for him."

"You don't know the half of it." She told Sharon about the crank phone calls and the mysterious driver who ran her off the road. She also mentioned Kelly's concern about his bosses. "The office politics don't worry me as much as the maniac who's out there. Ryan's life may be in danger."

Sharon's voice turned sharp. "The politics should worry you. You're forgetting that my dad's involved. He doesn't want the crash to be blamed on TCAS anymore than the FAA does. Tell your boyfriend to watch his back at work, too."

"Are you suggesting your father would really try to influence—"

"I'm sure of it. Have you been reading Ellen's stories about Circuitron? The company is a major TCAS supplier. They made the unit that was on board Coastal 276. It occurred to me the other night that my dad took several trips on Circuitron's corporate jet during his last campaign. I was only sixteen then so I didn't think much about it when he told me. But I'd be willing to bet there were some other payoffs. With that kind of cozy relationship, he's probably doing whatever he can to protect the company."

Sharon's assessment belied a maturity unusual for her age. Christy felt certain she'd do well as a reporter. "That would be a great story if we could confirm it."

"Run it before next week and it'll take the wind out of my dad's sails when he tries something at the hearings. He will, you know. It's too great a PR opportunity to pass up. Besides, TCAS is his baby. I seriously doubt he'll stand by and let it take the fall."

Christy was at once aghast and excited. Fearful more than ever about the man she held so dear, the journalist in her coveted the possibility of a scoop. She'd felt helpless watching events unfold around Kelly. Now she could do something tangible that might give the paper's accident coverage a major boost. She thought about the business reporters on their staff. Hamilton was the most knowledgeable. She hoped he'd be in the office when she got back to the *Chronicle*.

"Is there anything else you remember about your dad and Circuitron?"

Sharon rubbed a tender muscle in her left thigh and thought for a moment. "I believe he owns some of their stock. Dredge up his tax returns and just follow the money."

✈   ✈   ✈

THE RADIO IN KELLY'S CAR blared deafeningly during the drive to Bear's apartment. The rest of his first day back in the TRACON went well. He had to think a bit longer devising traffic plans, but the worst moment was the scare with Bosko at his side. Later, when he thought no one was looking, he raised one of his hands above the console and discovered with relief that he could hold it rock steady. After the shift ended, he bought several pitchers of beer for the gang at the Sports Edition, then decided to check in on Bear.

He answered the doorbell with a bottle of Budweiser in his hand and waved Kelly inside. His eyes were bloodshot again, but he'd healed from the scuffle at Charlie's. The apartment remained mostly unfurnished. Without asking, he pulled another Bud out of the fridge, twisted off the cap, and handed it to Kelly as they sat down at the kitchen table.

"I hear you went back to work today. How'd it go?"

"Passed my check ride."

He clinked the neck of his bottle against Kelly's. "About time you started making an honest living again. Just be careful. Hawkins can't be trusted."

Kelly nodded. "I don't know what his game plan is, but I'm staying on my best behavior."

"You'd better. Fuck up now and even the union won't be able to save your ass. Something this big, Hawkins will lift your ticket with the stroke of a pen and never mind NATCA."

"Yeah, I might be forced to take my case to the public." He said it sarcastically but added half-seriously, "Maybe it's about time they heard our side."

Bear slammed his bottle on the table, slopping beer. "Shit, Rain Man, eleven thousand controllers were fired in '81 and the public said right on. You think anyone's gonna care about two guys? They want a scapegoat just as much as the FAA."

Christy's accusation at the church stirred in his memory. *You screwed up.*

"Yeah, I hear ya. Let's hope the NTSB finds out what really happened and tells it like it is."

"Sure. In nine months to a year the board will finally come out with an honest report the public won't care diddley about." He picked up the cap to his beer bottle and flicked it with his thumb. The cap ricocheted off the rim of the wastebasket and bounced onto the floor. "Meanwhile, Hawkins deep sixes us so the agency can look like it fixed the problem. I went through the strike and I know how they operate."

"The strike was a long time ago."

"Things haven't changed. In all these years, after all the money they've spent and all the programs they've tried in their quest to make this a kinder, gentler FAA, things haven't really changed. The guys walked because of long hours, outdated equipment, money, and piss-poor management. What do we have today? Six-day weeks half the time, the same scopes when the TRACON was built in '71, paychecks that haven't kept pace with inflation, and too many inept bosses."

Kelly drank more beer and nodded glumly. Bear's points were largely on the mark. "I've never asked why you didn't walk."

"It's against the law. That wouldn't stop me now. Laws are made by people and they're not always right." He stretched an arm to the fridge and retrieved another Bud. "Speaking of which, women must have written the divorce laws because I'm getting shafted on my property settlement."

"I saw Donna on TV last week."

For the first time, Bear's deeply lined face brightened. "The little bitch deserves an Oscar. I gave Rykrisp's wife a standing ovation when she called the show to defend us. I'm a celebrity at Charlie's now." He laughed over his newfound fame, which developed into a violent fit of coughing that bubbled with phlegm. When he recovered, his face turned dour. "Donna's lawyer keeps twisting my balls. I'm about ready to throw in the towel with her."

The doorbell rang and Bear went to answer it. Kelly stayed in the kitchen, pensively sipping his beer. Until watching Donna last week, he'd never appreciated her willingness to go for the jugular. Until now, he never would have guessed she'd win. Bear was like a pit bull. He didn't give up easily. When he joined the Navy, he couldn't swim so he'd spent days in the pool overcoming his fear of the water. But the midair was a lot to handle, sapping his energy to fight other battles. Donna wouldn't have had a chance otherwise.

Indistinguishable voices from the living room rose into shouts. Bolting out of his chair, he hurried to investigate. Bear stood at the front door, shaking his fist at a television camera crew.

"You've got no right coming here."

The reporter clutched his microphone. "Do you have any comment on what your wife said about you last week?"

"That's none of your fucking business, you goddamned leeches! Get the hell out of here!" He lunged and shoved the cameraman.

"Hey, Bear. Don't!" Kelly grabbed his arms, but the nickname was well-deserved. He grunted, struggling to restrain his massive friend. "Bear, you're making it worse."

The red light on the minicam stayed on while the crew backed down the stairs. Bear kept sputtering obscenities as Kelly pulled him inside and slammed the door. They both stood heaving, looking awkwardly at each other.

"What the hell's the matter with you? Are you drunk?"

"Those bastards have got no business poking into my personal affairs."

"No, but do you have any idea how that'll look on the news? They love that ambush stuff and you acted like a lunatic. Hawkins will have a field day."

Bear stuffed both hands into his pockets and shifted defiantly. "It doesn't matter what I do. The agency's got their finger on my ripcord and I don't have a parachute. Neither do you. I told you your star would fall one day. Fuck Hawkins. Fuck all of you."

"I'm trying to help—"

"Yeah, well, you've worn out your welcome. Don't let the door hit you on the way out."

They stared at each other some more in stony silence. Kelly decided it was best just to leave and call him in a few days. He cracked open the door and saw no sign of the news crew. He glanced at Bear, standing forlornly in the barren room.

"Try to take it easy."

Kelly closed the door and plodded down the stairs. Once Hawkins saw the tantrum on TV, he'd write an evaluation pronouncing Bear mentally unstable. His friend would never sit at a scope again. With a feeling of helplessness, he trudged out of the apartment building and saw the TV news van driving away. Pulling keys out of his pocket, he stepped between two parked cars to get to his Acura across the street. Halfway there, the roar of an engine swelled from the right.

He jerked his head and froze in the path of a gray sedan bearing down on him. Instantly, his universe compressed into the few feet separating him from the car. *Better move because that driver can't stop in time.* The headlights loomed and he thought he could feel heat from the engine. It needed a tune-up. The valves clicked noisily.

Christ, move now—he's not even trying to stop!

The motor raced with an overpowering din. Kelly leaped toward his Acura and landed on the hood as the sedan streaked past in a blur, its side-view mirror slapping the sole of one foot. As he twisted to focus on the license plate, the car skidded around a corner and disappeared.

Gingerly, he swung his legs and wriggled his right foot to check for injuries. Other than a stinging sensation, his limbs felt okay. But his gut roiled with acid as the adrenaline rush subsided. He hung his head, cursing when realization fell into place. Gray sedan. The same one Christy described. Another warning. Unsteadily, he slipped off the hood and wobbled into his car. Before keying the ignition, he locked the doors.

TWENTY-THREE
DEAL

B RAD SCHWARTZ STARED IDLY through the grimy window of the No.
54B CTA bus that ambled south along Cicero Avenue, his left foot
resting on the empty seat next to him and his left arm balanced
casually atop his knee. The brakes squealed as the bus lurched to a stop at
Archer and the folding doors behind him hissed open. Another blast of hot
humid air invaded the half-empty coach, overwhelming its anemic air conditioning, while several passengers clambered down the stairs. An elderly
man clutching a white plastic grocery bag gripped the polished metal handrail and moved deliberately. The driver watched him in the rearview mirror,
his eyes flicking impatiently to the traffic signal that would turn red any
moment. As soon as the man stepped onto the sidewalk, the doors banged
shut and the bus lumbered across the busy intersection with a surge of its
diesel engine.

Ordinarily, the sluggish pace rankled Brad. Though he grudgingly admitted that the El could make faster time than traffic on the expressways,
he hated riding buses that stopped every other block. After buying a Camaro
during his first year in college, he'd steadfastly avoided the transit system
until the Denver Boot immobilized his car a month ago.

But today he tolerated the usual annoyances, his spirits buoyed by the
Chronicle that lay folded in his lap. He'd picked up a copy on the way to
campus this morning, quickly flipped to the classified section, and spotted
the ad referring to a three-legged cat named Phoenix. Brad smiled with
anticipation now as the bus labored toward the mall where he worked after-
noons and evenings as a salesman at an electronics store. Soon, he'd never
have to deal with the CTA again.

He snickered inwardly at the clever way he'd delivered his note on Sunday. Simply tossing it in Kelly's mailbox would have been lame. He liked the idea of messing with the controller's head and the cat was a perfect catalyst. He'd spotted it lounging on the deck behind the house while scoping out the place once before. When Brad saw the kitty again on Sunday, he coaxed it into the woods where he'd hidden. Then he attached the film container to its collar while dodging angry claws. The critter scampered straight for the deck as soon as he let it go. From the cover of brush, he had the satisfaction of watching Kelly's reaction when he discovered the note a few minutes later.

Trembling with excitement and nerves, Brad retreated to his mother's car that was parked near a row of bushes alongside the house after Kelly disappeared inside. He shook his head at the memory of unintentionally running a blue Honda Civic off the road. A close call that could have ruined everything. He hoped the driver hadn't gotten a close look at him. Good thing, too, that he hadn't sideswiped the Honda. Despite the note's warning, Brad figured that Kelly would alert the authorities. If he'd done so right away, the presence of a stranger at the end of his driveway would have drawn immediate suspicion. And he would have been hard-pressed to explain the accident to mom. She'd let him borrow her Dodge on the premise that he was going to the campus library—and only because she planned to shop for an RV with pops and didn't need it. He'd have to get a grip and not do anything stupid again when he traded the black box for the cash.

As he'd done repeatedly during the past few weeks, he reviewed his plan for the exchange once more. A crowded public place was a given to help him remain anonymous to the FBI goons who'd no doubt be swarming in force. He'd selected a site several days ago, but would wait until the last minute before informing Kelly so the Feds couldn't position themselves in advance.

He assumed the bag of cash would contain a hidden transmitter to pinpoint his location, and he'd devised a way to switch the money into another satchel. They'd have the serial numbers recorded, too, of course, but Brad planned to swap the bills in Las Vegas. At each of several casinos, he'd buy a few thousand dollars worth of chips, gamble minimally, then turn in the chips for clean cash. He estimated he could work his way down the Strip in a day and be gone before the marked bills were discovered.

Through the window of the bus he saw a woman walking her poodle and a wide smirk spread across his face. While concocting his scheme, he'd dreamed up a way for Stan's yellow Labrador to help him safely retrieve the money. When Brad told his friend that he'd dumped Gina and wanted to borrow the "babe magnet," Stan happily obliged. For the past two weekends, Brad had spent several hours at Marquette Park training Moose to perform a very special trick.

During the next few days at the store, he planned to acquire half a dozen wireless phones using his five-finger discount and activate them with phony accounts. By using a different handset for each call to Kelly during the exchange, the Feds would have a hard time tracing his location—even with their fancy electronic gear.

All that remained now was to let the controller know when the swap would take place. Saturday seemed like a good bet to ensure maximum crowds. He'd wait till Friday before telling him. Make the guy sweat a little. With a warped view of reality, Brad had legitimized his actions through gradual rationalization. He was really doing the victims a favor. If the dumbshit had let two airplanes smack, killing several hundred innocent people, then he ought to atone for his mistake.

The bus jerked to a stop at Ford City mall, rousing Brad out of his contemplation. Gloating over his plan, he hopped off the bus and strolled jauntily toward the store where he worked.

✈   ✈   ✈

FRIDAY MORNING'S TRAFFIC along the Northwest Tollway slogged through Elgin, slowed by typical rush-hour capacity and the requisite stop at a toll plaza near Route 31. Kelly edged into the lane to his left to pass a semi-trailer truck blocking his view and sighed at the flashing red constellation of brake lights ahead. Another car cut in front of him and he jabbed his horn, provoking an obscene gesture from its driver. He changed lanes again for another toll booth and acknowledged that his short fuse had less to do with this traffic than the elusive black box.

After dutifully placing an ad in Tuesday's *Chronicle*, the lack of response by the reprobate who'd stolen it baffled him. Special Agent Andretti tried consoling him on the phone, saying the thief was playing a psychological waiting game, but Kelly's frustration and anger ratcheted up with each passing day. He'd begun to speculate that the note demanding money was simply a sick joke from someone who had no intention of following through.

He pulled forward to the booth and irritably tossed several coins into the metal bucket. A dime bounced out and tinkled onto the pavement. *Shit.* He fished another one from the change compartment in the dashboard and dropped it carefully into the bin. Without waiting for the light to turn green, he jammed the gear shift into first and stomped on the gas pedal. At the same time, his wireless phone chirped and he snatched it off the passenger seat.

"Hello!"

"Kelly?"

Aggravation vanished as he pressed the phone tightly against his ear, eager to hear every nuance of the unknown voice. Intuitively, he knew this was the thief. "Speaking," he replied slowly.

"Put the cash in a backpack and don't rig it with dye or you'll just get it all over yourself. We'll trade tomorrow. Drive toward the airport from your home and I'll call you at one P.M. to tell you more. No tricks or the box is history. Got it?"

"Yeah. But where exactly are we—"

Click.

The long anticipated response and its attendant swiftness startled him. After switching off the phone, he looked at it to assure himself the call really happened. The male voice sounded youngish, but he hung up so quickly that Kelly couldn't distinguish much else. As soon as he arrived at O'Hare, he went to the NATCA office and ordered a few controllers out of the room so he could speak privately to Andretti.

"We knew you received a call because we've been monitoring the computer that handles the billing for your phone," she said. "It was placed from a pay phone downtown here in the Loop. My guess is the perp waited till today so we wouldn't have much time to prepare. And to play with your head."

"If that was his plan, he succeeded."

Andretti laughed gently. "Hang in there, Mr. Kelly. This should all be over soon. Meet me tomorrow at the First Chicago Bank branch in Schaumburg. It's at Higgins and Meacham, only about fifteen minutes from the airport. Let's make it twelve-thirty."

"Fine."

"By the way, I'm sorry I forgot to mention this the other day. We checked out the land line at your home. It's secure, so you can use it at will."

"Thanks, that's reassuring."

"And the crank call you got last night was placed from another pay phone on the North Side. Could be the same guy but my gut feeling tells me it's not."

"Okay."

"Let me know if anything else happens, but otherwise I'll see you tomorrow. Bye."

Kelly hung up and sat with his hands clasped on the desk in the small silent office, trying to clear his head and spool up for a shift in the TRACON. The door flew open and two controllers barged in, trading insults with each other. In no mood for levity, Kelly exchanged pleasantries with them and walked to the radar room. He paused just inside the doors to let his eyes adjust, the darkness swathing him in a comforting cocoon.

The past week had been more difficult than he'd anticipated. As always, the side issues bothered him more than the traffic itself. The incredible business with the box, the persistent crank calls, continuing unease with his bosses, and his self-imposed exile from Christy. They'd spoken on the phone everyday, but it was a poor substitute for holding her in his arms. Sam, Boskovich, and his fellow controllers watched him constantly. They were all waiting, it seemed, for him to make a mistake or crack up. Perhaps both. He smiled at the irony because talking to airplanes actually helped him stay calm. He was confident, sharp, happy to be working again. In here, he felt safe—most of the time.

Holding the specter of the midair entirely at bay was impossible. Flashbacks burst and faded like claps of thunder. After years of perceived invincibility, his genie of self-doubt had escaped from the bottle and no amount of reassurance could put her back. During the past four days, he'd handled his shaken faith without a flicker of the eye or a change in intonation, but the scotches he poured at home each night were a telling barometer. One of the stranger moments occurred yesterday while he was working East Departures. Talking to Coastal 317, the airline's five P.M. flight to Washington National, a feeling of vague weirdness swept over him, then soon dissipated.

He deliberately shook off his anxiousness when he noticed Boskovich approaching. Now that the city was sweltering under the full brunt of summer, the meticulously dressed supervisor had traded sweater vests for suspenders, generating a new round of caustic comments behind his back.

"Good morning, Ryan. Are you ready to work or would you rather just stand there all day?"

"I'm waiting for my supervisor to assign me on position," Kelly said evenly.

Boskovich arched an eyebrow and consulted his clipboard. "Take over for Christensen on the Foul Line." Before Kelly could move away, he held up a hand. "Pete Rykowski has been Lombardi's primary instructor in your absence, but he'll be unavoidably late this afternoon. So I'd like you to give Gene some time on Approach." He stared defiantly. "If that's all right with you."

Kelly ignored Bosko's sarcastic tone. The jerk was just trying to goad him into a fight. Smiling sweetly, he said, "As you wish, boss."

The day proceeded uneventfully and training Lombardi proved to be good therapy. It forced him to concentrate more on the scope instead of his emotions. Lombardi appreciated the change, too, and discreetly mentioned it while reeling in a stream of arrivals.

"It's nice being back with you, Rain Man." He glanced around and lowered his voice. "Pete's been kinda touchy lately. Guess I'll get paired with him again next week when you're at the accident hearings."

"Rykrisp will be at the hearings, too, since he's the NATCA facility rep," Kelly said. "But J.J. or someone else will keep you on your toes. Watch your spacing between Simmons and United."

"I got 'em. Simmons 4287, turn right heading one-two-zero and intercept the one-four left localizer. Traffic three o'clock, six miles southbound, on the final for one-four right at five thousand. It's a United heavy DC-10."

Bear would also be at the hearings and Kelly mused over how he'd fare. The video clip of his outburst had aired repeatedly, fanning a flurry of comment on radio and TV talk shows. An editorial in the *Chronicle* pronounced him unsuited to the demands of air traffic control, regardless of his involvement in the midair. Kelly was hard-pressed to disagree. Bear apologized for his blowup when the two had another visit the other day, but he continued to drink heavily. Kelly decided to drop by his apartment again after work and try to prepare him for the hearings.

Lombardi was doing very well. He'd made vast progress since his first day on Approach when the beacon went out and Kelly dismissed him as an ARTS baby. Now, he was comfortable with the pace and conscious of his spacing. He splatted United and a Continental jet in front of it, smiling with satisfaction at their separation of 2.1 miles.

"Simmons 4287 is cleared for a visual approach, runway one-four left, hold short of two-two right. O'Hare Tower at the marker twenty-six niner. G'day."

Lombardi splatted Simmons and a Delta target ahead. They were precisely two miles apart, which did not go unnoticed by Kelly.

"Looks like you're getting the hang of this." He raised his voice for the benefit of others on the Front Line. "Hey, Pizza Man needs more airplanes."

Kelly saw Boskovich turn in their direction and hoped the supe heard, too. Lombardi deserved the recognition. For the next hour, he talked nonstop, pounding the parallel runways with arrivals. He'd never worked so hard at a scope and never felt so satisfied. He was grinning proudly at Kelly when Boskovich stepped behind them.

"You're both immediately decertified."

The two controllers looked up with perplexed smiles. Kelly spoke first.

"What's the problem, Bosko? Did we forget to say 'runway' or something?"

"Loss of separation on final. I've seen several instances of two-mile spacing."

Kelly blinked, trying to wake from a bizarre dream. "You can't be serious. We run two miles all the time and no one says a word. You want it safe or legal? You can't have both without backing the final all the way out to Milwaukee."

Boskovich looked askance. "We have a federal waiver to reduce separation to two-point-five miles. Two-mile separation is not officially sanctioned. Greg Webber will take over."

Kelly craned his head toward Sanchez, sitting at her desk. "Hey, Sam! Did I miss the big memo? Since when are two-mile finals a deal?"

"What?" Confusion rapidly turned to comprehension when she saw Boskovich. She sprang out of her chair and hurried over to them. "You'll never make it stick, Ray. We'd have to decertify everyone in here."

He stood arrogantly, adjusting his tie with annoying fastidiousness. "We'll see about that. Care to join us in Hawkins' office?"

She tugged forcefully on his tie. "You bet your ass! Greg, take over here."

As soon as Webber completed the transition with Lombardi, the group marched toward the administrative wing. They encountered Rykowski along the way and he fell into step with them, grim-faced, after Kelly related what had just happened. When Hawkins found out, feigned concern barely disguised his delight.

"I'm dismayed to hear this, Ryan. An operational error is the last thing you need on the eve of the hearings."

Lombardi grimaced. Developmentals were protected by immunity. The instructor shouldered full responsibility.

"Every other controller in the TRACON is also disobeying your sudden insistence on going by the book," Sanchez said. "It's how we handle the traffic around here—or hadn't you noticed? When are you going to decertify them?"

"We'll start with this one."

"I'm flattered to be first," Kelly said. His steely eyes bored through Boskovich, making him take a step backward. "It takes a lot of skill to maintain two-mile spacing. Something you never mastered, pal. You were too busy kissing ass."

Hawkins clucked. "Your attitude is regrettable, Ryan. So's yours, Ms. Sanchez. As a member of the management team, I suggest you work with us to keep the system running safely."

His comment infuriated her. Having been discriminated against all her life, having watched her parents humiliated too many times by ignorant *Americanos*, she refused to stand by while Kelly was unfairly singled out. Equality laws pressured the agency to promote her and she hoped they'd protect her now. She leaned over and placed both hands on Hawkins' desk, spitting out her words.

"Maybe it's different for you, chief, considering you've never been a controller. But when I see someone get a deal for handling the traffic safely, quickly, and within our normal bounds of operation, I can't be a happy smiling member of the management team." She straightened, towering over him. "This is total bullshit."

Hawkins gripped the edge of his desk. "I'll deal with you later, Ms.

Sanchez—in private. Ryan, you're legally prohibited from discharging your duties until further notice. Gene, report for your next shift as scheduled—"

"You planned this all along, didn't you?" Kelly snarled.

A brief look passed between Hawkins and Boskovich before the chief snapped, "That's an insult to everyone in this agency who maintains the highest standard of safety."

"Yeah, yeah. Save your speech for the Rotary Club. If you're so goddamned concerned about safety, hire more controllers and get us some equipment that doesn't crap out all the time. I've got the flick. You wanted something else to hang me with at the hearings."

Hawkins propelled himself out of the chair and pursed his lips into thin pale lines. "Don't blame me for your irresponsible and dangerous behavior, Mr. Kelly. You've done this to yourself. And if I have anything to say about it, you'll never control airplanes again." He glanced testily at the others. "Now, if you'll all excuse me, I have work to do."

Kelly considered a retort, but decided it was futile and whirled around toward the door. Lombardi, Rykowski, and Sanchez filed out behind him. Boskovich hesitated, as if he hoped to engage the chief in a private conversation. He followed the others into the hall after Hawkins' mouth curled into a hint of a smile and his head shook imperceptibly.

Kelly bowed gallantly in front of the supe, held out an arm, and said brightly, "Assholes before age." He winked at Rykrisp. "Or is it age before beauty? I always get that mixed up."

"It's ladies first, assholes last," Sanchez said, her dark eyes blazing. She snapped one of Boskovich's suspenders against his chest and stalked down the hall. Kelly grinned and brushed past him, followed by Rykowski and Lombardi.

"This doesn't end here," Sanchez said when the others caught up to her, loudly enough for Boskovich to hear.

Rykowski frowned. "No, it doesn't. In light of this incident, the union will have to re-evaluate its willingness to move the traffic according to commonly accepted standards."

Sanchez grunted, anticipating monumental delays. "I know where this is going."

"It's nothing personal against you, Sam. But we won't stand by quietly while Rain Man's nailed to the cross. If Hawkins insists on holding us to the regs, then by God we'll follow 'em to the letter."

"I'm sorry," Lombardi said. "This is all my fault."

"You did what's required," Kelly said. "Think of all the people who got home to their families this afternoon because you had what it takes to get the job done. They ought to be certifying you." He slapped him on the back. "Let me buy you a beer."

Lombardi looked at his mentor in awe. "How can you be so cavalier about this?"

"Juvenile repartee does that to me. Besides, I know I can look at myself in the mirror with a straight face. That's something Hawkins and Boskoprick can never take away."

Sanchez touched Kelly's arm. "Why don't you go home and get some rest."

"Yeah, I suppose that's the sensible thing to do." He smiled bravely at Rykrisp and Pizza Man. "Keep pushing that tin, guys."

With Hawkins' final pronouncement echoing in his ears, Kelly's heart sank as he strode away. How could he have been so arrogant and naïve to think that returning to work this week wouldn't end badly? The brass had charted their course and he'd followed it perfectly, carelessly ignoring his instincts. Now he was paying the price of ego. He felt like having a drink, but was too weary to stop at the Hilton. Visiting Bear was unappealing, too, but his friend needed all the support he could get.

Traffic crawled out of O'Hare as usual for a Friday afternoon. Kelly broke free just beyond the airport exit and sped south on Mannheim Road. Bear's black Corvette was parked in front of his building when he arrived. He knocked on the door and waited. Muted laughter erupted from the apartment across the hall. He knocked again, thinking Bear might have walked to Charlie's. Silence. He turned to leave and a car backfired in the distance. Kelly stopped short.

The backfire had come from inside Bear's apartment.

Without thinking, he twisted the knob and the unlocked door opened. "Hey, Bear. You here?"

No answer.

He padded through the living room, still vacant except for the TV, lawn chair, and lamp.

"Bear, it's Rain Man."

The kitchen was empty, too. An unwashed coffee cup sat on the counter. He moved down the hallway to the bedroom. Empty. Bear must be drinking at Charlie's, he thought hopefully, but that noise had definitely come from his unit. A gurgling sound filtered out of the bathroom and Kelly pushed the door open with a hand.

"Oh, fuck." The silence in the apartment magnified his words.

Bear lay crumpled in the shower. His right hand cradled a pistol and remains of the left side of his head were splattered against the tile wall. Blood pooling on the floor flowed neatly down the drain.

Kelly's knees buckled and he slumped to the floor in the doorway, feeling nauseous. He forced himself to breathe slowly and stave off hyperventilation. *Jesus Christ.* Big, blustery Bear—Mr. Cocky—had finally cracked under the pressure.

The midair.

The knife from the FAA.

Donna. The talk show interview came to mind and he imagined her gleaming as she twisted the knife deeper. He stared at Bear's body in grief and pity, in anger over his friend's inability to stay strong, in guilt for missing the signals of what he'd been about to do. He wasn't sure how much time passed before he picked up the phone on the floor beside the bed to dial 911. When the operator answered, his voice was a hoarse whisper.

"There's been a suicide."

✈   ✈   ✈

CHRISTY RARELY WORKED ON FRIDAYS, but she was huddled now in the *Chronicle*'s Business Department with reporter Alexander Hamilton. All week, as their schedules permitted, the two had tenaciously unveiled a shrouded web of illegal campaign contributions and other financial transactions involving Senator Richard Masters. Armed with tax returns he was required to make public, they canvassed SEC documents to trace ownership of what appeared to be a dummy corporation linked to Masters. Now, as Christy pored over records available at the agency's Edgar site on the Web, Hamilton hung up the telephone, laced his fingers together, and cracked his knuckles.

"We've got it, Christy! I finally connected with that source I've been trying to reach for the past two days. Circuitron fired this guy six years ago, so he was more than willing to talk. He confirmed what Sharon told you about the corporate jet. Masters took four trips—all of them to political rallies that the company illegally charged off as regular business expenses."

"We'll need a paper trail. Circuitron will claim he's disgruntled and making this up. Why was he fired?"

"He says they let him go a month after he questioned his bosses about the trips. Corporate downsizing was the official explanation. Fortunately, he'd already made copies of the records. He's faxing us the expense accounts, flight manifests, everything. He wanted to go public at the time, but was afraid Circuitron would arrest him for stealing company property. He figures enough time has passed that they won't know for sure who leaked the documents."

"That's terrific, Alex. I'm afraid I'm not doing as well." Christy waved a hand at her computer monitor and a mess of papers strewn across the desk. "These SEC records don't show a solid link between Masters and Pinnacle Corporation, but there's no question Pinnacle owns a substantial block of Circuitron stock."

"I'll take a look at that stuff right after I call Circuitron. I want to catch their corporate flack before the offices close for the day."

It took several minutes for Hamilton to reach Circuitron's public affairs director. When he did, he endured the inevitable chitchat about his name. Hamilton's father, a banker, had chosen to call his son Alexander in honor of the first secretary of the U.S. Treasury. Hamilton's corporate style of dress, right down to the oxford shoes he wore, fostered the assumption that he might be a descendant of the American Revolution statesman. It had proven to be a handy icebreaker for numerous interviews, though not during today's call to Circuitron, which terminated soon after he asked for comment about the trips.

"He said he'll get back to me, but I won't hold my breath. Now let's see what you've found."

They carefully reviewed the SEC records for another hour, still unable to establish a firm connection between Masters and Pinnacle. Hamilton downplayed Christy's frustration.

"We've got enough to ask some pointed questions. Maybe even enough to run a story that'll force Masters to open his books. Metcalf will have to make that call."

"Did I hear my name?" They turned to see the managing editor standing behind them, smiling faintly. "I didn't realize you were in the habit of working so closely with reporters, Christy."

His tone carried an edge to it and she tempered her excitement. "Alex and I have a good story to pitch, Ralph."

"So I've heard." He motioned toward the door to the business editor's office, which was open and empty. "Let's talk about it in there." They shuffled in and everyone remained standing after Metcalf shut the door. His face was taut.

"It seems you've been asking Circuitron about some trips that Senator Masters took in their jet. Must have touched a nerve because our publisher called me right after he got off the phone with the senator, who insists there's nothing to the story." Metcalf sighed heavily. "Prendergast wants us to drop it."

"We've got proof," Hamilton said. "Documents that'll hold up in court."

"I'm sorry, but Prendergast insists. And let me know about anything else you're working on involving the senator." Metcalf held out his hands in a gesture of helplessness. "Alex, our publisher rarely interferes, but it is his paper. He has every right to choose what we print."

Christy remembered a story the paper published several weeks ago and motivations became clear. "The *Chronicle*'s trying to buy five TV stations in New England. Prendergast is worried that Masters might persuade the FCC to scotch the deal if we run a story detrimental to him. Does that accurately characterize the situation, Ralph?"

Metcalf regarded her circumspectly. "I didn't say that."

There was a knock at the door and Ellen Sanders poked her head in the office. "I thought I'd find you here, Christy. We just heard about a suicide." She waved a hand when Christy drew in her breath. "It's not your friend. The victim was that other controller involved in the crash. Sharon and I wanted to tell you before we go out to the scene."

"I wonder if Ryan knows," Christy said. "I'd better call him." She turned to Metcalf, who cast his eyes toward the publisher's office two floors above.

"We're through here. I'd characterize his position as final."

✈   ✈   ✈

T WO POLICE OFFICERS ARRIVED at Bear's apartment twenty minutes after Kelly's call and he answered their questions in robotic monosyllables. The officers then milled about the apartment waiting for the medical examiner to arrive. Radios on their belts stuttered harshly in the nearly vacant rooms. Kelly sat at the kitchen table as he'd done so often with Bear, nursing a beer from the fridge. He played with the bottle cap and wondered how such a burly, tough-fisted ex-sailor could feel so out of control that he'd pull the trigger on himself. Unexpectedly, two women appeared at the kitchen door. He didn't recognize the blonde on crutches, but he remembered the brunette. She'd come to his house that day.

"Hi, Mr. Kelly." Sanders slowly approached him. "The police let us in. I'm so sorry about your friend. We heard about it on the scanner." She motioned at her companion. "This is Sharon Masters."

Kelly stood and shook hands with both of them.

"Would you mind telling us about Frank?" Sanders asked.

He ignored the question and watched Sharon prop her crutches against the wall. "What happened to you?"

He caught a flicker from Sanders as Sharon replied matter-of-factly, "I lost my leg in the collision. I was aboard Coastal 276."

He flopped back onto the vinyl chair and squeezed his eyes shut. *Jesus, there was no end to it all. She's just a kid.* Masters. Of course. The senator's daughter he'd heard about on the news.

"The paper wants to be fair, Mr. Kelly. We'd really like to hear your side of things," Sharon said. "But from a purely personal standpoint, I need to know what happened."

He took a long pull on his beer. He didn't like admitting that he owed Sharon Masters an explanation, but deep down he felt he did. And Bear deserved a decent obituary. The fucking agency certainly wasn't going to give him one. All right, then. If that bastard Hawkins insisted on taking him down, he wasn't going quietly. Folding his hands on the table, he looked at the two women in turn. Sanders opened a notebook and uncapped a pen.

"The media, the public, none of you know the first thing about Bear. What the FAA told you and what his wife said were deliberately meant to mislead. Yeah, he had problems with Donna. That's not uncommon in marriages." He pushed the bottle cap around on the table. "What's relevant is that Bear was a first-class controller. I'm sure the brass won't mention the time he coaxed down a pilot who lost his wits after his plane iced up. Or the time he threaded an emergency landing through a dozen other airplanes circling in bad weather. Or the countless saves he made when pilots went to the wrong altitude or heading. For twenty-two years, that guy was an unseen shepherd of the sky, sending everyone safely along their way."

Sanders scribbled furiously. Sharon asked gently, "What happened the night of the accident?"

He recounted the sequence on the scope, the fluctuating Mode C readouts, his sentiments on TCAS. He told them about the crank caller and today's trumped-up deal. Sanders wrote down every detail.

"I doubt I'll ever get over what happened. All the lives lost. All the suffering." He took in Sharon's young face, so innocent and full of promise, and her crutches leaning against the wall. "Losing Bear. Losing my reputation and probably my job. But there's another aspect to all this. It's about misplaced faith in technology. The agency and the airlines bet the ranch on TCAS. Five weeks ago, they lost their gamble. And you can put money on it happening again."

"So it's your contention that TCAS malfunctioned and caused those planes to collide?" Sharon asked.

"Not my contention. I know that's what happened and the flight data recorder will bear me out."

Sanders laid down her pen after he fell silent. "We'll definitely be asking the FAA about all this." She flipped through the pages of her notebook, assessing the voluminous material, and turned to Sharon.

"We'll run the news story tomorrow, of course." She avoided saying "obituary" out of sensitivity for Kelly and Bear. "We've also got plenty for an in-depth profile on Mr. Kelly. I'd like to write the story, but your byline should go on it, too." Sharon beamed. "We'll use it Sunday for the extra readership, provided we can maintain the exclusive." Sanders turned to Kelly. "How do you feel about not talking with other reporters for at least another day?"

"There's no danger of that. Don't take this personally, but I still don't trust you people. This was for Bear."

"Perhaps you'll change your mind after reading our stories," Sharon said.

Kelly smiled politely as he reached for the bottle cap and flicked it into the air. Soaring, it fell directly into the wastebasket against the far wall.

Twenty-four

The Drop

K ELLY HEFTED THE SMALL RED BACKPACK and discovered that $50,000 weighed less than he'd imagined—seven or eight pounds at best. He set it down on the desk in the manager's office of the First Chicago Bank branch in Schaumburg and looked inquiringly at Special Agent Andretti, who sensed his curiosity and undid the flap. Inside were bundles of twenty-dollar bills bound with brown paper wrappers. Reaching in, he palmed one of the stacks and ran his thumb along an edge, fanning through the slightly used currency.

The mortgage on his house totaled more than all this legal tender and so did the combined value of his investment statements. But even though he felt comfortable with dollar amounts followed by several zeroes, touching real greenbacks conveyed the sense and worth of money far more vividly. He whistled softly.

"I've never seen this much cash, other than in the movies."

Andretti nodded shortly. "There's fifty bundles. A thousand bucks in each. We've recorded all the serial numbers and the backpack has a hidden transmitter so we can track it. This isn't Hollywood, of course, and we have no intention of losing the taxpayers' money."

Andretti's professional manner contrasted with her blue jeans and purple Northwestern University sweatshirt. Rodriguez was similarly dressed. Her comments and the suspicion that they carried guns hidden beneath their casual clothes reminded Kelly of what was about to happen, sending a sudden chill down his spine.

"We've set up equipment to monitor calls to your cell phone," she continued. "And there'll be a dozen of us keeping you under surveillance. But we'd like to cover all the bases. Would you be willing to wear a wire?"

He shivered again and replied unsteadily. "As long as you don't think this guy will search me."

"Doubtful," Rodriguez said, stepping in front of him. "He won't want to meet face to face and give you the chance to identify him. Unbutton your shirt, please." He taped a small wireless microphone to Kelly's chest and Andretti assessed him critically while he slowly redid his shirt.

"How are you feeling, Mr. Kelly?"

"Ready for takeoff, ma'am," he said with a brave smile. "And call me Ryan."

Her face softened. "All right, then. I'm Lynette. I know you've never done anything like this before, so just try to stay calm. You won't see our agents, but they'll be observing you at all times. In fact, don't look for us—you never know when the perp may be watching and that could spook him. Remember, this guy just wants the money, so do whatever he says and leave it where he tells you. We'll take care of the rest."

Kelly slung the backpack over one shoulder. "Sounds simple enough."

She smiled reassuringly and glanced at a clock on the wall. "We've only got a few minutes till he said he'd call you. Why don't you head on down Higgins toward the airport, nice and easy."

"All right."

"You'll do fine, Ryan. Good luck."

He walked out of the office with a wave of his hand, catching bursts of radio static as she informed other agents that he was leaving the bank. His heart began to pound and he breathed deeply, smelling ozone in the muggy air that signaled the onset of a storm. He tossed the backpack on the passenger seat of his car, started the engine and pulled out of the parking lot onto a thoroughfare jammed with Saturday traffic.

Despite Andretti's warning, he couldn't resist checking the rearview mirror for the agents who were following. Passing between tall cement pillars supporting Interstate 290, he decided they were in a brown sedan several cars back. Traffic sped up for a couple of miles through the Ned Brown Forest Preserve and then he drove by a sign welcoming him to Elk Grove Village, a suburb he deemed virtually indistinguishable from all the others in the area. Even though he was expecting a call, the chirping of his phone startled him and he fumbled for it on the seat.

"Kelly here."

"We'll do it at Woodfield. Go to the information center, lower level in the middle of the mall. Be there in ten minutes or you'll never get the box back. Got it?"

"Yeah."

Click.

"Woodfield," Kelly murmured for the benefit of whoever was listening to the microphone taped to his chest. He'd shopped at the sprawling mall in Schaumburg several times. Evaluating his location, he turned left onto Route 83, then left again in another mile onto Golf Road to head back west, not far from where he'd picked up the money. Billowing clouds overhead were ominously darker in this direction and rain began to sprinkle the windshield, but blue sky on the horizon indicated the storm would pass soon. Although Kelly doubted the extortionist would cancel their exchange if he was late, the relentless ticking of the dashboard clock made him uneasy. Finally, he swerved into a parking space at the mall near Marshall Field's.

He slipped one arm through the strap on the backpack, grabbed his phone, and jogged inside just before a downpour lashed across the lot. Several shoppers turned to watch him trot past racks of women's clothing and counters laden with cosmetics and jewelry before he entered one of the mall's main concourses.

He reached the center atrium and found the information kiosk on the other side of several terra-cotta brick planters that framed an open-air arena with mauve carpeted bench seats. A juggler riding a unicycle on stage drew repeated applause from the small audience. Pacing restlessly, Kelly caught his breath and took in the three levels of stores surrounding him. Two glass elevators glided up and down columns covered in travertine marble beneath a tiered white ceiling lined with skylights. Snatches of conversation from strolling shoppers swelled and faded against a backdrop of water splattering in a nearby fountain.

Chirp, chirp.

He held the phone to his ear and searched for the caller in the crowd. "Hello."

"I'm watching you, so be a good boy. Walk toward Penney's."

Click.

Kelly craned his head to locate the anchor store and threaded his way down the concourse. He glanced at people moving along the middle and upper mezzanines, wondering whether the extortionist and any FBI agents were among them. His phone chirped again as he approached the store.

"Yes."

"One-eighty back to where you were. Then to the right toward Nordstrom."

Click.

He felt surreal carrying so much money and following these terse commands while hundreds of people around him chatted and laughed, oblivious to what was unfolding in their midst. Kelly guessed the extortionist wanted time to size up the situation, but he was already growing impatient hiking through the mall. After turning to his right, the smell of toiletries and then coffee wafted over him. He barely glanced at provocative lingerie hanging in the window of Victoria's Secret before rounding a bend and stopping in front of Nordstrom. He fidgeted for two long minutes before his phone rang.

"Now where?"

"Escalator in front of you and head back toward the center court."

Kelly swore under his breath, then winced when he remembered the mike. He obediently walked to the escalator and grasped the handrail, watching the swarm of shoppers on the upper level. Several people caught his gaze and briefly stared back. A youngish man leaning over a glass banister kept glancing furtively his way. Kelly studied him whenever he wasn't looking. He appeared to be in his twenties, had short-cropped hair, and wore a rock band T-shirt and baggy black pants. When their eyes met once, the man quickly turned away.

After stepping off the escalator, Kelly moved aside and bent down to fiddle with his shoelace. In his peripheral vision, he saw the man turn again and then leer at a young woman in a halter and shorts walking off the escalator behind him. With a sigh, he stood and trudged down the mezzanine.

Chirp, chirp.

His heart skipped a beat when he spotted another man in a tan sport jacket holding a phone to his ear on the opposite side of the mezzanine. But the man slipped the phone into his breast pocket before Kelly answered.

"Yeah."

"Go to Eddie Bauer down on the left and buy one of those canvas lunch containers with the zippered top. They're on a rack near the door."

✈   ✈   ✈

BRAD SCHWARTZ REACHED INSIDE his green windbreaker and switched off the phone hidden in a large mesh pocket. Ambling along the upper level, he disconnected the phone from a cord attached to an earpiece with a built-in mike that enabled him to converse hands-free. He used a bandana to wipe the handset clean of fingerprints and surreptitiously dropped it in a trash container outside Lord & Taylor.

Brad wasn't sure what type of electronic gear the Feds used, but he suspected they could trace the signal from Kelly's phone to his location in seconds. To minimize the chance of detection, he'd used a different phone for every call so that the incoming number kept changing, forcing them to start each trace from scratch. As soon as the call ended, he immediately discarded the phone and took off his earphone.

Brad walked slowly, keeping an eye on Kelly on the other side of the mezzanine and covertly observing the horde. Despite his assumption that the Feds would be here, a cold hollowness ballooned in his stomach after he spotted two or three of them. They all acted the same: stone-faced, checking everyone out, looking in but never entering any of the stores.

One who fit the profile, with a large oblong face and broad sloping nose, headed in his direction now and Brad turned toward the window of a jewelry store, pulling a baseball cap lower over his brow. The agent's earphone gave him away and Brad realized with a start that he was still wearing his. He quickly reached up and slipped it underneath the collar of his jacket. The agent neared to within a few steps and Brad stared at a pearl necklace, holding his breath. In the reflection of the glass, he saw Big Nose stop and look at him, but the agent moved on after a passing glance.

Brad quietly exhaled and stepped away from the window in the opposite direction. He spotted the red backpack disappearing into Eddie Bauer and glanced behind him, relieved to see Big Nose still walking the other way. Sauntering down the mezzanine, he stopped opposite the outdoor clothing store across the concourse and looked in a window filled with chocolates carefully arranged in gold boxes. He turned again and saw Kelly emerge from the store carrying a shopping bag.

Brad strolled around the perimeter of the center atrium, positioning himself near an elevator where he could still see Kelly. This call would be the most critical and dangerous. The Feds had to be hovering, but he wanted to make sure Kelly transferred the money from the backpack to the smaller container he'd just bought. His eyes darted through the crowd. Several people potentially fit the profile, but he couldn't be sure until he saw their earphones. Kelly remained standing outside Eddie Bauer with one foot perched on a bench, occasionally looking around.

Facing a Planet Hollywood store, Brad felt for the remaining phone in his mesh pocket. The phone slipped in his clammy palm when he pressed the POWER button and he cringed, waiting for it to clatter to the floor, but it dropped safely back into the pocket. With a deep sigh, he peeked inside his jacket, dialed Kelly's preprogrammed number, and inserted the earphone again. He glanced behind him, sweating heavily, and listened to the soft ring in his ear.

"Okay, now what?" Kelly said.

Brad turned back to the window display. "Put the cash in the container you bought. Leave the wrappers in the backpack and ditch it under the bench. Then go to the outdoor deck at the California Café, down by Sears."

As Brad turned off the phone and pulled out his earphone, he noticed Big Nose watching him from his position outside Godiva Chocolatier across the mezzanine. The agent tilted his head and spoke into a small microphone on his jacket lapel, then strode purposefully in Brad's direction.

Oh, shit.

Brad tensed and looked around, furiously trying to figure out where to go. He could get out of the mall through Marshall Field's down the concourse behind him, but he'd never make it without running and arousing further suspicion. Somehow, though, he had to lose the phone, plus the fake mustache and geeky glasses he'd worn, before Big Nose or any other agent caught up to him.

The elevator doors hissed open and he made a snap decision.

Tossing the phone in a nearby trash container, he ducked into the car and silently screamed at several people to hurry as they jostled in behind him. Finally, the doors began to close and he heard someone hollering to wait. He stabbed at a button. The doors slid shut and he leaned heavily against the side of the car. Resisting the temptation to look out the windows while the elevator descended, he took off his baseball cap and glasses and stuffed them in a pocket.

✈   ✈   ✈

KELLY SAT ON THE BENCH, pulled the blue soft-sided container out of the shopping bag and unzipped its top flap. The inside was lined with a silver fabric designed to keep the contents cool and prevent moisture from leaking. It was large enough to snugly accommodate a six-pack. He watched people walk by, uncomfortable with handling so much cash in public, then reassured himself that the FBI would immediately arrest anyone foolish enough to grab it and run.

Slipping off the backpack, he set it on the floor between his legs and unfastened the top. He placed the blue container on his lap and kept a firm grasp on its nylon handle. Using his other hand, he reached into the backpack for one of the bundles and tore the wrapper with his thumb, hoping Andretti had followed through on her promise not to arm the money with dye. The wrapper broke harmlessly and he covered the bills with his hand as much as possible before quickly placing them in the container. It took several minutes to fill the container with three neat stacks and he was almost done when a young boy and his parents strolled past him.

"Mom, look at all that money!"

Kelly tightened his grip on the container and glared at the boy. His mother pulled him by the arm but the father glanced over his shoulder, bumping into another shopper before facing forward again. Kelly quickly transferred the remaining bundles and closed the zipper. After sliding the backpack beneath the bench with his feet, he stood and headed across the mezzanine toward Sears.

"Hey, mister. You forgot your pack." A young woman with long brown hair and frayed jeans held it up when he looked back.

"It's not mine."

She cocked her head. "I just saw you leave it here."

In no mood to waste time, he said quickly, "You can have it."

He heeled around and strode away, imagining her surprise when the FBI moved in if she decided to keep it. He didn't see the California Café while approaching Sears. He reached the end of the mall and began to fret. Doubling back, he spotted the restaurant down a short concourse to his left. A hostess smiled perkily when he walked in.

"Lunch for one, sir?"

"Yeah. Can I have a table on the deck?"

"You're in luck. It stopped raining and the sun's out again." She led him through a maze of diners and out a door to a half dozen round tables arranged beneath red, white, and blue umbrellas advertising Cinzano vermouth. With quick, efficient strokes, she wiped the table and dried off a chair. "Jessica will be your server and she'll be right with you."

Kelly sat down and looked out over the parking lot. Large puddles dotted the pavement and he heard cars splashing through them periodically. Thinking that he'd welcome a martini right now, he clutched the container and waited for the next call.

✈   ✈   ✈

THE ELEVATOR DOORS OPENED on the lower level and Brad stepped out, trying to stay between the other shoppers riding in the car. As they wandered off in different directions, he looked around fearfully, bracing for a shout or a sudden hand on his shoulder. None came and he forced himself not to run, instead walking steadily along the concourse toward Sears. He glanced back to the center court and saw Big Nose running down an escalator.

Increasing his pace, Brad canvassed the stores and darted into J. Riggings. He grabbed a beige cable knit sweater off a rack and hurried to a fitting room at the rear of the store. After pulling the curtain closed, he ripped away his false mustache and slipped it in a pocket of his jacket. Then he pulled off the jacket and hung it on a wall hook. Edging the curtain aside, he crept out of the fitting room and saw no sign of Big Nose.

"Wrong size," he said casually, handing the sweater to a clerk.

He strode out the door, looking to his left, and ran into another man coming from the right. Brad stumbled back and panic flashed across his face when he noticed the earphone.

"S-sorry, man."

"Pardon me," the Hispanic agent said.

Brad stood frozen for a moment, his brain unable to connect with his leg muscles and make them move.

The agent watched him curiously. "Are you all right, sir?"

"Yeah." Brad's voice squeaked in falsetto and he tensed to control the trembling that threatened to ripple through his body.

The agent's eyes narrowed. He pulled a leather wallet out of a trouser pocket and showed his badge. "I'm Special Agent Rodriguez of the FBI. What's your name?"

Swallowing, he managed to lower his voice to its normal range. "Brad Schwartz."

"May I see some identification?"

Struggling to keep from shaking, he handed over his driver's license. While Rodriguez examined it, Brad noticed a clerk in J. Riggings hold up his jacket and talk to another woman at the cash register. He shuffled in a circle to mask his growing terror and saw Big Nose weaving through the crowd toward him. Licking the sweat off his upper lip, he swiveled back to Rodriguez.

The agent returned Brad's license and studied him intently. He started to say something, then hesitated and held a finger to his earphone. "A female subject just picked up the pack," the voice in his ear said. He nodded at Brad and began to move away. "Mind your step, Mr. Schwartz."

Scarcely believing his good fortune, Brad paced swiftly down the concourse and into Sears, past aisles of household appliances, then outside to the parking lot. He didn't look behind him until he was halfway to his mother's car. Only a few people were in the lot and none appeared to be agents. He had to steady his right hand with the left in order to unlock the door. Slumping behind the wheel, he gulped for air with short shallow breaths. In the back seat, Stan's yellow Lab leaned over and licked the side of his face.

Forcing his nerves to settle down, Brad stroked Moose and drew the back of his arm across his forehead, soaking his shirt sleeve with perspiration. That had been really close, but he'd kept his cool and done it!

Now that he was out of the mall and away from all the agents, his confidence surged anew. He'd wanted to see Kelly take the cash out of the backpack, but he doubted the dumb shit would risk losing the black box by disobeying. All Brad had to do was pick up the container, dump the box somewhere, and call Kelly from a pay phone to give him the location. Lifting a towel on the floor in front of the passenger seat, he glanced at the dented metal box and then covered it again.

He looked out the window toward Sears. To the left of the entrance about thirty feet above a blank white wall was the outdoor deck of the California Café Bar & Grill. He'd spent ten bucks there on two lousy drinks while scouting a place for the drop. It was one of those expensive joints with fancy lighting and waiters who introduced themselves. As he watched, a woman showed Kelly to one of the tables. Brad started the car with trepidation and rolled down the window behind him. He retrieved his last phone from the glove compartment, powered it up, and dialed.

"I'm on the deck," Kelly said.

"Drop the container over the edge."

"What?"

"Just do it!"

Brad turned off the phone and dumped it on the ground outside the car. While backing his mother's Dodge out of the parking space, he watched Kelly walk over to the edge of the deck. After a moment's hesitation, he let go of the blue container and it fell to the sidewalk below. Reaching behind him, Brad opened the car door.

"Okay, Moose, go get it."

As the Lab raced through the lot, Brad drove in the opposite direction and turned around a few aisles away from the money. If the Feds tried to come after him, they'd have to negotiate several rows of parked cars. Befitting his breed's reputation, Moose bounded up to the container and snagged the nylon handle in his mouth, perfectly executing the plan.

When he started to run back to Brad's car, Rodriguez and Big Nose walked out of Sears. A black Chevrolet Suburban rounded the end of another aisle. Moving like a nimble quarterback, Rodriguez sprinted in front of the Lab and tackled him while Big Nose wrestled away the container. The agents struggled to hang onto Moose, but Brad had removed the dog's collar. Twisting out of their grasp, he bolted across the lot.

Brad's renewed courage vanished when he saw the agents. He turned in front of Sears to drive away, but a family leaving the store forced him to slow and veer around them. With Rodriguez and Big Nose in pursuit, Moose caught up to the sedan and jumped through the back window.

"No, Moose! Oh, shit."

Brad alarmingly realized the flaw in his plan. He hadn't considered what to do if the Feds chased Moose. Ever faithful, the Lab did exactly as he was trained. In his rearview mirror, Brad noticed the Suburban pull away from the curb and he floored the accelerator, swerving around the corner to the back side of the store.

✈   ✈   ✈

KELLY CLUTCHED THE RAILING of the restaurant deck and watched the sequence of events from above. As Brad's car disappeared, trailed by the Suburban, Andretti ran up to him holding a finger to her earphone.

"I hope your guys catch him," he said.

She raised her other hand and listened for a moment, then nodded. "They just did. Let's go."

Making their way down through the mall, they exited Sears and jogged past a loading dock toward a group of agents gathered around the front of Brad's car, which had been cut off by the Suburban. Brad was bent over the hood with his hands cuffed behind him. Kelly leaned against the door, panting from his exertion, and looked around for the flight data recorder.

"Christ, a kid did this. Where's the box, fella?"

Brad's eyes widened with fear, but there was a hint of smugness in his voice. "What box, mister? I don't know what you're talking about."

Big Nose plopped the container of money on the hood. "Then why did your dog go after this?"

"I dunno. He got loose by accident. He's not even mine."

For an instant, Kelly almost believed him until he recognized the voice. Overcome with rage, he lunged and grabbed Brad's shirt, slamming him against the hood. "Where's the goddamn box, asshole?"

Rodriguez and Big Nose pulled Kelly away and restrained him while he glowered at Brad. Another agent emerged from the Dodge, shaking his head.

"The kid's clean. Nothing in the car."

TWENTY-FIVE
DALLAS BUMP-UP

ILLING CROWDS PACKED the vast Continental Room of the Hilton Chicago at Michigan and Balbo to overflowing. NTSB accident hearings invariably drew substantial attention, but this one sparked interest from around the world. At the front of the room, several dozen news people were clustered near both ends of a long head table covered in green cloth. On one side, dubbed the UN by their American peers, were reporters and camera crews from the BBC, Reuters, Agence France-Presse, the German television network Deutsche Welle, and *Asahi Shimbun*, one of Japan's major dailies. CNN favored the international corner, too.

The other three major American networks were grouped on the opposite side, along with MSNBC, local TV stations and papers, and correspondents from AP, the *New York Times*, *Los Angeles Times*, the industry magazine *Aviation Week*, and the big three weeklies *Newsweek*, *Time*, and *U.S. News & World Report*.

Ensconced among her Chicago colleagues, Ellen Sanders reviewed the hearing agenda and witness list, mulling the first day story she'd write. Sitting next to her, Sharon Masters tested the operation of a tape recorder and jotted down names of dignitaries assembled in the first several rows of chairs for a feature sidebar. She felt a bit strange adding her father to the list when he appeared, easing his way through the horde.

After the senator saw her, he strode over with his young aide, Jeremy Parker, dutifully in tow. Masters conveyed his usual aura of confidence, but she detected discomfort in the affected way he smiled at her. They hadn't seen each other since she'd thrown him out of her hospital room that day after the accident and had spoken only briefly on the phone.

"Hello, Sharon."

"Hi, Dad."

Mindful of other reporters watching them, he shuffled and regarded her awkwardly. "How's the physical therapy going?"

"I won't need crutches soon." Shifting in her chair, she grimaced when the prosthesis chafed against the stump of her left leg.

"You're looking well."

"Thanks."

"Did you finish your classes?"

"My professors were very understanding and let me make up the work. Took my last final on Friday." She smiled proudly and arched her head toward Sanders. "Ellen and a few others from the paper treated me at the press club Saturday night." Duncan and Christy had rounded out the group, and they regaled Sharon with so much shop talk that she forgot all about her injury. "You'll be at graduation this Friday, right?"

Guiltily, Masters glanced at his aide. "I'm, uh, hoping Jeremy can rearrange some things. There's a hearing on the Hill . . . "

Sharon bit her lower lip, blinking back tears. "Dad, you promised."

"I'm sorry, Pump—Sharon. There are a lot of things going on."

She sighed heavily, determined not to make a scene. It certainly wasn't the first time he'd canceled on her. "Never mind. My friends will be there, at least."

"I plan to attend, Senator," Sanders piped up. "I'll take a picture for you."

He shot her a look of annoyance and turned back to his daughter, coughing nervously. "I'm doing my best to reschedule. In any case, I'd like to get together for dinner while I'm in town."

Perhaps it was only fair, Sharon thought. He'd missed so much of the journey that he didn't deserve to watch her celebrate reaching this crossroad. The sudden realization gave her strength to smile pleasantly. "I'll be busy covering these hearings. Let me get back to you on that."

Masters' face tightened and he pulled on his shirt cuffs. "Perhaps I'd better let you do your job then. Goodbye, Sharon."

"See ya later."

On the way to their seats, Masters and his aide passed six oblong tables set at right angles to the dais. Each was covered in the same green cloth, with a microphone, silver pitcher of water, and several glasses grouped in the center. Beads of condensation were already forming on the sides of the pitchers. Representatives from Atlantic, Coastal, Boeing, the FAA, the Air Line Pilots Association, and NATCA huddled at the tables while shuffling papers like generals preparing battle plans. The aim of this government hearing was to help determine why two airliners collided. No verdict would be rendered, but each organization bore a potential share of liability in the rising tide of civil lawsuits. To these interested parties, this was, indeed, a trial that would necessitate vigilant posturing for the record.

Numerous attorneys retained by next of kin were scattered among the 900 chairs lined up throughout the rest of the room. Don Szemasko sat with his lawyer midway back. Only a few dozen seats were cordoned off for those with influence, forcing spectators to form long lines outside the hotel several hours earlier. Every chair had been taken and several hotel staff members monitored the number of people standing along the back wall.

Christy and Jason enjoyed front-row seats in the reserved section thanks to Kelly's union connection. Metcalf reluctantly granted Christy a few days off during what would be a busy time at the paper only after she revealed her relationship with Kelly. Jason was excited he could attend, too, now that school had ended for the summer. He nudged his mother's arm and held up a small gift-wrapped package. She nodded and they walked over to Kelly, who was reading some notes at the NATCA table ten feet away. It was the first time she'd seen him wear a suit, single-breasted and dark gray with a blue and gold tie.

"That's a snazzy outfit, controller," she said. "Got a hot date tonight?"

His head jerked up. "Oh, hi. Didn't realize you'd gotten here. The only date I'd care to have is dinner with you two."

"We thought you'd never ask."

Jason held out the gift. "This is for you, Rain Man."

With a surprised smile, Kelly tore off the paper and opened the box. Inside was a red caboose with a tiny brakeman standing on the rear platform. "Thanks, Jason. This is great. You'll have to come up to the house again and try it out on the railroad with me."

Jason beamed and Christy placed a hand on his shoulder. "We'd better get back to our seats now. Good luck, Ryan."

Kelly winked and gave them a thumbs-up. To his left, Pete Rykowski and a man named Howard Jacobs, who'd politely ignored their private moment, discussed an NTSB status report on the investigation. Jacobs, NATCA national president, had flown in yesterday from Washington. Several months ago, he'd made an eloquent speech to Senator Masters and his Aviation Subcommittee, arguing that TCAS should be used in Traffic Alert mode only until the bugs were fixed. TA mode warned pilots of potential collisions, but did not issue avoidance commands. The FAA, airlines, and ALPA had resisted the proposal so far. When Rykowski noticed Christy walking away, he turned to Kelly.

"Curtain's about to go up on this little drama. Are you ready?"

"I'm not looking forward to it. Friday night and Saturday were enough excitement to last me through the summer." He clenched his fists. "I'd like to strangle that kid. Andretti told me this morning he still won't admit he took the box or where he stashed it."

Rykowski pointed to a copy of the *Chronicle* on the table with the headline "Student dogged by FBI" printed across the top of the page. "The media's having fun hyping the story. It's bound to turn up sooner or later."

Kelly grunted, his attention drawn to a conversation at the next table where Hawkins, TRACON chief Jeff Richardson, and a balding man he didn't recognize were sitting.

"What a nightmare getting here yesterday," the stranger said. "We pulled away from the gate in D.C. and sat on the taxiway for two hours before takeoff. Then we circled O'Hare for another hour."

"I apologize for the delay," Hawkins said, sounding embarrassed. "A temporary slowdown by controllers that's been resolved. Trying to generate publicity before today's hearing." He briefly turned his head to glare at the three men occupying the NATCA table. "Quite unconscionably, I might add."

Kelly peeked sideways at Rykowski, who laughed softly. "Unconscionable, my ass. We went legal is all. Three-mile spacing for one shift—on a Sunday to minimize passenger inconvenience—in response to your bullshit deal. We had planes stacked everywhere. Flow Control ordered a ground stop for flights coming in from La Guardia, Denver, LAX, you name it. One big fucking mess. I was in Hawkins' office when United's CEO called, demanding to know what the hell was going on. After the chief hung up and promised there'd be no more deals, we agreed to resume normal separation."

"We don't want the public to misinterpret our motivations during these hearings," Jacobs said. "But if your operational error last Friday isn't rescinded, we'll revisit the issue."

Kelly nodded, his spirits lifting at the show of support. It was a powerful tactic they exercised on rare occasions.

"Good morning, ladies and gentlemen." The deep voice boomed through a series of speakers mounted on black metal stands along the sides of the enormous ballroom and the hum of a hundred conversations faded. A man wearing a red bow tie who sat at the center of the dais adjusted his microphone.

"Welcome to this public hearing on an accident that occurred May fifth involving an Atlantic Airlines Boeing 727, registration number N7087A, and a Coastal Airlines Boeing 757, registration number N607CA. My name is Preston Collins. I'm a member of the National Transportation Safety Board and will be directing these proceedings. To my right is investigator-in-charge Frederic Esterhaus, who will handle most of the questioning. On my left are staff members Scott Carter and Sarah Trent, who will assist in the testimony. We have a lot of ground to cover, so let's get started right away with statements from the technical staff."

Carter and Trent in turn summarized the basic findings of the investigation teams. Neither aircraft suffered loss of flight control until impact, which they referred to as the "closest point of approach." The phrase drew an ironic smile from Kelly because it was based on the premise that airplanes weren't supposed to hit with TCAS. The Power Plant team concluded that all engines were functioning normally and there was no evidence to indicate sabotage caused the accident. Much of the audience grew weary with the mundane testimony that droned on throughout the morning and welcomed the break for lunch.

Christy and Jason joined Kelly, Rykowski, and Jacobs, all of whom snared one of the last tables at an Irish pub in the hotel. Inevitably, their conversation drifted to the missing black box. After Brad's arrest, Kelly called Christy to tell her everything that had happened. Miffed at first that he'd kept it a secret from her, she acknowledged her job left him no choice and teasingly pleaded for a scoop. Now, Kelly described the events at the mall once more to Rykowski and Jacobs.

At one-thirty, Collins consulted the agenda and summoned Captain Chet Wertheimer to the stand. A member of the Operations team, Wertheimer flew for Prairie Air and also belonged to ALPA's accident investigation group. He and a fellow pilot had conducted dozens of simulator flights at the airline's training base in Minneapolis to reconstruct what happened. Still photographers and TV cameramen perked up at the sight of the captain, dressed in a navy blue uniform with four silver stripes sewn into the sleeves of his jacket. He took his place at a small table positioned in front of one end of the dais, then stated his name and affiliation after prompting from Esterhaus.

"Captain Wertheimer, would you please review your findings."

The gray-haired pilot walked over to a large-scale photograph mounted on an easel. The satellite image of Chicago, with O'Hare in the upper left corner and Lake Michigan along the right side, was superimposed with dotted lines to show the flight paths of the two planes. Heads in the audience craned when he pointed to a location over the lake.

"One minute before the closest point of approach, Atlantic 59 was descending toward its clearance altitude of seven thousand feet. The aircraft's intended route would take it north along the shoreline until it turned west near Montrose Harbor onto final approach. Coastal 276 was climbing to its clearance altitude of six thousand feet on a due east heading. Once beyond the arrival flow along the lakefront, roughly abeam of Meigs Field, the departing aircraft would have continued climbing to its cruising altitude. This is a standard traffic pattern over Chicago, so for the past five weeks several of us have spent many hours trying to establish what was different about these two flights."

Wertheimer walked back to the stand, sat down, and held an index finger with his other hand.

"Our findings indicate the vertical speeds of the two aircraft triggered the TCAS Traffic Alert. Atlantic's fairly high descent rate of two thousand feet per minute was ordered by the arrival controller to position him expeditiously in the pattern. Coastal was climbing faster than normal because the aircraft carried only half its normal load. Based on the geometry of the encounter and nearby traffic, the computer ordered both pilots to increase their vertical rates rather than level off. This was a classic crossing RA, otherwise known as the Dallas Bump-Up Effect."

He angled both hands in the air, fingers pointing at each other, and moved his left palm over the back of his right hand to demonstrate the maneuver. Several spectators, notably lawyers, scribbled notes. Wertheimer held a second finger.

"Certainly, weather was a factor. A layer of scattered clouds hampered visibility. Cockpit voice tapes and the DARC printout indicate Atlantic's copilot saw the other plane first and immediately initiated a left turn. We calculated they would have missed each other if he'd been able to start his turn eight-tenths of a second sooner."

Two representatives at the Atlantic Airlines table leaned close to each other and whispered. Third finger.

"Coastal was climbing somewhat later than normal, so it was still in a nose-up attitude crossing the shoreline. Departing traffic from Midway Airport was a factor as well as a radio failure that temporarily delayed the departure controller. This contributed to the high vertical rate that set off TCAS."

Hawkins spoke quietly to the man Kelly didn't recognize. Fourth finger.

"Atlantic was told to turn north at the twenty-five-mile ring around O'Hare instead of the twenty. While this is standard under heavy traffic conditions, it was yet another factor that put the two planes in unique juxtaposition. A lot of little things added up."

Jason poked his mother's arm and said, "I told you." Wertheimer held out his hands.

"However, after programming all these data points into our simulations, we were never able to induce a midair unless one or both of us failed to follow the Resolution Advisory or delayed our response to it. Available information shows no such hesitation by the Atlantic pilots. We're uncertain about Coastal because the plane's flight recorder is . . . still at large, shall I say?"

Pockets of laughter broke out in the audience. With Collins directing, representatives at the interested parties tables questioned Wertheimer next, largely eliciting a repetition of what they'd just heard. The captain's most significant response came under prodding from the FAA man who complained earlier about yesterday's flight delays. He identified himself now as Charles Perry, legal counsel for the agency. Wertheimer testified that Coastal would have leveled off in time to avoid provoking the TCAS alert if Kelly had cleared the flight to climb from 5,000 feet to 6,000 four seconds sooner.

The hearing broke for a fifteen-minute recess, after which Collins announced the last team to testify would be Electronic Systems. Scott Carter matted down his wild red hair, scanned some notes, and cleared his throat.

"With one possible exception, all systems aboard both aircraft appear to have been functioning normally before the accident. The exception is Coastal's primary Mode C unit, which used the Gillham interface to provide altitude information to air traffic radarscopes and TCAS."

As Wertheimer had done, Carter held up his fingers in succession while he continued to speak.

"Point one. Two controllers say they saw erratic altitude readouts from flight 276 indicating the aircraft was six hundred feet higher than Mode C reported. Although there's no evidence as yet to support their statements, electrical short circuits involving Gillham devices have been known to occur. The most notable incident involved a near miss between two 747s over northwest China last summer.

"Point two. Coastal's logbook notes that the plane landed abnormally hard on arrival at O'Hare ninety minutes before its flight to Washington. After inspection, a maintenance crew concluded the gear was undamaged. However, it's conceivable the landing jarred loose a pin connecting Mode C to another system onboard the aircraft that verifies altitude. No cross-checking occurs if the connection is broken.

"Point three. TCAS ordinarily shuts down when there's a discrepancy in altitudes between the two systems but it will operate fine, perhaps even use faulty information, without verification from the backup. Therefore, it could have directed the Coastal pilot to fly into the other airplane."

Kelly sat up straighter and watched Carter intently. He hadn't heard any of this before.

"What were your other findings?" Esterhaus asked.

"Inconclusive. Part of the connector pin for the two systems was melted by fire. From what little remained, we were unable to determine whether it was dislodged by the previous landing or the force of impact when the aircraft struck a building. There was nothing extraordinary on the Direct Access Radar Channel from the TRACON. We need the black box."

"For the benefit of our audience, the FBI is continuing its search for the aircraft's flight recorder. Anyone with knowledge of its whereabouts is asked to please contact the authorities. Ladies and gentlemen, I cannot stress enough that evidence contained in the box is extremely critical to this investigation."

Kelly groaned softly. Carter's theory was plausible. There just wasn't enough information to prove it.

"The next witness will be Mr. Ryan Kelly," the chairman announced.

Rykowski placed a hand on his arm. "Knock 'em dead, kid."

Kelly momentarily resented Bear for forcing him to face the lions alone, but anger subsided into resignation. He caught a discreet smile from Christy while walking to the stand and tried to tune out the endless faces and cameras focusing on him. After stating his name and occupation, he was asked to describe what happened. Kelly outlined the entire sequence from the time he issued initial clearance to Coastal 276 until the flight landed at Midway. He spoke tentatively at first because of the cameras and an unavoidable feeling of being on trial, but gradually warmed to his subject and ended in a level precise voice. Esterhaus and Perry wrote down several notes.

"I have just two questions," Esterhaus said when he finished. "As you know, we've been unable to empirically corroborate what you and Mr. Lombardi told us about the erratic readouts. Is there anything else you can think of to help us resolve this issue?"

Kelly shook his head. "I really wish there was. I clearly remember seeing the altitude drop six hundred feet, then increase two hundred. I think that's when Gene leaned over and asked me if I'd noticed and I called Coastal to verify altitude. Nothing else seemed unusual."

"Very well, then. Lastly, what is your opinion of TCAS?"

"My opinion?"

Esterhaus smiled disarmingly. "Yes. Do you consider it a useful safety tool? What other experiences have you had with it?"

Hawkins squirmed uncomfortably while Kelly collected his thoughts. "That's a loaded question," he muttered.

"It has the potential to be a useful safety tool. We know we're only human and every controller is grateful for that second set of eyes." Kelly hesitated, trying to phrase his answer diplomatically. "But, in some respects, TCAS is severely limited. It can't understand human intent, won't recognize terrain, and doesn't cross-check any of the information it gets. The lack of altitude verification is particularly significant because we encounter Mode C variations all the time."

"What improvements would you suggest?"

"Make it recognize terrain and understand intent. Provide a longer alert time so pilots can ask controllers to confirm what the computer is telling them. I'm not against TCAS per se, but it worries me that the FAA has made pilots totally reliant on it. I don't know of any computer that's fail safe. Do you?"

"No, Mr. Kelly, and thank you for your comments. Some of the concerns you mentioned are being studied." Esterhaus consulted his watch. "It's almost four-thirty, so with the chairman's permission I'd like to hold off on questions from the interested parties until tomorrow."

Collins readily declared the hearings recessed for the day. Waves of people stood, stretched, and poured out of the ballroom.

✈   ✈   ✈

DINNER WAS SOMBER amid the boisterous atmosphere of the Berghoff restaurant on Adams Street. Picking apathetically at his steak, Kelly chatted with Jason about the model railroad and laughed politely at Christy's jokes. She tried to keep the mood upbeat while waiters dressed in white shirts and aprons bustled among the wooden tables and chairs, but by the time dessert arrived his gloominess had infected all three of them.

"What's going to happen tomorrow?" she asked.

"The FAA's hired gun from Washington will get a crack at me. Help the agency justify lowering the boom later on, no doubt. The senator will have another chance to preen for the cameras, too. Did you see him doing it today whenever they panned the audience?"

"Yes. He's so vain. And I'm so angry with our publisher I could scream." On their walk from the hotel to the Berghoff, she'd disclosed the Masters story that Prendergast quashed. "I called the paper during this afternoon's recess to tell him he's sitting on a terrific scoop, but he wouldn't budge."

"I'm not surprised. Doesn't this sort of censorship happen all the time?"

"Not that much. Oh, sure, we've occasionally been pressured to go easy on the Cubs when they were stuck in the cellar too long, stuff like that. This is different. Ellen wrote a damaging story about Masters' radar deal in Dallas a couple of months ago with no interference. But now that the paper's trying to buy those TV stations, Prendergast has lost his balls." Christy glanced at Jason and quickly covered her mouth.

Rolling his eyes, he said, "Like I haven't heard that before. Geez, I'm not a kid anymore."

"As a journalist," Kelly said, "shouldn't you be using proper terminology—like testicles?" He grinned with Jason when she stuck her tongue out at them. "I suppose leaking the story to another paper would be heresy?"

"I'd considered that. I wouldn't give it to the *Trib* because they're our main competition. I do have some contacts at the *Washington Post* and some other papers. But Prendergast threatened to fire me if I breathe a word. As much as I want to get the story out and help you, I can't afford the risk."

"That's so lame," Jason pouted. "You're always telling me to do the right thing, but now you won't."

"It's more complicated than that, honey. I've got responsibilities—a mortgage and a car payment and a smart young man who needs to go to college in a few years."

He folded his arms and scowled. "So get another job, if you have to. We've always managed somehow. Rain Man needs our help. And I thought newspapers were supposed to tell the truth—not hide it."

"You are growing up, aren't you," she said gently, combing his hair with her hand. "I'm so proud of you. But one day you'll learn that things aren't always as black and white as they seem. If I left the paper, my new job might be in another city and we wouldn't get to see Ryan as much as we do now."

"If Rain Man's fired, *he* might have to move."

"A lot of things can happen," Kelly said breezily. "Best to just take it one day at a time."

They fell silent, each immersed in their predictions of the future. At length, Christy changed the subject, determined not to end dinner on a sour note. "Jason's recorded a bunch of sound effects on our PC. His voice sounds like HAL when we boot up."

"After I fixed your mistake," he said, still perturbed.

"I'll never live this down."

"I was right in the middle of recording when you called me to dinner." He looked at Kelly in a plea for understanding. "I had to do it all over again so you wouldn't hear her in the background and it took me awhile to get the right tone."

Kelly listened with half an ear, his mind wandering to something he'd said this afternoon. *I think that's when Gene leaned over and asked me if I'd noticed.*

"I'm amazed by what that computer can do," Christy said.

You see Coastal's altitude jumping around?

Leaning over him in the TRACON. Near the mike. His voice might be on the tape!

"What's wrong, Ryan?"

He stared at her while solidifying his recollection. "Gene warned me about Coastal's altitude readouts just before the midair. If my mike was keyed and his voice is in the background on the tape, it'll prove we're not making it up. Right now, they think I'm delusional and he's a sympathizer. Jason, you're brilliant." He smiled proudly as Kelly signaled for the check. "I've gotta get back to the hotel and tell Esterhaus."

Suddenly elated, he handed the waiter a credit card when he arrived with the bill. He'd love to see the investigator's face if they could hear Lombardi's voice on the tape. After Kelly signed the tab, adding a hefty tip, they headed for the door. Back at the Hilton, he followed them to their car parked in the underground garage. He kissed Christy and shook Jason's hand.

"Thanks again for the tip, my friend."

"No prob, Rain Man."

"See you tomorrow."

After their car disappeared up the exit ramp, he headed toward the elevators. He'd checked in to the hotel last night to avoid the long commute from Woodstock. As soon as he got to his room, he called the front desk and asked for the investigator's suite. When Esterhaus answered and learned that Kelly was on the line, he became effusive.

"I'm glad you called. Have you been watching the news?"

"I try to avoid it."

Esterhaus chuckled. "Can't say I blame you. We have the black box. The FBI conveyed it to us late this afternoon and it's already been sent to Washington for analysis. I was told just after the hearing adjourned."

"Hallelujah! Where the hell was it?"

"The young man threw it in the back of a truck behind Sears at the mall. The FBI searched the trucks, but this one apparently left for the store's distribution center before they started looking. The center's closed on Sundays so no one noticed it until this morning."

"I don't believe this."

"I know. It's all very unprecedented. By the way, he was formally charged this afternoon. He cleaned off the box, but I gather that agents found a wireless phone with his fingerprints near an elevator at the mall. When the box was traced back to the location of his arrest, he broke down and confessed."

"I'm glad it's over. And, as far as I'm concerned, the kid deserves whatever he gets."

"Indeed. Why were you calling?" Esterhaus sounded intrigued after Kelly outlined his theory. "It's more anecdotal evidence, but it would certainly lend credence to the statements you and Mr. Lombardi made about what happened on the radarscope. Of course, it won't be on the tape unless your mike was keyed when he said it."

"I'm counting on that."

"It's late in Washington. I'll contact one of my staff people first thing tomorrow. Thank you for bringing this to my attention."

TWENTY-SIX
FINAL APPROACH

<hr />

A FTER EATING A LIGHT BREAKFAST and watching the news in his suite the next morning, Kelly rode an elevator downstairs minutes before the hearing was scheduled to resume. He eased through another capacity crowd that filled the Continental Room and stopped to say hello to Christy and Jason. Noticing the circles under her eyes, he held a hand to her cheek.

"You look tired."

She stifled a yawn. "I tossed and turned all night worrying about what might happen today." He followed her gaze to Senator Masters, coolly observing them from his seat farther down the front row, and felt a growing sense of disquiet. "I've been thinking, Ryan—"

A gavel banged sharply. "Ladies and gentlemen, this hearing will come to order," Preston Collins announced. "Mr. Kelly, would you please take the stand."

"Guess you'll have to tell me later," he said, squeezing her hand.

TV camera lights blazed on and once again he tried to ignore the hundreds of eyes on him while walking to the witness chair. "Keep your cool," Rykowski admonished softly when he passed the NATCA table.

"We'll take questions from the interested parties now," Collins said. "FAA."

Charles Perry tapped his microphone, sending dull thumps reverberating around the ballroom. His balding pate shone from the bright lights as he consulted some notes on a pad in front of him.

"Thank you, Mr. Chairman. I'd like to review your background, Mr. Kelly. On November 15, 1989, you were involved in an operational error while working in the tower at Seattle-Tacoma International Airport. Would you describe the circumstances?"

Kelly cleared his throat and unconsciously drew himself up in the seat, vividly recalling the incident. Controllers never forgot deals. Singular events that registered with cataclysmic intensity on the seismograph of their careers.

"I'd cleared a Beechcraft and a Delta 727 to land on the same runway when I should have sent Delta to the parallel. The Beech landed and was just turning onto a high-speed taxiway when Delta touched down."

"You were decertified after this incident?"

"Of course. The Beech hadn't cleared the runway before the second plane crossed the threshold so there was a loss of separation. I took a written exam and passed my recertification two days later. I also passed my check rides thirty days and six months after that."

"Why did it happen?"

"Shifting winds forced us to keep changing the direction of the arrival flow. I was tired and . . . made a mistake." He shrugged. Occasionally, we do. It's that simple.

Perry frowned, gesturing for more elaboration. When none came, he continued. "All right, then. On February 3, 1995, you had another operational error in the TRACON at O'Hare Airport. Would you describe this incident?"

"Separation between two airplanes on approach got down to one-point-eight miles. I'd issued a speed restriction to the pilot in trail, but he didn't slow soon enough." The line was razor thin between packing them in and a deal.

Perry arched his eyebrows. "Of course, it's your obligation to allow for adequate response time, isn't it?"

"Yes." He wasn't going to argue, but the pilot had taken forever to pull back on the throttles.

"I understand you were not controlling the traffic while on position last Friday in the TRACON. But you were supervising a developmental who in several instances reduced separation to below legal minimums. Why did you permit that?"

"Gene Lombardi performed exceptionally well. According to the log, he brought in fifty-seven airplanes during his last hour by maintaining two-mile spacing. We do that all the time. Why is it suddenly a deal?"

Perry slumped against the back of his chair and placed both palms flat on the table, his face aghast. "That's a half mile below minimums. I'm not aware that management has sanctioned two-mile separation."

Through the harsh glare of the camera lights, Kelly saw reporters scribbling notes. He looked directly at Hawkins and tried to avoid sounding defensive. "Not officially. But they know we do it—"

"The regulations are in place to ensure safety, Mr. Kelly. I must say that your cavalier attitude toward them is troubling."

Rykowski motioned him with a hand and he struggled to hold his temper. "Wait a minute—I wasn't finished. The airlines know we do it, too, and they like it just fine, thank you. We're not compromising safety. We're simply squeezing every last mile of space out of that sky so no one holds unnecessarily."

"The fact remains that you routinely ignore regulations. I have performance evaluations indicating that you repeatedly disregard official phraseology."

Kelly grit his teeth. Boskoprick again. "Look, we have to do a lot of talking on some very congested frequencies. So to keep everyone moving, I'll clear a guy to the ILS one-four right instead of the ILS *runway* one-four right. Or I'll tell him to contact the tower on twenty-six nine instead of one-two-six-point-niner. The pilots understand and they appreciate that we're getting them on their way as fast as possible. When it's busy, Mr. Perry, we don't always have time to use the Queen's English."

"Excuse me, gentlemen," Collins cut in. "While Mr. Kelly's performance as a controller is relevant, let's not stray too far from the focus of these hearings, which is the accident that occurred five weeks ago."

Perry smiled charitably. "My apologies, Mr. Chairman. I'm just trying to assemble a complete record of the employee involved."

"Which you're doing," Collins said peevishly. "It's time to move on. Any further questions?"

"One more." Perry looked back at Kelly. "Would you tell us why you disregarded regulations once again when Coastal 276 responded to its RA?"

What would you have done, pal? Kelly swallowed an urge to scream. Folding his hands in his lap, he answered in a tightly controlled voice.

"Every moment of my working day is devoted to keeping airplanes separated. That's my very essence. I couldn't just stand by and watch TCAS run them together." He knew it was reckless, but he also knew what he believed. "If they'd followed my instructions, I seriously doubt we'd be here."

"Mr. Chairman!"

Heads turned to the front row of spectators, where Senator Masters was bounding to his feet. Jeremy Parker tugged on the senator's arm, but Masters shook his assistant's hand away.

"Mr. Chairman, I apologize for interrupting these proceedings. I know this is highly unusual. But the remarks of the witness deeply trouble me. They should not go unchallenged. He has unfairly tried to blame this accident on a technically superior collision avoidance system with a proven track record. The facts do not support his conclusion."

Collins glared at the senator, tapping his pen on the dais. The grandstanding rankled him and he wanted to avoid politicizing the hearings on national television. "Senator Masters, the witness has a right to say whatever he wishes and the board will take it under due consideration, as with all testimony."

Masters cut an imposing figure striding to the FAA table in his tailored midnight blue suit. He scooped up the microphone and his commanding voice swelled through the ballroom.

"I merely want to ensure the record is balanced. The taxpayers and the airlines have invested a billion dollars in this system. As their elected representative and someone who's been closely involved with the TCAS program, someone who's suffered personally from the tragedies it's designed to prevent, I respectfully ask permission to address the witness."

"As you said, this is highly unusual."

Esterhaus leaned toward Collins and covered his microphone with a hand. "You might as well let him speak or he'll just hold court with the media out in the lobby. This way, we have some measure of control."

Collins didn't like it, but he saw no graceful way to reject the request. He tossed his pen on the dais with a sigh. "Very well, Senator."

Masters marched toward the witness stand, positioning himself so the cameras could get a tight shot of them both while he faced the audience. The body language was not lost on Kelly, who smoothed his tie and gazed serenely at the face he'd seen so many times on television. In the media pool, Sharon caught Christy's eye and they nodded in unison.

"You've made many unfavorable statements about TCAS, sir. Has it ever benefited you during a close traffic encounter?"

"I can honestly say it has not. I do know of a few cases where it's helped others, but NATCA reports from controllers on position indicate that eighty percent of RAs are unnecessary. Only five percent are genuine saves. We can't determine the validity of the others."

Masters sneered. "Considering the source, I question the accuracy of those figures. Since you admit there are documented cases where TCAS has saved the day, how can you sit there and claim the system is not an important safety tool?"

Collins rapped his fingers against the microphone. "Gentlemen, I implore you. Please don't turn this into a personal debate."

"I've never dismissed TCAS out of hand and neither have most of my colleagues," Kelly shot back. "If you walk into any center, you'll find some controllers who like it because they don't see nearly as many false alerts as we do in the terminal areas. But those false alerts worry us, which is why we're pleading with the agency to put it in Traffic Alert mode only until the bugs are worked out."

"There are fewer and fewer irregularities. Software update six-point-oh-four virtually eliminated unnecessary RAs."

Among other changes, the update lowered the difference in altitude between two planes from 1,200 feet to 800 before TCAS sounded an alarm. While that had helped, problems persisted.

"Nationally, we're still getting at least a hundred RAs a month," Kelly said. "Most of them do nothing more than place everyone on board the airplanes in potential danger and scare the hell out of a controller."

Masters held up his hands, then dropped them against his sides. "So, despite the fact that TCAS saves lives, you'd rather hobble its capabilities until a few minor issues are resolved. This is a very sophisticated system. Aren't you being a tad unrealistic demanding absolute perfection?"

"Let me tell you about reality, Senator." He ignored another cautionary signal from Rykowski, his words tumbling out with increasing vehemence. "One of the first things an air traffic controller learns is that we can't make mistakes. Obviously, we do. We're human. Now, controllers try to blow it off. We'll tell you it's just a video game they pay us to play. But it's not. We're in there to do a job and we're supposed to do it right *every time*. Since we're expected to deliver perfection, the computer should be held to the same standard."

Masters paced in front of the witness stand like a prosecuting attorney arguing for a conviction. "Your performance the night of the accident was hardly perfect. You admitted you ignored regulations by calling that flight crew."

"I know you and a lot of other people think it's my fault somehow. If I genuinely felt responsible, believe me I'd take the rap. But I'm convinced this'll turn out to be one of those things where no one's directly to blame." He shook his head sadly. "That is, unless you want to blame the people who put TCAS into operation. Your intentions were noble. The system has a lot to offer. But its flaws must be fixed and we should question our willingness to put machine ahead of man."

In the audience, Kelly's response galvanized Don Szemasko, who muttered to his lawyer, "That mealy-mouthed son of a bitch is trying to wiggle out of this."

The attorney continued writing on his yellow legal pad. "Don't worry. We'll nail whoever's responsible."

"I'm not going to let Kevin's death be just one of those things."

"Hey, it won't. You can count on a fat settlement."

Szemasko fidgeted, saying nothing. It was about more than just money. As much as he lusted after it, he felt duty bound to defend his brother's honor. Kevin, who'd fulfilled their mutual dream of becoming a firefighter, couldn't die in vain. Don was determined to avenge him. He turned his attention back to the witness stand, glaring at the two figures bathed in bright lights.

Several rows forward, Jason hunched on his chair and curled both hands into fists. "Rain Man's gettin' dissed big time, mom."

"I know, honey."

"We gotta help him," he whispered insistently.

Masters stopped pacing and towered over Kelly. "TCAS works very well, sir, and is highly regarded in the flying community. Since you're not a pilot, I suppose it's hard for you to visualize what a godsend it is in the cockpit. Are you sure this isn't just sour grapes because you don't have total authority as a controller anymore?"

"Senator, no one should have total control," he snapped, his voice dripping with contempt. "Pilots can't see everything. Your computer doesn't know everything. And controllers admittedly aren't perfect. TCAS can be a valuable member of that team, but let's all play by the same rules. Mr. Perry was busting my chops awhile ago for two-mile separation, even though it's a safe and accepted practice. Last April, your beloved TCAS put a couple of planes over Chicago within two hundred feet and a quarter mile—and that was far from an isolated incident. If a controller did that, he'd be yanked off position faster than you can say vote for me."

A number of spectators chuckled as he sat back and looked askance at Masters. "Now, if two hundred feet and a quarter mile is satisfactory, tell me and I'll use it. But if the legal minimum's a thousand and three, then for Christ's sake don't rely totally on some machine in the cockpit that can countermand my instructions and run 'em together. Like it or not, that's what happened over the pond."

"It seems clear to me that your interference ran them together," Masters snarled. "You directly violated regulations and confused that captain."

"Excuse me, Senator," Esterhaus said into his microphone.

"If pilots love TCAS as much as you say," Kelly said hotly, "then the last thing they'd do is listen to a controller."

"You'd like us to believe that, wouldn't you? Get yourself off the hook. Well, it won't work because you have no proof."

Esterhaus tried again. "Senator—"

"I have proof!"

Heads turned once more to the unexpected speaker in the front row of spectators. Christy walked tentatively to the NATCA table and picked up a microphone.

"I have proof, Senator, that you're not as squeaky clean as you'd like your constituents to believe." Her voice quivered slightly and she breathed deeply to steady it. "Isn't this just a personal vendetta against Mr. Kelly because of your relationship with Circuitron?"

Collins banged his gavel with obvious exasperation. "Ma'am. Senator. Mr. Kelly. This is totally irregular."

"Let's hear what she has to say," someone shouted from the press corps. Murmured comments buzzed through the audience.

Christy noticed Sanders and Sharon perched on the edges of their chairs with discreet smiles playing on their lips. She glanced at Jason, who was watching her in awe and pride. Turning to Kelly, she saw him looking at her fondly while mouthing, "Don't." As a vision of Carla and Kevin crossed her mind, she remembered her sister's gentle teasing about that first date with Ryan. *You asked him out? You've always been kind of shy. Were you drunk?* Oh, Carla, if you could see me now. To hell with the consequences. She owed it to these people, not to mention a professional obligation to unveil the truth.

"Senator Masters, my name is Christy Cochran and I work for the *Chicago Chronicle*. I have documents that conclusively show you flew on Circuitron's corporate jet to four political rallies during the last election without reimbursing the company. I'm sure you're aware that's against the law. I'm also familiar with your connection to Pinnacle Corporation, which heavily favors Circuitron stock as an investment. Would these issues have anything to do with your obvious zeal in protecting a major TCAS manufacturer?"

Masters licked his lips. "This is hardly the forum for me to respond to these wild and unsubstantiated charges."

His eyes had widened at the mention of Pinnacle. Gripping the edge of the table, she decided to go for broke. It had been many years since Christy bluffed to confirm a story and she prayed the tactic would work now. Collins pounded his gavel again, but she ignored him and pressed on, her heart racing.

"Just answer the question. Did you ride on Circuitron's jet or not?"

"I go on a lot of trips, ma'am. It's hard to keep track."

"A simple yes or no will do, sir."

He stared icily. "I may have, yes, but that was several years ago. You can't expect me to remember what financial arrangements were made."

"I can detail them after this hearing recesses. Trust me for now when I say the company has no record that you paid them. Your income tax returns indicate you own shares of Circuitron. Would you care to acknowledge that?"

"If you know all this, why are you bothering to ask?" he said huffily.

"Yes or no, Senator."

He sighed irritably. "My investments are in a blind trust. I don't know what stocks are in it."

"So we'll have to assume your tax returns are accurate. Will you admit that you own Pinnacle?"

"The whole point of a blind trust is to shelter knowledge of the investments from its owner." He turned to Parker with pleading eyes.

Christy clasped her hands and tilted her head coyly. "Come now, Senator. According to SEC records, Pinnacle has substantial assets. Surely, ownership of such a large concern could not have escaped your attention, blind trust or not. Are you telling us that you simply don't have a clue?"

Masters clenched his jaw and wagged a finger. "I'm not the sole principal, lady. You should get your facts straight before having the audacity to barge in here and interrupt these important proceedings." Realizing what he'd blurted out, the senator started to say something else, then clamped his mouth shut. He looked helplessly at Parker, who lowered his head and shook it slowly.

Christy blinked and caught her breath. "Thank you for clarifying that, Senator. Mr. Chairman, please accept my sincere apologies for this interruption." Replacing the microphone in its holder, she returned to her seat against a backdrop of stunned silence in the ballroom.

Masters stood rigid. Collins hesitated, too, unsure how to proceed. Esterhaus regarded the senator with a wry smile.

"On behalf of the board, apology accepted, Ms. Cochran. Now, ladies and gentlemen, returning to the focus of this hearing. I was given a message a short while ago from our Washington office. The lab has isolated Gene Lombardi's voice on the TRACON tape warning Mr. Kelly of erratic altitude readouts from Coastal flight 276. This confirms for me that the aircraft's Mode C unit was malfunctioning. I wish we knew how much bearing it had on the accident, but we cannot rule out the possibility of a TCAS failure."

Unwilling to surrender, Masters stammered, "Wait . . . um, if Coastal's Mode C really was malfunctioning, Atlantic's TCAS should have caught the discrepancy."

"Atlantic apparently encountered an instantaneous altitude gain of 600 feet from Coastal," Esterhaus pointed out. "TCAS has been programmed to temporarily ignore such aberrations because they can't really happen."

"But you said yesterday there was no sign of anything wrong on the DARC."

"The DARC doesn't record continuously," Scott Carter explained. "It takes a snapshot once a second. It could have missed the fluctuations."

Now Collins interjected, hoping to put the episode behind them. "Senator, this has been a most colorful debate, but it well exceeds the scope of these proceedings. I must kindly direct you to sit down."

Masters' face reddened. He looked at the three men, then at Kelly, then back at the dais. Deafening silence ensued while everyone watched and waited. Finally, he stalked resolutely back to his chair.

Collins rapped his gavel. "This hearing will adjourn early for lunch."

Bedlam broke out in the ballroom. Reporters from both sides of the room descended on Masters, pointing cameras and thrusting microphones and tape recorders at him.

"What about those plane trips, Senator?"

"Tell us about Pinnacle Corporation."

"How much Circuitron stock do you own?"

Masters stood and waved his hands, trying to flee down an aisle clogged with spectators. "No comment."

Several reporters followed him, but the majority surged around Christy. "What else can you tell us, Ms. Cochran?"

Fighting through the crowd, Sanders grabbed Christy's arm and spoke in her ear. "Prendergast just called on my cell phone. He's been watching this on TV and wanted to make sure you don't say anything more." When Christy nodded glumly, she shook her head. "Your Q and A ran live on CNN and the other networks are picking it up already. Cat's out of the bag, Christy. He's got no choice now. He told Hamilton to write the story and said don't worry about your job. He admired your chutzpah."

Jubilant and relieved, she faced the cluster of reporters surrounding her. "Sorry, but I've said enough already. You can read all about it in tomorrow's *Chronicle*."

Ignoring persistent questions and protests, she elbowed her way toward Kelly and Jason, who were standing together watching her. Oblivious to the cameras, she threw her arms around Kelly and they kissed to the accompaniment of popping flashbulbs.

"That was a gutsy move," he said when they ended their embrace. "Is this what you were trying to tell me earlier?"

She nodded happily.

"How did you know the senator would fess up about Pinnacle?"

"I didn't. It was a dice roll."

"At the high-stakes table, my darling. Remind me to take you to Vegas sometime." Hugging her again, he said, "Just remember this isn't over yet. The board still needs proof of what happened, so it better be on that box."

"It will be."

He smiled at the conviction in her voice. "All this has given me a whopping appetite. Can I buy you two lunch?"

"I've a better idea. Why don't we celebrate over dinner? I want to go home and freshen up, but I can meet you back here. Say about six-thirty?"

"It's a date." A man Kelly vaguely recognized kept glancing at them from several rows back in the audience. He nudged Christy. "Isn't that Don Somebody?"

She looked and nodded curtly, then turned her back on him. "Szemasko. My brother-in-law. I didn't realize he was here."

Kelly kissed her once more on the cheek. "I'll see you tonight." He was halfway to the NATCA table when she called him, her eyes twinkling.

"Hey, handsome! What's your room number?"

He caught Rykowski's leering grin. "It's 2112."

Christy and Jason waved goodbye and melded into the crowd.

The afternoon session was comparatively quiet. Kelly answered questions from Coastal Airlines representatives designed to establish for the record that Captain McKenzie properly followed ATC instructions, and he never felt on the spot. Rykowski lobbed him a few token queries to flesh out his years of good service, but the parties from Atlantic, Boeing, and ALPA declined to ask anything. Other testimony from several experts dwelled on the inner workings of TCAS and Mode C. Although the reporters grew bored trying to understand technical details, Kelly listened with interest, grateful to be out of the spotlight. When the hearing recessed about four-thirty, Esterhaus caught up to him on his way out of the ballroom.

"May I buy you a drink?"

"I could use a scotch. Actually, more than one."

Esterhaus smiled with genuine warmth. "So could I."

They wandered into a two-story atrium lounge at the hotel and found an empty table along the windows overlooking Grant Park. After their drinks were served, the investigator lifted his glass.

"My compliments. You really held your own today." They each took a sip and he chuckled. "I've never seen a hearing quite like that."

"Just trying to defend a few shreds of honor." Kelly said, gulping down a large swig of Laphroig.

"I didn't mean to disbelieve you about the readouts. I'm sure you appreciate I have to be certain in these matters. Part of that comes from my wife. She's a lawyer." He flashed a quick smile and tossed back the rest of his drink. "If I were a betting man, I'd put money on Scotty and his theory."

Kelly signaled the cocktail waitress for another round. "I hope you're right about that."

"There's something else I'd like to discuss with you," Esterhaus said. "A proposition. However this turns out, would you be willing to come to Washington when the hearings are over and talk to us some more about TCAS? If you're interested, there might even be a place for you on the NTSB staff."

"I'm flattered." Then he caught himself. "Do you know something I don't that'll affect my future as a controller?"

Esterhaus laughed. "No. The truth is we dearly need people with technical expertise."

Kelly thought about the opportunity. Even if the FAA let him keep his job, he wasn't so sure he wanted it anymore. Not when the same equipment could fail again. Not with people like Hawkins and Bosko around.

"Sounds very interesting. At least worth discussing."

The waitress arrived with fresh drinks and they clinked their glasses. "I'm flying back on Friday," Esterhaus said. "I'll make the arrangements for you to join me."

Like old friends, the two men fell into an easy conversation about aviation, baseball, and the relative merits of attractive females who strolled through the lounge. It was nearly six before Kelly returned to his room. He quickly showered to wash away the day's tension and clean up for dinner. Wrapping a towel around himself, he clicked on the TV and flipped through the channels. Today's hearing, highlighted by Masters' showdown, dominated all the news programs.

After slipping his suit back on, he ordered a bottle of champagne from room service and gazed out the window. Numerous white boats dotted the deep blue surface of the lake. His eyes followed a jet streaking eastward in the bright cloudless sky, past the point where the collision occurred. That the same catastrophe could happen again troubled him and he considered the offer from Esterhaus more seriously. He was a controller—that's what he knew how to do. But maybe by working at the safety board he'd be able to help make TCAS more reliable.

Lost in thought weighing options, he finally looked at his watch, startled to discover it was six forty-five. Christy was generally punctual. If anything had happened to her . . . Loud rapping sounded at the door. With relief, he ran and opened it.

"I was beginning to get worried—"

Kelly had seen only a few guns in his life and never from the wrong end of one. Webber took him duck hunting once and he'd handled firearms owned by several other friends. Now, he recoiled from the .38-caliber Smith & Wesson in Don Szemasko's hand with a profound sense of dread.

Szemasko stepped into the room and the door automatically sighed shut behind him. He reached around, clicked the deadbolt, and latched the safety lock. Kelly kept backing away to get as far as possible from the pistol pointing malevolently at his churning gut. Szemasko's face was flushed—the smell of bourbon wafted through the room—and his eyes gleamed demonically.

"Your time's come, ya piece of shit. You're to blame for what happened and we both know it."

The voice of a dozen crank calls rang in Kelly's ears. It was somewhat different now—he must have disguised himself on the phone—but the similarity was unmistakable. He was amazed that he remained so calm. His head resounded with a frenzied cacophony of escape plans considered and rejected.

Szemasko giggled sloppily. "I enjoyed sideswiping you outside that apartment last week. Might have left it at that, but then you tried to weasel out today. Can't let that happen."

Kelly clung to the hope that Szemasko was drunk. He stalled for time, trying to keep him talking. "Do you really expect to get away with this? What would it accomplish?"

"I owe it to Kevin."

Someone knocked on the door and a muffled voice called out. "Room service."

Szemasko raised his gun to Kelly's chest. "Tell 'em you changed your mind. Try anything funny and you're dead meat."

Kelly eased past him and they moved as one. Szemasko put a hand on the safety latch, preventing him from opening the door more than about four inches. A waiter in a black jacket held a tray with a bottle of Tattinger and two glasses.

"Your champagne, sir."

"I, uh, I've changed my mind."

The waiter shrugged and was about to leave when Christy walked up, smiling broadly. "Sorry I'm late. Traffic on the Eisenhower was terrible."

The waiter glanced at Christy, then back at Kelly. "Are you sure, sir?"

He felt Szemasko press the barrel of the gun against his side. "Yes. I'm sorry for your trouble."

The waiter heeled around. He frankly appraised Christy's low-cut silk blouse so the trip wouldn't be a total waste, then disappeared smartly down the corridor.

"Hey, even if you weren't thirsty, I could have used some of that." She took in his blank stare and confusion clouded her face. "Aren't you going to let me in?"

Szemasko jammed the pistol painfully against his ribs. "Christy . . . uh, I'm not feeling well."

She grinned saucily. "Let me in and I'll try to fix that."

"It's not good now."

Moving closer to the door, she peered through the opening. "What's wrong?"

"Christy, please go." Kelly twisted in terror against the gun and considered mouthing a warning, but there was no way he'd get away with it. Szemasko's burly face was so close he could see the stubble of his beard. Panic-stricken that she'd get shot, too, he said shortly, "I'll see you tomorrow." He let the door click shut and backed into the room again. "She knows something's wrong. She'll go get help."

Unperturbed, Szemasko grabbed a pillow off the bed and held it in front of the gun. "Don't have much time then, do we?"

Kelly realized he was still clutching the remote control unit for the TV. It was now or never. In desperation, he flung the remote to his right and ducked to the left, snatching a lamp off the desk. Szemasko's head darted away from the remote, then from the lamp cord that whipped out of the wall. Pillow feathers burst from a muffled pop and the window behind Kelly crinkled and cracked. He swung the lamp at Szemasko and knocked him to the floor—more from surprise than strength—and scrabbled to pull away the pillow so he could see the gun.

After he yanked the pillow aside, sending more feathers flying, the barrel waved menacingly at his left ear and he cringed when a second bullet roared past his head into the ceiling. Kelly managed to grab Szemasko's wrist and banged it against a leg of the bed. Grunting in pain, Szemasko pummeled the side of Kelly's head with his other fist. A third bullet fractured the wooden desk drawer while Kelly continued to batter Szemasko's wrist against the metal bed frame. The gun finally dropped to the floor and skittered underneath the bed.

Szemasko swore and kneed Kelly in the groin. He swept his hand beneath the bed, but couldn't reach the pistol. Scrambling to his feet, he dragged Kelly up. The room spun as they twirled like ballet dancers caught in an embrace. Szemasko had fifty pounds on him and was a formidable opponent, even drunk. Kelly rammed a shoulder into his chest and the mountain stumbled, but Szemasko recovered and pushed Kelly back into the window. Glass shattered, cascading onto them and falling to the street twenty-one floors below.

Snarling incomprehensibly, Szemasko grabbed Kelly's coat lapels and heaved him halfway out the broken window. Searing pain knifed across his back from jagged shards ripping through his coat. The lake spun crazily upside down. Kelly stretched an arm and grabbed onto the window frame, screaming in agony as more glass sliced into his fingers. He hit Szemasko with his other hand, but the blows had little effect. He lost his grip and flailed at the window frame and was shoved farther out until only his lower legs were still inside the room. Using all his remaining strength, he gripped the wall with his feet and wildly waved his hands, grasping for a purchase.

He felt Szemasko's hands on his feet and was bracing for free fall when he heard a commotion and the hands let go. Kelly slipped some more just as someone grabbed his belt and he looked up into Christy's beautiful, terrified face. She was preventing him from falling, but didn't have the strength to lift him back into the room. The weight and angle of his body continued to drag him toward a plunge to the street far below.

Then a man appeared beside her and reached out to help haul him inside. Kelly slumped to the floor below the window, smearing red streaks down the wall. Dazedly, he took in the two hotel security guards. One was holding a gun on Szemasko, sitting on the bed. The other hustled to the phone and called for medical aid. A sledgehammer lay on the floor and the door to the room was splintered where they'd smashed it open.

Christy dropped to her knees. "My God, you're bleeding! He shot you!"

Kelly breathed heavily, recovering from vertigo, and it took him a minute to find his voice. "Coupla cuts is all." He draped an arm around her to prop himself up and crimson droplets stippled her white blouse. She gingerly hugged back, fearful of hurting him. At length, he asked, "Did you bring the champagne?"

Her short laugh broke into a sob. "Oh, Ryan. As soon as you closed the door, I called security on the house phone near the elevators. God, I nearly died when I heard the gun go off. I thought you were dead." Holding his face with both hands, she kissed him tenderly on the lips. "I love you, Ryan."

He touched his nose to hers and smiled broadly, despite the pain. "I love you, too, Christy. I have since the day we met."

TWENTY-SEVEN
DCA

THE GREEN RADARSCOPES tugged at Kelly's heart, yet he still felt strange being in the TRACON. So much had happened in the week since Hawkins sent him packing. He slowly surveyed the room as if he were taking it all in for the first time, listening to the familiar patter of voices and picking out Rykrisp, Pizza Man, and J.J. on the Front Line. He'd miss this if he walked away. But he'd proven to himself that he could still handle the job after surviving the unthinkable, so maybe it was time to try something new.

Sanchez walked over and introduced herself to Christy and Jason, who were standing beside him. Pointing to the bandages covering his left hand, she asked, "How are you, Ryan?"

Details of his ordeal with Szemasko had been widely publicized. Doctors sewed his fingers back together with sixteen stitches, plus another twenty-two across his back. The hand was temporarily useless and gradually diminishing pain knifed through him whenever he moved. Szemasko was now languishing in Cook County Jail, not far from Brad Schwartz's cell, awaiting trial on charges of attempted murder.

"I'm okay. The last two days of hearings were downright boring compared to the first two, but I'm not complaining."

"I'm afraid I have something to tell you." Her face turned serious and he grimaced while she kept him in suspense for several long seconds. "Hawkins decided there was no deal last Friday. You're welcome back whenever you like."

Kelly grunted. "What prompted his change of heart?"

Sanchez tipped her head toward Christy. "The phones started ringing after the story about you and Bear ran in the *Chronicle*. Then your appearance at the hearing opened the floodgates. We've had hundreds of calls. A few have been negative, but the vast majority say we should let you guys do your job and keep the traffic moving. Hawkins finally spoke to Administrator Chalmers this morning. Not long after, he told me they were dropping the deal."

"I'll be damned."

"I knew they'd never make it stick," she said, raising her voice for the benefit of Boskovich, who was sitting morosely at the supervisors' desk with his tie uncharacteristically askew. "What brings you by today?"

"We're flying to Washington for the weekend. Esterhaus wants to interview me for a job."

"I've never been there," Jason said.

Sanchez raised her eyebrows. "Will we ever see you in here again?"

"I don't know, Sam. You know what they say about how you can never go back." He checked a digital clock above one of the scopes and automatically translated universal time into the local hour. "We'd better move along. Our flight leaves soon."

"Take care, Ryan. And good luck, whatever you decide to do."

J.J. waved them over as they turned toward the door. "I wanted to say goodbye before you left."

Kelly nodded uncertainly. They'd barely spoken since their argument after the accident.

She shook hands with Christy and Jason. "Hi. We met in here before."

"I remember," Christy said coolly.

J.J. called an airplane and then looked anxiously at Kelly. "Bosko asked me to help the brass take you down—that was the day you came back to work. When he suggested it could help my career, I told him where to stick it. Regardless of what happened between us, I would never sell out a controller who was doing his job." She turned to Christy. "Sorry I was short with you when we talked on the phone. I was going through a difficult time. It looks like things have worked out between you."

Christy slipped a hand through Kelly's arm. "We get along very well."

"I can see that." J.J.'s voice sounded a shade wistful, but she smiled warmly. "I'm happy for you both. I overheard you talking to Sam—have a safe trip. What's your flight number?"

Kelly pulled their tickets out of his sport jacket. "We're on Prairie 473 to DCA and 101 coming back on Monday."

J.J. jotted a note. "We'll take care of you."

✈   ✈   ✈

FREDERIC ESTERHAUS LEANED ACROSS THE AISLE as the Prairie Air DC-9 climbed over Lake Michigan. Kelly, Christy, and Jason occupied the opposite row. The investigator adjusted his wire-rimmed glasses and peered through them with anticipation.

"The lab has finished a preliminary analysis of Coastal's black box."

Kelly held his breath. The roar of the jet faded to a whisper as he waited for the verdict on his innocence or guilt.

"Understand this isn't a probable cause report, but it appears that Mode C misdirected TCAS. We counted five erratic fluctuations during the last minute of flight." Esterhaus paused briefly. "Even though you warned the pilot, there was no hesitation. Captain McKenzie followed the computer's instructions to the letter and climbed right into Atlantic 59. It's what killed him and everyone else."

Kelly sank heavily into the seat. "That's a relief for me. I just wish it could never happen again."

"I agree, Ryan. There's always been a difficult balance between safety and expediency. Every improvement has a cost and the FAA usually doesn't order changes until the loss of lives exceeds that cost. The benchmark they use is one-point-five million dollars per passenger. The airlines have invested a fortune in TCAS. It'll take a lot for them to turn it off, even temporarily."

A flight attendant hovered politely. "Are you Ryan Kelly?"

"Yes."

She motioned at Christy and Jason. "Captain Lansing suggested the three of you would be more comfortable in first class. It's a token of his appreciation for the direct routing ATC gave us into National. Would you care to follow me?"

Embarrassed, Kelly shrugged at Esterhaus, who made a point of inspecting his coach accommodations. "Go ahead and enjoy yourselves."

"I'll see you when we get there."

Christy had never flown first class and stretched her legs in front of the spacious leather seat after they were escorted to the forward cabin. Jason snuggled next to a window on the right, losing himself in the view outside. Kelly noticed Senator Masters two rows ahead and hoped he didn't see them. He wasn't in the mood for another confrontation. After he clasped his safety belt, Christy leaned against him.

"Pretty nice pull, controller. How'd you manage this?"

"One of the perks. Remember when J.J. asked for our flights? We try to give a plane direct routing when we know there's a controller on board. Sometimes, it's genuine because the person has to get back to start a shift and was delayed by weather. Mostly, I just get free drinks."

"Do you play favorites very often?"

"I doubt there's one among us who doesn't give the rare flight special treatment. It's not always because a controller's on board. Besides emergencies, we might give a pilot faster service if we recognize his voice and remember that he helped us out of a jam one time." He grinned and she did, too.

"What's so funny?"

"Well, J.J. was coming back from Jamaica last year on Atlantic and we cleared her flight direct to O'Hare. The pilots called her to the cockpit. When the door opened, they were both crouching and waving their arms in genuflection."

"I feel a gentle tug on my leg."

"J.J. swears it's true."

Christy's laugh was interrupted by a flight attendant handing her orange juice in a glass tumbler. Kelly asked the attendant to thank the captain for the upgrade and inquire if he could observe them for a while. She motioned him forward a few minutes later and he was strapping himself into the cockpit jump seat when Lansing turned around to shake his hand.

"You're the one I saw on TV at those hearings, aren't you?"

"Yes." He tensed for the reception.

Lansing's sunglasses focused on him steadily. "I gotta tell you, Kelly, I like TCAS. Having that extra set of eyes is nice. Frankly, I've seen you guys screw up. But I also have to admit you made some good points. I'd like a longer alert time myself. Maybe a lot of it was just hearing your perspective. You guys are on my flights now and then, but I'm sorry to say I've only been in a tower once."

"You're welcome anytime."

"I plan to take you up on that."

They were descending over the Virginia countryside and had switched frequencies from Washington Center to Approach when the synthetic voice rang out.

"Traffic, traffic."

The first officer kept flying the plane while Lansing scanned the clear blue sky, squinting in the morning sun. Kelly had never been in the cockpit during a TCAS event and was at once curious and fearful. He studied the fish-finder and looked out the window, but he didn't see the intruder.

"Descend, descend."

The first officer obediently pushed the control yoke forward, increasing their vertical speed from 1,000 to 1,500 feet per minute. Lansing keyed the radio mike.

"Washington Approach, Prairie 473 is descending for an RA. We're passing through ten thousand eight hundred."

"Roger, 473. Be advised I show no traffic in your vicinity."

"TCAS indicates the intruder is just above us at twelve o'clock."

"I don't see anything in that quadrant. Nearest traffic is six miles ahead and two thousand feet below."

"Four seventy-three is still looking."

"Clear of conflict."

Lansing grunted and notified the controller, who told them to level off at 10,000. Kelly sighed quietly. The pilots were in the midst of a checklist when TCAS squawked once more.

"Traffic, traffic."

"Here we go again." Lansing resumed searching the sky.

"Descend, descend."

The nose tipped forward and the altimeter unwound.

"Two o'clock!"

Lansing had barely shouted his warning when a private plane flashed on the right. The first officer jerked the control wheel to veer away. A twin-engine Beechcraft zoomed so close in the windshield that Kelly imagined he could reach out and touch the wing. Then it disappeared below them. He waited for a jolt and finally let out his breath when it didn't come.

"Prairie 473 is reporting a near miss," Lansing said into the mike. "Looked like a Beechcraft Baron."

A desire to be with Christy and Jason, to see them and hold them, suddenly overwhelmed Kelly. He shakily unbuckled the safety harness. "I should get back to my friends in the cabin."

TCAS sounded a third time while he was twisting out of the jump seat. No nearby traffic displayed on the fish-finder, and Lansing warily turned it off.

"Damned thing is going crazy."

"I suspect it's met the enemy and it is us," Kelly said.

"What do you mean?"

"TCAS is supposed to transmit signals, then wait for a response. Occasionally, it does both at the same time and gets confused. It thinks *we're* the intruder."

Lansing straightened himself in the left seat. "Rest assured we'll get you down in one piece, Mr. Kelly. Nice meeting you."

Masters was shouting at a flight attendant when he emerged from the cockpit. His tray table contained an empty glass and a wet spot stained his suit. "I have an important hearing as soon as we land. I'll look ridiculous."

The attendant remained poised and dabbed at his jacket with a napkin. "I'm very sorry, Senator. The plane banked unexpectedly."

Kelly glanced at Christy and Jason, who appeared to have no idea what happened. A sharp turn and nothing more. They deserved to know, but unless they asked he'd wait until they landed before saying anything. He couldn't resist with Masters. He leaned over the crew member's shoulder, keeping his voice low so he wouldn't frighten the other passengers.

"For your information, Senator, we just survived a TCAS near miss. Ask the captain if you don't believe me." He held a thumb and forefinger half an inch apart. "We came that close to scraping paint."

Shock flashed across Masters' face. His mouth opened, but nothing came out until he finally grabbed the napkin from the attendant. "I can do that."

✈   ✈   ✈

CLUSTERED AROUND A SECLUDED TABLE at The Bombay Club, one of the capital's finer Indian restaurants, Christy and Kelly each savored a snifter of brandy while Jason sipped Coke. All of them were sated after a sumptuous feast of subcontinental delicacies complemented by relaxing piano music. Christy rubbed her throbbing feet together and rested her head on Kelly's shoulder. While he'd talked with Esterhaus and the NTSB chairman over lunch and throughout the afternoon, she'd followed Jason around the National Air and Space Museum. Now, she smiled contentedly at her son.

"Are the three of us going to live together?" Jason asked.

"Why do you think that?"

"You two look happy."

She felt Kelly's hand squeeze her thigh in confirmation. "One doesn't always follow the other."

"I told Dave that, but he says you will 'cause you're doin' it. Only he didn't use that word."

Kelly sensed Jason testing limits. "I can imagine what he said."

"It was the 'F' word." He acted nonchalant and waited for their reaction.

Christy swallowed a hefty swig of brandy. She knew it was her duty to educate Jason, but the subject matter and public environment left her flustered. Her condition amused Kelly and he decided to clarify a point, feeling oddly like a father.

"Your mother and I love each other. People who do often express their affection by making love, which is the dignified way of saying it. It's a private matter between them that's no one else's business."

Christy gazed tenderly at Jason, impressed by Kelly's simple explanation. "How would you feel if Ryan and I decided to live together?"

"I think it'd be awesome. Don't you, mom?"

She reached for Kelly's hand. "Well, I've never been happier."

"Do you have a girlfriend, Jason?" Kelly asked.

"Nah. They're only interested in the jocks."

"Not all of them. You'll find one to charm."

He shrugged. "S'cuse me while I use the *lavatory*."

Kelly toyed with his snifter after Jason left. "Did you put him up to that?" He knew she hadn't, but he enjoyed teasing her.

"*Moi?*"

"Anyway, after Don played yo-yo with me the other night and after our near miss this morning, all I could think about was not seeing you again. I didn't like that thought. The two of you are a big part of my life now. I want us to be together."

Her blue eyes held his. "So do I, Ryan."

"We have some practical considerations to work out."

"Like your place or mine?"

"And whether I'll be in Chicago. Esterhaus made the job offer official. I'm seriously considering it, even though the pay is less. I might be able to help fix TCAS and some other safety issues."

She sighed, proud yet frustrated by his determination. "The *Washington Post* is a good paper, but they may not want me. At least I have a friend there."

"We don't have to decide on any of this tonight."

"That's good." Her fingers strayed beneath the table. "Because right now I'm more interested in what you were explaining to my son."

He raised his bandaged hand. "I'm not sure how energetic I'll be."

"Don't worry. All you'll have to do is tell me if it hurts."

Jason returned to the table and they lingered briefly before hailing a cab back to the L'Enfant Plaza south of the Mall. After Jason climbed into bed, his mother sat on the edge. She no longer felt awkward.

"I'm staying in Ryan's room tonight."

"Okay."

She bent to kiss him on the forehead and he didn't turn away. "Good night, Jason."

"Night." He watched her fetch an overnight case and reach for the light. Propping himself up on his elbows, he said, "I like Rain Man a lot, mom. He rules."

Her smile was a mixture of relief, joy, and anticipation. "I think so, too."

Jason settled under the covers again and she turned off the light and walked through the door connecting their rooms. Kelly stood near the window admiring the city. The room was dark except for two small candles flickering on a coffee table. A soulful saxophonist played softly on the radio. She changed clothes in the bathroom and stepped beside him wearing a semi-sheer camisole, her breasts clearly visible beneath the thin fabric. He offered her another snifter of brandy and she set it on the table.

"I want something else now."

Christy guided him to the bed and their mouths locked onto each other. Tugging open his terry cloth robe, she eased Kelly onto his back and gently sat astride him, running her hands across his chest. Slowly and deliciously, they began moving as one in the warm dim light to whispered yearnings that were neither dignified nor obscene. Long after the candles burned out, they settled onto their sides like spoons and drifted peacefully asleep.

✈   ✈   ✈

THE FLIGHT TO CHICAGO on Monday was thankfully routine. The three of them didn't get to enjoy first class again, but the captain announced their direct clearance over the PA system. After pulling into the gate at O'Hare, they encountered Gene Lombardi waiting in the Jetway, grinning through his mustache.

"This is a surprise," Kelly said.

"I wanted to make sure you knew what the agency just did."

He braced himself. "What now?"

"They've ordered the airlines to use TCAS in Traffic Alert mode only until further notice. Chalmers announced it this morning at a news conference in Washington. We heard through the grapevine that Senator Masters was pretty shaken up after your near miss on Friday. And he's been taking a lot of flak in the press over his connection with Circuitron. How much do you want to bet he put some heat on the agency?"

"That's a sure thing. You didn't have to chase out here to tell me, though."

Lombardi pointed toward the terminal. "There's a mob of reporters waiting for you. The phone's been ringing off the hook in the TRACON, so Sam finally told them what flight you were on."

"Oh, great." Kelly debated whether to thank her or seek revenge.

Lombardi strutted up the Jetway. "I also wanted to let you know I passed my check ride today. I'm fully certified."

"Congratulations, Pizza Man. You're buying at the Sports Edition tonight."

When they entered the gate area, someone hollered, "There he is!" Camera lights switched on and the reporters surged forward, forcing passengers to dodge around them.

"Mr. Kelly, would you care to comment on the FAA's action concerning TCAS?"

"I'm relieved," he said, moving off to one side. Relieved for all the passengers, for his fellow controllers, yes. But relieved mainly because the two most important people in the world to him were safely back on the ground. "It will still provide warnings, only now pilots and controllers have a chance to make sure the threat is real."

"How does it feel to win?"

He shook his head. "This isn't about winning or losing. It's about people who died because we relied solely on technology to solve a problem. Computers are fast. Usually, they're accurate. But they're not perfect. We need to be aware of their limitations."

With an apologetic wave of his hand, Kelly ignored a dozen other shouted questions and slowly propelled Christy and Jason past the minicams and microphones and into the anonymity of the crowded concourse.

AFTERWORD

A
F
T
E
R
W
O
R
D

PERSPECTIVES FROM THE OUTSIDE

An Afterword by Paul McElroy

In many respects, this novel is a work of nonfiction. To paint a genuine portrait of the largely unseen and often misunderstood world of air traffic control, I borrowed heavily from real life. *TRACON* includes authentic controller and pilot phraseology, ATC and cockpit procedures, references to air safety issues and aviation accidents, even real radio frequencies and airline flight numbers. And, yes, all of the humorous controller vignettes actually happened. Although the characters are products of my imagination, they're composites of some of the 15,000 professional men and women controllers in the United States—and 45,000 others around the world, for that matter, who all share a common mission and bond.

Fortunately, the midair collision depicted in *TRACON* has not occurred—yet. When the collision avoidance system called TCAS went into operation in the late 1980s, teething problems frequently caused dangerous near misses. Computer software updates and other changes based largely on suggestions from controllers—who were not consulted when the system was developed—have improved the reliability of this much-needed safety tool. And, as this book tries to point out, we're better off with TCAS than without it. But no machine is fail-safe, and TCAS false alerts that lead to near misses still occur. The scenario in *TRACON* is based on several frightening incidents, including one over northwest China in the summer of 1999. Two 747s flown by British Airways and Korean Air whisked past each other, wingtip to wingtip, a mere 600 feet apart.

There have been some changes in air traffic control between the time I began researching *TRACON* and the publication of this special edition commemorating the twentieth anniversary of the 1981 PATCO strike. Some are minor, others more significant, and at least one is potentially sweeping in scope. Sadly, some of the issues that led to the historic walkout and firing of 11,560 controllers—including outdated equipment, excessive overtime, and inept management at a few too many control towers and radar rooms—still exist today. A thoughtful essay by Rebecca Pels Lust, which follows, offers illuminating insights into this regrettable chapter in aviation history.

The main stage for this book—the O'Hare TRACON—has moved from the base of the airport control tower to a new and much larger building in Elgin, Illinois, about twenty miles away. The controllers are happy to have more modern radarscopes and radios, and to avoid traffic congestion on the expressways around the airport. But some wistfully remember their old haunt, where they could walk outside and see airplanes. The cramped quarters helped foster a camaraderie that's more elusive now because the controllers don't all work within shouting distance of each other.

The O'Hare control tower described in the book still stands, however, operations are conducted at a new and larger tower nearby. It's so roomy, in fact, that shorter controllers standing on one side of the tower cab must perch atop a plastic stool to observe planes on the other side of the field.

These and other new ATC facilities around the country are welcome news to the traveling public and a profession that, until recently, grappled with unreliable equipment often older than the controllers using it. With the first stages of a long-awaited system modernization moving forward in fits and starts, the Federal Aviation Administration has shed its dubious distinction of being the world's largest purchaser of vacuum tubes during the late nineties.

Relatively newer computers now provide aircraft and other information on radarscopes, a task that used to be handled by antiquated mainframes. Other modern PCs provide controllers with real-time weather and traffic flows. And many scopes now sport color rather than the traditional monochromatic green, although the software running them needs to be updated to take advantage of this new

A F T E R W O R D

capability. Meanwhile, it's as if controllers have a color television tuned to a black-and-white channel. These enhancements have occurred largely under the stewardship of current FAA Administrator Jane Garvey, who has also made strides in improving labor-management relations with the National Air Traffic Controllers Association, the successor union to PATCO.

Even so, much more needs to be done.

A plan to upgrade the radarscopes and computers at the nation's 185 TRACONs is behind schedule. Computers running the scopes at the FAA's 21 en route centers are written in an obscure programming language called Jovial, and people conversant in this Sanskrit-like dialect are rapidly retiring or passing away.

Other improvements are long overdue. Many airports do not have ground radar, which severely hampers a controller's ability to monitor planes moving on runways and taxiways in low visibility. This is despite the fact that the National Transportation Safety Board has deemed runway incursions the No. 1 safety problem confronting aviation today. During a blinding snowstorm one night in late December 2000, for instance, a Boeing 737 departing from T.F. Green Airport in Providence, Rhode Island, suddenly aborted takeoff to swerve around a 757 that had inadvertently strayed onto the active runway. Luckily, the alert crew of the departing plane averted a collision and no one was hurt. The outcome likely would have been tragic had the plane been landing. Veering past the other jet at such a critical time would be nearly impossible. If the tower had been equipped with ground radar, however, a controller could have warned the pilots of the other plane when they missed a taxiway turnoff in the heavy snowfall.

Another much-needed upgrade involves oceanic control. Pilots flying over the Atlantic and Pacific can pinpoint their location by using satellite-based Global Positioning System navigational equipment. But controllers at the three en route centers that handle these flights—New York Center in Ronkonkoma on Long Island, Oakland Center in Fremont, California, and Anchorage Center in Alaska—must still use circular slide rules to help calculate the planes' positions and track their progress with grease pencils on Plexiglas charts.

Upon seeing this archaic system, former Republican Rep. Susan Molinari of New York described it as "something out of the Flintstones." The FAA appears close to upgrading its oceanic control centers but, as of this writing in the spring of 2001, the agency has not selected a vendor.

And, in the FAA's world, the term "upgrade" can have a special meaning.

Two years ago, the news media reported widely on equipment being installed at all en route centers. Most accounts glossed over the fact that the Display System Replacement, or DSR as the agency calls it, was just that: an updated video display lashed on top of the old radarscope equipment, akin to buying a new monitor for your obsolete personal computer. The 20- by 20-inch square color displays were built in the mid-1980s as part of the FAA's plan to automate certain aspects of air traffic control and essentially reduce the controller's function to that of a hall monitor. The Advanced Automation System project became so complicated and unworkable that the agency abandoned it. Three scaled-down portions of the project were salvaged, but the agency wasted $1.6 billion. For nearly fifteen years, the DSR monitors and the-then state-of-the-art RISC 6000-chip computers that run them collected dust until they were hauled out of storage for the en route center "upgrade."

Most controllers like the newer monitors and aren't complaining. But DSR's evolution is characteristic of the agency's cumbersome procurement process, which typically drags on for five to seven years—or longer—before new equipment is brought online. The Advanced Automation System project and other agency boondoggles are one of the reasons Congress has been reluctant to spend more money on air traffic control and airport improvements.

Another reason, observers charge, is that Capitol Hill hoards multibillion-dollar surpluses in the Airport and Airways Trust Fund to mask the size of the federal deficit or to meet other political needs. To its credit, Congress passed a bill known as AIR-21 in the spring of 2000 that was signed into law by President Clinton. AIR-21 significantly increased FAA spending to about $40 billion over the next three years and mandated that the money we all pay into the trust fund whenever we fly be spent solely on aviation. Unfortunately, politics inside the Beltway continues to create turbulence for the flying public. One year later, the Office of Management and Budget temporarily chopped $300 million from the FAA's budget—until President Bush directed the agency to restore the cuts.

It will take awhile for air travelers to see the results of this belated spending spree. Equipment used at airports and in the air traffic control system is sophisticated, and usually requires a long lead time to install and test before it becomes operational. Ironically, as NATCA President John Carr has pointed out, all the equipment modernization in the world will do little to solve the No. 1 complaint of travelers: airline delays. In 2000, they reached a record 450,000, or about one of every four flights.

The General Accounting Office, our government's watchdog agency, agrees with the FAA that two-thirds of those delays were caused by bad weather. The reasons for the remaining one-third are many, including airplane mechanical problems and crew shortages.

Beyond that, the airlines and their trade group, the Air Transport Association, blame the FAA for not keeping pace with demand. That's partly true, but it's not the whole story. Just as metropolitan freeways are clogged during rush hour, major airports suffer a similar phenomenon. Airlines often overbook runways much as they overbook seats. Every evening at six o'clock at Dallas-Fort Worth Airport, for example, fifty-seven flights are scheduled to leave. Even though DFW is a sprawling operation with seven runways and three control towers, it cannot physically handle that many departures within the 15-minute grace period before flights are considered late. And so, every evening, at least twenty-two planes are delayed.

The situation is similar elsewhere. At 7 P.M. at O'Hare, sixty-two departures are scheduled—twice as many as the airport can handle. At Hartsfield Airport in Atlanta, which edged past O'Hare as the world's busiest in 2000, runways are overbooked about one-third of the time. New York's La Guardia, already saturated with a thousand flights a day, was swamped when regional airlines added another 600 in a competitive free-for-all. The carriers eventually cut that figure by two-thirds after delays there skyrocketed but, not surprisingly, La

Guardia earned the worst record for delays of any airport in the country.

Airlines say they schedule flights based on customer preferences. Travelers are glad they do, but again there's more to the story. In today's hub-and-spoke environment, flights are also scheduled to maximize carrier efficiency. As a result, herds of airplanes arrive at major airports one hour, then scatter the next, in several waves throughout the day. The hub-and-spoke system also creates a domino effect, which is why many people prefer to fly early in the morning before delays stack up.

In the end, we have met the enemy and it is us. We're flying more than ever—nearly two million people a day in the United States— and our numbers are expected to surge half again as much by the end of this decade. Look at a list of the world's busiest airports (takeoffs and landings in 2000) and you'll find all but three of the top twenty are in this country. The exceptions are Charles de Gaulle Airport near Paris at No. 8, London Heathrow at No. 17, and Frankfurt Main at No. 19.

So what's the solution?

Some industry observers have advocated a concept known as peak-hour pricing, meaning that airlines, corporate, and private pilots would be charged higher landing fees during times of congestion. Presumably, these costs would be passed on to airline passengers so that, if you want to leave at rush hour, you'd pay a little more. While this may help, it's a Band-Aid approach.

Another solution involves greater use of regional airports. The top sixty major hubs handle ninety percent of airline travelers. That's where most of us live and work. Some savvy travelers try to favor smaller airports a little off the beaten path—MacArthur Airport on Long Island rather than Kennedy or La Guardia, for instance, or Providence airport about an hour's drive southwest of Boston instead of Logan. But they're often stymied by limited service or significantly higher air fares.

The only long-term answer is to build more runways. A grand total of two new airports opened in the United States during the last quarter of the twentieth century: Dallas-Fort Worth and Denver

A
F
T
E
R
W
O
R
D

International. In the 1990s, just six new runways were poured at major airports while the number of passengers soared 44 percent. Is it any wonder that we're fast approaching gridlock?

Responding to an increasingly frustrated traveling public and growing pressure from the airlines, some politicians are making noise about privatizing the air traffic control system. One of the oft-cited benefits is that modernization would happen much faster. Indeed, Nav Canada and Airservices Australia, both of which took over their respective government's air traffic control operations in the mid-1990s, now use state-of-the-art equipment that makes U.S. controllers salivate. Instead of slide rules and grease pencils, oceanic controllers in Brisbane, Australia, see real-time aircraft positions on their computer displays and can tell pilots to change course with a simple click-and-drag of the mouse.

Privatization proponents also like to rave about cost savings. Nav Canada estimates that airlines spent about $225 million Canadian less in fiscal 2000 than what they would have paid under the old Air Transportation Tax. What often goes unmentioned is that general aviation pilots who frequent smaller airports pay a lot more than they did before.

Modern equipment is great and travelers should benefit from cost-efficient air traffic control. But such preoccupation with the bottom line makes me uneasy. I worry that controller staffing would be streamlined, bringing smiles to the bean counters while leaving pilots and passengers short-changed. I'm concerned by simple comparisons trumpeting the success of privatized systems elsewhere, but which fail to address the volume and complexity of our airspace. And a privatized system would do little, if anything, to alleviate traffic delays.

During thunderstorms over New York in the summer of 2000, Nav Canada declined to allow U.S. controllers to route some flights north of the border because there wouldn't be enough traffic to justify paying a Canadian controller overtime to handle them. So much for solving the delay problem. In his foreword, John Carr mentioned an Airservices Australia internal memo raising the possibility of denying help to pilots in distress because of liability concerns, a proposal I find terrifying.

I agree that our air traffic control system needs improvement, but such incidents do nothing to convince me that privatization is the answer. Right now, I have the option of avoiding rock-bottom, cheap-fare airlines whose safety records don't give me a warm and fuzzy. A privatized ATC system would deny me that flexibility. The FAA is charged with ensuring safe and efficient air travel, and it has helped to create the safest aviation system in the world. Instead of throwing that out the cargo bay door, we should hold the agency accountable—not succumb to knee-jerk frustration and sell a national public franchise to the lowest bidder. Let's not compromise safety in our haste to fix the system and ignore the biggest problem plaguing air travel today—delays.

Despite having written a suspense novel involving an airline disaster, I'd rather fly any day of the week than deal with the life-threatening chaos on our highways. As we approach the 100th birthday of manned flight in 2003, let us hope the skies always remain so safe.

P.M. / April 2001

A
F
T
E
R
W
O
R
D

TROUBLED UNION

The Pressures of PATCO:
Strikes and Stress in the 1980s
By Rebecca Pels Lust

A

F

T

E

R

W

O

R

D

On August 3, 1981, almost 13,000 air traffic controllers went on strike after months of negotiations with the federal government. During the contract talks, Robert Poli, president of the Professional Air Traffic Controllers Association (PATCO), explained the union's three major demands as a $10,000 across-the-board raise, a thirty-two-hour workweek (down from forty), and a better retirement package. While the press and hearings in Congress focused almost exclusively on the demand for a pay raise, certain commentators recognized that the air controllers' walkout was not solely, or even primarily, an economic issue. *Newsweek* noted that "controllers concede that their chief complaint is not money but hours, working conditions, and a lack of recognition for the pressures they face." *Time* wrote that the thirty-two-hour week was "a reduction that the controllers seem to want more than the pay increases. ... most PATCO members see this issue as the key to lowering their on-the- job anxieties and enhancing safety." One striker later explained that the $10,000 demand "was always negotiable; anyone who believed it would come to pass was dreaming. Of primary importance to most was a reduced work week and an achievable retirement."[1] Such views had little effect on negotiations; forty-eight hours after the walkout, President Reagan fired the 11,350 ATCs (almost seventy percent of the work force) who had not returned to work. In case the message was still unclear, he declared a lifetime ban on the rehiring of the strikers by the FAA.

The dramatic circumstances surrounding the strike attracted much commentary, at the time and subsequently. This attention, however, for the most part, failed to uncover or illuminate the fundamental issue under contention: control of the workplace. A study of the relationship over several years between air traffic controllers and their employer, the Federal Aviation Administration (FAA), and the language, reasoning, and actions used by controllers both before and after the strike, as well as the FAA's responses,[2] reveals the centrality of this fight which has traditionally characterized strong labor action in the past. Despite the assertions of many that the issue of control has little relevance in the "modern" high-tech workplace and has been superseded by other concerns, it was the galvanizing force behind many controller protests over the years and led to the explosion in 1981 with the strike. Indeed, instead of a redefinition of workplace relations in the twentieth century, the same struggle over control continues, only in less evident, and perhaps more dangerous, ways.

Historians have long debated whether workplace control is still a key issue in late twentieth century management-worker relations. Many scholars and much of society have surmised that the development of new technology and modes of production would alter the terms of, or even eliminate, this conflict. The rapidly changing character of world markets and new economic and technological advances would preclude the usefulness of the traditional adversarial relationship fostered by unions and managers at the point of production and replace it with a participative model which reduced the need for work rules, grievance systems, and wage standards. With the restructuring of the workplace as a "caring community," traditional dissatisfaction would "dissolve in an atmosphere of unity and good feeling" and do away with conflict and division. New technology would allow workers to perform more creative, useful, and interesting tasks; reduce hazards at the workplace; and even lead to less hours and more leisure time.[3]

Harry Braverman, in his classic book Labor and Monopoly Capital (1974), disputed this optimistic view of change in the twentieth century workplace. He instead presented work (in capitalism) as inherently geared to the creation of profit rather than the satisfaction of man's needs, thus ensuring a fundamental conflict of interest between workers and capitalists. As management systematically attempted to reach the potential of its labor in the face of antagonistic relations, it looked to scientific management theory, as well as technology, in order to better control labor. The widespread adoption of Taylorism had only initiated the process of deskilling jobs and removing autonomy, responsibility, and judgement from the shop floor, which then continued through other, more sophisticated, and less obvious, methods.[4]

Historians David Noble, Harley Shaiken, Barbara Garson, and Ronald Howard have all supported variations of Braverman's thesis, primarily by studying the effects and implications of technology and automation on blue and white collar workers. Like Braverman they argue that the primary impetus behind job definitions and the structure of developing technology has generally been to limit worker autonomy further. Cost reduction and profit, frequently management's explanation for implementing changes in job structures, have thus been only rationalizations masking initiatives basically designed to strengthen managerial control.[5]

A study of the reasons for the ongoing strife between the FAA and air traffic controllers, highlighted by the strike, demonstrates how important the issue of workplace control continues to be in late twentieth century worker-management relations. Moreover, it indicates how factors such as technological advances and the discourse and substance of labor-management bargaining since World War II have served to mask this struggle, often to the disadvantage of the workers involved.

The PATCO controversy is particularly useful to illustrating such an assessment for several reasons. First, while air traffic controllers are employees of the FAA, ostensibly the overriding goal of both groups is to assure the maximum safety of air travel. This presumably removes the traditional conflict of interests between management's search for profits and workers' job satisfaction, and would seemingly make for harmonious relations. Since this was not the case, obviously other factors worked to divide the two groups.

Second, the FAA possessed a monopoly over the training and hiring of air traffic controllers (except for a small percentage who worked for the military). With specialized skills and usually limited education, most ATCs had little choice but to work for the government. They therefore had a large stake in work conditions and benefits. The same factors gave the FAA a strong hand in dealing with its work force.

Third, the majority of controllers found their work intrinsically interesting. Most described their occupation as challenging and exciting. As one explained, "the expression is used about printers that they get ink in their blood. We have airplanes in our blood." A striker noted in 1984 that, "I have been unable to find a job or position that offers the same excitement and personal satisfaction that controlling aircraft did."[6] Such job satisfaction indicates that the complaints of air controllers ran deeper than unhappiness with the occupation per se.

Finally, advancing technology played a key role in both the cause and the resolution of the strike. Controllers, for the most part, paid little attention to the implications of automation on their occupation, although PATCO occasionally faulted the FAA's emphasis on equipment instead of people. Most controllers believed in the centrality and necessity of human skill and judgement to the system. Indeed, they welcomed almost any equipment or programs that might assist them in their work. At the same time, though, an overwhelming number of individual ATC complaints singled out stress as a primary motive for striking. Greater air traffic volume and increased demands on ATC capabilities made possible by new technology, coupled with faulty equipment and autocratic management that limited workplace autonomy, were the obvious causes of such stress. Yet neither PATCO nor the controllers made this connection explicit or strongly challenged management privilege to decide the nature and purpose of computers in air towers.

Meanwhile, FAA officials clearly saw automation as a means of eliminating dependence on skilled controllers. As an editorial in *Aviation Week and Space Technology* commented, "few federal bureaucrats have the chance to fire seventy percent of their departments and replace the victims with lower-salaried recruits—or with computers and black boxes." In 1982 J. Lynn Helms (head of the FAA) announced a twenty-year program costing between $15 billion and $20 billion to replace the system's aging computers and further move towards automating air control.[7]

✈   ✈   ✈

While the strike suddenly made relations between PATCO and the FAA headline news, there was nothing novel about their opposing stances and uncompromising positions. PATCO and the FAA had had a turbulent relationship since the formation of the union in 1968. In 1968, 1969, 1970, 1974, 1975, and 1978, ATCs conducted nationwide slowdowns and sickouts in efforts to gain better pay, training, staffing, retirement benefits, less hours, and in response to FAA actions such as the involuntary transfer of certain union activists. By 1980, the union had achieved significant benefits for controllers, including one of the best retirement systems in the country and the best collective bargaining position of any union in the public sector. At the same time, an "us vs. them" mentality prevailed between PATCO and the FAA. This divide was reinforced by PATCO's establishment of a group of "responsible militants" (referred to as a strike force at times) in 1978 to help organize and lead membership, and the FAA's creation of a management strike contingency force in 1980 as both groups anticipated renegotiating the controllers' contract when it expired in February 1981.

Two studies conducted during the 1970s confirmed the existence of deep-rooted problems. A task force commissioned by the secretary of transportation in April 1968 to explore ATC complaints released its official findings in January 1970. The Corson Committee Report warned that employee-management relations with the FAA were in "extensive disarray." Concerned about an extremely low controller morale and its possible effects on public safety, the committee urged a sharp reduction in work hours, the upgrading of equipment and facilities, the reduction of required overtime, the expansion of intervals between shift rotations, and the revision of pay criteria. Most significant, it recommended making these changes by working with appropriate employee organizations. The report also criticized PATCO for "ill-considered and intemperate attacks on FAA management." But it placed the majority of blame on the failure of FAA management to "understand and accept the role of employee organizations" and its tolerance of "ineffective internal communications."[8]

The FAA commissioned a more extensive study in 1972. Headed by Dr. Robert Rose, the five-year, $2.8 million project led to similar conclusions. The 750-page Rose Report found that the job of an air traffic controller was not uniquely or debilitatingly stressful. However, the researchers added that many of the stresses that were associated with the job, indicated by high levels of drinking and depression, were due to autocratic management, and a system which included little reward and a fear of burnout. The Rose Report labeled morale as "low" among nearly forty percent of controllers.

The FAA paid little attention to such warnings and implemented few of the reports' recommendations. FAA officials seemed to view the reports alone as somehow conducive to ameliorating workplace relations and continued to act in ways that both the Corson and Rose reports had condemned. For instance, in 1979 FAA Administrator Langhorne Bond arbitrarily terminated an immunity provision which had been included in the 1978 three-year FAA/PATCO contract. This program was designed by controllers to encourage ATCs, pilots, and administrators to exchange information and thereby learn from each others' mistakes without fear of retribution or ridicule. It set up an outside, disinterested committee under the National Aeronautic and Space Administration (NASA) to process accounts of mistakes and act as a buffer between the FAA and system users. Controllers and pilots could report errors and in most situations remain immune from disciplinary action. Regularly published reports compiled from this data then circulated throughout the aviation industry, making system users aware of common pitfalls.[9] Bond's refusal to honor the contract provision not only further eroded FAA-ATC relations, it led to a drop in reported incidents, thereby undermining aviation safety.

At the same time, the FAA was demanding that controllers handle increasing traffic loads with staffing that was already below the agency's own standards. When the union pointed out the problem, the FAA revised its facility staffing standards to legitimize the situation.[10]

A fundamental struggle over workplace control best explains such seemingly irrational actions (the FAA's *raison d'etre* being to enforce and maintain the safety of air travel). As several historians have documented, in labor-management relations conflicts over control are extremely volatile and management reactions are not necessarily "rational" in strict economic terms. Indeed, management understands labor's threat in this arena as a challenge to the system underlying its own power and status.[11] Barbara Garson has specifically argued that the contemporary combination of nineteenth-century scientific management and twentieth-century technology is basically an effort to centralize control and move decision-making up the bureaucratic hierarchy. The "specific form that automation is taking seems to be based less on a rational desire for profit than on an irrational prejudice against people."[12]

Interestingly, during the years before the strike, FAA acquisition of better, more advanced equipment was surprisingly slow. Only when the possibility of a strike loomed did the FAA make a concerted effort to implement better technology into the air towers. While bureaucratic inefficiency and financial limitations explain part of this delay, it appears that an important reason was that new technology would have done little to increase managerial leverage over controllers. Indeed, such upgrades might have lessened FAA control. Only when the strike made it absolutely necessary did the FAA invest substantially in new technology after spending considerable effort on ensuring such equipment would mean less reliance on controllers' work.

A closer look at the FAA's plans concerning the use of computers in air traffic control supports such an analysis. An April 1982 issue of *Technology Review* described an important aspect of the FAA's new program:

"Between 1989 and 1995, an automated en route air traffic control (AERA) facility will be implemented to carry out normal routing and conflict-avoidance without controllers' intervention. . . . Such a system implies that the entire task of routing air traffic will be done with minimal human intervention, changing the controller's role from that of an active participant to that of a monitor. Only if the computer system shuts down or judgments beyond the programmed instructions were required would direct human intervention be expected."[13]

This effort to minimize the role of controllers, though, actually conflicted with the development of optimal technical alternatives which would improve the safety of air travel, as a 1982 Rand Corporation report pointed out. Rand blasted the direction of FAA research and development, writing that:

"The AERA scenario presents serious problems for each of the three major goals of ATC—safety, efficiency, and increased productivity. By depending on an autonomous, complex, fail-safe system to compensate for keeping the human controller out of the route decision-making loop, the AERA scenario jeopardizes the goal of safety. Ironically, the better

AERA works, the more complacent its human managers may become, the less often they may question its actions, and the more likely their system is to fail without their knowledge. We have argued that not only is AERA's complex, costly, fail-safe system questionable from a technical perspective, it is also unnecessary in other, more moderate ATC system designs."[14]

Rand proposed an alternative called Shared Control in which the role of the controller would be expanded so that "he is routinely involved in the minute-to-minute operation of the system" using an increasing suite of automated tools. Obviously, Shared Control had little appeal for an FAA more interested in limiting worker autonomy than promoting public safety.[15]

The FAA's reluctance to implement managerial practices that might be less abrasive and improve FAA-ATC personal relations during these years is more difficult to explain. In part, this reluctance might have stemmed from a basic fear that personnel management techniques might irrevocably undermine the hierarchical structure on which management control and power rested. Yet many other businesses have successfully used such approaches to consolidate control over labor. It appears that in this case the FAA's employment monopoly is a main reason for rejecting such a system. ATCs have no alternative to working for the FAA, thus a seemingly more responsive management is unnecessary to maintain its labor force.

Another oft-cited component which may have contributed to the continuation of autocratic management is a military orientation within the FAA's air traffic control system. One management specialist recommended that forty percent to fifty percent of supervisors be replaced because of the high proportion of people with a paramilitary management value system. He explained that such an approach indicated a deeply engrained autocratic belief system and obstructed compromise or worker input. (Many supervisors had, in fact, been in the military. Interestingly, though, the specialist, David Bowers, found it ironic that the "paramilitary style that seemed to be prevalent in the FAA is not one that I have encountered with any frequency in the Navy nor in the work that I have done with the Army.")[16]

Other reasons for the FAA's resistance to reform may be a lack of any kind of training program to teach management skills and responsibilities, the practice of simply promoting controllers to positions as supervisors— "They are accustomed to vectoring aircraft. . . . [then] they attempt to manage by vectoring people. But people don't vector. Nevertheless, they have a management philosophy that emphasizes top-down direction, top-down control, autocratic behavior, and says that this is indeed what gets results."[17]—and an inefficient, top-heavy bureaucratic structure which inhibits communication.

Finally, the FAA's dual mandate has contributed to its choice of management styles. Created to enforce and monitor air safety, the FAA is also charged with promoting air travel. The resulting interaction of the airline industry, the administration of aviation traffic, and air traffic controllers has often led to outcomes that undermined air safety and exacerbated ATC stress and aggravation. For instance, the FAA has consistently reacted swiftly to stifle PATCO demands, such as regulating flight schedules to even out the volume of air traffic throughout the day, that would slow traffic. This twin purpose also led the FAA to blame any problems in air traffic on the individual controllers rather than the system or employment practices.

By 1981, management-labor relations had deteriorated to an all-time low. ATCs complained of staff shortages, dangerously out-of-date equipment, limited opportunities for transfer, and harsh authoritarian leadership. Using new equipment, supervisors selectively and discreetly, monitored all communications and had the authority to discipline controllers for anything from nonstandard phraseology to rule breaking. Union activists were generally monitored more closely, enabling FAA officials to selectively log mistakes and build cases for future leverage.[18]

The result was increasingly militant views in the numerous surveys PATCO leadership authorized in preparation for the 1981 contract negotiations. In March 1981, seventy-eight percent of PATCO membership indicated their willingness to back a strike.[19]

When negotiations opened with the FAA in February 1981, President Robert Poli brought a list of ninety-seven demands to the table. Of this list, seven grievances dealt with economic issues, two with working hours, five with equipment, and sixty with various working conditions, including items such as facility lighting, dress codes, and staffing levels. As the talks stalled, Poli stressed the demands for an increase in pay, better retirement benefits, and a shorter workweek. In June, the FAA made a final offer of a $2,500 pay raise (in addition to the $1,400 ATCs were slated to receive as part of an overall federal pay hike), a fifteen percent increase in pay for night work, and a guaranteed thirty-minute lunch period. When Poli presented the package to the members of PATCO, ninety-five percent voted to reject the terms.

The FAA refused to make any further concessions in the talks that followed, and on August 3, eighty-five percent of PATCO's members went on strike. When President Reagan threatened to fire all ATCs who did not return to work within forty-eight hours, only 1,650 did. The remaining 11,350 lost their jobs.

The FAA immediately implemented its newly revised plan designed to offset the effects of a strike. Through the use of flow control (regulating and distributing evenly the number and schedule of daily flights), a minimal force of 10,000 remaining controllers, supervisors, and military personnel (a total of 7,000 fewer than before the strike) were able to maintain over eighty percent of scheduled air traffic. Although working six-day, forty-eight-hour-plus weeks, work force morale was high as the remaining controllers and management worked closely together to keep the system aloft. The "honeymoon" period soon ended, though, as temporary expedients attained a normal status. The FAA removed restrictions on air traffic, yet hired few replacements. Worse, the firing of the strikers eliminated a large percentage of the most experienced journeymen, placing a heavy burden on those who remained. The forty-eight-hour week continued in many areas for years, as did mandatory overtime. Not surprisingly, by 1983 controllers were discussing plans to create a new union. In 1987, ATCs (almost all non-strikers or new employees) moved to form the National Air Traffic Controllers Association (NATCA). Their grievances mirrored those of the strikers and exposed again the FAA's ability to rely on technology and monopoly to avoid conceding control over the workplace.

Congressional hearings, surveys, and interviews of controllers conducted before and after 1981 show that the workers' concerns which led to the strike (and many earlier and later protests) stemmed from a vital interest in bettering their lives at work and away from work by reducing the stress involved in their occupation. The air controllers' overwhelming rejection of the FAA's offer of a substantial pay raise in 1981 was indicative of the true interests of the rank and file. Instead of "following the ritual in such cases of dropping its more innovative demands [a shorter workweek and earlier retirement] in return for a higher money wage, the membership greeted the compromises that its leadership was prepared to make with swift disapproval."[20] An overriding interest in gaining more power within the workplace in order to minimize stress helps explain this decision. Indeed, as Philip Foner, David Roediger, David Montgomery, and Benjamin Hunnicutt have shown, the call for shorter hours has historically been one of control and related to broader notions of work and leisure. Controllers frequently linked these issues as well, albeit implicitly.

Most observers, though, attributed the rejection of the contract to controllers' greed and belief in their ability to hold the government hostage to their demands. One reason for this viewpoint was the Reagan administration's and the FAA's tremendous success in influencing media coverage. Such media reports reinforced most Americans' tendencies to view salary and work-related stress as the controllers' primary grievances. The widespread acceptance of such complaints as commonly experienced and unavoidable drawbacks to work led the majority to believe that they did not justify the uproar and inconvenience that the controllers were causing.

A critical component contributing to and ensuring the acceptance of this view was PATCO's own demands and rhetoric. Poli's emphasis on economic benefits served to subsume the basic struggle over power in the workplace; mask the links among stress, autocratic management, and workplace control; and undermine the moral position of the strikers in the eyes of the country. By basing a strike on an action critique of specific FAA techniques rather than an ideological and theoretical critique of managerial control and its relationship to stress, PATCO earned few supporters and the basic issue of manager-labor power remained unaddressed.[21]

A look at the most publicized aspects of the strike—economics, stress, and management—shows how these issues obscured and distorted the controllers' main concern of workplace control and helps explain why problems persist in the ATC workforce. It also demonstrates how management and labor's focus on economic issues since World War II has bankrupted labor's discourse and limited its ability to address concerns outside of a narrow range of concerns.

✈   ✈   ✈

Numerous commentators criticized PATCO's demand for a $10,000 raise, as did many strikers afterward who said that salary was really not a concern at the time and not the reason for the walkout. The FAA and the Reagan administration seized immediately upon the $10,000 figure and successfully used this issue to prevent support for the strikers. The media focused almost exclusively on the pay raise and the violation of the no-strike pledge, to the exclusion of the controllers' other concerns. The result of such coverage is clear from one striker's wry observation: "I'm still amazed when I talk to union people in my present line of work (phone service sales) of how much they really misunderstood about our job action. They only remember the $10,000 raise and the four-day workweek." To both unsympathetic members of Congress and the public, PATCO members were "overpaid, secure public sector employees trying to use their monopoly position to secure more than Congressmen were making."[22] These perceptions were in part responsible for the overwhelming public approval of Reagan's handling of the strike; 65 percent in a public opinion poll; mail, according to one representative, ran 1000-to-1 in favor of the administration.

Most strikers denied that money was a critical component in their decision to strike. Yet Poli insisted that his demands, headed by a pay raise, reflected the desires of his constituency. Arthur Shostak, who conducted five surveys of PATCO members in 1979 and 1980, backs up Poli's assertion that salary was important to the strikers. It is tempting to concede then that workers did see the strike as an economic solution to their inability to change working conditions, and merely backed down when faced with public hostility.

However, controllers' statements to the press and in congressional hearings contradict this view and indicate how central the issue of managerial power was to the decision to strike. For instance:

"Controllers suddenly find their work schedule is changed on very short notice instead of with the more common and regular two-week notice . . . at some locations . . . the sixth workday does not show up on the work schedules, but you are expected to show up. If you don't, you get a telephone call. We have had some controllers tell us they have scheduled minor surgery just so they can get two days off in succession.

"The fear of retaliation or retribution [by the FAA for testifying] is very real in the minds of these controllers. It doesn't take much to have some administrative action taken against you when traffic is being handled at such high volumes.

"We are not dealing with robots here, we are dealing with human beings. That is what we are screaming out for."[23]

Such comments make it clear that salary was not the critical issue for ATCs. Why the attention to financial benefits then? The basis of the focus and expression of PATCO's demands rested upon prevailing norms of workers' interests and power. Since World War II, labor leaders have placed a disproportionate amount of emphasis on economic gains, and the collective bargaining process has gravitated toward these areas. At the same time, management has carefully guarded its prerogatives from the bargaining process.[24] In this context, it seems likely that in envisioning a future strike, controllers felt that wages could and should be one aspect of it. Yet wages were not the decisive factor for most, and their other demands, derived from a far more vital, ideological interest than economic gains, evoked their passionate and surprisingly unified response.

Individual controllers pointed to stress far more often than salary when justifying the strike. Indeed, in the same way that Reagan emphasized PATCO's economic demands to gain support for his actions, PATCO, both leaders and members, pointed to the unique stress that air traffic controllers experienced daily in order to legitimate its demands. Their reasoning rested on two premises: that the nature of air traffic controlling as an occupation made it inherently and uniquely stressful, and that FAA management through indifference to acute staff shortages, dangerously out-of-date equipment, poor training methods, and harsh authoritarian leadership exacerbated that stress. The results of this stress were physical and psychological problems and the undermining of public safety.

Since its founding in 1968, PATCO promoted this stress-relief thesis at every opportunity. Indeed, PATCO's entire case for deserving benefits given no other federal employees hinged on the general acceptance of this two-pronged reasoning. Yet ATCs consistently emphasized the first premise, underscoring the stress inherent in directing air traffic, and neglected the second which related management to the stress. For example, in 1981 strikers constantly spoke of the adverse tolls of their profession. Bob Consart, after twenty-nine years as an ATC, cited his occupation as a primary reason for his divorce and a year of psychotherapy. He explained that "this is a young man's game—like professional ball-playing." An August 1981 article in the *New York Times* reported that "controllers say the heavy responsibilities of their jobs create stress, and they usually retire in their 40s, often with medical problems they say are related to the stress." Another controller told the *Los Angeles Times* that the strain of his job was so great that it was a factor in the breakup of his marriage and had raised both his pulse rate and his blood pressure.[25]

Poli elaborated upon this theme in testimony before a congressional subcommittee in 1981:

"Controllers constantly face countless situations which require them to make decisions affecting the lives of thousands of people . . . Day in and day out, they must guard against even the smallest error, for a mistake could kill hundreds. There is no room for guesswork, nor is there time to sit back and leisurely consider a traffic situation. Decisions must be swift, positive, and correct. . . . Being able to accept such an intense level of responsibility is at the heart of the controller's job. However, its residual effects are felt in every aspect of his life. Over time, while dreading the terrible consequences of one incorrect control decision, the controller loses the fight to the knowledge that he is human and in the long run, fallible. The strain created by this internal war generates insidious effects on the controller's entire life. They can manifest themselves in physical or mental disorders, social withdrawal, marital trouble, or concealed alcoholism."[26]

Arthur Shostak and David Skocik claim that the union argued that stress was caused by the autocratic FAA system, rather than the job itself. But as the passage and statements above indicate, this distinction was often unclear or omitted, opening the way to critics who urged rejection of the stress-relief argument for several reasons: 1) the most comprehensive study of controllers, the Rose Report, found medical proof of the job's hazards "conspicuously elusive;" 2) widespread abuse of medically-related retirements discredited PATCO's claim that 89 percent of controllers never survived until normal retirement; 3) the love that controllers professed for their jobs and the long waiting list of applicants to the FAA's academy for controllers undermined claims of its killer characteristics; 4) stress as the ATCs explained it was hardly unique to the controller's job, as satirist Mike Royko put it, "almost as many people head for bars at 5 P.M. each workday as get on commuter trains or expressways. . . . A lot of people would like to give the striking controllers a pat on the back, but their own hands are shaking too much."[27]

Citing such points, the FAA maintained that workplace reactions to stress were simply an individual matter and thus did not require organizational changes or reforms.[28] Adherence to a strict medical definition of stress forwarded this thesis and undercut PATCO complaints that referred to quality of life issues outside the workplace such as family.

In 1981, controllers were primarily protesting the conditions under which they worked and their inability to change those conditions rather than the work itself. It was the environment over which they had no control—faulty equipment, long hours, mandatory and unscheduled overtime, fear of arbitrary reprisal, fear of losing the ability to handle the job adequately, and being left without a means of supporting self and family—which led to intolerable stress, burnout, and health problems. But, when thrown together, labeled stress, and unlinked theoretically to autocratic management, observers failed to see these concerns as unique or worthy of work stoppage.

Americans' widespread suffering from and acceptance of stress as inherent in work rather than caused by factors such as certain managerial techniques also bolstered the FAA's position. Indeed, studies have shown that workers tend to blame themselves rather than management or technological design when feeling burned out and incompetent. Stress is seen as "their own inability to function according to the norms established by the company. They feel they are individually failing to live up."[29] Such an approach effectively delegitimized ATC grievances in this area.

Most analysts of the strike have concluded that the controllers were really protesting against the FAA's autocratic management. Commentators criticized PATCO leadership for submerging this complaint in favor of economic gains. In 1983, for instance, an article in the *Washington Monthly* noted that "although complaints about low pay and long hours are conspicuously rare when controllers are asked to name their biggest frustration with the system, complaints about bad managers are almost universal."[30]

The many congressional hearings also settled upon FAA management as the main problem in the air traffic control system. The Rose Report, two other FAA-commissioned studies (the Jones Reports), and two General Accounting Office surveys pointed to the rigidity and inflexibility of the FAA as the reason for the tremendously low morale in the workforce. However, even as these groups correctly identified the problem as a labor-management conflict, their recommendations failed to improve the situation. By focusing on management practices, researchers and congressmen tended to view low morale and the strike as a response to "an organization that they [the controllers] experienced as uncaring, unconcerned for its people, uncommunicative, and unreceptive." David Bowers, one compiler of the 1982 Jones Report, attributed the real problem to "an inability to bargain or contractually mandate human concern, considerate behaviors, and mutual affection."[31]

These types of evaluations lended themselves to personnel management sorts of solutions such as providing human resource counselors, scheduling "rap sessions," and establishing management training programs. Although the Jones Report also suggested that the FAA should "publish a manual of employee rights and responsibilities that clarifies the basic rules within which everyone works together" and maintain flow control,[32] such concrete improvements were rarely stressed and never implemented. Thus, the emphasis during the congressional hearings placed on the need to improve the nature of FAA management often served to prevent further probing into alternative causes or solutions which might involve acknowledging the need for a restructuring of workplace relations, which in turn might challenge aspects of capitalism and free enterprise central to a general American philosophy and way of life. It was much easier, and in the interest of many, to ignore the politically charged issue of workplace control and concentrate discussion instead on problems with solutions less difficult to reconcile with the prevalent framework of employer- employee relations.

The lackluster results of this focus were predictable and indicative again of the underlying struggle for workplace control between workers and management. For example, the FAA's creation of Human Resource Committees (HRC) and Facility Advisory Boards (FAB) in local control centers in order to improve communication between workers and management and address employee grievances had little, if any, positive effects. A report based on interviews at one center related that:

"The FAA's Human Relations Program at the Indianapolis Center is the joke of the facility. Employees laugh openly at FAA's efforts to make the program workable on paper while they continue with their prestrike policies of employees' relations. . . . the end results show minimal, if any, improvement. The more senior people do not openly complain about the lack of improvement because for them it is business as usual. The newer people don't openly complain because they know FAA doesn't like the boatrocker and because the older personnel are keeping quiet."[33]

More revealing was the FAA's reaction when one Chicago controller organized a national conference of FAB representatives in order to network and thereby improve the communications within respective facilities and with management, and improve the air traffic control system as a whole. The FAA instructed the controller to cancel the convention (he did) or risk punitive action. This was despite the fact that the conference was to be held on the controllers' own time and at their own expense. Again, the discussion in the congressional hearings about this event revolved around the complicated bureaucratic structure of the FAA and its lack of support for the controllers' initiative, missing the whole point of why the FAA felt the need to cancel the conference. Despite the supposed mutual aim of public safety, the FAA was not about to give up its power to dictate working conditions. Indeed, its denial of the existence of any problems and its refusal to negotiate on issues of working conditions underscore this point.

The FAA used personnel management devices as cooptive and repressive measures rather than a means of sharing power. The controllers' turn to another union in 1987 reflects the failure of this supposedly cooperative approach to mitigate the management-labor conflict in the ATC system.

✈   ✈   ✈

The FAA, Congress, researchers, the media, and workers overshadowed and masked this traditional struggle between management and labor by concentrating on these various issues, effectively depoliticizing and quantifying the employer-employee conflict. Each problem appeared to have a scientific or readily available solution which would resolve the disagreement and lead to harmonious workplace relations. Common discourse contributed to labor's ineffectiveness in forcing fundamental root problems in the workplace to be directly addressed. Language and discourse, which in the early twentieth century served to unify workers and forward their causes, has become less powerful and incendiary since World War II. In the case of air traffic controllers, scientific studies and surveys transformed worker consciousness into "morale." Worker discontent and dissatisfaction became stress, a medical problem generally accepted as a factor of everyday life. Statements made by individual controllers, however, contest these interpretations of the strike's causes and indicate the potential, though unrealized, of a theoretical, political, and ideological critique of managerial control that is rarely expressed in the late twentieth century.

What is most striking about the grievances made by air traffic controllers before, during, and after the walkout is the dramatic language they used to express their concerns. In 1981 congressional hearings, Poli responded to an attack on the legitimacy of PATCO's demands by saying that controllers "are not starving, but they are starving for a working condition that does not leave them destroyed individuals when they leave the job after fourteen, fifteen, sixteen years." Dennis Lebeau, striking after twelve years as an ATC, simply said, "it's our lives at stake and they're worth the sacrifice." The wife of a 28-year old traffic controller in Chicago explained that the strike was not simply a matter of principle but a "matter of survival." In 1984, a striker wrote that "given the same set of circumstances at any given time, I would do it again. There is no doubt history will prove PATCO was right in their actions. Maybe legally wrong, but surely morally right."[34] A placard carried during the strike read: "We're on strike against (F)ear, (A)ntagonism, and (A)dversary."

Consistent use of such passionate, suggestive terms indicates a deeply rooted frustration with FAA management. These men (almost all the controllers were men) were not suffering from economic deprivation or a lack of respect. They loved their jobs. One controller's wife explained that " . . . they were like gods . . . they were like giants; they were like nobody else . . . macho, crazy, eager, proud, dedicated."[35] These very conditions may have contributed to many controllers' decision to strike, as did an almost universal confidence that they were vital to the functioning of the system. These factors may also have embedded the firm conviction that they were entitled to the power to enact changes in the workplace which they believed would better their own lives and enhance the safety of the system. The irony, of course, is that theoretically the FAA had the same goals (operating under the assumption with which most agreed that a happier workforce would enhance safety, while dispirited and overworked ATCs would harm the system's effectiveness). Yet in the eyes of controllers, the FAA's dictatorial character undercut both goals to an intolerable degree. Thus the feeling of morality, survival, and the need to act.[36]

This power struggle emerged clearly in the many congressional hearings dealing with the status of the ATC system and the government sponsored surveys of the ATC force. Controllers in both instances told again and again of the arbitrary and authoritarian nature of management that little by little eroded their ability to perform their job, their control over life away from work, and their dignity, and the stress that resulted. The FAA's constant attempt to limit worker independence is evident, as is the controllers' interest in gaining more autonomy.

In 1979, a subcommittee of the Committee of Public Works and Transportation held hearings about the adequacy of equipment and staffing in the ATC system. Interestingly and significantly, when the committee's staff attempted to collect information from twenty ATC centers around the country to compare statistics on FAA equipment and procedures in preparation for the hearings, the FAA issued orders advising centers not to provide any information. In his opening statement Representative Tom Corson (Ill.) noted controllers' complaints that there were "no set standards used by supervisors in deciding numbers and qualifications of people necessary to work at a given time."[37] Corson emphasized that shortages of qualified staff, inadequately maintained and out-of-date equipment, insufficient training programs, safety hazards all contributed to a low morale.

Less than a year later, during an investigation of computer failures in the ATC system, Representative Bob Whitakker (Kan.) pointed out that the official FAA response to most near misses was that "they chose to blame the controller for the near tragedy and only listed the computer malfunction as a contributing cause." ATC Charles Mullick from Oakland testified that "controllers are now hesitant to report dangerous or possibly dangerous situations for fear of reprisal by the FAA." Mullick added that "the FAA has taken away our second career [the physical ability to pursue another occupation once unable to continue air traffic controlling due to its debilitating effects], our safety reporting program, and a number of freedoms guaranteed under the U.S. Constitution."[38] Such remarks only showed in part the conflicts and confrontations that ATCs experienced daily.

Controllers saw management's abuse of power as affecting not only job performance, but hurting the quality of life away from work. In 1980 testimony to Congress, Poli explained that for workers in larger towers with inadequate staffing "who maybe for four or five months are working six days a week and ten hours a day, there isn't enough money to pay them for what they have to go through with the disruptions of their family and how it affects them as individuals in the continuing operation of their job." When asked what benefits controllers would hypothetically strike for, Poli responded that fewer hours, better retirement, and improved equipment would be main issues, along with "the ability to spend more time with their family . . . if they could work less time so they can be home more, I think that would be a big issue."[39]

While Poli may have used this appeal to gain congressional sympathy, the words of controllers during and after the strike demonstrate that the quantity and quality of time away from work was a vital concern to many. One wife described how her husband had gone from "a completely passive person, a guy who was crazy about his job, to someone who would jump on you at the drop of a hat." A controller described how "somedays I go home and walk in the door and my wife takes one look at my face—and my clothes, which are sweated through from the neck down—and she doesn't say a word. She sends my son to his room and she makes me a drink and we don't talk for two hours." Another added that "my wife says she'd rather have me whole, healthy, and with her than going back to work under the conditions we had." One wife complained that "by the fourth day of a work week, he has no patience and it's almost as though his head is going to explode. Our whole family runs according to Kennedy Tower's traffic." Many controllers traced such problems to mandatory overtime and rotating shift work that undermined parenting and neighboring roles.[40]

Several responses to a 1984 survey of former controllers saw a better family life as one of the few positive results of the strike. One wrote that "I regained a family that I had lost by working weekends, holiday, and night shifts. I have learned to communicate with my family now, as I had no time for family life as an ATC. My wife and children have related to me many times how [much] easier I am to get along with . . ." Another simply stated, "Family situation vastly improved," and a third that "this was the greatest thing I have ever done for my family. We get along better, no drinking problem. Health problems have disappeared. Better relationship with friends and new friends are easier to make."[41] Obviously, ATCs understood and resented the costs of management's power.

In 1983, Congress began to ask controllers to testify in hearings on the ATC system. One controller who testified wrote a telling letter to the chairman of the subcommittee immediately after the hearings had ended: "The way Mr. Helms [the chairman of the FAA] slanted his testimony against the Washington Center controllers, it was as if to make them feel ashamed for taking their annual leave. . . . we as controllers should not be boxed into a canyon of workload that makes us feel less of a human being if we don't take on unsafe volumes of traffic and risk our health by gleefully working all the overtime. It is not normal, and for Mr. Helms to denigrate those of us for taking our leave (that we've earned) proves my point that they now 'expect' us to be supermen."[42]

Dr. David Bowers, who helped conduct research for the Jones report, related what one controller who had not been a member of PATCO and not gone on strike had told him: "He said that in the days leading up to it [the strike], the management divided them into two kinds of people:

good guys and bad guys. The good guys were management, team supervisors, and the controllers who were known would not go on strike. There was the honeymoon period in the immediate wake of the strike, two or three weeks or whatever . . . of teamwork and good relationships. [Then] he said, suddenly, they woke up and the world was divided into good guys and bad guys again. This time, the managers were the good guys and the bad guys were team supervisors and controllers."[43]

Hearings in 1989 brought more of the same sorts of protests and allegations. A 1988 GAO survey included the words of one supervisor who explained that "employee input is not really being sought out and that budget constraints make permanent changes and station moves practically impossible . . . [moreover] drug testing [which had recently been instituted] being performed on a work force with no history of drug-related errors and accidents [is] professionally insulting." The report also set forth the view of one controller as widely representative of the work force as a whole: "Morale is horrible, traffic is intolerable, management insensitive. We are overworked, understaffed, and abused. We even have a supervisor who says you can't stand up to relieve the tension and ache after spending two-and-a-half-plus hours at a sector by yourself without any help. . . . Worst of all—nothing will change after this survey. Too bad." Numerous controllers repeated this last sentiment.[44]

Finally, Steve Bell, president of the newly formed union, the National Air Traffic Controllers Association, testified:

"It is no wonder that NATCA won certification and that we now have half of the work force as members. The FAA was the best recruiting tool around. Controllers were feeling helpless in the face of this disinterested monolith. NATCA gives them the only opportunity to effect meaningful and lasting change. . . .

"It is as if FAA managers are absentee landlords who had no idea what their tenants are complaining about . . . And, as with an absentee landlord, we will probably get little relief."[45]

It was the imposition of management control over all aspects of a worker's life—the effect of overtime on job performance and outside lives, the arbitrary/short notice of overtime demand, inability to obtain sick leave or take breaks, a lack of clear job definitions and responsibilities, the facility, and practice of perceived unfair managerial reprisal—

against which ATCs continued to fight almost ten years after 11,400 workers struck—and were fired—for the same reason. As Harley Shaiken writes, "these seemingly picayune squabbles are, in reality, disputes over more fundamental questions of power and job security. The real issue is who will organize work on the shop floor"[46] and, by extension, life away from the shop floor.

✈ ✈ ✈

The FAA's responses to the controllers' grievances and repeated congressional reprimands and recommendations demonstrate perhaps even more dramatically the degree to which control over labor may influence managerial actions; for asserting FAA control was not a question of profit, but in fact posed a blatant threat to public safety. That members of the agency were willing to take such a risk by consistently ignoring controllers' obviously valid criticism, such as faulty equipment, demonstrates an awareness of the challenge that the controllers presented and a refusal to give up any part of their authority.

The FAA's handling of the strike is the most obvious proof of its outlook. Rather than reopen talks, the FAA instead maintained air travel using an overworked, undertrained, skeletal work force. It, too, denied the legitimacy of workers' grievances, refused to negotiate working conditions, and dismissed the strikers as "chronic complainers and crybabies." Deliberate underreporting to Congress and the public of near misses and other safety violations since the strike also showed the extent to which the FAA was willing to violate its mandate to ensure safety in air travel in order to maintain control over its labor force.[47]

In addition, the FAA immediately intensified efforts to automate the system more fully in order to decrease its reliance on trained skilled controllers and monitor workers' actions. One example that instigated tremendous controller protest was the implementation of computers designed to record operational errors. The FAA claimed that the purpose of this program was to detect unreported errors and thereby promote safety. The "squeal-a-deal" or "snitch machine" as it became known, reported any error, no matter how insignificant, immediately to a supervisor. Despite the supposed immunity from reprisal, supervisors and managers then exercised enormous discretion in recording and reprimanding such errors.

Controllers saw the implementation of drug testing as yet another way in which the FAA displayed its distrust of, disrespect for, and control over workers, as did its use of a Survey Feedback Action Program. While the agency said that the purpose of the survey was to "give every employee a chance to identify problems and also have a voice in correcting them," after collecting the supposedly anonymous responses, the FAA returned the original comment sheets in the controllers' own handwriting to the facility managers, thereby destroying all confidentiality. NACTA president Steve Bell noted that:

"The ramifications are obvious. Controllers who were critical of management and facility policies were identified and could now be subject to prejudicial treatment. Reprisals can be very subtle, such as watch schedules, performance evaluations, promotions and transfers, etc. The breach in confidentiality also means that controllers will think twice about ever filling out one of these forms again."[48]

Perhaps the best evidence of the depth of the struggle between FAA management and the air traffic controllers for control of the workplace is the remarkable similarities of the workers' complaints, despite years of congressional investigations, recommendations and supposed improvements. As a GAO representative explained to Congress in 1986, "in reviewing the written comments, one of the things that surprised us was the fact that you really could not discern a difference between the comments of a relatively new controller, one hired since the strike, and one who has been around the system for quite a few years. The tone was virtually the same. The issues were the same. We were quite surprised about that."[49]

The most recent survey of air traffic controllers, completed by 80 percent of the work force in 1988, led the GAO to conclude that "the same problem areas that the GAO recognized in 1984, and many of the same problems that contributed to the controllers' strike in 1981, still plague the ATC system." Congressman Guy Molinari (N.Y.) added that "the most salient point of the GAO report . . . shows . . . the perceptions of management and controllers are worlds apart. It is hard to understand how facility managers and controllers in the same building perceive work conditions so differently."[50]

David Montgomery has pointed out that "the battle for control of the workplace neither began nor ended in the opening years of this century."[51] Although technology, management theory, modes of production, labor's position, and cultural views of work and workers have all changed the appearance and terms of this struggle for power, the fundamental conflict remains the same. These same changes in society, though, have also served to overshadow this dispute, leaving it, at least in the case of the air traffic controllers, unaddressed and unresolved. Nevertheless, controllers clearly saw, if only indirectly, this problem and understood it as vitally linked to their broader expectations and aspirations of life and work. Thus inspired, in 1981 13,000 of them risked job security, income, and arrest to reassert this right, and less than ten years later a new group of workers created a union to better continue the struggle for control.

"The Pressures of PATCO: Strikes and Stress in the 1980s" was originally published by the Corcoran Department of History at the University of Virginia. Reprinted with permission of the author.

A F T E R W O R D

Notes for "The Pressures of PATCO"

1. R. Magnuson et al., "Turbulence in the Tower," Time, 8/17/81, p. 17; Arthur Shostak and David Skocik, The Air Controllers' Controversy: Lessons from the PATCO Strike (NY: Human Sciences Press, 1986), p. 68.
2. The importance of ATCs to public safety and their position as federal employees led to numerous congressional hearings in which air controllers voiced their concerns. Government organizations, FAA-commissioned panels, and PATCO also conducted detailed studies and surveys of the air traffic control workforce, compiling rich sources of data from which it is possible to elicit the views of air controllers and management.
3. Ronald Howard, Brave New Workplace (NY: Viking, 1985), p. 7. See, for instance, Michael J. Piore and Charles F. Sabel, The Second Industrial Divide: Possibilities for Prosperity (NY: Basic Books, 1984).
4. Harry Braverman, Labor and Monopoly Capital (NY: Monthly Review Press, 1974); Stephen Wood et al, The Degradation of Work? (London: Hutchinson, 1982), pp. 13-14.
5. See David Noble, Forces of Production (NY: Knopf, 1984); Harley Shaiken, Work Transformed (NY: Holt, Rinehart & Winston, 1985); Barbara Garson, The Electronic Sweatshop (NY: Simon & Schuster, 1988); Howard, Brave New Workplace.
6. Hearings 1983-1984, p. 1372; Shostak, p. 138.
7. Howard, pp. 251, 253.
8. Shostak, p. 54.
9. Shostak, p. 97-98.
10. Shostak, p. 98. It is worth noting that at the same time that the FAA refused to employ more ATCs to handle the growing volume of air traffic, the number of FAA managers hired increased considerably.
11. Howell Harris, The Right to Manage: Industrial Relations Policies of American Business in the 1940s (Madison, WI: University of Wisconsin Press, 1982), p. 27.
12. Garson, p. 13.
13. Hoo-min D. Toong and Amar Gupta, "Automating Air-Traffic Control," Technology Review, April 1982, p. 54.
14. Robert Wesson et al., ÒScenarios for Evolution of Air Traffic ControlÓ (Monograph, Rand, R-2698- FAA, November 1981), p. 2.
15. The FAA was in all likelihood probably not purposefully risking the safety of air travel, but instead used rationalizations to deny this effect and justify their efforts to maintain their authority such as asserting that the ATC system had been overstaffed before the strike and so there was no need to hire additional workers.
16. U. S. Congress, Committee on Public Works and Transportation, Rebuilding of the Nation's Air Traffic Control System (Has Safety Taken a Back Seat to Expediency?) (Washington: U.S. Government, 1985), pp. 55-56
17. Ibid., p. 59.
18. Shostak, p. 102.
19. Ibid., p. 82.
20. Stanley Aronowitz, Working Class Hero (NY: Adena Books, 1983), p. 68.
21. Ibid., p. 67.
22. It should be noted that the average salary for controllers at the time of the strike was $31,000. Shostak, p. 114; David Morgan, "Terminal Flight: The Air Traffic Controllers' Strike of 1981," Journal of American Studies (August 1984), p. 175.
23. Hearings 1983-1984, pp. 222, 228, 259.

24. Hearings 1981, p. 190; David Bowers, "What Would Make 11,500 People Quit Their Jobs?," Organizational Dynamics (Winter 1983), p. 8.
25. Newsweek 8/17/81, p. 23; New York Times 8/4/81, p. A-1; Los Angeles Times 8/6/81, p. 1-1.
26. Hearings 1981, p. 15.
27. Shostak, p. 90.
28. Ibid., p. 91.
29. Howard, p. 89.
30. Phil Keisling, "Money Over What Really Mattered," Washington Monthly (September 1983), p. 16. Keisling went on to condemn the controllers as preoccupied with their own comfort and security and allowing economic interests to overwhelm legitimate ones such as too much traffic at peak hours.
31. Bowers, p. 16, 17.
32. Hearings 1981, pp. 524, 521.
33. Hearings 1983-1984, p. 459.
34. New York Times 8/6/81, p. D-21; Shostak, p. 96.
35. Shostak, p. 22.
36. Several studies of the air traffic controllers have examined the personalities of the people making up the ATC workforce. The Rose Report, in particular, looked closely at psychological make-ups when it tried to determine the presence and cause of stress. It found that in general ATCs "are highly intelligent men who control their anxieties by meticulous compulsive behavior, men who—though they tend to be bold and dominant individuals by nature and have no great intrinsic respect either for authority or regulations—are nevertheless, as members of a closely working team, group conforming by necessity." (Hearings 1983- 1984, p. 968) The study also found that many controllers had an intense and chronic feeling of alienation from their FAA managers and hated the supervisory system. They believed the FAA would scapegoat them if anything went wrong, but, "as people who take pride in their job, they take pride in not being intimidated." (Shostak, p. 23) Indeed, many observers have pointed to the collective psychological profile of ATCs as a critical component in the decision to strike. A tendency to take action and a disdain for authority made a dramatic statement likely whereas another workforce might have opted for a different method of protest. Undoubtedly, the FAA's style of management and refusal to compromise or make changes aggravated the situation as well. The FAA's behavior during the contract negotiations was the final straw.
37. Hearings 1979, p. 250; Hearings 1981, p. 3.
38. Hearings 1980, pp. 28, 5.
39. Hearings 1980, pp. 24, 25.
40. Chicago Tribune 8/6/81, p. 1; New York Times 8/13/81, p A-1; Shostak, pp. 21-25.
41. Shostak, pp. 145, 149.
42. Ibid., p. 282.
43. Ibid., p. 1221.
44. Hearings 1989, pp. 11, 20.
45. Ibid., pp. 128, 47, 119.
46. Shaiken, p. 32.
47. Shostak, pp. 184-185.
48. Hearings 1989, p. 136.
49. Hearings 1986, p. 28.
50. Hearings 1989, p. 3. For a more recent look at the safety of air travel which is very critical of the FAA, see "How Safe Is This Flight?" Newsweek 4/24/95, pp. 18-28.
51. David Montgomery, Workers' Control In America (NY: Cambridge UP, 1979), p. 4.

AFTERWORD

WHAT'S
IN A COVER?

This was a question we pondered long and hard. We knew the image needed to convey the genre and subject while also distinguishing *TRACON* from an airline disaster book. *TRACON* is a story about air traffic control. About man versus machine. About man's faith in technology and the systemic issue of how far we should go in entrusting our lives to a computer. The search for a comfortable balance between cognizance and the human capacity to adapt to changing conditions and the lightning speed yet literal logic of a microprocessor.

We took this core theme as our starting point and brainstormed concepts intermingled with recognizable elements of air traffic control: radar, targets on the scope, the sweep repainting the screen, a commercial jetliner. The resulting image that our artist, Henk Dawson, delivered took our breath away. It is as arresting as it is prophetic and, we believe, works on so many different levels.

An eye, wide open with terror, morphs into a radar screen, illustrating the tense, codependent relationship of man and machine. The pupil drawing the plane into a black vortex, the center of a storm, the mind's eye of air traffic control. An atmospheric glow emanating from the top of the iris, curving like the edge of the earth as viewed from a craft high in the sky. And the conflict alert symbols ablaze on the targets of two jets seconds away from catastrophe.

We are grateful to Ray Gibbons in the O'Hare TRACON for sending us images of the radar screen to help Henk recreate an authentic look. And to Henk, who ran with our concept and rendered our task effortless, and his wife, Kristen, whose eye graces the cover of our book. Henk has created many other wonderful and well known pieces (the Internet Explorer logo, for example), but we must say with obvious bias that we think this is his best piece yet.

— *The Publisher*

Please visit us at
www.japphire.com

- Read behind-the-scenes information about the book.

- Listen in live to air traffic controllers around the world.

- Read humorous and heroic vignettes about ATC as told by controllers.

- Check out links to a variety of aviation sites on the Web.

JAPPHIRE

6942 Coal Creek Parkway SE – No. 1000
Newcastle, Washington 98059 U.S.A.
Tel: 425-430-0007 / Fax: 125-204-8577

Please visit us at
www.japphire.com

✈ **Read behind-the-scenes information about the book.**

✈ **Listen in live to air traffic controllers around the world.**

✈ **Read humorous and heroic vignettes about ATC as told by controllers.**

✈ **Check out links to a variety of aviation sites on the Web.**

JAPPHiRE

6947 Coal Creek Parkway SE – No. 1000
Newcastle, Washington 98059 U.S.A.
Tel: 425-430-0007 / Fax: 425-204-8877